ATLAS in REVOLT

American Secession

BOOK II

GREGORY C PHILLIPS

Blue M Publishing, LLC – Chicago

Library of Congress Cataloging-in-publication data
Names: Phillips, Gregory C.
Title: *Atlas in Revolt*
Description: First edition | Blue M Publishing (Paperback), Chicago, IL [2016] |
Series: Book two of trilogy set | Contents: *Atlas in Revolt – American Secession Book II* | Summary: Shea searches to find her husband while the leader of the country consolidates his power. Yet, both are undermined by the efforts of an ambitious bureaucrat seeking the throne for herself. Shea and a former Congressman create a movement to spotlight the tyranny of the Administration, creating growing unrest and rebellion. | Audience Note: Recommended for readers fifteen and older | Language Note: Infrequent offensive language.
Identifiers: ISBN 978-1-945385-01-8 (Paperback)
Subjects: LCSH: sh85001072 Adventure stories| BISAC: FIC031060 FICTION / Thriller Political | FIC055000 FICTION / Dystopian | FIC037000 FICTION /Political | GSAFD: 00000cz a2200037n 45 0 680 Dystopias
Classification: LCC PS370-380 | DDC 813/--dc23

Phillips, Gregory C.
Atlas in Revolt: American Secession Book II, Gregory C. Phillips
Contents: Part Two – A Nation in Decline | Part Three – Change is Good

ISBN 978-1-945385-01-8 (Paperback)

Printed in the United States of America
www.blueMpublishing.com

Fabulous Book Cover Design by HIP Distribution
Published by Blue M Publishing, LLC, Hammond, IN

Blue M Publishing
6205 Indianapolis Blvd
Suite 100
Hammond, IN 46320

Contents

Atlas in Revolt – American Secession
Book II

Book Summary

Shea searches to find her husband while the leader of the United States moves to consolidate his power and shred the *Constitution*. Yet, both are undermined by the efforts of an ambitious bureaucrat who seeks the throne for herself and intends to send the nation deeper into despotism. Together with a former Congressman, Shea creates a movement to challenge the tyranny of the Administration. Emotions run high as those who create the country's wealth are the ones drowning in exorbitant taxation, while others are satisfied standing in line for government handouts. Not since 1860 has the country been so polarized.

"Secession ... secession now!" they chant. But will it come to that?

In this second installment of the Atlas Series, the factions take sides, and when the ultimate decision must be made, chaos reigns. Can war be far behind?

*****

Rating: PG-15* for use of harsh language and graphic images of violence and threats of violence. Some drug and alcohol use is described. There are some scenes with sexual references or implied sexual activity.

*Rating is provided by the author as a parental guide and is not based on any established rating systems. PG-Parental Guidance is suggested. Suitable for readers over 15.

PART II – A NATION IN DECLINE

CH 1 The Cost of Money

A t the senior management level, EG, Inc. was not the place for the meek and unassuming. It was competitive to the extreme and was proud to foster such an environment at the very top. It was true that they hired only the best and brightest, but political savvy was much harder to come by. There was little correlation between brains and cunning, although if one had both, one was much more dangerous. Deception was key, as outright sabotage of someone else was frowned upon. To get ahead, Machiavelli had to be your close confidant and companion. If not Machiavelli, then at least Sun Tzu.

Thorne had learned the lessons from those masters early on in his career, and he'd successfully made it to the top using those strategies. To his superiors he was all about saying *Yes*. If it were something that could be damaging to him, he would spin it in his favor or pawn it off to someone else who was unknowing. Regardless, he made sure he remained blameless. In fact, his colleagues often referred to him as Slick Kilby, as he seemed able to get out of just about anything.

On the other hand, toward his subordinates he was ruthless and self-serving. He was friendly when the occasion demanded – around holidays and company social events. Otherwise, he made sure they knew where they stood with him. They were terrified of him, and the only way he kept them was to ensure the company paid them handsomely. His direct employees enjoyed the highest raises in the company, and they could easily earn up to twice what they could make in the outside world. So, they were prisoners, enslaved by a man they despised and yet thankful at the same time. They hated going to work in the morning, but when they returned home, they saw their big houses, nice yard and gave thanks. In many neighborhoods, their neighbors struggled, as fewer and fewer could afford the lifestyle they lived. His employees were only worried about someday rolling snake-eyes – particularly, the next time their boss needed someone else to blame for his latest mistake or debacle.

As CEO, Thorne only had to worry about the board of directors which re-appointed him every year at their annual meeting. He had packed the board with his friends, so rarely did they express dissatisfaction with the way he handled the company.

However, as the economy had continued to falter and the company's stock price had begun to decline, he had started to catch heat from the very members he had counted on to keep him in power. Feeling that his influence with the board was slipping, Thorne knew that the last thing he needed was to be caught spending forty million dollars of the company's money illegally. His payment to Ratner had to be buried deep, so no one could find it.

"Stevens," said Thorne, looking at his live hologram, standing on the far side of the room, "I need a place to park about forty mil. It's not a lot, but I don't need for it to be found by inquisitive outside accountants or anyone from our audit committee."

"Yes, Mr. Thorne. I'll have to see what I can do," said Stevens. "I'll probably run it through some offshore accounts with large balances. But, don't worry, sir. It will be handled. "

He didn't ask what it was for. This wasn't the first time he'd been asked to find a 'home' for some amount that his boss was going to spend. The numbers at EG were so large that it was relatively easy to find hiding places for smaller amounts like this. However, things had gotten stricter, and shareholders had finally wised up to the shenanigans of executive officers of such companies, especially of protected GovCo's. As a result, outside auditors were also being held accountable for a company's misdeeds. They were digging deeper and asking more questions. Still, in a company with 116 billion in sales, forty million represented a drop in the bucket – less than one in three thousand.

"Good. I knew you would," answered Thorne, not having to say anything more.

As for Stevens and Chou, Thorne believed he had his inner circle of henchmen to do his dirty work. Between the two, they were to get the vital engine information discretely from Ratner and funnel the funds to her through offshore accounts or other means to mask the trail. It was clean. It was efficient. All would be good.

Then, his private line rang.

"Thorne speaking," said the CEO gruffly, in the harsh tone he always used when picking up a call. He hated to be annoyed by pointless interruptions and people asking him stupid questions.

"Mr. T," as Muntz privately called Thorne, "this is Roger Mertz. Do you have a few minutes?"

Gunter Muntz often used the alias Roger Mertz when conducting illegal or illicit acts on behalf of others. He had no problem with covert types of operations like this, and it didn't matter whether they were for a good cause or not. It was all about the money – pure and simple. The ends always justified the means to him.

He had never been accused of having a conscience. His only minor regret was killing Sergei, but he'd gotten over that quickly too.

"No, I don't. And how did you get my private number?"

"It will only take a second. You see, I know about the little transaction you have going with the deputy secretary, Ms. Ratner."

"I don't know what you're talking about. Now, I need to get back to a meeting," said Thorne, curtly.

"Yes, you do. The problem is that Ms. Ratner doesn't have the information she promised you. And the person she was going to get it from was found in a lake just outside of town this morning. His name was Sergei Navarov."

Thorne knew who Navarov was. Being in the industry, he was well aware of Sergei's connection to the Disones and their laboratory. "Go on."

"Well, if I can work out a deal with you directly, we can both benefit. You can get the complete plans to the SECE engine, and I can walk away with some cash," said Muntz.

Thorne laughed. "You expect me to deal with someone I don't even know? I don't know anything about you. And I certainly don't know anything about this SECE engine, or whatever you called it. This call is over." He started to hang up.

"Check your virtual mail," said Muntz, harshly. "It's in the best interest of your family if you do."

Thorne was not accustomed to being talked to that way, and it only made him angrier. Yet, the veiled threat to his family was always a concern. He had in place security for his wife, three children and two grandchildren. His position demanded it. Running a major, global corporation was riskier than ever, with kidnappings for ransom becoming more and more frequent in the U.S., just as they had been for years in Central and South America.

At the same time concerned and annoyed, Thorne tapped a few icons on his PCD. At the top was an image of a letter sent allegedly from one Roger Mertz. "Open," he commanded, and the image unwrapped itself and about twenty pages began stacking themselves in 3-D form in front of him. The first picture was an official cover page from the Department of Technology Assessment, stamped with the department's seal and dated within the previous eighteen months. The filer was Lenoir Research Laboratories; the subject was the *Super-efficient Combustible Engine Series, Mark IV.*

Thorne scanned the next several pages quickly, reading the filing and getting up to the part where it began to outline the details of the invention and the software used. However, the last page ended before any real substance was revealed.

"Yes," Thorne said coolly. "I have received your mail. It's interesting, but not conclusive. I need more pages to determine that ..."

"You have enough," said Muntz. "Now, are you willing to participate in this unique auction event?"

"I don't deal with criminals," answered Thorne.

"Yes, you do. You do it all the time, Thorne. Now, you'll need to come to Wachusett Reservoir, off Route 110. There's a little dirt road that runs south of the lake. Be there at 1 AM tonight, and come alone. If there's anyone with you, the deal is off. Oh, and bring the forty million you offered Ratner. Do you understand?"

"You must be mad! There's no way in hell I'm doing that! I'd be walking right into an ambush. You could just kill me, take the forty and vanish!"

"True, but instead I propose that you pick your wife up at the same time you're there."

Thorne sat stunned. "My wife?" he asked, urgently.

However, this time Muntz hung up, and the line went dead. They had been on audio only, so there was no image of the man who had called. Thorne sat frozen in his overstuffed, leather chair trying to decide what to do. His body trembled. It was the first time for as long as he could remember that he truly felt helpless and vulnerable. For years he had been invincible, running a huge company with minions all around him doing his personal errands and handling most problems and issues as they arose. Now he faced something he couldn't delegate off to his staff, nor discuss with anyone -- not even Stevens or Chou.

Quickly, he said, "Call Patty." His automated system sent him the image of his home on the left side of a split screen with the image of his wife, Patty on the right. The phone rang and rang, but there was no answer. "Call Patty at home," he then said urgently. His pulse was racing. He could only think the worst at that moment. "Come on Patty, answer."

"I'm not available, right now," mouthed the image of his wife in a pre-taped recording. "Leave me a message, and I'll get back to you."

"Sh*t!" yelled Thorne, turning off the phone. "Janet, get in here," he bellowed to his assistant, sitting just outside his office. He always liked her to come in personally rather than send her avatar image. "I need you to track down Patty.

Find her. Send guards from our security company if you have to. I need to know where she is right now!"

"Yes, Mr. Thorne," she answered.

"Close the door," Thorne said to the computer after she'd left the room. As the doors swung shut, he went to the liquor cabinet on the far side of his office and poured himself a scotch. Once that was gone, he poured another.

The minutes passed like hours and the hours like days. He kept calling Patty, but she still didn't answer.

"Janet, have they ..." he would start to ask, but Janet would only cut him off in mid-sentence, replying that security had not yet found her.

"I'll let you know as soon as they tell me something, Mr. Thorne," she told him repeatedly.

His marriage to Patty had not been good during the previous several years. They had mainly gone their separate ways. He had made enough money to keep her happy, even when, as CEO, he had often hopped the corporate jet and traveled the world visiting their far-flung manufacturing plants and distribution facilities. Yet, he still loved her – at least he had convinced himself that he still did. He hadn't had any affairs, anyway, and he thought that counted for something.

Finally, it was five o'clock, and his staff was leaving.

"Where the hell is everyone going?" he shouted, watching as some were walking down the hall. "Janet, you're staying until I get answers!"

"But, Mr. Thorne, tonight is my anniversary. I promised my husband that I'd be home so he could take me out."

"Cancel it!" Thorne yelled back. "I need to know where Patty is!"

Janet put her purse back on the desk and sat down, calling her husband on her PCD to let him know that she had to stay late. Thorne wanted information on his wife, and he wanted something now.

Within ten minutes, Janet came into his office. "Mr. Thorne, I've just heard back from the security team. They found your wife's car abandoned about five miles outside of Boston in Marlborough. However, I'm sorry, she wasn't anywhere around the area. Should I call the police?"

"No!" he said. Then he added, "Did they find anything else at the scene? Her purse, clothing, anything?"

"No sir," she replied. "They said that all they found was the car."

"It was the Mercedes – the silver S Coupe, I assume. Is that what they found?"

"Yes. But they said it had a flat tire. Maybe that's all there is to it. She had a flat tire and went for help?"

"She would have called me," said Thorne, lowering his eyes and clasping his hands. "That's all then?"

"Yes, sir."

"Okay. Well, you can go home. I'll see you in the morning," said Thorne, looking away from her and out the window.

It was an unusually kind gesture from a man who was known for his vicious attacks and unreasonable demands. But, Janet didn't question it. She quickly put her things away, threw her mauve Coach purse over her shoulder and left – leaving her boss alone in his office.

***

It was late, but the visual of his General Counsel popped up on the screen in his office.

"Mr. Thorne, this is Chou. I've got some news for you. It's about Deputy Secretary Ratner."

Abruptly, he sat up and opened his humidor, pulling out a long Ashton Maduro cigar. He clipped the end and lit the tip, sucking-in in spurts until smoke billowed from the gray-ashen tip.

"Talk to me," he said, staring at the screen. His face was lined with stress, and his old-fashioned narrow patterned tie askew on his collar.

"Yes, Mr. Thorne. I just got off a secure call with Secretary Ratner. She was not in a good mood today."

"She's never in a good mood, and neither am I. Make it quick, Chou."

"She said her price just went up. She's not asking for the amount originally agreed. Now she said to add another zero."

"What?" Thorne shouted, exploding over the new number, "four hundred million?" He sat, astonished at the outrageous demand.

"Yep. She said take it or leave it. She said the engine is worth billions in world-wide profits. She said you'd know that as well as she," said Chou. Her face was emotionless, even though she had expected that reaction from him.

Thorne was quiet for a moment, calming himself. "I see," he said. "I'll have to take this under advisement, then."

"She said not to wait too long. She said to tell you she has another bidder – one from overseas who's willing to pay her that," said Chou.

"She's a wh*re," claimed Thorne. "And as for you, Chou. I'm not paying you to let these negotiations go against me like this. It's your job to keep things in order. How could you let this happen?"

"I am working with her, sir. I think she'll come around. I outlined why we would be better to deal with than someone she didn't know overseas. I told her that our money was good, solid. There was no way to verify the integrity of the person she was dealing with. And, I said that she risked losing everything, as you wouldn't just sit and wait if she were bluffing or her other deal went south. I stated categorically that we could withdraw our offer as well."

"You know I won't do that, Chou. That patent is too valuable."

"Are you willing to give a counteroffer?"

"Let me think about it. I've got other things going on right now," said Thorne, disconnecting the line. "Bitch," Thorne mumbled, turning off his phone.

But maybe all this is a good thing, he thought. *Ratner can't hurt me now, if I have another deal with Muntz. I'm risking a lot, but if Patty's been taken – well, it will be the best deal I can make all around.* Now more than ever, he hoped the deal with Muntz was legit.

"Stevens, I need forty million dollars," said Thorne, calling his CFO at nearly ten o'clock.

"Yes, Mr. Thorne. I can have the wire done for you in the morning," said Stevens.

"No, Stevens. I need it in cash tonight. In fact, I need it within the hour. Bring it to my office."

"Uh, tonight, sir?"

"Yes. Do you have a problem with that?" asked Thorne.

"Uh, well, …"

"Do it, Stevens. I don't care how. Just do it!"

Stevens came into his office an hour later carrying a briefcase. "Here you are, sir. Forty million dollars." He opened it, showing the contents. "They're bearer bonds, sir. They can be claimed by anyone who physically has them in their possession."

"That will be all Stevens," Thorne answered.

Thorne shut the case. "What time is it?" he asked.

"It's eleven thirty, sir," Stevens replied.

"I have to go," Thorne said. "And Stevens, make sure you bury this as we discussed."

"I already have, sir."

*****

CH 2 Remaking Government

"Today commences a new dawn in America. It begins a new era in a country thirsty for change. And it will go down in history as the day America finally realizes its true potential as the leader of the world.

"It has taken us three hundred years, and during that time we have evolved from the lowest state of a republic with laissez faire capitalism to a much higher state of social and moral consciousness. As your president, I will lead this great country in a revolution – a revolution to reach that which was previously thought impossible – a utopian state of equality for all. It shall be a land where no child is hungry; no child is without an education; no child is denied healthcare; and no child is forced to work in horrible conditions, enslaved by ruthless business owners of all kinds! Each child should be able to pursue his or her dream, no matter what it is. It is the obligation of the people's government to provide for its children and to enable them to realize the possibility   that   exists   within   their   soul.

"It is my solemn commitment – one that I make to you, the children of this great nation -- that I shall leave no one behind. We must all, as a community, care for each other. The rich must look after the poor, the strong after the weak, the wise after those less gifted. We who walk the halls of power must tend to our flock. We must make sure our sheep are protected and that the wolves of capitalism are not permitted to devour the weakest among them. I will do that.

"Yes, my friends, utopia is within reach, and together we shall attain it!"

... *First Inaugural Address*
President John (Jack) Fourier 2041

During the four years of his first term, President Fourier spent most of his time pushing through edicts regulating day-to-day life among the citizenry. True to his words, he did seem to know what was best for his flock. Unhealthy foods were virtually eliminated from the country. Forced exercise became accepted. And, reduced working hours to just twenty-four per week, lowered stress levels for most Americans. The executive orders from the Oval Office were invasive, but people accepted that president Fourier and his Administration knew best what was good for the country ... for them. These things he sold to the people as easily as PT Barnum had sold curiosity tickets to his circus during the nineteenth century. People were drawn in by his likeability and magnetism. Just as had other charismatic leaders throughout history, Fourier had created himself as a demigod-like image, and with it, his people had become his obedient sheep – willing to follow him blindly wherever he wished to lead them.

By 2044, Fourier had positioned himself as the unquestioned champion of the little guy. As a populist, he manipulated the results of his failed programs and dismal economic record during the first four years to show unheralded success. With a compliant media, any questioning of his so-called facts was drowned- out as unpatriotic. As a result, the election against a demonized candidate from the Constitution Party became a landslide victory for the incumbent. Even his coattails had been long, marshalling in commanding majorities in both houses of Congress – enough for a supermajority in the Senate. His power was now assured.

The voting public believed they were getting four more years of the kinds of changes they'd come to accept as those that were 'good for them,' especially if they came with all sorts of government benefits and handouts. It was taking the good with the bad, and to them, it all balanced out. However, things changed after Fourier finished misstating the last few words of his second oath of office -- "... defend *a* Constitution of the United States," and omitting the "So help me God" part.

Within twenty-four hours of his second swearing in, President Fourier began phase two of his grand scheme to radically change the country. During the first one hundred-day honeymoon period, he expanded the number of departments within the Executive Branch from fifteen to thirty-two and renamed them *ministries*, rather than *departments*. He renamed all of them to be more in keeping with, as he put it, "the modernity of the times." As a result, departments like the Department of Defense, became the Ministry of International Policing; the Department of Energy, the Ministry of Energy Stewardship; the Department of Homeland Security, the Ministry of Domestic Policing; the Department of Education, the Ministry of Enlightened Learning; the Department of Housing and Urban Development, the Ministry of Residential Justice; the Department of Labor, the Ministry of Organized Labor; the Justice Department, the Ministry of Affirmative Justice; and the Department of Commerce, the Ministry of Fair Trade. New ones added were the Ministry of Facts & Statistics, the Ministry of Minority Rights, and some other society-changing ministry that the president said would be forthcoming. No one seemed to know anything about the new ministry other than to say that it was necessary to bring Americans back together – to unify the nation under a common cause. When asked when Congress would approve the new ministries, Fourier told the press that no authorization was needed. They were ministries and, therefore, he said, they did not come under the jurisdiction of Congress. No one challenged him. He merely told the people and Congress to trust him, as "I know what I'm doing, and everything I do is for the greater good."

The two most troubling departments were the IRS, now the Ministry of Taxation and Enforcement and the new Ministry of Facts & Statistics. These were the most powerful ministries in the Executive Branch, and each had gotten large increases in funding to grow their staffs and their control over others.

The Ministry of Taxation and Enforcement (MTE) had become a behemoth of an institution. With more than 325,000 employees it was larger than the military in size and considered far more lethal. It was a ministry used by the president to beat down opponents. One misplaced word and the MTE would be knocking on a citizen's door, asking for financial records to support a tax deduction. Simple and innocuous errors found in tax returns could result in lengthy jail time. Cases the MTE considered intentional tax evasion would result in sentences up to and including life in prison, and its interpretation of tax evasion was used liberally. As the penalties imposed were harsh, the treatment by tax agents could be even harsher. The most frightening words for most people to hear were "I'm from the MTE, and we need to talk."

The Ministry of Facts & Statistics was an altogether different animal. There had always been groups within each department that had dealt with compiling and distributing national statistics on employment, inflation, gross domestic product, money supply and thousands of other numbers upon which the country relied to make decisions. The new Ministry of Facts & Statistics (MFS) brought all of these groups under the central control of one minister. It was housed in the Old Executive Office Building, right next to the White House and had a high-level Cabinet person in its chief, Riley Chapman. Dr. Chapman had a multitude of credentials and diplomas from prestigious universities all over the developed world. He was cocky and arrogant, and his believed his numbers were never to be questioned – whether accurate or not.

Chapman knew which side he needed to be on to succeed, and it wasn't the Constitution Party. At this point, Fourier had a strangle-hold on the government. With super-majorities in both houses, Fourier could not be challenged. And what was most important was that people continued to believe he had all the answers. For that to happen, the statistics had to reflect prosperity and improvement, whether it was real or not. Therefore, every statistic that came out of Chapman's ministry had to support that premise. So, numbers were shaded, samples skewed, and favorable interpretations made whenever possible. When the results did not support the Administration's narrative, they were 'sent back for review,' which meant reanalyzed to get the answer for which the president was looking. Usually that meant changing the assumptions to get the best answer, whether excluding certain groups that caused the number to go in the wrong direction or changing the calculation altogether under the guise that it 'better represented the true nature of the statistic being reported.'

For the president's new social programs, he would insist on a short time horizon to minimize the impact on the federal deficit; for tax bills, the horizon was extended as far out as possible to improve the impact on the nation's debt. As a result, it was rare that the economy, unemployment, interest rates, poverty levels, educational performance, crime statistics or any other measure of how well a president is doing would be shown in decline or in a poor light. During World War II, Goebbels called it propaganda; now it was called truth.

But by far the biggest headache for any of the ministries was JC Sumner. Sumner questioned just about everything that came out of Chapman's ministry. At first, the minister himself would respond to petitions from the Congressman for backup detailing how the numbers were derived. However, this lasted only two months into the president's second term. Getting back vague explanations or fuzzy details behind the computations, Sumner not only didn't give up, but he pressed harder for answers. Soon, Chapman just ignored Sumner's requests, knowing that he would never be cited with a Contempt of Congress charge as his president's party controlled Congress.

Yet, Sumner persevered. He kept up his attacks on Chapman and many of the other ministries. Eventually, he would get some shred of information – a scrap here or a morsel there, but it was never enough to defend or justify the statistics being issued.

One ministry was particularly obstinate in revealing anything to the Congressman – that was the Ministry of Technology Assessment. In fact, he'd even received death threats shortly after he'd begun pursuing them for information. None of the threats could be traced back to the ministry, but he was always suspicious of the serendipity of the situation – particularly knowing the reputation of its deputy secretary – now a full minister – Angel Ratner. Of all the ministers, Sumner found her the most troubling, once remarking that she made his skin crawl.

"I've got some news, if you care to hear it," said Sumner's chief of staff, Marston. "But, on second thought, maybe I shouldn't ruin your day."

Sumner was just coming in the doorway to his congressional office. It was one of the smallest offices in the Longworth building, one of three used for House member offices. Since the House Speaker assigned offices, members of the opposing Constitution Party got virtual closets. The congressman threw his coat on the coat rack and went into his windowless cell.

It had only been two weeks since Sumner had returned to his office after being released from the hospital. Everyone, especially Maria, had told him to stay home and rest for a while longer, but he had ignored them. "I have the people's business to take care of," he'd said. "No, you're just being stubborn," Maria had answered him.

"How are you feeling, by the way?" asked Marston, embarrassed for asking as an afterthought.

"Oh, well, thanks for asking," quipped Sumner. "I'm great. How about you, Randy? How are you and the family?"

"We're well too sir. Sorry for not asking sooner."

"There's a lot going on right now, Randy. It's easy to get caught up in it all. So what's on your mind?"

"Well, I've got bad news and bad news. Which do you want first?"

"The good news, Randy. I always want the good news."

"I was afraid you'd say that. So for that, the only thing I have is that the weather looks like it's turning warmer on us. After our brutally cold winter, it's about time things improved, eh?"

"Yeah, so much for global warming, I guess," said Sumner, now flipping through his electronic video messages. "So, fine. What is the bad news then?"

"Well, you saw that Ratner got promoted to full minister. She's now the minister of the new Cabinet-level ministry – the Ministry of Technology Assessment. It's one of the seventeen new ones Fourier created. That means ..."

"Yeah, that means she's got even more power."

"Right."

"That's a problem. She was a threat to every American citizen and his freedom before. God help us now that she's sitting at the adult table in the White House," said Sumner.

"That's what I thought too. But what's worse is that new ministry the president alluded to in a speech a few weeks back – it's the one no one knows anything about."

"Yes, I can't seem to get any information on it. It's all so *hush-hush*. I don't know what to make of it."

"Well, the word I got today is that your favorite new minister may be angling for it," said Marston, watching the expression on his boss's face.

"You mean Ratner is trying to get the new ministry?"

"Yeah. That's what I heard."

"I don't think so. She's only now getting into the big leagues. I can't see Fourier putting her in the position of a major ministry – especially a brand new one. There would be too much at risk," said Sumner.

"Maybe. I just don't know. That's just what I heard."

"What's the other piece of bad news?" asked Sumner.

"I also heard that Fourier will announce that he is to change his own title. He no longer is to be called president."

"What?" cried Sumner. "What the hell does that mean? We've been calling the head of our country Mr. President ever since George Washington was in office. He set that precedent. There's no way Fourier would change that."

"I'm not sure that's what's meant, sir," exclaimed Marston.

"Then what do you mean?"

"I mean, that he may declare that he is no longer to be referred to as the President of the United States."

"Then what would we call him?" asked Sumner, looking perplexed.

Marston started to smile, but then held it back.

"Is this a joke?" Sumner asked, now believing his chief of staff was just leading him on.

"Uh, no. I don't think so. But now that you mention it, we could come up with some suggestions on what he should be called. Don't you think?"

"There are several things that come readily to mind. Yes, that's true," said Sumner, now grinning too.

"Should we have an office contest to see …"

"No," said Sumner, still smiling. "I think you've taken this far enough. Let me know if you find out anything more. Meanwhile, please keep any suggestions you may have to yourself. The last thing I need is some sophomoric prank coming out of this office to make us all look bad."

"Yes sir. But sir?" asked Marston.

"Yes?"

"Sometimes you just take all the fun out of things."

"I know," replied Sumner. "But that's my job."

*****

CH 3 A Disembodied Voice

The screen in his office announced that a call was coming in, but there was no image. Patrick, sound asleep at his home library desk, looked up, groggy and disoriented. It was nearly midnight, and he had told his wife that he would be upstairs in bed soon – but that had been over an hour earlier.

The number coming in showed as 'blocked' which meant that the caller did not want the number known. Still, this late at night Patrick thought the call might be important, so he said to the computer, "Answer."

"Answering call," his computer replied.

"Hello?" he asked, wondering who would be calling so late.

"Patrick? Is that you?" asked the voice. It was familiar, yet distant – sounding as if it were coming from halfway around the world.

"Yes, who is this?"

"Patrick, it's me, Sergei." The voice sounded panicked and distressed. "They've been holding me prisoner these past several days. I escaped, but I'm not sure where I am and I need your..." Then, there was a pause.

"Sergei, are you hurt? What's happening?"

"I'm torn up, Patrick. They beat me pretty good. I don't know exactly where I am either, but I think I'm still someplace around Boston. It's wooded, and there's a large body of water just up ahead ... wait a minute, there's a sign. It says Wachusett on it."

"That's the Wachusett Reservoir! It's just west of Boston, past Framingham."

There was another pause before Patrick heard, "Yes, past Framingham. That makes sense. Another sign says that Route 110 is just a mile to the north of here."

"Okay," said Patrick, only slightly more sober than he'd been an hour earlier. "Stay right there, Sergei! I'll be there in about thirty minutes."

"Patrick ... hurry! I can hear dogs in the distance. It won't take them long to find me." The line went dead.

Patrick grabbed his coat and ran to the car park door. But there he stopped, debating whether to leave Shea a note. He glanced over at the six-foot antique, grandfather's clock ticking away in the corner. *I just don't have time,* he thought. *Sergei is in trouble. His life is in danger.* Instead, he quietly closed the door behind him and hopped into his car. "Wachusett Reservoir, Route 110," he said, clearly and distinctly.

"Wachusett Reservoir, Route 110," came the car computer's reply. "Arrival time should be approximately twenty-three minutes."

The car's auto-pilot kicked in and took him out of the garage and down the street. Patrick was drunk, but he wasn't controlling the car. It would take him where he needed to go and use the most efficient routing possible. His heart raced, and the adrenaline ran freely within his system. Gun laws were so restrictive that he hadn't carried one in years, even though this was a time he sorely wished he had one. Instead, he kept an old ax handle in the trunk, just in case.

The small Mercedes took several lefts and rights before exiting through the front gates of the guarded complex. The guard waved him through after the steel-reinforced concrete barriers receded into the ground and the demagnetizing plates swung to the side. Nearly everyone lived in guarded complexes with ten-foot high cement walls, barbed wire strung across the top, together with broken glass embedded on top within the concrete itself. Crime had become rampant, and the justice system had all but given up on it. The courts were jammed, and so were the prisons. There was no money left for either, so citizens took matters into their own hands.

Patrick's car waited for the onboard cameras to determine no other vehicles were approaching and pulled out onto the main street. It was late, and few were out and about on a workday night. After a few minutes, Patrick calmed himself. He would have to get himself under control before he arrived at the reservoir. He didn't know what he might face, and he wanted to be in charge of all his faculties.

He took a deep breath and closed his eyes. "Let me know when we arrive," he commanded the computer.

"We will notify you when we arrive at your destination," answered the computer in a pre-selected, female British accent.

What Patrick didn't notice was a car turning on its lights immediately after his pulled out of the complex and onto the main road. Waiting only briefly, the black sedan began following at a distance behind, tracing every move made by the Mercedes as it made its way toward the Wachusett Reservoir.

***

Chou turned off her computer and disconnected the phone connection. Artificial intelligence had come a long way during the previous twenty years. Robots developed by the early 2020s had passed the Turing test, one proposed by Alan Turing in the 1950s to challenge scientists to create an artificial intelligence that could interact with a human without the human realizing it was not human. Chou's friend was an AI expert, and it was easy for him to adjust an AI's voice modulator to sound like Sergei and interact with Patrick as if her were talking with his old friend.

"Nicely done," she said, turning to her friend. "I think he bought it."

"It was no problem at all," said the expert. "Next time, give me something a bit more challenging."

Glancing over at Muntz's hologram, Chou said, "It's done. Disone should be headed in your direction. Let's get this done cleanly this time, shall we?" she said, sarcastically.

"It's as good as done. We'll kill several birds with one stone," said Muntz.

"Just don't kill the bird that's on his way to see you," said Chou.

"Don't worry. But I can't guarantee there won't be other birds left dead in the road at the end of the night. Birds get called along the roadside all the time, you know. All I care about is getting my hands on that forty mil."

"We are getting the forty million, remember? Don't forget I'm in this thing too. But just in case you do forget, you need to remember that Ratner gave me a copy of your FBI file to keep you tethered. It's in my vault. You won't get very far if you forget to cut me into the transaction."

"Understood," said Muntz, abruptly.

Then, the line went dead.

*****

CH 4 Sheriff of the Parish

Maria came into her husband's study and sat in the soft, Queen Anne's style chair next to him. He was resting on the striped but dimpled loveseat, his knees pulled up into to his chest to squeeze his stout frame into the limited space. Maria chuckled at the caricature in front of her – the well-known and honorable Congressman lying before her, all crumpled up on a five-foot sofa, snoring soundly. She was tempted to snap a picture to hold for some future roasting event or perhaps his upcoming sixty-fifth birthday, but she thought better of it. His eyes were closed, and he looked peaceful and content – something she hadn't seen in him for a very long time. *I'll let him sleep*, she thought.

But then she noticed he was partially lying on his PCD, so she got up and pulled it from under his body to make him more comfortable. On the razor thin, clear screen was the image of a man dressed in a Louisiana sheriff's uniform. *Odd*, she thought, but then she remembered the oil refinery explosion in Baton Rouge that Sumner had talked about and connected the dots.

"JC ... JC," she whispered gently, trying not to make her interruption so jarring.

Sumner rolled his head toward her sounds and fluttered his eyes. "Yeah ..." he mumbled, still not awake.

"JC, I think this is something important. JC?"

Finally, Sumner opened his eyes and began to focus. "Maria, good morning," he said, trying to unfold himself from the couch.

"Easy now," she said, putting her hand on his chest to keep him from moving too fast, too soon. "All I wanted to do was show you this ..."

She held up his PCD with the sheriff's image.

He blinked, and then said, "Yeah, I called and talked to him several nights ago, when I was still in the hospital. I asked him about the refinery explosion, but I could tell someone had gotten to him. He didn't want to give me anything, even though I tried to persuade him. He said he'd call me back on it, but I never heard from him."

"So, you haven't talked to him since then?" she asked, still looking at the picture on the device.

"No, it was at the hospital, after you left. I stayed up until ten-thirty before I nodded off."

"He called today, probably while you were sleeping. You didn't answer," said Maria, handing him his phone.

Sumner reached for the PCD to confirm the time. Indeed, the sheriff had called, but he'd left neither an audio nor video message.

"Crap," said Sumner. "Call Gauteaux," he said, telling his PCD to make the callback.

"Calling Sheriff Peter Gauteaux," answered the device.

The line rang several times, but there was no answer.

"He'll call back," said Maria, hopefully.

"Let's hope so. He's the only lead I have right now," said Sumner.

***

It was the next day when Sumner got the callback for which he'd been waiting.

"Sumner," he answered, turning on the video connection.

The image of Sheriff Gauteaux came on the screen, and Sumner pushed a button to create a 3-D image that floated in midair.

"Congressman, I don't have much time to talk. I do want to assist, if I can. But ... "

"But what?"

"You do understand the dangerous situation you're putting me in, don't you?"

"I'm sorry, but ..."

"Listen, whatever I tell you, you didn't get from me. Do you hear?"

"Yes, of course," answered Sumner.

"Alright, then what I know is this. I arrived at the plant at about ten that night. The fire was burning out of control when I got there. Water from the refinery pumper trucks and even the backup pumping station that brings up water from the Gulf of Mexico wasn't enough to put it out. We knew if we couldn't get it under contained fast, it would be, well, bad. We were all afraid the fire would engulf the whole place. And ... it did. The explosions came fast and furious. It was like being back in the war. All we could do was get to a bunker and try not to get blown apart."

"Go on."

"They said that over a hundred died when the first blast went off."

"Is that true?"

"I don't know. All I know is that when I walked out of the bunker later that night, it looked like the place had been carpet bombed. Dead bodies were everywhere. It was then that I was told to go back to the station – the parish police station. I objected, telling these men in black suits that had arrived out of nowhere that this was now a crime scene, and I had to seal off the area."

"Who were these men in black suits?"

"Feds. I don't know where they were from. They just showed me their badges, which said FBI, but I don't think they were from the Bureau. But at that moment, it really didn't matter. Several black helicopters landed by the plant headquarters and more men in dark suits jumped from the choppers, briefcases strapped to their wrists. They stormed the control room, and before I could call for backup, they drew guns on me."

"What about the others there with you?"

"It was just the general plant manager and a bunch of his supervisors. They took one look at these guys and black and did whatever they were told. They weren't going to flinch without first asking permission."

"What did the men tell the plant manager?" asked Sumner.

"I really don't know. They pulled me away, pointing their M-18 submachine guns at me. They told me that they were relieving me of my responsibilities. They said they would take it from there. Needless to say, I got in my cruiser and left."

"That's it? That's all you know?"

"No. I have friends in Homeland Security. They were helping me track down who gave the orders to send in the men in black suits. They alluded to the fact that the decision was made at the minister level or above."

"Or above? Really? What do you mean?"

"I mean exactly what I just said … *or above*. They suggested that the actual decision to pull the whole thing off was made on Pennsylvania Avenue."

"The White House?" Sumner asked.

"I don't know."

"The president has been saying for years that he's wanted to break the backs of big oil."

"I don't know, congressman. I swear," said the sheriff. "At this point, my contacts at Homeland Security won't return my messages anymore. I'm afraid for them at this point. I assume they've been threatened like I have."

"Who threatened you?"

"I can't say."

"Sheriff, I can't help you if you don't tell me."

"You can't help me anyway, congressman. But I can tell you this ..."

"What's that?"

"I was told to give you a message if you contacted me. I told the person that I would not tell you a thing, but that I would convey this message."

"Go on," said Sumner.

"Pardon me, Congressman Sumner, but I was told to give you this number to call if you had any questions. And that's all I would do. The number is 312-555-1789."

"Okay. I appreciate your time. You are a brave man, sheriff. The country is indebted to you for your service."

The sheriff began to break down, his face bunching up as he fought to hold back the tears. "I have a wife and kids, sir. If you breathe a word to anybody that I said any of this – they will be killed. Please don't."

"Okay," Sumner responded. "I promise. I won't." He hung up. It was unfortunate that Americans were being threatened by their own government for telling the truth. It wasn't something new, but it was something that was becoming more and more wide-spread.

He looked down at the number. He didn't know why he was hesitating, but something inside him was holding out a caution flag. Why? he thought. Why should I be frightened? I'm a U.S. Congressman, for God's sake. Surely, they wouldn't knowingly harm someone in my position, would they?

Sumner took a deep breath. "Call 312-555-1789," he said.

"Calling the number, now," responded his computer.

The phone on the other end rang seven times, and Sumner was about to hang up with there was an answer.

"Hello?" Sumner asked, when no one on the other end seemed to respond. "To whom am I speaking?"

There was no video connection, but there was an audio track. It was a prerecorded message, using a digitally synthesized voice.

"Congressman Sumner. We've been expecting this call. Understand that this is a phone number will not be traceable and the PCD will self-destruct following the conclusion of this message. Please hold for this important message."

Sumner didn't have to wait long. It was a screeching, high-pitched noise, followed by three beeps. Then, he heard:

You have been warned! Don't continue on this path, or we will kill your beloved Maria! We will slit her tender throat in broad daylight, regardless of any feeble security you think you have in place. Likewise, Sheriff Gauteaux will find his wife, Marilyn, and his precious little daughters, Caitlin nine, Amanda six, and Jennifer two, in a trash bin behind some abandoned warehouse. It would be a shame if that happened. Don't you agree?"

There was another shrill, ear-piercing sound before all was quiet – deathly quiet.

*****

CH 5 Wachusett

The car turned off sharply onto the dirt road, which led down to the reservoir. Even though it was dark, the dust swirled visibly in the red afterglow of the taillights. As it rolled down the hill toward the lake, it shut off its headlights and slowed, making sure that it didn't miss any unusual sign or marker along the way. Eventually, it slid closer to the water, its engine propelled only by photovoltaic cells buried in the trunk. It was quiet, almost silent, as it drifted nearer to the water's edge. But just as the dirty-gold path ahead swerved off to the right but before the expansive block of pure blackness – the reservoir that loomed beyond -- two headlights flashed on only yards away. The car stopped dead in its tracks. Then, the lights ahead blinked out as suddenly as they'd come on. For more than a minute, nothing happened, only the chirping crickets pierced the silence and the inaction.

Finally, a car door opened. The light from the full moon overhead reflected off the high-gloss of the car door's ebony paint. Emerging from beneath the gull-wing door was an inky, dark figure. Clad only in black, it pushed a button on the outside of the sleek coupe, making the door glide down silently into its cradle in the chassis. Hesitating for a moment, the image walked quickly toward the opposing car.

Standing outside the rear passenger side of the car, the figure waited while the back window dissolved, revealing the pale, worried face of Kilby Thorne. "Who are you?" Thorne asked the dark image, standing just outside his door.

The figure said nothing. Its hands in its pockets, it merely stared inside the car from under the shadowy hoodie pulled sharply forward to cover its face.

"You understand that there is a gun spotting you inside this car right now," said Thorne, nervous, but aggressive.

"I couldn't have expected anything less," said the figure.

Finally, there was enough reflection from the moonlight for Thorne to see that it was a man with a scruffy, dark beard.

"Where is she? My wife," Thorne asked, trying not to overreact.

"She's here," said the man, casually.

"Where?" the CEO demanded.

"I'll show you where-when we make the exchange," said the man.

"I don't think that's the way this works," said Thorne. "I want my wife. Otherwise, you'll have a bullet through your head."

"And you'll have a dead wife," came the answer.

Thorne paused. "Okay. So, what's next?"

"Give me half now; half when you get your wife."

"Where is she?"

"Half now," said the man, adamantly.

Thorne huffed and then reached down under the seat. The man outside pulled his gun and pointed it toward Thorne's forehead. "Don't do something stupid!" he yelled.

"Relax," said Thorne, calmly. "I'm just getting my briefcase. I assume you want the money the old fashion way – in bills?"

"Hand it over slowly," said the man, waving toward himself with is free hand.

Thorne opened the briefcase and took out half the money, handing forty bundled packets of five thousand dollar bills to the man, who stuffed them into a crumpled, brown bag he took out from under his jacket. As money had become more worthless than ever before, the Federal Mint had begun printing 500-dollar, 1,000-dollar, 5,000-dollar and even a few 10,000-dollar bills.

"Wait here," said the man. He walked back to his car and got in. A few minutes later, he got out and moved back up the hill toward Thorne's car.

Thorne pushed the button again to dissolve his window. "Where is she?" he asked, agitated.

The man touched his lapel's com device. "It's a go," he said, simply, mumbling into the mic. Then he turned to Thorne and said, "You have exactly three minutes. Follow this road down to the water. You'll find it turns to the right and follows the reservoir for about a quarter mile or less. You'll see a tree stump on your right side – farther up into the woods. You need to drop off the rest of the money there. But I wouldn't take too long. About fifty yards ahead you'll see a car rolling into the water. Your wife and a 'friend' are in it. You'll get your love and your SECE plans at the same time … but you may want to hurry. Our offer expires in three minutes … Oh, and by the way. If you decide not to stop to drop off the money, the car is detonated to explode with both of them inside. It's all up to you now."

Thorne started to answer, but the man briskly walked away.

Thorne was panicked. His mind was a blur. *Had the man really told him he only had three minutes to drop off the money and save his wife?*

"You heard the man," said Thorne. "Step on it! We have to get to my wife!"

The driver sped off down toward the reservoir at full speed. He drove so fast that he almost missed the turn, nearly flipping the car into the water. But he was able to make the turn and fly down the half-paved road at a torrid pace. Even in the dark, the dust roiled into the air, scattering the moonlight in all directions and making the scene a confusing cauldron of noise, dense haze and raw delirium.

"Faster!" Thorne shouted at the driver. "We have less than two minutes!"

The car continued, skidding on the loose gravel as the tires tried to torque, gripping whatever pieces of earth they could to push the car onward. The lights of the car showed nothing ahead but the dirt road and the blackness beyond it. Thorne watched carefully out his window, trying to spot the tree stump he dare not miss.

"We've only got a minute left?" screamed Thorne, looking at his watch. "Did you see any kind of stump?"

In the distance, the road seemed to end, veering sharply again to the right and away from the water. But before that, their headlights scanned the front-end of a black car rolling slowly toward the water. The front wheels were just starting to break the surface of the water, but the car was moving fast enough to make a splash as it struck the liquid surface.

"Vance, stop the car!" cried Thorne, pulling back on his driver's shoulder. Thorne jumped out of the car and ran toward the submerging vehicle. Inside, he could see his wife in the front passenger's seat; her eyes were closed. He began banging on the window, but he couldn't wake her. "Patty! Patty! Wake up!" But he got no response. The car continued to slide into the cold water. Thorne tried to open the door, but it was locked from the inside. He started pushing back on the car, trying to keep it from moving, but it made little difference. Then, he saw a red dot appear on the back of his wife's head inside the car.

"Sh*t!" said Thorne, realizing he'd missed the tree stump along the way and now his wife would die whether by drowning or being shot. "Vance, we've got to go back and find that tree stump!"

Tearing his soul apart, Thorne left his wife and stumbled back up the road to find the tree stump. It wasn't as close to the road as the man had suggested. Instead, it was tucked away back into the surrounding woods.

"It's right here, sir!" cried Vance, motioning to his boss.

Thorne ran to the stump and dropped the suitcase – the other twenty million dollars. Then he found his way back to the black sedan. It was sinking fast. Already, the water was up to Patty's shoulders in the front seat, and there looked to be no way to get her out alive.

His body wracked with panic, Thorne didn't know what to do. It was the first time that he truly felt helpless. All he could do was watch as his wife slipped quietly into the dark waters of the Wachusett Reservoir, as they filled her lungs and extinguished her life forever.

Thorne pulled his hair and tore at his face. "Vance! What can we do? We have to save her! We have to!"

The driver ran over to help, but even with both of them pulling back on the car as hard as they possibly could, it continued to roll forward, ignoring their pleas and attempts at heroics.

Then, there was a ringing sound coming from Thorne's PCD. He wasn't going to look, but it kept ringing. The car was already halfway into the water, the black wetness rising quickly inside the passenger compartment and beginning to cover the bottom cushions of the rear seats. Now, Thorne was frozen with fear – trying to save his wife's life yet annoyed by the persistence of the phone call that wouldn't leave him alone. Finally, seeing no hope and no solution, he answered the call.

"What do you want!" he yelled.

"Did you drop off the money?" a man's voice asked him.

"Yeah! I did it minutes ago. Now let my wife go! I held up my end of the bargain! Now you hold up yours!"

"Very well," the voice answered before hanging up.

Thorne turned back to the car. He began wading into the lake, trying frantically to open the rear door. Several times he pulled on the handle, but it yielded nothing. The water was now up to his wife's neck. Soon she would be breathing in the deadly waters from the lake. "Patty!" he shouted with sweat dripping off his forehead. "Patty, can you hear me?"

"Try the door again, sir," said Vance. "I thought I heard a click."

Thorne pushed the button on the outside to engage the door. He heard the battery whirl inside the car and the passenger door start to pop open. Then it stopped. "You've got to be f*cking kidding me!" shouted Thorne, as the water continued to rush into the car's compartment. The lake water had flooded the engine and battery compartment, making the connection to the door short-out.

"Come on!" Thorne said, pleading and pounding his fist on the car. "Work, you son-of-a-bitch! You've got to work!" He tried the button again, but the passenger door went up less than another foot. "Vance, help me with her. We have to drag her out from under this door!"

Vance squeezed in through the opening. "I'm stuck!" he said, gasping for air.

"Hold on, Vance. You're fine. We can do this! We can!" said Thorne, doing everything he could to help.

Vance calmed himself and pulled the emergency quick-release on Patty's restraint. He then grabbed her by the waist and eased her out through the bottom of the doorway. She was unconscious and, as dead weight, she felt like almost twice the hundred or so pounds she normally carried. Together they had to push her head briefly below the water's surface to rescue her from the clutches of the lower edge of the door.

Pulled free of the door, she began coughing as she fought for her next breath of air.

Thorne pulled her free, just as the car started to vanish below the surface of the water. As the hood and windshield disappeared below the rippled surface, he saw another figure on the driver's side, unmoving. But it was too late. At that moment, the car sank from view, folding itself into the deep clutches of the watery graveyard beyond. At the end, there was a only a small *blurp* of white foam that got expelled up to the surface. That was the end of it.

Patty coughed, a deep hacking attempt to clear her lungs. And Thorne took her in his arms, ready to do anything to make her feel better and once more among the living.

"Honey, are you alright?" asked Thorne, compassionately.

"I ... I think so," she answered him, being held in his arms, but lying on the ground next to the bank of the lake. Then, she shook her head, as if trying to get out of a fog. "Kilby! Kilby! I think there's a man inside the car! You ... you have to ..." she gasped.

"*Shhh*," Thorne answered holding her. "*Shhh*, Patty. You have to save your strength. There's ... there's nothing I can do. If somebody was in there ... well ..."

Patty began to sob softly. It was all coming down on her, crushing her with the reality of what she'd just been through – just endured. "I ... I know someone was in there. I know it!"

"Patty, you need to calm yourself now," said her husband.

"I just don't know anymore," she said about nothing in particular.

Thorne pulled her close – never wanting to let her out of his sight again. Even though he could sometimes be a monster at work, when it came to his wife, he was protective, even doting. At the same time, he watched as his chance of getting the SECE engine plans vanished below the currents in the reservoir. Presumably, the other passenger had held its secrets. There had really been no choice, but then, he sensed that the shrouded man or the mysterious Roger Mertz or perhaps the one-in-the-same, knew that all along. If so, he had been clever, and it had worked.

Thorne helped his wife back to his car, while Vance started the engine. They really didn't need a chauffeur – the car did everything on its own -- but his position had demanded it. It was a tradition at GovCo's. The leader, just like within the higher circles of politics, got the perks of office. After getting his wife situated in the backseat, with a blanket thrown around her to keep her warm, he motioned for Vance.

"What is it, sir?"

"Wait here," Thorne answered, getting out of the backseat and closing the door behind him. He walked back up the dirt road and then into the brush to where they'd found the stump. He shook his head before returning.

"Well?" asked Vance.

"It's gone. But I knew it would be. Vance, it's time to go home. It's been a long night."

"Yes, sir," his chauffeur replied, and the car turned on its lights and moved on up the path toward the main road.

All Thorne could do now was think about the forty million dollars disappearing somewhere into the deep woods. He had no money, no billion-dollar engine, and worse yet, no briefcase. Yet, he glanced over at the seat next him and smiled. She was sleeping quietly. He realized he had saved something far more valuable.

*****

CH 6 Ministry of Unity

An urgent press conference was called by the White House, and the president demanded that all *friendly* media outlets send their reporters. Physically attending such conferences was no longer necessary, as virtual press rooms were made available; however, most journalists preferred attending to see better the nuances in the president's facial expressions and body language that were more telling than what he was saying to them.

But, there was another thing that did not change — the punctuality of the president. The press grew increasingly agitated when Press Secretary Ken Biester appeared and announced that the six o'clock conference would not start until seven. At seven, he announced the new time was eight. Finally, at eight-thirty, Biester came out to give them more bad news.

"At this time, the president has another engagement from which he is unable to break-away," said Biester. "However, he has instructed me to convey his thoughts on several important matters facing the nation and our people."

There were groans throughout the press room, and even more over the video and audio feeds provided to the virtual press rooms on the SI-net. Fourier always had a plan, and there was a reason he'd chosen not to attend. The press had learned this during his time in office, and as with most things, they wouldn't learn the truth until months or even years later.

"On the economy," Biester said, "the president has a clear vision on how to sustain the robust recovery we've been enjoying." Of course, this was a statement the White House had repeated over and over. Most people did not believe it, as they were not living the 'dream' he said was theirs to be had. Certainly, the reporters had reported it that way. But, even they were becoming cynics, if not patent disbelievers. "He will be disseminating an executive order to deal with the residual unemployment problem and inflationary issues of the day. While these are not serious, the president wants to be proactive to ensure these do not get out of control. He has said that if we don't address these problems head-on now, we may have larger problems later."

These remarks made several reporters in the room shake their heads. Things were already out of control, and to state that the president was being *proactive* was such a mischaracterization that they weren't sure how they would try to report it. It was a tight-rope walk -- playing the friendly journalist game helped them avoid being personally harassed by the Department of Taxation Compliance; however, writing obvious falsehoods undermined what shred of credibility they had left.

"What President Fourier believes we need," said the press secretary, raising his voice, "is equality of pay! CEO's of companies should make the same as their mailroom workers! The president is outraged by these executives getting huge paychecks and bonus packages for doing nothing! If we just took away the divide between what CEO's make and their workers, we would be able to fix the problems we have in the economy. In fact, a good example is Thomas P. Berkshire, the CEO of Norwood Industries. He made 56 million last year, while his administrative assistant only made five hundred thousand. Kilby Thorne of EG, made 36.5 million last year. And there are hundreds of others."

These two men had long been financial supporters of Fourier and the Administration. However, Biester's citing them did not come from some random selection; it was intentional. The companies of both men had not contributed nearly as much to Fourier's political action committee as they had in previous years, nor had they donated to the National Committee of the People's Party. It was the type of revenge, the president enjoyed. Within days, he would most likely contact each man and convey the importance of upholding his company's long-standing tradition of supporting what he considered just and honorable causes.

"The president believes these numbers are unacceptable in a country where the average worker takes home only 180 thousand dollars per year. The poverty level is at 137 thousand for a family of four. These tycoons do not *need* the kind of money they make. This Administration feels these are good examples of obscene capitalism and greed at its finest. That is why the president will be introducing an order that will level the playing field -- paying those at the top the same as those at the bottom. *That*, he feels, is what is just and right. That, he says …"

But, he was interrupted by another voice coming from behind him. It was deeper and more commanding.

"… is what is right for America and for my people. Thank you, Kenneth. I'll take it from here."

"Yes, Mr. President," said the press secretary, as he stepped aside.

It was as if the king had entered the room. It was rare these days that Fourier appeared at a press conference. There was little to be gained, as he already had them in his pocket. In fact, one reporter once quipped that Fourier could probably shoot someone in the front row and the headline that day would read: *Reporter Acts Impertinently and is Disciplined by President*.

"This is a monumental day," the president said, grasping the edges of the podium with his large, rough-knuckled hands. "This is a day for which I have been waiting a very long time. America is ready for significant change, for a remaking that it so desperately seeks. America has matured as a country. It is no longer tone deaf to its workers and their plight. It does not curry favor with the bosses while the employees starve. We are a humanitarian-driven nation – not one obsessed with money and riches.

"In fact, I have been setting the foundation for this action for many years. When I brought up the idea as a young senator many told me it was wonderful, but that it could never happen in this country. 'The nation is too corrupted by the industrialists,' they said. 'There is too much power held by the corporate moguls to ever trickle down to the common man,' said others. And some told me that everyone is just too afraid to do what's right. But I knew it was possible, and today it is a reality.

"Today, I am announcing a new program that will ensure that every American receives the same compensation as every other. Class struggle will no longer exist. The rich will no longer gloat over the poor. There will be no favoritism given those with money and power. They will not receive special treatment or gain unfair access to the good life when others who are less fortunate are shunned and deprived of such benefits. My critics claim that what I've been doing is against the Constitution and against what the Founders wanted. Now, I believe I can agree with them without fear of retribution.

"Our Founding Mothers and Fathers did not have the benefit of the deep and profound thinking of Karl Marx and Friedrich Engels at the time they created the patchwork of modern government that was born from the bosom of the U.S. Constitution. The word *communism* rose to prominence during the nineteenth century, but was demonized in this country. Those who preferred the *status quo* of an unjust world were ignorant then as they are now. They were the ones who propagated the myth that communism was evil and that people suffered under its care. It has been distorted at every turn. It has been presented as a scourge of the world, when it was actually the savior of the world. It is a compassionate philosophy – one that holds a sensible, tangible perspective on the theories that the dark-ages of religion once offered. Although we all know now that religion and the belief in some god somewhere is misguided and dates back to pre-civilization, we as a species have struggled to get beyond that. We are at a higher level of consciousness than man was, say, even two hundred years ago. And as we must cast off the shackles of religion, so too we must throw away the enslavement of capitalism. Just as slaves broke the whip of their plantation owner, we must break the whip of the business owner."

There was little sound in the room, as the reporters listened to the words of revolution espoused by their president.

"It is disputable, but acknowledged, that capitalism *may* have been useful to bring the country into the period known as the Industrial Revolution. However, we live in the Current Era. Capitalism has no place in a civilized society. It is an economic philosophy that is harmful to our way of life. Only a few rich executives thrive in that environment, as they skim off the cream and leave sour curd for the rest of us. They become billionaires, and we're left with whatever scraps we can sweep off the floor at midnight for our children's next meal. As they said at the turn of this century, it's those one percenters that get everything and leave nothing for us!

"That's why our children are starving, dying by the thousands from malnourishment each day and from hazards created by deleterious products that are produced in our vile, smoke-belching factories. Even with all we have tried to do with the environment, companies are polluting our water, our air, and our school playgrounds. Millions of young children die every year from these contaminants. That is an undisputable fact. And, while the fat-cat owners earn billions off of you – the hard-working people who suffer in the country's sweatshops – your children suffer in silence. I have done my best to protect the middle class and the poor from the self-serving acts of the rich, but it has come to a point that more must be done. We must protect our children and safeguard their future. We cannot let the filthy rich steal the wealth of this country. It will not happen on my watch! I commit that to you today!"

There was general, polite applause in the press room. Although such plaudits used to be frowned upon as a sign of bias, reporters used them occasionally to reaffirm their commitment to the president's agenda and his narrative.

"Therefore, effective immediately, I am issuing an Executive Order which I call the *Unity Plan*. This plan will create an even-playing field for everyone. All Americans will get the same benefits, regardless of their position in life. And, to pay for the plan and police all companies to ensure it is enforced, I am announcing the assumption of all corporate assets large and small by the people of America."

It was then that Fourier expected a cacophonous outpouring of cheering and whistling by the news groups present. He actually believed they would rise from their chairs and jump with excited jubilation at the news. However, instead, they sat in stone silence.

The look on his face was one of puzzlement, but he was polished enough as a politician to realize that the reaction he anticipated was not going to be forthcoming. So, he merely cleared his throat and reached for a crystal goblet of ice water that had been placed on the table next to him.

"All assets owned by these businesses will be subsumed by the Ministry of Government's Funds, or what you used to call the Department of the Treasury, and all profits made by these entities will be earned on behalf of the citizenry of this great country. It will be my responsibility as leader of this great nation, to make sure the government acts responsibly as the trustee of those assets – to safeguard them on behalf of the American people.

"Only by sharing this wealth with *all* Americans can this nation remain strong. The assets and income from all companies – large and small -- will allow us to pay off our debts and fund new social programs that will provide relief for all Americans. These new programs will raise people off the dirt floor of poverty and give them the gold and marble that they deserve -- a lifestyle that, until now, was exclusive only for the rich.

"Therefore, I've created a new ministry to direct this program and ensure its success. This new body will be the Ministry of Unity, and with four hundred thousand employees it will be directed by …."

Fourier looked to his right where the curtain was pulled back again, and out stepped Angel Ratner.

There was another shockwave that rippled through the room. Without another word from the president, people there understood that this new ministry would be powerful, and its new minister would, therefore, assume a mantle of authority like no other in the Cabinet. The combination was frightening. Ratner was the last person anyone wanted given that power. It was a dangerous person to whom such trust was about to be given.

"I have known Angel Ratner for many years. She is extremely competent and is well-suited to take-on this new responsibility. I now present to you, Minister Ratner, the new head of the Ministry of Unity. Ms. Ratner …"

"Thank you," said Ratner, stepping forward and beaming. "I am honored to assume the role of minister for this great new program. Not since the glory days of the FDR and the 1930s, have we had such leadership in the White House as we do now. I applaud our president for making such a bold gesture to right the wrongs of this country and make us, once again, the most moral, human, and caring country in the world.

"What I will share with you is that the president's Ministry of Unity will forge a new covenant with the American people. I've already discussed this with the president, and we will enforce new orders from his Oval Office. Among these will be: First, a mandate of one year of salary for any employee terminated by a commercial business – large or small. Second, lifetime pensions equal to at least ninety-five percent of a worker's salary. Third, a reduced workweek, permitting employees to work no more than thirty hours per week but require a flat pay for thirty hours, whether worked or not. Fourth, an increase in the required number of paid vacation weeks to eight, excluding the fifteen days formally recognized as federal holidays. Fifth, a reduction in the retirement age to fifty, with the company paying a supplemental bridge until social security kicks in at age seventy-five. Sixth, the government will assume the majority of seats on all GovCo boards of directors. Seventh, all companies, large and small, *must* be union shops. Henceforth, each state will enact union-required work laws to replace existing ones. New unions will be setup and sponsored by my ministry as needed. And lastly, the Ministry of Stock Trade Policing will monitor GovCo stock trades and ensure no profits from stock trading exceed four percent per year.

"But, this is just the start. We will be considering more dramatic measures during the weeks and months ahead. It is a very exciting time. Things are going to change, and it's all for the good," she said enthusiastically.

Ratner stepped away from the podium and let Fourier close the meeting. The president did not take questions after the conclusion of his remarks. Instead, he and his new minister walked off the stage, smiling and chatting like two old, collegiate friends.

As the days passed, there were no more details on the forthcoming Unity Plan, as promised by the president during the press conference. Neither President Fourier nor Minister Ratner elaborated on how making all pay equal would fix anything, nor did they explain how taxing corporations at 100 percent of profits and seizing all of their assets would help the future growth of the country. However, the direction of the program was all that was necessary -- and it was honey for the journalistic bees. The media swooped in and gobbled it up, splashing headlines that read *President to Right the Wrongs of Capitalism* as well as *Equal Pay for All!* across the headlines of their flagging e-papers.

The few blogs that continued to escape the jamming of government SI-net censors took the Administration to task over the comments. Doing the troublesome chore of calculating the impact of the president's changes on the economy, most blogs were in agreement that there was only one outcome – free commerce, as it was once known in the country, was dead. Congress didn't have to get involved and it chose not to, as the mandate was issued as an executive order.

Finally, after two months, the Unity Plan was unveiled with its fifteen thousand pages of laws, one hundred thirty thousand pages of regulations and four-and-a-half million pages of interpretations that had the same force and effect of law. Since it would take years to sort out what the law really did or did not do, the result was that the Ministry of Unity had free-rein to do as it wished – when, where and how it wished.

By implementing the Unity Plan so quickly, no company had been given the time to move assets or take precautionary measures to limit losses. Shareholders were wiped out overnight, and the public stock exchanges were quickly shuttered. By extension, land and other assets held by the rich were confiscated as the

Administration claimed that they had benefited personally from businesses they had run, so those assets and profits too must come under the control of the feds.

Ratner orchestrated marches within all the major cities to demonstrate faux, public approval by for their actions. Banners were printed, placards made, and chants rehearsed to make it look like home-grown, spontaneous events. Media coverage was coordinated to guarantee that every street corner was covered by the best angles for the cameras. Thousands showed up, but only after social media announced that all participants would receive a free PCD phone and one thousand dollars for participating without mentioning that it was all at taxpayers' expense.

Minister Ratner quickly assumed consolidated her power and setup commissions to oversee and manage each company in each industry. Wages were fixed at the same level, regardless of the person's duties. And, although nearly all at the bottom of the pay scale assumed they would get huge increases, they did not. Instead, the wages of everyone at the higher levels were lowered to boost company profits for the government. All profits were taxed at 100 percent and forwarded to Washington. Manipulation of the books was also carefully policed to ensure executives didn't create other means to reward themselves. Soon after the new orders were effective, others were promulgated to ban and replace public accounting firms that had historically done audits of companies with yet another ministry that would do that – the Ministry of Financial Compliance.

Experienced, senior managers at many companies quit and sought positions in subsidiaries outside the U.S. That loophole was quickly closed when the minister issued orders to revoke the passports of all leaving the country on self-declared business trips. They would never be able to return to the U.S. and never able to visit their families again. Then, all visa applications for trips outside the country suddenly became holiday trips. The ministry was working on how to address that problem.

So, the economy ground to a halt. With the output of the country, as measured by the gross domestic product (GDP), falling by nearly 23 percent, a new crisis was born. But out of crises came other opportunities for the Administration. Blaming companies and the rich for hording their wealth and not turning over assets and income to the government, Minister Ratner mobilized what was formerly known as the National Guard into a group called the Red Shirts Brigade.

"I approve," said the president, looking over the proposal from his Minister of Unity. "I think we should recruit thousands to this cause. We need to police the people and commerce from every angle, and it will take an army of people to do this. If we don't have a million in the Red Shirts Brigade, we don't have enough to make sure people are doing what they should be doing.

"Minister Ratner," said the president, "you need to build an internal, military group that will be our eyes and ears. We have to know what everyone is doing, when they are doing it, and where it will happen. Then, we have to crush any revolt. It must be silenced before a whimper is heard. Do you understand?"

"Yes, sir," said Ratner. "I understand completely."

*****

CH 7 A Body Found

The peeling of church bells blared from the speakers of her alarm clock, acting like daggers piercing her head. "It's time to get up," said her computer, as the piezoelectric windows of her home changed darkness into daylight, letting the sun from outside drench her bedroom with color and brightness.

"Shut up!" Shea yelled, temporarily silencing the sound. But, then she just rolled back over on her side as if nothing had happened. Five minutes later, the bells sounded again, reminding her of Quasimodo's words from Victor Hugo's timeless story of Notre Dame – the bells ... the bells! he would say covering his ears as the church rang out, calling to its faithful.

"Shut the f*** up!" she yelled, more vehemently this time. She lay there only a minute more, before she rolled off the side of the bed and walked to the bathroom to get ready for the day. Some twenty minutes later, she emerged and stepped quietly over to the bed to kiss her husband goodbye before leaving for the office. Yet, when she approached, she found his sheets and pillows undisturbed from the night before.

He must have just fallen asleep in his study, she thought.

Shea put on her earrings -- small diamond studs her husband had given her for their tenth wedding anniversary -- and hurried downstairs to get toast a sesame seed bagel before running in to the office. Like many things, it had become a ritual.

After pulling the lightly toasted bagel from the small oven, Shea bit into it as she approached the doors to Patrick's study. "Patrick?" she called, "I'm about ready to leave. I'll see you in the office, Okay?" She opened one of the two French, walnut doors that led into his private office. "Patrick?" she asked again, poking her head inside.

Her husband wasn't there; the big, overstuffed leather chair behind the desk was empty.

She called out his name again, this time in the direction of the rest of the house, but no one answered. Opening the inside door from the house to the garage, she saw that his car was gone – the British-racing, dark green -- nearly black -- Jaguar he had owned for over twenty years. *I wonder where the hell he is?* she thought. *He'd better have left me a note. Maybe I just missed it.*

She walked back into the house and scanned the kitchen counters. But, there was no sign of any message.

Shea went back to the garage. "Open door one," she said, watching as the double-wide garage door rose. But, just outside, at the end of their driveway, a black-and-white police car was parked, it's red and blue lights strobing from within the windshield glass.

Shea stood still, watching to see where they were headed. An uneasy chill came over her, but she shrugged it off. *It's just coincidental,* she forced her mind to believe. *He'll be moving down the street any moment.* However, the car didn't move. It remained parked in front of their house, the men inside talking to their computer and each other.

Finally, the doors to the police cruiser opened, and Shea's heart nearly stopped. Both officers got out of the car and made their way up the long, serpentine driveway toward her.

No, she thought. *No! This is not happening!* Her mind struggled with what was unfolding before her eyes. She had witnessed scenes like this before, both on TV and in the movies, but she never thought they would be replayed for her in front of her very own home.

"Hello, officers. Is there a problem?" She tried to hold herself together, but there was something wrong -- something *very* wrong.

"Ma'am?" said the older officer, in a dry, formal voice. "Are you Shea Disone?"

"Yes," she answered, almost robotically, "I am. Why? What is it?"

The officer looked down at the ground. Even though he'd done this many times during his career, it was never easy.

"I'm afraid … ma'am," he started. "Is your husband Patrick Disone?"

At that moment, she knew what was coming. "Something's happened to him. Hasn't it?" she asked numbly.

"I'm afraid so, ma'am. We need you to come with us down to the station."

"Why? What is it?" she asked frantically.

"Ma'am, we believe that your husband may have been in an accident. We need for you to identify a body. We think we found him this morning. I'm sorry."

Shea's face drained of all feeling and emotion. The world around her began to spin, she grabbed her head to make it stop.

"Ma'am? Perhaps you should sit down. You don't look very good," said the other officer, standing beside his copartner.

Shea knelt on the grass to steady herself. "What … uh … what happened?" she stuttered, still light-headed.

"I'm sorry, ma'am. We don't know a lot at this point, other than his car went off the road near West Boylston, down at Wachusett Reservoir. There was a side road that looped down toward the water. Someone jogging there this morning spotted a purse and other personal articles washed up on the shore. Then, they saw a vehicle submerged in about twenty feet of water. We pulled the car out of the lake, but we still don't know what caused the accident. Was he drinking last night, Ms. Disone?"

Shea knew he'd been drinking, but he'd never drive drunk. "I don't know, officer. All of this is such a shock," she said, trying to hold back tears.

"I understand," said the younger cop. "Right now, we need you to come down to the station. We have a few more questions and we'll need you to ..."

"I know," she said abruptly. "Does it have to be right now?"

"Well, sometime today. I'm sorry to have to ask this, but it's policy," said the older officer.

Shea didn't answer and instead looked away, staring down the street at the neighborhood in which they'd built their home and their lives together. "Okay, yeah. Uh, I'll be there. I will," she mumbled, the words coming out as disjointed as was her thinking.

After the police drove off, she crumbled, throwing herself onto the grass and sobbing uncontrollably. She felt as though someone had taken a knife, carved out her heart, and tossed it into the middle of the street where it would be run over several times. The emptiness was dark and deep. It was a place she'd never been before, and a place from which she felt she might never be able to return.

She shut her eyes and kept them closed for a while, hoping things would be different when she re-opened them – that the sun would be out, the officers would be gone, and Patrick would be smiling, standing in front of her and explaining that he'd only gotten lost and was happy to be back home. But when her eyelids rose, she only saw the police car moving down her street with the two officers inside.

This time she shouted, "Why! Why!" looking up at the sky and pounding the resilient blades of green grass around her. She continued, flailing her arms and cursing both heaven and earth, as her emotions overtook. Then, exhausted and empty, she closed her eyes once more and faded into darkness.

*****

CH 8 Trolling for Dollars

"I support what you and the president are doing," said a young, Hollywood producer, just beginning to make a career for himself in the sunny state of California. "It's about time he initiated a plan to bring down those high-and-mighty CEO's who do nothing for America."

Ratner had thrown a private party inviting People's Party members and wealthy contributors, all of whom had asked and been granted special exemptions from having to turn over their personal assets to the government. They were there to make sure their requests were stamped with the Minister's seal in exchange for some contribution to the Party coffers.

"But what are you going to do about the ongoing plunge in the economy?" asked an older, well-heeled benefactor, worried about his business even if he did get his exemption.

"It doesn't matter much now," answered Ratner. "The rest of the world is either Islamic or riddled with dictatorships," said Ratner, motioning for the butler to pour her another glass of a 2042 Malbec Reserve, "and Germany and Austria look like they are going to merge and form the New Prussian Democratic Republic. The German Chancellor has made statements about adopting their own Unity Plan, much like what we have in place. There is no place else for money in this country to go. It will stay here and be reinvested. You don't need to worry."

Ratner watched as the butler poured the wine, filling the glass only a quarter of the way up. She gave the butler a disgusted look and waved at him to give her more. He kept pouring until she waved him off. "That's good," she said when the glass was half full. Then she returned to her point. "So, you see, there really is no other place on Earth to go. Capitalism can't hide anymore. We've closed off all the escape routes. Now, all we have to do is watch as the flame of free enterprise around the world goes out for good – once and for all!"

"What about Canada?" asked yet another patron, a middle-aged woman whose jewels suggested she had easily qualified to be among those in attendance. "They have been doing quite well economically. They've been going the other way from us, adopting more and more free-market ideas."

"It's Canada, for Christ's sake," said Ratner. "I certainly wouldn't worry about them."

"We shouldn't be worried about anyone, Minister," said the woman. "Well, except for maybe China, Russia or Saudi Arabia."

"What about them?" asked Ratner, taking a sip of her wine. "They have nothing on us."

"China's military is twice the size and power of ours now. And, Russia's and Saudi Arabia's armies passed us several years ago. If they team up ..." said the woman.

Ratner interrupted. "That's why we've done everything we can during the last two years to become more like them. It's ironic, isn't it? For so long, they strived to be more like the old USA when they had it right all this time -- a benign ruler and a party that knows what's best for its citizens. The people at the top of the ruling class have the education and degrees, you know. We have the smarts to figure it out. It's a burden, really. All those stupid, ignorant people out there," quipped Ratner dismissively, "they rely on us to help them make it through life. They wouldn't be able to survive without us. So we have to tell the rest of those low-life, impoverished saps how they should live their lives. The vast majority of them doesn't even know what a constitution is! Nor do they know the first thing about an economy, let alone how to even *spell* the word. And worse yet, they don't care. Some say it's tragic that our people are so stupid. Of course they're idiots; that's partially by design! For years we've given them the gruel of propaganda and spoon fed them with crap that is meaningless. Ignorant masses are the most pliable medium anyone could ask for. We can mold it however we wish! It's only when people learn the real truth and get educated that they cause problems. Hell, why do you think the first thing most dictators do when they get power is kill all of the intellectuals? Because if there are people out there who can put together some morsel of logical reasoning, the ruling class is doomed! That's why! So, yeah! We have to keep them stupid. It allows us to stay in power and make the right decisions for them. If they have no education, they need our help. They need us! That's all there is to it."

"I agree," said the producer, "but how do you justify it when people ask questions like why salaries in government jobs are so high and exempt from the Equal Pay Act the president put into effect? A lot of people think you shouldn't get exemptions, as government officials."

"Because first of all, no one will ask such a question. It's a stupid question that doesn't deserve an answer," shouted Ratner, incensed by the implication, "and if someone *is* so stupid as to ask it, then ... like I said ... *we* are the ones who must lead the rest. Without people like us, we'd be back living in caves. That's where that new Freedom Party would have us, anyway. What's most important is that the Unity Plan succeed. With *that*, we can get this country to where it needs to be."

"And you've shored-up your support for it, then?" asked the older gentleman.

"What are you implying?" asked Ratner.

"Nothing, minister," he answered quickly, not wishing to have his exemption reconsidered. "Of course, we are here to serve the president and his Administration to the very fullest."

"Then serve him!" scolded Ratner. "He relies on you, his supporters, to make sure that other people are convinced this is the right path. "You can't let anyone believe otherwise."

As the evening wore on, the conversations became skewed toward ensuring that all who attended pledged their loyalty to the president and his programs – both philosophically and monetarily. Standing in the spacious entryway of her new multimillion-dollar home, Ratner picked up a lead-crystal decanter that sat on her ornate, mahogany George III writing desk, circa 1821, for which she'd paid half a million dollars and dumped out the contents of twenty-three commemorative coins from the president's first inaugural. They were made of polished bronze with the image of Fourier on one side and the White House on the other.

"This is just a parting gift," she said handing a coin to each attendee. "And you can just transfer your bit-coin donation directly to the People's Party Committee or to the Ratner Foundation. Contributions of over a million are greatly appreciated," she added without batting an eye.

These were Ratner's well-rehearsed closing remarks. She had setup her ersatz foundation long before and had gotten the director of the IRS, now the Ministry of Taxation Compliance, to approve her foundation as a non-profit charity. She'd never given away any money, and it's trust balance was well in excess of ten million dollars. It was what she called her *rainy-day fund*."

Attendees were fearful not to give and even more fearful not to give enough to her causes, especially her foundation. She had real power now, and she wasn't hesitant to make others fear her.

As each attendee used his or her PCD to transfer a substantial contribution, generally selecting her foundation rather than the People's Party, Ratner stood, making a mental note of those who gave and how much.

One young man approached her in the entryway, his husband or partner in tow at his side.

"Ah, Doctor Ferguson. It was so good of you to come," said Ratner, extending her hand. I apologize for not having spent more time talking with you this evening. I hope you enjoyed yourselves."

"Oh, don't worry," said the doctor. "We're all-in for what you're doing. You are sure that doctors are included in the government worker exemption from the Equal Pay Act, right? We are all on the government payroll now. I work for the federal hospital here in town, Obama University Hospital, and although we don't have nearly enough doctors, I believe that what you're doing is spot on target. We have to rein in corporate fat-cat salaries, and your involvement in all aspects of people's lives is also quite necessary. I see a lot of things, and most times it's bad choices people make. If we could only prevent them from making those in the first place, our ER rooms would be a lot less crowded."

Overhearing the conversation, a young woman interrupted, "Pardon me, but did you say the ER rooms are overcrowded because people make bad choices?"

"Why yes," said the doctor. "That's been my experience, anyway."

"I see," replied the woman, with a note of skepticism in her voice. "And how long have you been practicing?"

"Oh, I just finished my residency last year. I realize that's not a lot of time, but that's what my experience has been."

Ratner was about to interrupt, but decided she was no longer interested in their side conversation, so she abruptly left to go on to other, more promising bankrolls.

"And you are a doctor?" asked the man.

"No, no. I'm afraid not. I was going to go into medicine but ..."

"I see," said the young doctor, condescendingly. "Well, I'm sure you found a profession that required less dedication and mental acuity – something better suited to you."

Although startled, the young woman smiled courteously. She'd been assailed by young doctors before, those believing they knew everything right out of medical school and would find a cure for mental diseases, such as conservatism. Ever since healthcare had come under government rationing, it had been difficult to find good doctors and treatment within twelve months. Still, these doctors were big supporters of Fourier, particularly as they were on the government payroll and now exempt from the Equal Pay Act.

"Interesting you would say that knowing nothing about me?" she asked him pointedly. "Why would you infer it was because I lack dedication or intellect?"

The young man laughed, as did his partner. "I apologize if I offended you," he retorted disingenuously. "I assure you that neither I nor anyone here who holds a degree in higher education would want to offend you."

"Oh, no. You merely embarrassed yourself."

Now it was he who was taken aback. "Pardon me?" he asked.

"Yes, well, I have my PhD in Physics from Cal Tech. My specialty is the Unified String Theory. I do admire medical doctors, however. My father was one, until he was driven out of the profession. But he always told me that the ER rooms were no longer emergency centers. Long ago they became replacements for GP hours, oh, I mean general practitioners. He was dealing with minor cuts and bruises, coughs, aches, and other maladies that used to be treated with over-the-counter medications. Now, everything must be prescribed, so people have to go to the ER. The last surgery he performed was about twenty years ago."

"Well, surgeries aren't done much these days. Technology has made that obsolete," said the doctor.

"To some extent, that's right. But when we're told that gall bladder removals are obsolete, so they will no longer be done, yet no other options given to removing or repairing the gall bladder are offered – I begin to think it's just code for 'we can't afford to do that surgery' or 'your father is too old and it would be wasted money.'"

"How could you say that?"

"Doesn't it take about eighteen months to get surgeries scheduled these days … even emergency ones?" she asked.

"Yes, but …"

"And don't people die every day because they can't get treated?"

"Absolutely not!"

"Really? Then why did my father die from a necrotic gall bladder that they refused to operate on?" She was visibly upset.

"I'm sure there was a medical reason," said the young doctor.

"Yes, and he and 355 thousand others last year got the same answer. They too died or will."

"Listen, we can't treat everyone. We just can't. So, we have to prioritize. That's all."

"Then why to members of the People's Party have an eighty percent greater chance of having surgeries than those who aren't in power? Even if they are in their 100s?"

"That's a lie," said the young man.

"Perhaps, but not from what I've seen and read. By the way, what medicine do you practice?" she asked him.

"I'm a pathologist," he answered. "Specifically, neuropathology."

"A neuropathologist? So you deal with dead brains then?" She said it, knowing better but trying to get a reaction out of him. And she got it.

He fumed and became indignant. "The study of pathology is very big now," he answered. "We must find out more about what causes certain diseases of the nerves, brain, and spine."

"I see. Well, that's good. But let me ask you how you know so much about *living* patients and ER rooms?" she asked. "I mean, you spend most of your time in the lab, don't you?"

"Yes, but you hear things of course. I have many doctor friends in the hospital."

"I think you're in the right field at the right time," she said.

"Why is that?" he asked, skeptically.

"Because if people can't get treated, more and more are going to die from their illnesses, right? So you should be kept very busy for a very long time to come, I would suspect." And with that, she took her coat and left.

*****

CH 9 Rogue Reporter

As Congress became less busy, the White House shot into high gear, cranking-out orders one after another. Rapidly, there was a plethora of decrees – one more invasive than the next, but they no longer came directly from the Oval Office. In fact, it was evident that the job of issuing those orders had been delegated to the ministries. Sure enough, Fourier's stamp *was* on all of them, but so were the names of his ministry chiefs. In particular, there was one minister above all others who was most prolific – Minister Ratner. She understood that her power was derived from the number and extent of her promulgations. *The more the merrier!* she believed.   And the meager four hundred thousand employees she had been given initially had not been enough. Swelling the ranks of her ministry were her new Red Shirts – a formidable and growing menace that had taken on a life of its own.

DrudgeUnderground **Report …**

> *Today, President Fourier issued new orders placing further restrictions on the way business is conducted in this country as well as offered clarification of many orders already sent out. Meanwhile, the U.S. economy continues to reel from the previous orders issued, reporting its eighteenth consecutive quarterly loss during the last three months. These numbers were obtained from the independent FAES organization, and they differ sharply from those issued by the Administration earlier this week.*
>
> *The new orders and clarifications are:*
>
> 1. *All workers are to be unionized – from the executive office to the janitor's closet. Managers who do not own more than 5% of their company's stock are required to be represented by a union in every discussion they have with owners of the company.*
> 2. *Terminated workers must be granted a minimum of twelve (12) months of pay, regardless of the circumstances.*
> 3. *A pollution tax will be imposed on businesses using energy – the amount will start at 14% and increase based on the company's profit level.*
> 4. *Work weeks may be no more than 30 hours. Overtime will be at double wages instead of time and one-half. Worker pay may be no less than that for 30 hours, regardless of how many hours are worked.*
> 5. *Eight weeks of paid time off is mandated for all workers, whether they have worked for the company two weeks or twenty years.*

6. Union grievances ignored by owners may be appealed to federal court for binding rulings.

7. As previously stated, workers must retire no later than age 50, and the company is obligated to pay 95% of their last year's wages each year until their death. The Social Security Fund and amounts previously earmarked for payment to retirees will be canceled. The government can no longer afford to fund the lavish lifestyles of those receiving payments. This burden is now shifted to business owners.

8. All retirement funds of retirees that exceed $100,000, including the old IRAs and 401(K)s and the newer 1401(K)s, and 2401(K)s, shall be immediately taken over by the federal government. This will be known as the Retirement Fairness Plan. The Administration will evaluate who is of greatest need for these funds and will redistribute them accordingly. The first payments will go to those who are at least 48 years of age and have nothing saved for retirement. Those wealthy retirees and those who are over 50 who wish to put money away for retirement, may contribute to their 1401s and 2401s, but one-half will be taxed to fund the Retirement Fairness Plan.

9. The Administration will give away free PCD's to everyone who cannot afford one. President Fourier believes it is one of the unalienable rights to be able to make calls to another person. As such, he announced a new tax – 20% on existing PCD holders – to fund devices for those less fortunate.

But, it was the tenth point that frightened people most of all.

10. The White House announced the formation of a domestic police group, to be called the Red Shirts. This group will supplement local police districts and make sure that the laws are obeyed. Fourier, through his mouthpiece Angel Ratner, declared that the Red Shirts would be proactive in their insistence of compliance with every law on the books.

Minister Ratner, speaking on behalf of the president, exclaimed: "We will not rest until we are assured that every citizen is obeying the law. No longer will we permit the practice of allowing some to violate laws if they pay an appropriate penalty. No one is above the law." Then, she added, "But of course, special cases will be considered based on the merits."

Like most things, people believed there would be special treatment for those well-connected; as for the rest, they believed very little of it. They were accustomed to certain people getting favoritism, whether they were movie stars or basketball stars. As football, hockey, and several other sports had been outlawed for their violence, only a few sports remained that were followed with any regularity by the polity. These celebrities were considered distinct and separate from the regular Joe or Jane who were made to turn over all of their assets as commanded by the government. They got to keep theirs with a wink and a nod.

It was later that Ratner was interviewed by several journalists on the progress of the Equal Pay Act. In her response, she cited many statistics, none of which were true, that appeared to support the brilliance of the measure. Employment was rising, workers were happier about their jobs, management and the rank-and-file were lockstep in their approach to problems and the productivity of companies was through the roof – or so said Minister Ratner.

But the interviewer then questioned her on the exemptions issued, excluding many from the new laws.

"And we understand that many exemptions were made to the Equal Pay Act. Why is that?" asked the reporter.

"Well, we would assume that would be obvious," Ratner answered, minimizing the question. But the reporter surprisingly did not shrink from the question and move on, as Ratner had expected.

"Perhaps, but to this reporter, it isn't. Would you elaborate?"

Ratner was at first taken aback, but then, being put on the spot, calmed herself. "If you insist," she answered. "Certain exemptions are necessary for any legislation to go smoothly after adoption. There are always cases that need to be evaluated. Not every case is the same. Many require digging deeper into the special circumstances that require greater scrutiny. As we often see, there is more to these matters than meets the eye. Of course, I could go into each one, but that would take us all night – heck, all month – to review," she said laughing, "so, let's just accept it for what it is."

Doggedly, the reporter, who was relatively new to the Washington scene, would not let go of the issue. "We do, Minister Ratner. We truly do. But what about government workers? They are not affected by this law. Is that correct?"

"That depends."

"Is that a yes or a no, minister?"

"I'm saying yes -- that they are exempted from the law. But rightfully so."

"And that would be because ...?" asked the reporter.

"Because they make no money! Compared with the for-profit, wealthy business owner and his or her employee, the government worker makes a fraction of that. She doesn't get the corporate jet ride home from work after a busy day. She doesn't make the riches promised to those in business. None of that."

"Great. Thank you for that," answered the reporter. Fresh out of journalism school, the reporter believed in the so-called pure, unadulterated world of the journalist as presented to him by his university. He was there to find the truth. But the truth had a wide strike zone in university classrooms. In classes things were decidedly skewed to the Left, but that approach had been explained as just part of the journalistic process. Students were told to get to the 'truth' of a story, and that 'truth' almost always lay with the liberalistic view of thinking -- *that* was where the truth inevitably lay, so *that* was where the reporter was encouraged to seek the answers.

However, something bothered this reporter, and he couldn't quite let go of his moorings.

"I'm sorry, minister. But there is something that comes to mind. It was something that I read recently, and I need to follow-up with you about, especially based on your last statement."

"Okay," said Ratner, now concerned with how the interview was diverging from the pre-approved script.

"A recent study conducted by the Ministry of Organized Labor found that public servants already enjoy pay levels that are nearly twice those found in private industry. Benefits of healthcare were automatically covered for government workers, while business workers had to pay for theirs. Vacations days for government workers totaled eight weeks per year compared with just two weeks for private industry and pensions were ninety percent of annual pay within the government while these were funded by the worker in private industry. The study showed that the average government employee made 152,653 dollars per year in salary, plus one hundred percent health and disability coverage, eight weeks of vacation and a retirement payout of ninety-five percent of their pay until their death. Also, job positions were guaranteed.

"By contrast, private industry workers had no pension plans other than the ones they funded themselves. They had to live off of whatever they had saved over the years, as Social Security benefits were closed some years ago. With the recent confiscated of IRA and 401(K) pension funds, the average non-governmental worker retires with virtually no benefits. If they haven't saved in other ways, they are forced into Medicaid and Welfare as the ways to stay alive through their retirement years. Industrial workers averaged only 84,512 dollars, when they could find fulltime work."

Ratner brusquely interrupted. "That may have been true, but with the Equal Pay Act and other measures we're putting in place, these things are no longer true. The non-government worker has been brought up to the same standard as those

56

within the government. It just shows you how business has failed their own people time and time again."

The reporter scratched his head. "But the things I just listed were all things enacted by the federal and state governments that created the retirement problems for business workers. They weren't caused by business. You do understand that?"

Ignoring the comment, Ratner continued. "I fully agree that business has been the genesis of all of our evils. From unequal pay to retirement – things are not as capitalism promised all of us. They are among the many lies that have been told to us over the years."

"So you still defend the socialist model of governance?" asked the reporter. "And you don't see that the government in any way has contributed to the current economic malaise of the country?"

"Absolutely not!" said Ratner, almost shouting. "The government is the solution to problems, not one that is creating more."

"I see," said the young journalist. "Therefore, more government involvement is the key to our getting out of this situation?"

"Well, first, I disagree with your precept that we are in a 'situation.' I believe there are issue, sure. But we are not in a state of despair – not by a long shot! Second, I adamantly defend the Administration and its ability to control and moderate our economy. You must understand that we want neither an economy that is too robust nor too weak. Either one is disastrous. No, we need t firm hand on the tiller to navigate us through the dangerous waters of worldwide commerce. That's why we need a strong person in the Oval Office, like President Fourier," said Ratner.

"Minister Ratner, thank you so much for sharing your thoughts with us tonight. I think we have a much better appreciation for what President Fourier is thinking and planning with regard to our economy and the place America holds in the global economy."

*****

CH 10 Four!

President Fourier steadied the high-tech alloy driver behind the white, dimpled ball and pulled the club back, cocking his left knee inward while keeping his right foot firmly planted. His swing was by no means professional, but he had played enough to have boasted a plus-three handicap – pretty good by most amateur standards. The metallic sound of the driver contacting the surface of the ball resonated in the air as the ball soared straight out from the tee-box before slicing slightly to the right.

"Crap!" said Fourier, unhappy that the ball didn't go down the middle of the fairway.

"It'll be fine," said one of his golf partners, Kilby Thorne. "This hole is pretty forgiving over there on that side. You'll have a good angle and a clear shot to the green. You're only about one-fifty out."

Fourier nodded, but he was still pissed, throwing his club at his caddie.

Next, it was Thorne's turn even though he'd beaten the president on the previous hole. Traditional golf protocol dictated that the winner of the last hole tee-off first. But, that applied if you weren't playing with the president of the United States. He had bogeyed the last hole, and by all counts he should not have been teeing off first. However, as everyone was learning, there was a new protocol just around the corner, especially when the current one no longer fit the model.

Thorne waggled the club and smacked the white dot down the middle of the fairway, passing Fourier's by more than ten yards. Then, it was the turn of the Minster of Facts and Statistics, Daniel Cho. His golf was abysmal, but he understood his role was to make the president look and feel better about his game and win whatever small-dollar bets were placed on various holes. True to expectation, Cho's shot went far right, well beyond where Fourier's had landed.

"I guess it's up to me to show you two where to put the ball," said Bailey Griffin, Fourier's regular golf partner. Griffin was having a dismal round, having bogeyed five of the last six holes.

"Right," said Fourier, sarcastically. "I'll believe it when I see it."

Griffin pulled the club back and let it go, hitting the ball solidly. Surprisingly, it cut a fairly straight swath down the left-side of the fairway, rolling off the cut grass into the first cut of longer rough.

"Not bad, Griffin," said Fourier. "I guess we'll keep you around for another hole or two."

Thorne walked off with Griffin, while Fourier headed toward the other side of the fairway with his caddy, a long-time friend who was on the White House payroll.

"So, what's going on with that Disone case?" Thorne asked Griffin, walking stride for stride next to the tax chief. He had known Griffin for several years and had even played golf with him and the president on occasion.

"Disone case?"

"Yeah, Patrick and Shea? Come on Bailey, you know full well who there are. They came under a tax audit a month or so ago and were in D.C. for over two weeks while they visited your ministry."

"How do you know all of that?" asked Griffin, nonchalantly as he looked for his ball.

"I have a lot of resources."

"Yes, I quite understand that," said Griffin. "So, tell me, Kilby, what's so special about them? They probably owe the government a lot of money – that's why we singled them out for audit. That's why we audit anybody. You know that."

"Sometimes," said Thorne. "But, in this case, they were involved in a dispute with another ministry over a patent filing. Were you aware of that?"

Griffin looked at him without emotion. "I was not. No."

"I see," said Thorne. "Then, may I ask if you found what you were looking for?" The trauma to his wife was still fresh, and he wanted to get whatever information he could, while he could.

"As a matter of fact, no," said Griffin. "But if you find a Titleist 3, then I will have found what I'm looking for."

Thorne laughed. "I hear you, Bailey."

The two looked quietly for Griffin's Titleist golf ball, but it had mysteriously disappeared, probably stolen by one of the well-known gopher gods that all golfers knew prowled golf courses.

Griffin dropped another ball, and whacked it, sending it bouncing up toward the green but rolling into a sand trap that straddled the right side of the emerald island.

"Crap!" said Griffin, putting his club back in his bag and climbing in his cart. "But really, Kilby, you know I can't discuss cases," said the tax man.

"Yeah, I know. We've just been working on our own high-efficiency engine, that's all," said Thorne, taking an eight iron from his bag. "Was the Ministry of Technology Assessment involved?"

Griffin looked over at him. "What? Why would you think ..."

"Because I know Minister Ratner. I realize she's now in charge of Unity, but I assume she was running Technology Assessment when the review was ordered. She can be very persistent, you know."

"Yes, she can. But that doesn't mean that she had anything to do with my ministry's investigation of the Disones."

"Investigation?"

"I mean *review* – a simple review. That's all," said Griffin, correcting himself.

Thorne had a short second shot to the green, which he struck nicely, sending the little, white ball soaring into the air and landing softly within twenty feet of the cup. "You do know that the combustible engine they developed could be worth billions on the world market, don't you? The problem is that Fourier banned all fossil fuel-based engines in the U.S. ... I mean sold within the U.S. So, they can only sell them overseas anyway. Still even that market would be huge."

Griffin steered the cart over to the other side of the green where his ball was buried in the bunker. He evaluated the sand shot and pulled out the old sand wedge. "I believe that they can't sell it anywhere, since they don't have a patent on it."

"That's true. They don't. But what if *we* could get that patent? I have the connections to sell it everywhere and to manufacture it in my overseas plants. You have the ability to protect me from government coercion. And, of course, for that, I would pay you handsomely."

Griffin smiled. He knew he had already been paid well by EG to overlook its excess-profit problem, but based on what he was hearing from Thorne, he pieced together that the CEO didn't know anything about that. So, he feigned ignorance. It was all a game, and Griffin played it as well as anyone.

The tax minister took his shot out of the trap, leaving a spray of sand wafting in the air. He looked on while the ball popped up and plopped down on the green, rolling swiftly toward the hole. But, it sped along, off-course some three feet to the right of the flag, before coming to a stop fifteen feet passed the target.

"Damn!" said Griffin. "I just don't have the touch today."

Thorne shook his head. "Well, I don't know about that, Bailey, but what I do know is that we can create a nice nest egg for ourselves. What do you think?"

"Kilby, your problem is Ratner. You know she's not something – someone -- to mess with."

"Won't it be easier now that she's out of the way?" asked Thorne. "I mean, now that she's over at Unity?"

"I wish it were true, but no. Ratner's got even more power now. She has her fingers into everything. She keeps up on things going on at Technology Assessment too, and makes sure that nothing she did is undone now."

"But surely, somehow, you can get access to that patent filing, right? You're the Secretary, I mean, Minister of Tax Stuff, right? There's got to be a reason you'd have to get to the file online, right? Don't you have password access to all sorts of things like that?"

"No!" said Griffin emphatically. "And, I'm not risking everything right now to roll the dice on this."

"Okay, okay!" said Thorne, standing over his putt. "I get it."

Thorne eyed the stroke and quickly hit the ball. It rolled slightly left before rimming out of the cup.

"Nice try," said Griffin.

"I guess it was," answered Thorne. "But I didn't score, did I?"

Griffin knew what he was saying. "That's only partially true," said Griffin. "I do have people inside the tech ministry, as you do. Between the two of us, I'm sure we can get the information."

"And what about securing the patent?" asked the Thorne. "How do we do that if Ratner is still involved?"

"Well, we'll either have to talk with Ratner and cut her in on a share, or, we have to eliminate the problem altogether."

"Eliminate the problem?" asked Thorne, tapping in his golf ball.

"Yes. Eliminate the problem."

Thorne stood up, after pulling his ball out of the cup. "I understand," he answered. It was a response he never thought he was capable of giving, but after the previous several weeks, he found himself involved in a higher circle of power and ruthlessness. The game there was played at a level of seriousness graver than he could have imagined. Others had been willing to kill his wife only days earlier. Life was merely … well … a commodity. It was something that was traded freely on the open market. Everyone's life was for sale – it just depended on the price. "By the way," added Thorne, "nice hole. Maybe it's a sign."

Griffin only laughed. "We'll see," he replied. "We'll see."

*****

CH 11 For Congressman Sumner

It was an anonymous package, left by the door of his congressional office in Washington. Marked *For Congressman Sumner*, it had no other information scrawled on its surface. The large, beige envelope was sealed, with tape spread across the flap, apparently for added insurance.

Sumner's Chief of Staff Marston walked down the hallway, half-asleep, his mind swirling with all that he had to get done that day. He held out his thumb to have it scanned by the sliver-thin reader affixed to the door frame, but froze when he spotted the orphaned package. It was something drilled into each congressman's brain every day of every week and month – *Call Capitol Hill Emergency if you or your staff discover any unusual letter or package anywhere in the building.*

"Oh, sh*t!" Marston said, backing away.

The bomb squad arrived some twenty minutes later and, using their chemical-sniffing wands and hand-held x-ray machines, were able to determine the envelop was no threat – neither an explosive nor a biological or chemical weapon.

"It's all clear," said the police captain. "You can open the package."

"Hey, man. Thanks," said Marston, stooping to grab the delivery before going into the office. Once inside, Marston lifted the black-plastic hangar from the backside of his door and hung up his jacket before returning to his desk. He looked at the strange package, wondering whether he should open it in advance for his boss. He decided against it.

Like Marston and other staff members, Sumner came in early as well, usually around seven-thirty. He was annoyingly fastidious about how things should be handled, and would have been pleased at Marston's by-the-book response to the potential threat outside in the hall.

The chief of staff gave his boss a few minutes to get his coffee and be settled before presenting him with the envelope. "I thought you should see this," Marston said, handing over the mysterious delivery.

"What's this?" asked Sumner, sitting up in his chocolate-colored, leather chair.

"I don't know. I had it x-rayed and tested for toxins, but it was clean. I didn't open it. I thought I'd leave that to you."

Sumner ripped open the envelop and pulled out a stack of papers. "Paper? Really? In this day and age? Who uses paper?"

Marston only shrugged his shoulders.

The Congressman flipped through the stack, page by page, sometimes reading, sometimes peering at a photo digitally inserted into narrative. It didn't take long, and he was totally absorbed, his facial expressions changing from skeptical to serious and then back to skeptical, all within minutes.

"Well? What is it?" asked Marston. "What did they send you?"

"It's the smoking gun," said Sumner. "The only problem is, I really need a smoking tank turret. Guns just aren't big enough these days to get anyone's attention." He handed the papers back to his chief of staff. "What do you think we should do with it?"

Marston looked over what was there. The first page was a computer printed message, simply addressed to Congressman Sumner. All it said was: *Thought you'd find this interesting.* The next several pages were electronic messages between Fourier and his Minister of Environmental Protection. In them, Fourier asks his minister what they can do to kill the oil industry. The minister responds with a list of possible actions – none of which include the sabotage of a refinery. Many were close to, if not went over, the border that distinguished moral and ethical judgment. Indeed, the minister did note that certain pipelines joints could be weakened to cause a spill, gas monitors at the oil wells modified to sound an alarm for toxic gas where there was none, seismic activity data in research projects doctored to show potential danger from fracking, and executive orders issued setting pollution control standards so high that the industry would be unable to comply – all were possibilities.

"I'm not sure," answered Marston, after skimming the data. "Fourier asks how to kill-off the oil business in this country – but we already know he wants to do that. He said that in his State of the Union last year. His minister then gives him a laundry list of options, but we can't prove he actually did any of these things." Marston looked back up from his reading. "I'm not sure, either."

"Yeah, it only shows they *were* hatching something. There's just nothing here on a refinery in Louisiana. It's obvious to me that it was to be the start of a campaign to amerce and close down all of the plants for egregious violations to our health and safety." Sumner pointed his finger toward the documents. "Right there, on page four, it says '*make sure they look like egregious violations.*'"

Sumner sat and thought for a moment. "No, I'll have to think about this. We don't have enough to go on right now. The last thing I need is to present a case with holes in it and sit back while I get persecute by everyone around me. No, let's wait."

A week went by. Then, Marston 's day began with a déjà-vu. Again, he found another envelope at the office doorstep. Cautiously, he proceeded through the standard drill with the bomb squad, but this time he opened the package and reviewed the contents himself before giving them to Sumner.

"You wanted a smoking tank turret? Here's your smoking turret," Marston said laying another stack of paper in front of the congressman.

Sumner took his time looking over what he'd been given. Then, he frowned.

"What's wrong?" asked Marston. "I would think you'd be thrilled with what someone dropped from heaven?"

"I see how you might think that," said Sumner, turning to the last page. "These photos show the cars and license plates of the government vehicles that were stationed just outside the Baton Rouge plant that night. They were all ministry cars. Someone also gave us this nice list the names of people involved, including correspondence between them in planning it."

"Exactly!" said Marston, enthusiastic at what they had gotten. "It's all there. All of it!"

"But, can we believe it?"

"What?"

"Are they fakes? Forgeries? Is all this just an attempt to frame Fourier? Is it an attempt to ruin me?" asked Sumner.

"I don't see how, congressman. It all looks airtight."

"There are easy ways to manipulate all the stuff we have here. Why didn't they send it digitally?" asked Sumner.

"They didn't want it traced," Marston answered.

"Perhaps, but it's also a lot easier to digitally alter everything, right? What if they can come back and say that it's all a fabrication – that you doctored the evidence?" said Sumner. "Once we present this, you know that all of the source documents – the real evidence -- will get destroyed or 'lost'. That's the way the Executive Branch has protected itself for years, especially since they have their own boys covering for them in Congress and in the media."

"So, you're just going to give up? Is that it?" Marston said, surprised at Sumner's apparent capitulation.

"I didn't say that. I only said that ..."

Marston interrupted, something very usual for him. "That's not the person I signed on with sixteen years ago. I *believed* in you then, JC. And, I believe in you now. You can't just let this slide by. It's done too many times now-a-days. That's not right!"

"Why is it?"

"Why is it what?" asked Marston.

"Why is it that everyone looks the other way now?" asked Sumner, thinking about what his senior aid had said. "Maybe because they've seen their careers derailed, yes? Or perhaps because they've seen their families and lives destroyed? To watch as everyone around them gets hurt as critics pile on high and deep?

"The Administration will drag everyone into it. You, your wife, your kids, your brother, sisters, parents – everyone. It's actually worse than the Cosa Nostra. At least the Italian mob had a code of honor. Wives and children were largely left out of it. Now, no one is immune."

"I understand. I have a wife and three kids as you know, and I wouldn't put them at risk either. So, what can we do? How can we fight them?" asked Marston.

"We have to find out where this stuff came from – discreetly. I don't want anyone to know what we have at this point. However, you need to start digging. See what we can get from anyone at the EP Ministry. Also, from the data stick I was given when I received this lovely souvenir," he said, pointing to where the bandages still covered his bullet wound. "The info from that said that Homeland Security was involved too. You need to check that out."

"Okay," replied Marston, who turned to leave. Then, he looked back at the man who had guided him throughout his career on the Hill. "But what then? What if this is legit and Fourier was behind it? What will you do then?"

"I don't know," answered the congressman. "We'll have to cross that proverbial bridge when we get there."

***

It took a few weeks, but Marston finally was able to get some answers. He reported back to Sumner as soon as he had something, eager to tell him what he knew.

"Boss, I was able to trace the package back. I have friends who are ex-FBI, and they still know people inside. Anyway, they ran the package for prints, DNA, paper stock and ink analysis – you know, all the usual stuff. The only thing that showed-up was from the paper and ink analysis. As it turns out, there's only one ministry that still uses that type of paper envelope. All the other ministries have gone to synthetics or, of course, electronic media. Can you guess which one?"

Sumner was in no mood for guessing games. Instead, he smiled politely, and shook his head.

"The Ministry of Technology Assessment. That's ..."

"... Ratner's old agency," said Sumner, finishing Marston's sentence. "Ratner sent the package? But why?"

"I followed up with some people inside her old ministry. She's very ambitious, if you didn't know. They all say the same thing."

"What's that?" said Sumner.

"She wants the top job."

"Fourier's?"

"Yeah," said Marston.

"She's the Minister of Unity now, for God's sake!" exclaimed Sumner. "That's the number two position behind Fourier."

"That's right. So, if Fourier is impeached and removed from office, she's ..."

"She's the next in line," said Sumner, rubbing his chin, thinking.

"It is getting more interesting, isn't it?" Marston asked, rhetorically.

"But you also have to consider that Fourier controls both houses of Congress. He won't be impeached and certainly won't be convicted in the Senate," said Sumner. "There's no way Congress can get him out of office."

"True, but he'd be damaged goods."

"Does that matter? He does what he wants, when he wants anyway."

Marston nodded in agreement. "You're right about that. So, why did she drop this in our laps?"

"That *is* the question – isn't it?" asked Sumner. But, it didn't take long for the congressman to find an answer. He smiled. "It all makes sense," he said.

"What does?"

"If she sends it to anyone, what will happen to them?" asked Sumner.

"Just as we said, they'd have a rough go of it with everyone attacking them and the evidence."

"So why not give Sumner the meat? Raw meat! Something he'd be tempted to jump on and expose. It would damage Fourier and it would ruin him and his career. Two for the price of one," said Sumner, speaking about himself in the third person.

"That does make sense," Marston responded. "That makes perfect sense."

"Yes, it does. But do we want to play her game? Is there any way to play it and come out without battle scars?" asked Sumner.

"I … ," started Marston before he paused. He thought for a moment before continuing. "Sorry, I can't think of anything. We can't push anything in Congress because we don't have the votes. We have no sway with the media, and we don't have a bully pulpit of our own to reach out to more than our own believers. All we'd end up doing is shooting ourselves in the head. The People's Party would jump all over us, the media would try and convict us in the press, the Fourier Administration would launch an offensive to investigate us, and Ratner would be able to sit back, smile and watch the carnage. I just don't see any upside, boss."

"Right now, I don't either. But there has to be some upside here. How can we turn it into one?"

Marston shook his head. "I don't know. I'll have to think about it."

"I think we'll just have to bide our time. Somewhere along the line, someone may make a mistake. Our timing has to be right," said Sumner.

Marston left Sumner's office, but in his gut, he felt that the refinery explosion would be just another dirty trick from which nothing would come. No one would be brought to justice, no sentences would be handed out, and the perpetrators would get off without as much as a hand-slap.

Someone should pay, Marston thought to himself. *But no one will. Everyone will just forget about it and go on as if nothing happened. Meanwhile, countless families in the South were grieving for the ones lost. Fathers, mothers, brothers, sisters, sons and daughters – all would be missed. Hopefully, these families would eventually forget too.* However, Marston knew that their pain would never end.

*****

CH 12 Searching for Answers

What seemed like hours passed while the sun marched along its path through the blue sky, reaching its apogee at its noon rendezvous with a point directly overhead and waning steadily in the afternoon, falling toward the horizon. Shea's eyes fluttered as she awoke to the sound of someone talking to her, a sense of panic in the voice coming from just above.

"Shea? Shea?" came the words through a blurry fog.

There was a haze all around her, and she mentally fought to cut through it.

"Is she coming around?" asked a second, higher-pitched voice, standing farther back than the first.

"Yeah, I think so," said the first person, again. "Shea? Wake up! The ambulance is on its way."

Shea could hear the siren in the distance, and it grew louder as she came to her senses. The face above her was just now coming into focus. It was her next door neighbor, Claire Hathaway.

"Uh, where am I?" she asked, trying to sit up.

"Easy now," said Claire, kneeling over her. "The medics from the ambulance will need to check you out."

"No," Shea protested. "I'll be fine. I just … must have passed out, I guess."

But Claire held her steady while the medics jumped out of the crimson-and-white striped ambulance. The screeching sound went silent, but the red strobe mini-lights on top continued to flash.

"What do we have?" asked one of the EMT's from the hospital.

"We don't know. I just came out to get my mail, when I saw Shea over here lying in her yard. I rushed over to see what was wrong, but she didn't move. I called my neighbor here, and she came over. That's when we called you," said Claire, stepping away to let the two ladies work on her friend.

The medics used their hand-held scanners to assess Shea's brain, heart, and other vital organs. The scanners also assessed other vital signs and whether there was any internal damage or bleeding. It was several more minutes before they felt sure she was going to be Okay.

"I think she'll be fine, now," said the first medic. "But ma'am, you have to come to the hospital. We need to check you out. Do you understand that?"

"No, I can't," said Shea, remembering she was supposed to go down to the morgue.

"I'm sorry ma'am. But you have to come with us. It's the law. You can't refuse treatment."

"What? Why? I'm fine."

"I wish we could give you the choice, but we can't," said the medic. "You'll have to come with us. With the national health plan, anytime we go on an emergency run, we have to bring the person back with us for observation."

"Dead or alive?" Shea asked, cynically.

The medic didn't find it funny. "You're not dead, so you have to come with us. Otherwise, I'll have to call the police."

The comment struck a chord with Shea, and she ached inside. "My … my husband is dead. I just found out today. The police … they told me," she answered.

The medics looked at each other. Suddenly, humanity and kindness returned. "I'm sorry," said the woman who was treating her. "Of course, you understand, but we didn't know. That's probably why you collapsed?"

"Yes," Shea answered, not telling them it had been hours since the police had been there.

"Well, in that case, we'll just overlook this. You don't have to come to the ER. But if you have another spell, you should go to the doctor. Again, ma'am, we're sorry."

The medics packed up their things and left, leaving Shea and her two neighbors behind.

"Oh, Shea! Patrick? Patrick is …" asked Claire, stunned by the news.

Shea could only nod.

"Is there anything we can do?" asked the other neighbor, Julie Preston.

"No, I just have to get down the morgue. The police ordered me to go down there today."

"We'll drive you, Shea," said Claire. "I'll have my car pull up to get us."

They drove down to the police station first, where they found a middle-aged woman officer sitting at a desk, flipping through the electronic pages of the latest *Nouveau Vogue* magazine. Her nametag read *Officer Thomson*. Blonde, with streaks of highlights, she was otherwise unattractive and plain. Years behind the desk had only enabled her tendencies toward lethargy and sloth. Overweight and insouciant, the officer ignored the three visitors and continued turning pages, swiping her computer tablet with her chubby fingers. She looked up at them briefly and smacked a few bubblegum bubbles before glancing at the clock on the wall – its numbers showing 4:57. "Damn!" she said under her breath. But then in a louder voice, she said, seemingly to no one in particular, "I'm sorry, we're closed."

"I was told to come down today. Two officers stopped by my home this morning about my husband," said Shea, standing in front of the bullet-proofed, glass cage in which the officer sat. Shea took off her sunglasses; her hazel eyes were red and puffy from crying. With a quivering lip, she asked, "They told me that my husband may have died, and I was told to come down to the station."

The woman officer had seen many grieving widows and girlfriends over the years, and such a display had little effect on her anymore. She had become cold and hardened to life's miseries, especially those coming upon what looked to her like rich people. *They deserved what came to them,* she often thought. *If only they had to suffer what she had in her life, then they would understand.* To her, money and wealth meant never having any problems or challenges. The rich lived in a state of perfect bliss – a nirvana that only social justice could fix. Meanwhile, she had to live in a cramped apartment, albeit fully paid for, including utilities, by the Ministry of Residential Justice, or rather the rich person standing before her.

"You got a name, miss?" asked the officer, putting down her tablet.

"Yes. His name is … was … Patrick Disone," Shea said, correcting herself.

"No, *your* name, ma'am," the woman said curtly, rolling her eyes.

"I'm Shea Disone, his wife."

"Okay, I need you to fill out this paperwork, Ms. Disone. I'm also going to need three pieces of photo ID, your travel documents and proof of citizenship. And by the way, you only have two more minutes. I close the place at five."

Shea took the computer tablet and quickly found a seat in the lobby while the officer left her post to make arrangements for the identification. As a potential homicide, there were specific procedures that had to be followed to the letter. And if that were the only thing the desk officer had learned during her tenure with the department, it was not to mess up a procedure – regardless of how inept, inefficient, and stupid it seemed. Her job depended on getting it right – all the forms, signatures, filings, copies – everything. If that's all she did during the day, her job was secure.

Once the officer returned, she pushed the button on the speaker which broadcast into the waiting area. "Ma'am? I believe the body is still in autopsy, so I can't make those arrangements at the moment. You'll need to come back tomorrow or the next day."

"What? But I was told to come down today … before closing, in fact."

Just then, another policewoman opened the door to Officer Thomson's little sentry post and thrust at her a note. She looked at the desk officer with the gesture suggesting, *You need to read this*. Then, she left.

Officer Thomson read it, and then pushed the intercom button again. "Oh, I guess I was mistaken. It looks like he's in the cooler after all. He's there waitin' for you," she said insensitively. "If you're done with the paperwork, I can take it for review. Then, we may be able to get you in there." She looked at the time from a digital clock that seemed to hang in midair in front of her. "Sh*t!" she said quietly. "It's gunna' be a late night."

"Yeah, here's your paperwork," said Shea, half-throwing the digital clipboard through the small opening in the glass vault.

"Well, we have to verify who you are first. Once we do that, we can let you see the body to confirm its identify. You'll need to step in here so I can take your fingerprints."

"You need those too?"

"Yes, ma'am." Then the officer lashed out. "And by the way, missy! I'm having to stay late tonight because of you! So don't give me any trouble! 'Cause I can make plenty of it for you, believe me!"

Office Thomson took the electronic clipboard with all of the family history, relatives' names, addresses, birthdates and other personal information pertinent to the Disone family and gave it to a clerk in another room to run through the interstate criminal and civil database. They also ran it through the U.S. citizenry database to verify prints of those law-abiding denizens who had never been arrested for a crime. As connections with international criminal databases from other countries had long been severed, they had to make do with what they had.

After an hour, the woman officer finally reappeared. "Ma'am?" she asked. "There seems to be a problem with…" She squinted at the text on her video screen. "… the previous address you gave for yourself. You said it was 1789 W. 45th Street in Boston. Is that correct?"

"Yes. That's right," Shea answered.

"Well, that's not what our database shows. It says 1879 W. 45th."

Shea said nothing. She pulled out her passport, travel visa, and driver's license – all stating her correct address of 1789.

"Okay. I'll have to correct this in the system," said the woman, leaving her desk again. Another thirty minutes went by before she returned. The officer punched into the computer some new information and then nodded. "Yes, that's right. Okay. Well, you can come with me. Everything checks out."

Shea turned to her friends. "I'll be alright. You two go home."

"Are you sure?" asked Claire, not wanting to abandon her friend. "We're happy to stay."

"No. You've done enough. Again, thanks. I'll see you later this week, perhaps."

As her neighbors left, Shea followed the officer through a doorway into the adjoining building and then downstairs to the morgue. The coroner wasn't there, but an assistant was, busy working through a stack of forms that lay on his desk, all required by the layers of bureaucracy.

"We have someone here to identify the body in A18. Would you pull it out for us?" the woman officer said, coolly.

The young man put his pen down and smiled. "No problem."

He picked up his roster of residents at that point and scanned the list with his index finger. "Yes, A18. Will you come with me?"

He strode over to a wall of metallic lockers, each labeled with an address of sorts, with the A's on one side of the wall and the B's on the other. Locker A18 was clearly marked with a black on white sticker, and he touched a button just to the upper left corner of the locker to open the door. The front of the locker dissolved into a transparent window inside which lay a body, shrouded with a white sheet. Seconds later an invisible device inside pushed the body out from under the sheet and through the transparent window into the room for viewing.

Shea had expected a more subtle approach to the revealing and was stunned by the rawness of the process. She recoiled, afraid to look at what was thrust in front of her. Her knees became unsteady once more, and she felt light-headed.

"Do you need a chair?" asked the assistant.

"No … I think I'll be alright," answered Shea, struggling to regain her balance.

The body was gut-wrenchingly foul. No one had told her how or where they had found the body, and she had expected it to look just like her husband. Yet, it was far from it. Resembling some bloated, white alien from a distant planet, the corpse was horrifying. Thick, slimy white skin covered the body, and in many places was peeling off. The cadaver's head was half again larger than that of a normal person, and there were contusions on its cheeks and nose. Bruises were evident around the head and neck, but nothing more was visible.

Shea ran from the room and vomited outside in the hallway. The scene had been shocking and had ripped from her any sense of innocence she had ever had. As her thoughts turned to Patrick, she threw-up again. It was something she couldn't let her brain process. It was too much.

The medical assistant came out into the hall. "Miss? Are you alright?"

Shea continued to cry.

"Is there anything I can get you?" he asked, sympathetically.

The woman police officer also came out, letting the door automatically close behind her. "Well, was that your husband?" she asked cruelly.

"I ... I'm not sure," she answered.

"Well, you have to tell us one way or the other. I want to get out of here tonight!"

Shea wiped her tears. "Let me see it again," she said.

"Are you sure?" asked the assistant. "I don't think that's a good idea."

"I want to see the body again," Shea said firmly.

The medical assistant led her back into the room. He hadn't moved the body, so it was still out for anyone to see. Shea slowly walked up to it and, this time, looked carefully at its features. It was gruesome, but she pushed herself to suspend her fears.

After a few short minutes, she began shaking her head. "That's not him," she answered. "That's not Patrick."

"How can you be sure?" asked the policewoman, trying to get a positive identification in order to get home.

"Its nose isn't the right size. Its ears are a different shape ... I can just tell. It isn't Patrick. That's not my ..." but then she stopped again.

"What?" asked the officer.

"I ... I ..." she began, trembling again.

"What is it?" shouted the officer.

"That's Sergei Navarov," Shea said, then covering her mouth as tears ran freely down her cheeks. She turned away from the stainless steel bed unable to look anymore. "He was our technology officer at Lenoir Labs. He's been missing for weeks."

"But the ID found on him was that of a Patrick Disone," said the officer.

"That's not him," said Shea emotionally.

73

"Well, I think the body may be too misshapen for you to really ..."

"I can get you any personnel records you need from the company," said Shea, adamantly. "I'm also sure, that you'll find the dental records match those of Sergei too. That is not my husband."

Confused and flustered, the medical assistant made notes on his computer screen. "Okay," he answered. "Well, I guess, we'll have to proceed with dental and other records, then. I'll need all the information you have on Sergei, including his next of kin."

"We'll also need those of your husband ... just in case," said the officer.

Shea looked back at the medical assistant for some answer – any answer. She was relieved that it was not her husband; yet, there was still pain. It was still a dear friend of hers – someone that had died tragically. "How did he die then?" she asked.

"I'm not allowed to give you that information if you're not the next of kin," said the medical assistant. "I wish I could give you an answer, but the rules won't let me. Again, I'm sorry."

Shea took a tissue from the box that was placed next to the white, ceramic sink in the corner of the room. "Well, I only know of one sister that Sergei had, and they were estranged. We'll have to get you the emergency contact in our company files, but it may very well be me."

"Still, rules are rules," said the assistant.

The information was sent electronically to the station within the hour, and the coroner was called in to provide greater detail. It was another three days before Shea was asked to come back to the police station. There she was greeted by the detective assigned to the case.

Sitting at a small, black-metal desk, Shea waited for the detective to arrive. Although late, he was at least apologetic for his tardiness.

"I see that you identified the body as Sergei Navarov. Indeed, his dental records did match those of the body we're holding," said the detective. He was a young man of Hispanic descent, sporting a short, black beard and close-cropped hair. Handsome with energy bursting from every pore, he looked driven and hungry to make his mark on the world. "What else can you tell me?"

"Sergei Navarov was my head of technology at our lab here in Boston."

"And, of course, he knew your husband," said the detective. "But, it seems strange that both he and your husband would disappear at about the same time, in different ways."

"Yes. I agree."

The detective flipped through the electronic file, reviewing relevant data points as they talked. "But you are aware that we found your husband's wallet in Sergei's pocket, aren't you? How would it have gotten there?"

"I ... I have no idea. I don't even know how Sergei died, other than the fact that he obviously drowned," said Shea.

"He was found in a dark foreign car, registered to your husband. Together with your husband's wallet, you can understand why we thought it was your husband ... but I don't suppose you'd know why he'd be in your husband's car?"

"No!" said Shea, insistently. "And, obviously, my husband has not yet been found either. True?"

"No, we haven't found him either."

"Where were Sergei and the car found?"

"We found the car submerged in the Wachusett Reservoir. It looks like it had sped down a hill and didn't stop, ending up in the lake."

"Was anything else found?" she asked.

"Ms. Disone, that's about all I can tell you. This is an active investigation, and I can't divulge any more than I have already. I'm sorry."

"So, what are you doing to find my husband?"

"We're doing all we can."

Shea wanted to say that it wasn't enough, but she held her tongue. "And there was no other sign of my husband being there? Nothing in the car? Nothing around the site?"

"Again, I really can't ..."

"Can you at least tell me if you've been able to contact a relative of Sergei's?"

"Not yet. We're still trying. If we are unable to find his sister, then we will contact you again. Thank you, Ms. Disone. We'll be in touch," said the detective, bringing the interview to an end.

Shea didn't expect answers. But, she really needed them — now more than ever. *Where is Patrick? Where could he be? What could have happened to him to end up with him missing and Sergei's body in his submerged?* It didn't make any sense, and she feared it never would.

After giving more details of her husband to the Missing Person's Division at the station, Shea went home. The coroner had suggested she contact her personal physician to get some sleep aids, but she brushed it off as something she would do later. Right now, she had a new mission -- to find Patrick.

She spent the next several days just sitting by the phone, waiting. The police had told her they would put out a BOLO on him, but Shea wasn't convinced they would actually commit manpower to the case. After all, he was of the *Hated Class* as she had been told repeatedly by people government, in the media, and those in Hollywood – she was a one-percenter who owned a business and had realized some success. Her failure had been that she had not been *more* wealthy and connected; now, she hadn't enough money to buy even a modicum of favoritism from a precinct police captain, let alone enough to buy a congressman or a minister. But that's what it would take.

Yet, that level of manipulation was not within her. She had principles, and she had always been true to them. Even the pressures and stresses imposed on her now would not make her stray from a straight and narrow path. It was an ethical code that was taught to her by her mother and father. She believed it would be a dishonor to them if she started violating it now.

Although the detective had shared some information with her during their initial meeting, the police had gone silent ever since. Shea had asked for any information the police had found from the car or from the autopsy and test results from Sergei – anything that would shine light on the whereabouts of Patrick. It took over three weeks, and finally she received a confidential e-letter, which read:

> *Dear Ms. Disone:*
>
> *The Coroner has completed her tests and autopsy of the body of Sergei Navarov. Although we are unable to share the specific results of her work, we have concluded that he died of natural causes. His death certificate, which was made public today, will reflect this conclusion.*

"Are you freaking kidding me!" she shouted, as she read the letter on her screen. A man drowns in another man's car in a reservoir late at night; the dead man has contusions and bruising all over his face and neck; the other man has disappeared, and they claim Sergei died of natural causes? Give me a break!"

I'm not taking this anymore. I won't! she thought. *If I don't fight now, I'll never find Patrick nor will I find out what happened to our dear friend Sergei. I owe it to both to get the answers, regardless of how long it takes or what answers I get.*

It was time she took matters into her own hands.

***

Shea pulled her chair up to the dining room table and spread out the high-res photos she'd taken earlier that day. Already two days into her own investigation, she had quickly discovered one thing – no one wanted to help her. The more she pressed for information, the more divergent the trail became and the harder it was to get people to talk.

At first, she had focused on Gunter Muntz. She found that he had recently left his old employer at Nasco, Inc., but they had no record of where he'd gone next – no forwarding information was on file. His apartment, in Pacific Heights, San Francisco, was still under rent, but the landlady said she hadn't seen him in months and hadn't received the last two months of rents. Shea had traced his travels to Boston's Logan Airport, but there it had run cold. She suspected he had been the one Sergei had seen during their presentation meeting to the financial firms, but she had no proof. Electronic data from the video cameras had disappeared, and no one in the government had agreed to provide her any satellite photos of the area during that time period. As for Gunter's friends, she had tracked down only one, an Asian woman, but she could only find a first name – Ellen. At that point, the Gunter trail had run cold.

Other pieces of information had also led to dead ends. Patrick's PCD records from that night showed he received an incoming call sometime before midnight, but the details had been 'corrupted,' or at least that's what the telecom company told her. One camera at a hydrogen fueling station showed a dark Jaguar driving past at about 11:47 p.m. It was on the highway near the reservoir, but the picture wasn't clear enough to identify the driver, and she didn't have the technical equipment to enhance the digital image. Their house surveillance cameras had only shown Patrick leaving the house in his car around 11:23 p.m.

But, the mystery remained -- why had he left?

Shea had asked Emery, their lawyer, to help if he could. She wasn't hopeful, as he had let them down before, but he did tell her he'd look into it. Two days later, however, he called. "Shea? It's Emery. I had to call in several favors, but I may have gotten at least something on the number you requested – the one the phone company said was corrupted. I must say, it was like pulling teeth to get what I have for you. It isn't much I'm afraid, but it's the best I could do."

"Emery, anything is better than nothing at this point. I appreciate the effort. So, what do you have?"

"The only thing I could get was that the call had an area code of 9202."

"D.C.?"

"Yeah. The call came from the District of Columbia. But I was able to get you a little more info. The next two digits -- seven eight something – tell us that came from a government building – most likely the Ministry of Technology Assessment." He paused. "I think we've been down this road before."

"You've got to be sh*tting me?" she exclaimed. There was a sudden chill that came over her body, sending goose bumps up and down her spine.

"I knew you'd react that way. That's the way I reacted too when my friend told me."

"Would Patrick have known that? I mean, would he have seen the number when he answered?"

"No, I'm afraid not. He would have had no idea who was calling. The number was blocked. The person could have told him it was the laundry down the street for all he would have known."

"And that's just like Patrick to answer an unlisted call too. I always warned him not to answer when there was a number that was unlisted," she said. "Crap! How do I find out who made the call?"

"I can ask a few more people, but I'm afraid if I do, we'll get even less information. People are really clamming up over this. I don't think there's much more I can do for you."

"It's as though they're scared of something. Isn't it?" Shea asked him.

"I'm not someone who believes in conspiracies, but ..."

"But what?"

"I think there's a lot going on here that no one wants to talk about. Your husband's disappearance is, quite possibly, only the tip of the iceberg, Shea. But, I'm afraid I'm out. I can't risk anything more. My business – my family – they're all I have."

"Emery, I understand. Thanks for the info," said Shea.

"So, what are you going to do now?" he asked.

"Right now, I'm committed to seeing this thing through. I have to find Patrick. That's it. And if that means I have to go on a tough, long journey to find him, I will."

"I wish you luck," said Emery.

She hung up with him. But she sat and thought for a while. Was her journey going to end with answers – whether propitious or injurious? Would it end with more unanswered questions than she had now? Or would it end with her finally finding her husband – alive and well – or tragically with him – and possibly even her -- dead?

Only time would tell.

*****

CH 13 Capitalism Reform

The government's attack on Lenoir Labs and the Disones was much like a bull fight – to thrust as many swords into the beast as possible to weaken it to the point of near-death; then, foist the fatal blow into the creature to the cheers and adorations of the crowd. Fourier had planned it thus.

By plotting a strategy to destroy one prominent and promising business, the president set in motion the start of a broader, more concerted campaign to destroy entrepreneurship -- the foundation of a capitalistic system. To kill a revolutionary engine that might foster a new wave of industrial development and prosperity in America -- one that could foster ingenuity and generate new technology for other disciplines and markets -- would be the *coup de grâce* they wanted. Destroying hope for others would be instrumental in cementing the dependency of the masses on government. Often times, capitalism destroyed that dependency, by holding out the promise for a better life if one worked hard and actually created something for society. No, it was better if the *hoi polloi*, or proletariat as Marx and Engels would say, believed that their best chance was to take as much as they could from their government, rather that working for it themselves. One was a sure bet; the other required effort. Therefore, destroying capitalism at its seed, was necessary. Regulating small business out of business would be instrumental in their eventual goal to dismantle the evil of capitalism and replace it with shared ownership or socialism – a concept which they believed was higher on the evolutionary ladder of social engineering.

At the same time, the next thrust of the sword would be to assume control over larger corporations that dominated American commerce. With the exception of GovCo's, which were already in the bag for the politicians, the takeover of other critical manufacturing and service industries was essential. These were the targets of the Ministries of Taxation Compliance and Environmental Protection . But to get to all of these companies required more than just tax audits and fines for environmental misdeeds -- these alone would be too slow to effectuate change. Instead, more draconian steps were required, and Fourier could think of no better project for his second in command than that.

"I'm sorry, but the vice-president could not be here today as he had other appointments," said Ratner, standing before the White House Press Corp in the press room. She was lying, of course. There was no way President Fourier would allow Vice President McFarlen anywhere near his flagship efforts of changing the country. While McFarlen had never created a problem for the president, neither did he instill any confidence in his ability to manipulate the people to ram through what was needed to consolidate power and assure their positions.

"We have been working for months on new regulations to improve business practices in America," Ratner said. "As Minister of Unity this was assigned to my ministry, and we have worked tirelessly to offer something that will fix all of the problems resulting from our free and unfettered business environment.

"We thoroughly examined the current situation and consulted hundreds of experts in the area to get a wide-spread consensus on what needs to be done with business. While many improvements have been made as a result of earlier executive orders, we now see that a firmer hand is required to make the system fair for everyone.

"In addition to pursing legal action against those that have not followed executive orders against business that is not in the best interest of the American people, all business practices must also be reasonable and proper. Therefore, we now order that every company, regardless of size: One, give annual donations to foster and promote the political process in America. Two, permit government auditors on site to assist the company in improving its operations to become more globally competitive. And three, share with relevant government ministries those patents, inventions, creations, ideas or other intellectual property that may be beneficial to Americans as a whole. Oh, and of course, follow all previous orders for equal pay, union presence and all other directives issued by this president."

As Ratner talked, the reporters recorded. They lapped-up the criticism of capitalism, as a dog does with water. Although they were paid by the evil machine of corporatism, they abhorred it.

Yet, most people outside of the major outlets heard the new restrictions for what they really were – translated as:

> One, companies must give to the People's Party, as the tax ministry will be watching and punish you if you don't; Two, the government will direct what your company does to ensure it's in the best interest of those in power. Three, businesses are required to give away all competitive advantages they have in new technology, so they can be used by cronies of politicians to make money for themselves. Four, they must become social organizations, like charities, but will never benefit from contributions from customers or their government, as their cause was never deemed worthy.

Still, Ratner continued.

"To assist companies in complying with our requirements, I am proud to announce the formation of the Commission for Equitable Business Practices that will ensure that President Fourier's executive orders are followed. These will further our commitment to overhauling what is wrong and broken with commerce in this country. This Commission will make sure that all companies operate fairly and properly. Since they already take advantage of the infrastructure created by government and built by the poor and working class of this great nation, it is only right that business works with government for the benefit of *all* people, not just themselves. Business uses the roads, waterways, bridges, cities, and systems of education and justice that are the very foundation for our prosperity. Yet, they are unwilling to pay their fair share! Selfish business practices that add gold to the pile they already have are against the idealism we believe is right for all Americans and must be stopped! That idealism is self-sacrifice and sharing – not hoarding and looting. This change will demand hard work and compliance by the entire business community.

"As for the Committee of Ethical Business Practices, it will report directly to the president. It will not be subject to Congressional oversight or control, and its proposals will not be challenged in court. Of course, it is within the authority of the president to give his stamp of approval to any or all elements presented in the Commission's final report.

"But, we must be clear. There is *no* place for profit in business. It is a misguided, if not pernicious, idea, encouraged by primeval capitalists whose sole purpose is to rape and pillage society at large. The concept of taking from the poor and less fortunate to aggrandize and enrich themselves is over. The top one-percenters *will* share their wealth! They don't need that brand new Gulfstream 24 jet or that ninth house along Malibu beach. The only ones too stupid to grasp the concept are those Neanderthals on the Right – those pre-historic, knuckle-draggers who don't understand that *Homo sapiens* have actually evolved from their cave-dwelling days."

This led to some subtle chortling in the room.

"Yes, yes. I know it's hard to believe there are people out there who still strive to make money on the backs of other hard-working Americans. They care not for the plight of others. They think not of the suffering of those less fortunate than they. And, they give not a damn for anyone but themselves! How miserable of a life they must have! They claim to believe in a god, yet they don't follow their god's ways and teachings. It's twisted, grotesque and wrong! And, worst of all, it's hypocritical at the extreme! They accuse us of being hypocrites. But it is *they* who ignore the poor to enrich themselves – contrary to what their religious leaders preach at their Sunday church services. It is truly ironic, that it takes those of us who are humanists, who are atheists, who are statists, to forge the way to a more compassionate country and more empathetic government. It's not the Christians or Jews! But, unfortunately, that's where we are today.

"The good news is that the chariot is about to arrive, and the knight in shining armor is about to fix everything. The Right has woven a web of lies so thick that the weak-minded believe it! They pontificate on how human nature is driven by reward and punishment. How primitive! Perhaps that was true when the Mongol hoards invaded Eastern Europe in the thirteenth century. But we have evolved to higher-level beings since then. We have learned from our mistakes, including that of capitalism. Where capitalism may have been acceptable three hundred years ago, the concept is now antiquated.

"We Progressives *are* the ones who have evolved. We *are* on a higher plain. Even Darwin could understand that! It's the difference between an amoeba and Einstein. Right-wingers are single-celled organisms unable to develop into anything higher on the food chain. While Progressives – Liberals - have developed their brains to an extent Conservatives cannot understand, nor can they ever fathom. Their feeble minds cannot wrap themselves around such complex thoughts.

"No, it's time that we force business into our epoch of civilization – to bring them out of the Paleolithic or … Okay … I'll give them at least the Mesolithic … Period. *We* are the intellectuals of our age. *We* are the ones who are enlightened enough to understand that our ideas, our thoughts, and our opinions *are* the future. Progressivism - Socialism is the ultimate level of human existence, and it will drive the world to peace and harmony during our time. There will be the five thousand years of utopia as prophesied in their Bible. It will be the final and ultimate status of a civilized society. We will no longer be judged as a first-world or third-world country or as industrialized or developing nation. No, only those nations that embrace social justice and fairness among the most down-trodden in our cultures will grow to achieve that next level – a oneness with each other and Mother Earth."

Again, there was widespread applause through the ranks of the mostly partisan group.

"So, it is up to us to force those who have everything to give it to those who have nothing. It is right, it is fair, and it is the thing to do! That's all we've been asking for all these years, and we finally have a president willing to stand up to them. He is fearless, risking everything for the betterment of society and those less fortunate. From his orders to reforming taxes and making the rich pay more to requiring every worker earn the same – it's all just a good first step! Now, he's asking that we go further. It's time that the rich are humbled and those who are becoming rich to be stopped before they embrace that evil! There should be no divide between rich and poor. If everyone were the same, there would be no class envy, no resentment, no anger. We would … we *should* … all be equal. Only in that way, can we live in peace and harmony in this great land of ours!"

Unusual even for the press corp, there was a massive eruption of cheering. It was as if their hopes, dreams and wishes had all suddenly come true. And Ratner looked on, soaking up every decibel. Her speech had sounded presidential, and had Fourier heard it live, he may have wondered about her motives.

"And that's why I'm here, working with the Fourier Administration to fix the injustices with which we've lived since 1776. So, with my help, President Fourier and Vice President McFarlen will be able to present to the American people a blueprint for how to change business from one of selfish greed to one of benevolent compassion. Thank you."

***

Ratner arrived back at her ministry and threw her purse down on the sofa in her office.

"It went very well," said Margola, coming in with her tablet to record the long list of *To Do's* she was expecting.

"Get me a coffee," said Ratner, not acknowledging her vice-deputy minister's compliment.

Margola returned with white, porcelain cup in hand. Her boss took it but neither thanked her nor even acknowledged the gesture. "What did you do while I was gone?" Ratner asked, abruptly, scrolling through her video-mails.

"Well, we got that draft of the oil industry executive order off to the White House for president Fourier to review. It should shut down the entire sector once and …"

"I need everyone on staff working on the Commission's report I discussed at the press conference. We have to come up with directives for Ethical Business Practices. This is the top priority right now."

"But minister, don't we have as much time as we need? That's what the president told you," said Margola.

Ratner finally looked up at her, answering in short bursts of sound. "What's it to you?" she asked, savagely. "You'll do as I tell you!"

"Yes, minister," answered her assistant, used to the abuse. "May I ask if the president has decided who will be on the commission with you?"

"Me."

Margola laughed. "Yes, I know -- you. But besides you, who else will be on the commission?"

But Ratner didn't laugh. She wasn't even smiling. "I told you … me," she said adamantly. She paused and put down her portable imaging device. "I don't think you quite understand, but it's important that you do. *I* will be the one appointing people to *my* commission, but we aren't going to be holding any meetings. I'm going to create the report myself. It will be the next greatest document ever written -- the next Beveridge Report – and it will revolutionize how business is done in this country."

"Really?" replied Margola, startled by the brashness. "That's great. It's time that we change things in America. But, won't business marshal its resources to fight you?"

"Yes. But the resources of the U.S. government are far greater than anything those companies could cobble together. Once you take out the GovCo's there isn't enough left that will make any difference."

"But you're not going to fight the GovCo's, are you? That would be, well, difficult to say the least."

"No … at least not at this point. You have to be smart about things, Marg. That's how I got to where I am today. The first thing is to create a hostile environment for business in this country."

"Hostile?"

"Yes. We have to change the current environment that allows businesses to do what they want, whenever they want. They work for us, the government, not for themselves! After all, they are part of America, just like the rest of us. They need to act like it! Instead of being ingrates, they should stand-up and be patriots. Instead of looking for profits, they should look to help the less fortunate." She was beginning to get more and more agitated, launching into an extension of what she'd said on the podium earlier that morning.

"After everything this country has done for them. After every opportunity this country has given them. The only thing they want is money for themselves – to use our fine country, to bleed it, to drain it, to take from it everything they can to make a profit. It's not right. But that is about to end."

"What about a slogan?" Margoal asked, interrupting. "Something like … *Humanity is Good, but Profits are not.*"

Ratner thought for a moment and then said, "*Compassion is Good. Profit is Evil …* I think. A slogan will be the first order of business for my Commission." Then she looked at Margola with a grin. "Perhaps I'll keep you after all, Marg. At the very least, I think I'll have you fill the only active slot on my Commission."

*****

CH 14 The Oil Burns Out

Sumner tried to reach Shea, but he'd gotten no answer. He'd left several video-mails, but she'd not returned his attempts to contact her. It had been over two weeks since he'd checked out of the hospital, and he was still nursing a sore abdomen where he'd been shot. His wife had told him he should be thankful that he was still alive, and he indeed was; however, he was more worried about Shea and her missing husband, Patrick. The Congressman had heard about the disappearance of Patrick from people he knew at the precinct house, and he couldn't help but think it might all be connected to that silver data stick he'd given him. He blamed himself for that.

He thought Patrick would be able to decode the contents and then work with him to hunt down the perpetrators or, perhaps, even go public with the story. Unfortunately, they hadn't been able to do either before he'd disappeared. It was true that Patrick had given Sumner some cryptic information, but it had been garbled and difficult to understand. Yet, the congressman felt sure there was other incriminating data on the stick, but it, along with Patrick, had vanished.

Once Sumner was back in his office on Capitol Hill, he charged his most senior staffer, Randy Marston, with digging into the accident – to find whatever information he could. However, after petitioning the oil company involved, the Ministry of Environmental Protection, the local news agencies, the workers who streamed in and out of the plant, and others, Sumner's chief of staff had gotten nowhere. Marston had even traveled down to the plant in Louisiana only to be turned away at the gate. The plant was off-limits, except for special authorized personnel, he'd been told. In the distance, he'd seen heaps of charred equipment and blackened pipe, but that was about it.

"I'm chief of staff to Congressman Sumner!" he'd protested. "What kind of special authorization is required?"

"I can't tell you that," was the answer from the guardsman.

"What do you mean, 'you can't tell me?' How in the hell am I supposed to be able to get authorization if you won't tell me?"

"You can't," said the man, standing just outside the guardhouse.

"So, you're telling me, that a congressman of the United States can't get information about an incident that may have killed Americans at this refinery?" asked the chief of staff.

"Yes," said the plant supervisor, unmoved by the plea. "But if your guy was from the ministry, then maybe we could get you something. And, it's clear you're not from these parts, son. We abide by different laws down here. What's important here is where our bread is buttered – that is, who's the one buttering it. And it seems to me that you and your boss don't butter my bread. If you don' t butter the bread, you don't get any to eat. Understand?" The man's southern accent was heavy and labored.

"Got it," said Marston, turning away from the guard and going back to his truck. He immediately got on his PCD and called his boss. "Congressman, this is Randy. I'm outside the plant, but I can't get in. They won't let me talk to any of the higher ups. I've tried to reach the bosses directly, but none will take my calls. I'm basically dead in the water. What do you want me to do?"

"Come home," said Sumner. "I suspected this would happen. Something's going on down there, but we'll have to use other means to get the answers."

Marston drove out of the parking lot and headed back to his hotel. The truck pulled in automatically to a slot just outside the reception area and shut down its lights and electric engine. The chief of staff started to get out of his car, when another truck pulled up right next to him. Two men jumped out, both dressed in black shirts and pants, sending a jolt of panic down Marston's spine.

"What do you want?" asked Marston, nervously.

"Are you the aid to Congressman Sumner?" asked one of the men whose features were hard to discern in the dark, moonless night.

"Yes."

The man handed Marston a slip of paper that had been folded several times. "Take this," said one of the men.

Marston looked at the page, and before he could lift his eyes again, the truck roared off down the road with puffs of dust roiled up behind it. He shook his head and unfolded the paper. Inside, it read:

> You need to contact Charlie Taglu, Assistant Plant Manager. 9225-555-4095@ctaglu.usa.

Marston remembered Sumner mentioning something about Taglu, but he couldn't recall exactly what it was. Even so, he thought it curious how such a message was being delivered to him. *Why would they just run off down the road after dropping it off?* he thought. He had a lot of questions, but now no one to answer – except, perhaps, Charlie Taglu.

It was the next morning after Marston had checked out of his room that he tried to contact Taglu. The line rang several times, and finally the line was answered: "This is Charlie Taglu. I'm not able to answer the line, but leave me your video message ..." Then the voice changed, and another, higher-pitched voice completed the notice. "... You may find me at 5918 Rue Crozat, Apartment 201."

Marston had three hours before he had to be at the New Orleans airport, so he thought he'd swing by the apartment to see what Taglu had to say.

The area was run-down, lined with the litter of broken bottles, trash, and other garbage that had accumulated along the side of the road, and the houses were unkempt with cracked and pealing shudders and porches that looked as if they would collapse if someone set foot on them.

5812 ... 5824 ... 5866, Marston said to himself as he watched for the numbers on the tilted and bent mailboxes as they passed by. *5902 ... 5912 ... 5918,* he thought as he, at last, came to the house he sought.

It was a small, light-green clabbered cottage, no larger than a double-wide trailer. It was nearly square with no more than a living room in front, a dining room, a kitchen and two small bedrooms, all serviced by a single bathroom. The garage was not attached, and its door was open, revealing an aging, silver Chevy Impala stored inside. Marston got out of his car and walked circumspectly toward the sloping, cement porch that had settled less-than graciously over the years. Rapping the back of his fingers on the door, he waited for a reply.

"Mr. Taglu? I'm Randy Marston. I'd like to speak to you about something that happened at the refinery," asked Marston. He waited for an answer, but none was forthcoming.

"Mr. Taglu? Are you there?" Still nothing.

Marston pushed the button on the lock, expecting nothing to happen, but the door cracked open, as if inviting him inside.

"Mr. Taglu?" he asked again, letting the white door slide inward effortlessly.

He walked in, not knowing exactly what to expect. To his surprise, the home was Spartan with few pieces of furniture and a simple, ochre and olive-colored wool rug, albeit frayed along one side, thrown haphazardly into the middle of the floor between two recliners.

"Hello?" asked Marston, going through the front room to the hallway that connected the two bedrooms. One was completely empty; the other had bedsprings and a mattress laying directly on the floor covered only by a rumpled white sheet and periwinkle comforter. There was a dresser nearby – a cheap, four-drawer oak model that had probably been purchased at a local flea market. Several of the drawers were pulled out with random clothes stuffed inside, but no sign of their owner.

Marston looked at his PCD and the time. He would have to hurry if he wanted to make it to the airport, so he hustled back down the hallway to the living room. Passing by the kitchen, he peeked in and noticed there were plates sitting on the stove — two with food still on them. He moved closer to realize the rank odor coming from the area. It grew stronger the closer he got, but it wasn't the typical stench of rotten food that he'd smelled before. No, this was something more wretched.

Moving into the kitchen, Marston rounded the corner and spotted the flimsy, aluminum kitchen table. There, with his back toward him, was a man in a white T-shirt slumped over the end of the table, face-down on the faux marble Formica top.

A cold chill came over Marston as he inched toward the figure. "Mr. Taglu?" he asked again.

As he came closer, he saw that the table was covered with a dried, red pool that had spread over most of its surface. Streams of crimson had eased over the sides, dripping onto the cheap, plastic tile squares directly underneath. But it was the sight of the man that made Marston nearly vomit. With its bluish-white arm outstretched, holding his knife with *rigor mortis* tenacity, the corpse was frozen to its chair, the right side of its head crushed by what most likely was a baseball bat. Cracked open like a watermelon, the inside of the skull and brains were exposed, still oozing tissue and membrane fluid over the victim's ear. Written crudely in the blood on the table were the words: *You're Next!*

Marston ran from the house and jumped in his car. His heart was pounding and his own head exploding with the throbs of fear and panic. *What do I do now?* he thought. *I have to get out of here!*

Driving as quickly as he could, he got on his PCD and called his boss. "JC! Pickup!" he said with sweat dripping from his face.

"Sumner here," said JC, answering after several rings.

"Boss," said Marston, shaking, "Taglu's dead. But there's more. There was a message sent along with the body ... I think anyone who pursues this case is in danger. I'm not joking. I have to get back to Washington. At this point, I'm afraid for my life and my family. I'm coming home now!"

***

Sumner decided to go directly to the ministries to get answers, even though he knew few would be forthcoming. Even so, he would submit his petitions and, at least, be on record for having done so. It would play his hand to some extent, but they still didn't know what, if anything, he knew.

Then, one night the Congressman turned on the evening news, which still doled out the usual gruel to the older generation across the country. Sumner kept up with it, as he had an older voting constituency in his district, and he wanted to know what propaganda they were being served by the mainstream media.

"I am Walter Jennings, and this is *News Today*, this day, October 18, 2048," said the newscaster with a dramatic flair.

Jennings had risen quickly through the ranks of reporters, having covered the White House and brief stints in the Middle East or what was left of it. He'd always presented optimistic perspectives on the way the U.S. was viewed around the world and the merits and successes of its foreign policy initiatives. He kept the biased narrative flowing for those on 1600 Pennsylvania Avenue and, as a result, he kept his high-paying job.

"Tonight, we begin with the latest numbers released from the Ministry of Facts and Statistics. The unemployment rate remains at one hundred-year low of just 2.3 percent while inflation is only 1.4 percent. The Minister of Fair Trade said today's numbers reflect the robustness of the U.S. economy and the success the Administration has had in taming inflation. Minister Marcus also said that he was working closely with the Bank of the United States, previously known as the Federal Reserve, to ensure interest rates are kept low to stimulate business."

Sumner shook his head. "*Bull sh*t!*" he mumbled under his breath. *Everyone knows that the unemployment number is really around 23.5 percent using the U6 number and that inflation took off three years ago and hasn't eased one bit. It's closer to 16 percent according to the FAES,* he thought to himself.

The FAES was the Foundation for the Accuracy of Economic Statistics, a group with which he'd worked and even sat on their board of directors. It had grown out of a necessity to get real numbers – both for the public and private sectors. The government had long manipulated the numbers to show themselves in the best light possible. No one believed the statistics coming from the Ministry of Facts and Statistics (MFS) – not even members of Congress used their numbers anymore. MFS reports never reflected the reality of the nation's economy; instead, they showed what the Administration needed them to show. If the Administration needed inflation to be high to further an agenda item, then inflation numbers for the period would be high. If low numbers were needed, then low numbers were given. And if later action required a change in the numbers, that could be accomplished too by issuing technical corrections to adjust previous months' statistics. It was all slight-of-hand and easily convinced those who were uninformed or outright ignorant.

"What are we going to do about all of this?" Sumner asked, looking down at the sad face of his golden doodle, Enzo, who was sitting on the couch next to him. His dog was all of three years old and still had the energy of a pup. A glossy-auburn color, the canine followed him everywhere while he was at home, licking his arms and hands to get any kind of attention thrown his way. Enzo yawned, licking his nose and lips and curling up closer to his master.

"And with the economy running along nicely," continued Jennings, "the president is proposing new expenditures to help the less fortunate. Mr. Fourier has rolled-out a ninety-point plan to address the nation's poor and downtrodden. He said today that business isn't doing enough to hire those people who are out of work, and he is proposing through executive order to make all businesses hire at least five percent more staff to their payrolls no later than the first of the year. Mr. Fourier argued that for businesses to make a profit, they must produce more goods and services. To do that, he insists, they need more workers. This will benefit both the poor people who are looking for work and the government which will receive more tax revenue from their earnings. These measures will buoy the overall economy and be good for everyone. Of course, the president is requiring that anti-discrimination rules for businesses extend beyond the traditional race, gender, age, religion, and sexual preference, but also include non-citizens, those with criminal backgrounds, the mentally unstable, and many other groups. He stated that, quote, 'no one in this great country should be denied work – for any reason.'

"Now, on to other news …" the anchor continued.

"They just can't seem to find it within themselves to tell the truth, Enzo," said an angry Sumner to his dog. "Facts and figures don't matter anymore. And, unfortunately, my little friend, most Americans are too stupid or too disinterested to understand they're being duped." Sumner looked back into the large, black eyes of his friend. "But, I'm happy to tell you that you're probably smarter than two thirds of them and definitely smarter than the one we have in charge now!"

He pulled off the cork from the wine bottle he'd begun the previous night. The Merlot would be good for at least one more night, he reckoned. He began to pour when the phone rang. "Answer phone," he muttered, commanding the computer to bring up the image.

"JC?"

"Yeah Randy, it's me. Go ahead."

"I'm on my way to the airport, but there's a car following me. It's a black sedan, probably government."

"It's probably nothing, Randy. The car's not threatening you is it?"

"It keeps speeding up and then backing off. It definitely is trying to intimidate me," Marston said nervously. Then he added, "Sh*t!"

"What's wrong?" asked Sumner.

"He just rear-ended me. Should I pull over?"

"No, keep going. Get to a police station," said Sumner.

"Sh*t!" Marston said again, this time more excitedly. "He's trying to push me off the side of the road!"

"Override the auto-pilot and hold the steering wheel tight!" shouted Sumner.

"I'm trying, but ... we're on a long bridge and ..." there was a banging sound and the picture of Marston took a jolt.

"Randy!"

Marston's face was twisted with pain and white with fear. Every muscle in his face was pulled tight, and his contracted pupils mirrored the intensity gripping every other part of his body.

"I've just got to hold on ..." he said, gritting his teeth.

There was a clicking noise on the line and the picture of Marston inside his car became fuzzy with black and white lines bisecting various quadrants of the frame.

"Randy?" asked Sumner, as the line seemed to go dead. "Randy, are you there?"

There was no answer, and the picture went dark.

Sumner tried calling him several times, but he got no response. The calls just went to Marston's mail system.

Sumner calmed himself and thought through what he could do. "Call Sheriff Gauteaux."

"Calling Sheriff Gauteaux," answered the computer.

The line rang several times, but there was no answer there either – only the answering service. But strangely, it wasn't the Sheriff's voice or image that came up, it was that of an attractive, young woman with perfect skin, hair and makeup.

"The phone you have reached for – Sheriff Peter Gauteaux – is unavailable right now, but if you wish to leave a message, please do so. Thank you and have a great day," she said with a programmed smile.

"A robot," said Sumner. "But where the hell is everyone?"

He tried calling others he knew down there, but again no one was picking up.

Sumner kept trying to reach his chief of staff. Still, there was no answer.

Later in the day, Sumner sent two staffers down to Louisiana to find out what had happened to Marston. They reported back daily, but could find no trace of his head staffer, the sheriff, the security director at the refinery, or anyone else connected with the incident at the plant. The trail had gone cold. It was as if all had been beamed up to some starship and whisked away to a far-off galaxy.

Marston and the others became just a few more mysterious, lost-persons cases that would be intentionally buried in the back of a file drawer at the local police station. Sumner never heard from his trusted staff person again, nor was he ever able to learn the whereabouts of Sheriff Gauteaux. When he pushed to get information on the Gauteaux, he had been told that the sheriff had been reassigned to an undercover case and could not be reached. All other efforts led him to the same place - a dead end.

*****

CH 15 The Search for SECE

The elevation of Ratner to Minister of Unity changed everything. Thorne decided not to pursue his crafty little plan with Bailey Griffin to cut both Ratner and him in on his development of the SECE engine. Ratner was someone after power and money. Griffin was cut from the same mold but was less predictable. Thorne could offer Ratner something when she was in a minor ministry, such as that of the Technology Assessment; however, now she was in the *top* ministry, and she didn't need any influence that either one of them could offer. She now had more than both of them combined.

Griffin tried to contact Thorne several times, salivating at the opportunity to rake in millions for his own retirement, but each time he was told that the CEO was out of the country and would get back to him. However, Griffin still had the power of the taxing authority, and he wasn't afraid to use it. Exasperated and humiliated by the delays, Griffin sent one of his lower-level subordinates over to EG to personally deliver a *Notice of Audit* to the CEO. As expected, Griffin received a call the following day.

"Hey, Bailey, how have you been? I'm sorry I haven't been able to get back to you. I've been out of the country. We have been having some issues in our South Indian plant. I've been eating curry for the past two weeks – you know how that can be!" Thorne said, mustering a laugh.

"Yes, Thorne, it's good to hear from you. I've been to South India several times. I haven't been to the north for a long time now – at least not since the take-over by the Pakistanis. It's just too dangerous in those Muslim controlled places."

"Yes, I've been told as much," said Thorne.

"So, what can I do for you?" asked Griffin, knowing full-well why he was getting the call.

"It seems that we received a notice of a ministry audit. They – you – wish to audit EG for the past two years. The notice also states that – let's see here – yes, that the ministry will also be auditing all officers of the company for the same years." He paused, and then added, "Is this really necessary, Bailey?"

"You know Thorne, I have little to do with who is audited and who isn't. It's really a matter of the computer we have determining who is the best candidate for it. I don't get into the details. Instead, we have certain algorithms we use to flag those returns that we think should be looked at," said Griffin, coyly.

"Yes, I realize that. Yet, I can't understand why we were picked. We are a GovCo, after all. GovCo's don't get picked for audits. It isn't in the agreement!" said Thorne.

"Agreement? I'm not sure what you mean."

"You know -- the mutual understanding that exists between big companies, like mine, and the ministries. We give you lots of money to fund programs and campaigns, and in return we get to have influence on legislation you pass – especially exemptions from crappy bills you pass that burden business. It's always been that way."

"Is that the arrangement?" asked Griffin, being obdurate.

This time, it was Thorne's turn to stop and reassess his approach. "Uh, yeah. It has. It's been that way since ... well forever. So, I suggest you call off the dogs and let everyone get back to business." His anger was growing more evident.

"I see. Well, Thorne, I think we may be able to work out something. I'll talk with my people to find out why you and your firm were identified for an audit. If there is something I can do there, of course, I will ... Oh, and have you had any luck with your discussion with Minister Ratner?" He was clearly fishing for information and creating a segue.

"I've been in negotiations with her, yes. We've been moving toward an agreement; however, the appointment to her new position seems to have changed things a bit. I'm not sure where we are presently. If I were to guess, I think we may need another approach."

"I see. So, where do you think we go from here?"

Thorne hadn't thought through exactly what his next steps would be, so he had to stall.

"Maybe we should just do it without her," said Thorne. Even *he* didn't know what that meant. He didn't have the software details for the SECE engine and, worse, he had no claim on its patent. "But we'll need some sort of an agreement – you know, a quid pro quo. You won't audit EG and I'll increase your cut on the SECE deal we've been discussing – say, seventy-thirty."

"That's close," Griffin answered. "Fifty-fifty," he said, adamantly.

"I'll have my attorney draft something and ..."

"No," said Griffin. "You know this can't be done above board. It has to be *sub-rosa*. You know that. In fact, I'll have my personal counsel put something together. It will be a vague agreement on a 'business venture' that we will have. It will say we split things fifty-fifty. I'll send it to you as soon as I have something."

"Agreed," answered Thorne. He was being boxed-in, and he didn't like it. But he was running out of options.

As soon as the call ended, he called in his chief legal counsel, Chow. "So, what do we do?" he asked her.

Chow had already made her deal with Muntz, and it had paid off handsomely, although she had yet to pocket the money. Thorne had unknowingly funded Muntz's and her retirement plans to the tune of $40 million. She was going to give notice as soon as the money was safely in her Swiss bank account.

"Good question," she answered, debating whether to take the question seriously.

"I'm not looking for an observation," he shot back. "I'm looking for a plan, Chow. Griffin thinks I have the complete details for manufacturing a fully functional SECE engine. As you know, that plan died with Patrick Disone in that car that went into the reservoir the other night. His chief technology man, Navarov, I hear, is also dead. That doesn't leave me with much since Ratner is now more powerful than ever."

"True, but she's not richer than ever."

Thorne looked at her. "Yes, but power leads to riches – it always does."

"A bird in the hand is worth two in the bush, sir," said Chow. "If you can give her money now, she'd take it over some future promise, I imagine."

"It's not a promise, Chow. She's got the secrets to the engine. All she has to do is either fund her own company here in the states to produce it or sell the secrets to someone other than us. Either way, she'll make billions."

"What if she doesn't have it?"

"What do you mean?"

"What if she doesn't really have all the pieces to the SECE?" asked Chow, planting the seed of doubt in Thorne's mind.

"How could she not? She's got access to the complete patent filing."

"Sure, but if the filing were incomplete or certain data added that made the filing inconsistent, the information would be useless. The Chinese and Russians have been violating our patent laws for decades, hacking in to get patent information. Patent filers began altering the data slightly to make it more difficult for anyone to re-create what they've done."

"But if the info in the filing wasn't right, it would nullify the patent in protecting the real intellectual property. In effect, there would be no protection for them, so why would they do that?"

"Because no one would figure it out until they had sold millions of engines. By the time someone deciphered the codes to determine what software really worked, they will have been multi-billionaires. Also, who's to say they wouldn't file an amended patent petition after they've been producing them a while. They'd protect their asset and be well along the way to dominating the marketplace."

"You almost sound like you were the one who came up with the plan, Chow," Thorne said skeptically. "It sounds too perfect to me."

"Unfortunately, I didn't, sir, or I'd be on a tropical island someplace." But that was exactly what was on her mind, and she figured she would be there within the month.

"So, what do you propose?"

"If Ratner is bluffing, which I think she is, then you won't have anything for Griffin. There won't be any company upon which to build the SECE empire."

"That's not a solution to my problem," said Thorne, growing impatient. "I need something I can take back to Griffin. If I don't, he will audit me and the company until there is nothing left to audit. He'll destroy us if he can. That's the way he rolls."

"So, why don't you just buy the technology?"

"From whom? Lenoir?"

"Yeah."

"They won't sell it. We've tried."

"Perhaps not everything."

"I don't understand," said Thorne.

"Let me try," replied Chow. "And if I do, I want five percent."

Thorne started to fume. It seemed like everyone had leverage on him, and he didn't like it. He was used to manipulating others, and wasn't accustomed to having demands dictated to him.

Thorne nodded his agreement solemnly. "Now get it done!" he barked.

"Absolutely," said Chow.

"And I want it done immediately. I need to be able to go back to Griffin and get him on board. Get the ball rolling," ordered Thorne, now pacing behind his desk.

"Will do, sir. Is there anything else?"

"No, just get out!"

Chow left the office and walked down the hall toward the white doors of the private elevator that went directly from Thorne's office on the 135th floor to the ground floor. She tapped the silver and pearl broach on her gray suit and turned off the recording device. She had all she needed from her conversation with her boss. She just wondered how much her other boss would be willing to pay for it. Her only question was whether to cut Muntz in on it. *Nah,* she thought. *I think Muntz already got his, and I don't have mine yet. And, until I have my share, this is going to be mine.*

*****

CH 16 Nadir

Days passed and there was still no word from Patrick. The company was forced to lay off half of its staff as sales of Lenoir's older HECE engine overseas began to falter. Customer fears that the company might go under pushed more to other models of less capability, but with larger, stronger companies behind them. Reminiscent of the early days, Lenoir Labs was down to a skeleton crew, and the two executives, Shea and Meghan Armstrong, the CFO, struggled to keep things together.

Shea had managed to get additional monies from friends and colleagues who were willing to invest in the business, knowing full well they might never get their money back. But friends were friends, and in the circles in which Shea traveled friendship still meant something. It was a bond that kept them together for life, regardless of their troubles. Like a marriage, her relationship with *this* extended family was special. As she didn't have any real family left, this was all she had. They were employees, former employees, colleagues, close business contacts, neighbors, and other friendships she'd developed over the years. They had benefited from introductions and contacts the Disones' had made on Capitol Hill and with others with which they'd done business domestically and abroad. She had stayed in touch with all of them, and now they were there for her – or at least as best as they could.

But now she was fighting something bigger. She was up against the biggest Goliath of all – the U.S. government. Even though her company's carcass had been stripped and cleaned many times over, the Ministry of Taxation and Enforcement continued to appear on her doorstep on a regular basis. State auditors were also circling overhead -- from Texas to Massachusetts. They had been in and out of the office, scrounging for scraps to tax. States were desperate for money to fund their bloated staffs and welfare programs, and by this time, the feds had contacted all of them. Eventually, states began suing other states to justify why they should be entitled to a greater share of the spoils. At this point, it had become a day-to-day battle to fend them all off. But Shea was never disillusioned enough to think that she was winning the war. She only hoped she could maintain the status quo until things turned the corner – whatever that meant.

Unfortunately, the day of infamy finally came. She had arrived late one morning, opening her office door after she'd gotten her blue ceramic mug of coffee from the small, employee kitchen. Meghan walked directly into her office without knocking. "Shea, there's someone here. He says he has to see you." Her face had a wrinkled, worried look.

"Who is it?" asked Shea, still scanning her messages on her computer screen.

"He wouldn't say. He just said he needed to see you."

Shea got up and went out to the front lobby where a young man in a navy, chalk-striped suit was standing. He looked like he was hardly old enough to vote, his suit ill-fitting, shirt slightly wrinkled and a skinny blue tie that was askew under his white spread collar.

"Yes, I'm Shea Disone. Can I help you?" she asked.

The man said nothing but held out his hand clutching an envelope.

"What's this?" she asked.

"A message," said the man.

Shea took the envelope.

"Consider yourself served," said the man before turning round and leaving.

She opened the delivery and pulled out a thick stack of pages. Turning it over, she saw the headliner.

>   RE: Patent Infringement Lawsuit

"What?" she said to herself before reading on.

>   Dear Dizones: (sic)
>
>   This is to notify you that charges are being brought against Lenoir Research Labs, Inc. (the Company), and both Patrick Dizone (sic) and Shea Dizone (sic) personally, as directors and shareholders of the Company for infringement of intellectual property rights in connection with the combustion engine technology the Company is attempting to develop and commercialize. EG Corporation has filed the attached restraining order and complaint in the state of California claiming that Lenoir Research Labs, Inc. used intellectual property developed by EG Corporation in the construction with their HECE high-efficiency combustion engine in violation of the U.S. Patent Act of 1952, Section 35, subsection 231(a) direct infringement of intellectual property rights.
>
>   As such, EG Corporation is seeking compensatory, punitive, liquidating and any other damages suffered by EG Corporation in the amount of $65.8 billion for the infringement of its property rights by Lenoir Research Labs. The enclosed papers will be served formally to the Company formally as the court is reviewing the company's request.
>
>   To avoid a lengthy and costly legal battle, we are willing to work out a reasonable compromise with your Company.
>
>   Very truly,

Ellen Chow
EG, General Counsel

Fire burned within her, as she read the paper. After finishing all thirty pages of allegations that accompanied the letter, Shea threw the document down onto the floor.

"F*ckers!" she said aloud. She'd never used that term before in her life, but she couldn't help herself. "Bastards! How the hell could they do this?" she screamed.

"Are you Okay?" Meghan asked, running back into her office.

"No. But, then again, I haven't been for a while. You already knew that," she snipped.

Meghan shook her head. "It's been a rough time."

"I'm sorry," said Shea, realizing she was being difficult. "I didn't mean to be short with you. I'm just at my wits end, that's all."

"Is there anything I can do?" Meghan asked.

Shea looked at her trusted administrative assistant – someone with whom she'd shared many of her private feelings during the years and her emotional turmoil during the last several weeks and months. "No," Shea answered. "At this point, I don't think so."

It was several minutes later when Meghan came back into the room. "Shea? I think you should turn on the TV. There's a story that ... well ... I think you should see."

"TV on," said Shea, activating the holographic image projected into her office.

> *... that EG says was in violation of the patents that it had perfected several years earlier. The lawsuit claims that Lenoir Research Labs purposefully copied the design and software of EG, Inc. and was selling it on the open market. In addition, EG said that the technology is protected by Import/Export Control Laws and that Lenoir Research Labs was selling the engine to foreign governments in violation of statutes. Finally, EG claims that the Ministry of Taxation and Enforcement has also levied tax liens and penalties against the company for tax evasion and other crimes.*

Shea was shocked. She had just received the notice! *How could it be on the news?* she thought. *The whole thing must be being orchestrated to bury me and the company! It's the final nail!*

The young reporter in a dark suit, mismatched chartreuse tie and powder blue shirt looked back into the camera and added, "It looks like there are real problems at Lenoir Research Labs. The executives refused to return our calls for more information, and they declined to come on the air to discuss the matter."

"What!" shouted Shea. She looked at her assistant and asked, "Did you get any messages from the media today?"

Meghan shook her head. "Absolutely not!" she said. "I've been in all day. I've cleaned out all my video mails, emails and everything else that's been sent my way. And you know me, I would have told you if someone from the media had called!"

Shea believed her assistant. She was meticulous in keeping records and checking things. There was absolutely no reason to doubt her. Much more likely was that the TV station had just fabricated the entire thing after the letter had been leaked to them.

Shea stomped over to her computer and began dictating the latest edition of her new blog, *Freedom Worth Fighting For*. It wasn't that original, but she did have a steady following of twelve thousand subscribers. They appreciated her articles on the latest shenanigans the government was pulling on Lenoir Labs and her, personally. Several were underground media reporters who took her stories and ran with them on blogs of their own, referring their readers to her blog as well. A network of such blogs had grown up in recent years, all using the latest technology to avoid blocking software from the government-owned SI-net.

This day, Shea began her blog by reciting the TV news report and what they'd said about her company. She addressed every allegation , stating the facts and circumstances behind what was actually going on and what had actually happened. Finally, her streaming video put a face to her cause, interviewing many of her employees, their children and families, and the hard times they were suffering from wage cutbacks and the stress of facing layoffs from a company being put out of business by their government. The emotions were deep.

"Hello, I'm Annie Reynolds," said the CFO shyly as she appeared in the video. Her auburn hair was pulled back sharply into a short ponytail behind her head, and she wore no makeup. Dressed in a beige blouse with a pussycat bow tied at the top and a plain, navy skirt, Annie looked the part of a less-than-stylish financial analyst. "I'm the chief financial officer of Lenoir Labs. I've been working for the company for nearly fourteen years now. I started in the accounting department as a clerk. I got my accounting degree while working here and raising three daughters. After years of hard work, I made it up to the top financial job here. It wasn't easy. I used to get up at five to study until seven; get the girls' lunches made for school; help the youngest get dressed and make sure she had everything in her backpack – you know how hard that can be. At eight, I'd drive them off to school and get to work by nine. I was only an hourly accountant at that point, so my hours weren't flexible. I worked through lunch so I could get home by five-thirty to help the girls with homework and fix dinner. After dinner, I had to drive them to soccer practice or singing lessons. I'd sit in my car doing my homework for my college classes or the work I had to get done for the company. The girls would go to bed at about nine. But, from then until midnight I'd be online taking my college courses. Sometimes after that I'd have to study for tests or write papers until two or three in the morning. I was exhausted most of the time – trying to make it on three hours' sleep a night.

"So finally, I graduated and got promoted to company controller and then CFO. My girls are still in school, and my hours haven't changed much. There are still long days for me. My oldest was looking at colleges, but with my pay cuts from the company, we will have to put that off. Government grants, scholarships and loans aren't available as you can only get those if you're unemployed now.

"My middle girl, who's sixteen, is struggling at school, and I try to help as much as I can – there just isn't as much time as I need to take care of that and the needs of my other two children. Food stamps aren't available either because I have a job.

"I've thought about quitting. At this point, I figured I'd make more in government benefits than I would working – with unemployment, food stamps, education credits, gas allowances, entertainment vouchers, PCD monies, and other handouts. But, I don't think that teaches my girls what's important in life – that hard work is important to build your character and prepare you for what life can dish-out to you. It's not all about what you take from the government that makes life worth living – it's what you can give back. Right now, I can't give back much, but at least I'm not taking anything from the other people who are hard at work doing the same thing I am – feeding their families and paying more than their share of taxes.

"What the government has done to us – to this company -- is criminal. They are trying to destroy a good company and all the people in it. But we aren't asking for a handout. We aren't asking for anything but your understanding and your emotional support. We are survivors, and we will survive this. But it will be hard, not only on us but more importantly on our families.

"All I can say is pray for us, and thank you for your support."

The picture faded to black. It was poignant and direct. It told the truth, and there was nothing more powerful than that.

The next scene was that of a thirty-something young man, an Asian American with an infectious smile and energetic personality.

"I'm Jimmy Win," he said, grinning broadly, "but you have to spell that N-G-U-Y-E-N. And *no*, it's not Nujen!" he said playfully, mockingly his own name. "For the past eight years, I've worked with some wonderful people here at Lenoir Labs. The Disones, Dr. and Mrs., have been exceptionally generous to all of us, especially during their hardship as of late. For months, they paid us our full salaries, even though the company was making very little – its sales virtually cutoff by the Ministry of Technology Assessment. Right now, none of us knows what the future holds. Dr. Disone has disappeared under mysterious circumstances. Our head of technology was found murdered in a submerged car only weeks ago, and the government has waged a full-scale war against us for being entrepreneurial and successful. I guess it isn't American anymore to be successful – I don't know.

"I'm thirty-eight, have my doctorate in electrical engineering from Stanford University, with my undergraduate studies at Cal Tech. I'm married to a beautiful woman, Leona, and together we have four children – Lea, aged five, Marcy, aged seven, Tom, aged ten, and Clara, thirteen. Like many of my colleagues, we've had a tough go of things lately. My wife's parents have serious health issues and both are staying with us as an extended family. Unable to get doctor appointments within the next fifteen months and completely unable to get any surgeries scheduled under the nationalized healthcare system, we have been exploring alternative health options. But these are costly. We've exhausted our life's savings and are now faced with personal bankruptcy. We still have student loans to repay and the government has threatened to take our possessions if we don't come up with money they claim we owe for back taxes. We've disputed that we owe anything, but we can't pay an attorney to file a complaint against the ministry. We are powerless to put up any resistance.

"However, Shea Disone has shown us that strong will and courage can overcome anything. She is facing troubles far greater than I am, and every day she comes to work with a smile on her face and a warm, friendly word for everyone in the office. She doesn't let others get her down. She's a fighter – she's a winner. And that's the kind of team I want to be on.

"If there's anyone who can inspire us to not give up, to fight those who seek to put us down and enslave us, and to stand-up to bullies like the government ministries who have stolen our freedom and our rights, it's Shea Disone.

"I know this sounds like a political ad, paid for by the Disone for President Committee, but it isn't. It's just a heart-felt endorsement for someone who is very special – someone who epitomizes strength of character and purpose. She will not back down in the face of great odds against her. She will not let the government destroy the company she and her husband have built – for us, their employees, for their customers, and, of course, for their own sake. She is a great lady. I just ask that you offer your support to her in any way you can. Please, help Lenoir and its employees. Let your congressmen know that their government is out-of-control and violating every human right we have. We're just like you. We care about our families and our country, and we're sickened to see both destroyed by this leviathan of a bureaucracy that is strangling the life's blood out of us."

The image of Shea appeared again. It was obvious she was embarrassed by the praise she had just been given by her employees. "I … I don't know what to say," she said, haltingly. "I must tell you that I am not seeking your monetary help. That would be charity, and that's not something that I will accept. There are too many truly needy people in this country who need your gifts of money, food, clothing and other necessities. No, I … we … are seeking your moral support. You need to standup and be heard. You need to stop being silent, hoping someone else will pick up the banner and carry it for you. *If not you, then who? I ask.*

"If you're upset that your taxes are being squandered on others who don't want to work and only want to sponge off the fortunes of others, I ask you what you are doing about it? Are you lying in bed watching TV and collecting government handouts while the rest of us pull the wagon for you? Are you afraid and waiting for someone else to be the standard bearer for the causes you believe in? What if we all took that view? Would we be any closer to getting our country back?

"Somewhere, deep inside you there is a spirit. There is a yearning to fight for what is right in this country. The USA wasn't founded on subsidies and benefits. It was founded on grit and determination. Our great grandfathers and mothers fought in two horrific world wars for us to keep our freedom, and what has our generation done? We sit and rely on someone else to stuff a government check in our mailbox. How pathetic have we become?

"So what's it going to be? Are we going to get involved or are we going to watch as the city burns around us, hoping we don't get singed? I for one am not about to get burned. I for one am not going to sit back and take the abuse our government doles out to those of us who are the most productive in society. I for one am sick and tired of rolling over and 'taking it' for the team. I give my fair share to the poor through my charitable donations. I don't want to be forced to give to the new religious order of the country – the U.S. government.

"So, I ask you – all of you -- to get involved! Get off your ass, call a friend and get them off their ass. Then, tell them to call someone to get them off theirs, and so on, and so on. We have the power to change things. But until now, we have just chosen to be silent and suffer. Our Founders didn't do that in 1775 and 1776. They risked their lives and those of their families to break from the tyranny of the British. It wasn't easy, and it wasn't certain. But they did it anyway.

"I implore you to do the same. Let's start to make a difference in America. Let's bring back the old United States of America – the USA – and reunite as a nation that can make a difference and is once again relevant in the world. Thank you."

Sumner stopped the video that he'd pulled-up online. "Wow," he said. "That's impressive."

"Yeah, I thought so too. That's why I wanted you to see it," said his new chief of staff.

"Get Shea Disone on the phone. We need to talk."

*****

CH 17 Betrayal

Chou and Muntz nervously sat in the waiting room outside of Minister Ratner's office. She had sent two of her black-suited men over to each of their apartments to personally bring them in to discuss what was happening with finding Patrick Disone. After the news headline in Boston that a car had been pulled from the Wachusett Reservoir, she had followed the story closely, sending in her goons to do an investigation of their own into what was going on. They had reported back that Patrick was missing.

Although they'd asked, neither Chou nor Muntz had gotten any answers from their abductors as to why the minister wanted to speak to them so urgently. They could only wonder and fear what the dragon lady had to say.

As for their partnership, it had taken Chou weeks for her to get the twenty million dollars Muntz owed her from the forty million heist of Thorne. After threats to his person and family, he'd finally come forward to pay her what they'd agreed. It was the first time she'd seen him since, and it was an acrimonious reunion.

"What do you think she wants?" asked Muntz. "I've been feeding her information on what we're doing every week. I don't understand what the problem is."

"We haven't been doing anything, so what have you been telling her?" Chou said sharply, still not forgiving him for his behavior.

"That we're working on it. You know – giving her bits and pieces of crap now and again. It's all bull sh*t, of course. But, she's not going to know. I just needed a little more time to make my arrangements and get out of the country. I bought property in Costa Rica, down on the beach. In a month, I'll be sipping a Mai Tai soaking up some rays where nobody can find me."

"Good for you," Chou said sarcastically.

One of Ratner's three administrative assistants came into the room and motioned for them. "The minister will see you now," she said.

The new building housing the Ministry of Unity was huge and ornate for a structure of the twenty-first century. Instead of glass and steel, it was decorated like a more modern version of the Biltmore Estate, as constructed by George Vanderbilt in 1895. Of course, the Minister's office together with her staff, consumed over twenty thousand square feet of space. The rest of the monstrous edifice was occupied by the other three thousand government employees who worked there. And, at Ratner's direction, no expense was spared. Hundreds of millions were spent building it, and hundreds of millions more in perfecting the intricate stonework, woodwork, artwork, and fine finishing details that would transform the building into a work of art.

Chou and Muntz passed through several small offices and strolled by many exquisite paintings by Renoir, Degas, Cezanne, and other impressionists, many valued in the millions themselves. But they were less interested in the scenery and more focused on what lay ahead in Ratner's office.

"Come in," Ratner said from behind a partially open door.

Chou and Muntz walked inside. The office was cavernous. The ceiling rose twenty feet into the air, arcing into a steeple-like crest with huge, wooden timbers set across the top to hold together the peaked roof. Tapestries graced the walls that once adorned castles in southern France, and the minister's desk stood as a monument to the exquisite craftsmanship of the same country during the eighteenth century.

Tense and edgy, the two sat in the plush, Queen Anne chairs that sat in front of the hand-carved, mahogany desk of the high-powered bureaucrat. They said nothing as they waited for the minister to address them.

"It's been a while since we all sat down and chatted," Ratner said gleefully. "I've been getting reports from Muntz here about what you're doing to find Patrick Disone. We all know that Navarov was the one they found dead in the submerged car, so it's important that we find the other one who knows the details of the SECE. So, what do you have?"

Chou let Muntz articulate an answer, as he was the one who had provided her all of the reports.

"Minister Ratner," he began, "we tracked him from the reservoir, where we believe he was involved in trying to fake his own death, using his friend's body as a substitute. There were tire marks up the road from another car we believe he used to leave the scene. It appears to be a late model Ford with Bridgestone tires. That's all we have at this point."

"I see," said Ratner, looking at him. Her poker face revealed nothing in her thinking. Then she looked at Chou. "What clues are you following-up on?"

Chou squirmed in her chair, but regained her composure quickly enough to answer calmly. "Yes, we have several clues we are working on."

"Like?"

"I'm sure Gunter has filled you in."

"Actually no. That's why I'm asking you," Ratner said flatly.

Chou glanced at Muntz but got no reaction.

"Well, there was the description of the car at a natural gas compression station about five miles away from the reservoir. He was probably filling up. The cameras had footage of the car coming in and leaving, but nothing good on the driver. No clear pictures."

"Do you have the pictures?"

"No, they were demagnetized somehow. We don't know how. But, we're still looking for other citings."

"What about any usage of his money cards anywhere? Hotels? Restaurants?"

"No. Patrick's wallet was found in the submerged car, right?" asked Chou.

Ratner smiled. "Yes, that's right," she said. "But you know what," she added, "let's cut through the crap here."

A cold chill went down Chou's spine. "What do you mean?"

"You two are lying to me."

"No, we've been working on ..." said Muntz.

"Shut up!" shouted Ratner. "You two have done nothing since you dumped Navarov's body off in that sedan which ended up at the bottom of the reservoir. You've been lying to me ever since."

"No, I ..."

"Stop it!" said Ratner. "You've let me down. Both of you. You were paid to get the software codes for the SECE. You got good money from me. And you've failed me."

"But there were extenuating circumstances."

Ratner just looked at him.

"Listen, Minister Ratner, we've had a difficult time finding anything. We're doing the best we can," said Muntz.

"Interesting, Muntz," said Ratner, "but my sources tell me that there were $40 million reasons why you haven't been forthcoming with me on this. Is that right?"

The blood drained from Muntz's face. "I don't know what you're talking about."

"Yes you do," said Ratner. "Both of you do."

"Minister, it was Muntz who arranged it. He's the one who ..."

"It doesn't matter!" Ratner answered, waving Chou off. "It really doesn't matter. You see; I understand. I get the fact that you wanted to make a little money off of this. I thought your plan was rather innovative. I wish I would have thought of it myself. Usually, I pride myself on coming up with schemes to compensate myself for my efforts. In this case, I put my chips with you two. I was right, but I was wrong too. So, this is what I'm offering you. You will give me twenty million of the take, and I'll forget all about your deception. I think that's a pretty fair deal. Otherwise, I have the power to take it all from you anyway and throw you both in prison where you'll rot for the next eighty years. I think that's a pretty good deal, don't you?"

The two sitting in front of her twitched uncomfortably. Each waited for the other to speak first.

"I still don't know what you're talking about," said Muntz.

"She knows," said Chou, coming clean. "She has eyes and ears everywhere. Let's not kid ourselves." Then, the lawyer turned back to Ratner. "Okay, yes. We did pinch a few dollars. I'm willing to cut you in. That's not a problem. I just need your assurance that you will leave us alone."

"Of course," said Ratner. "Let's just make arrangements to transfer the funds. Give my assistant your account numbers, and we'll make the exchange."

"That's all? That's all you need?" asked Muntz.

"That's it," the minister answered.

"Alright. Then we're square?" questioned Chou.

"I won't tell you again. Now get out!"

Chou and Muntz hurried out of the office before Ratner had a chance to change her mind. They gave their information to the assistant at the front desk and ran out the front door.

"I'll call you later," said Muntz before they split.

"Sure ..." said Chou, skeptically. "I've heard that before."

Muntz smiled and jumped in his car, screeching his tires in a hurry to get out of the parking lot.

***

Twenty-four hours later, a body was found in a forest preserve not far outside the beltway that encircled Washington, D.C. The police concluded that the man had slipped while climbing the cliffs along the turbulent leg of the Potomac river that bordered Rock Creek Parkway. His skull revealed fractures consistent with falling from a considerable height. There were other signs of struggle and trauma, but none were pursued.

Muntz never contacted Chou as he promised. He couldn't.

*****

CH 18 Closed

Shea struggled to keep the business going, but it was no use. With the threat of litigation and the yanking of the U.S. export permit that came with it, Lenoir couldn't sell the HECE or the SECE engines anywhere. In fact, the company had become a pariah in the business world. Quickly, customers had stopped calling and vendors had rapidly followed suit, especially after the company had repeatedly held their payments.

Running out of money, Shea dipped into the last of her savings to try to salvage the business, but the day came when Annie Reynolds entered into her office and closed the door.

"Shea, we have to talk," Annie said grimly.

"I know what you're going to say," Shea replied, diverting her eyes. "I've been waiting for you to come into my office to deliver the bad news."

It was something Annie had rued doing, but finally she was left with no choice. "I'm afraid so, Shea. We're out of money. My forecast shows that we have enough to make the next payroll, and then we're done. There is nothing left in your savings accounts. You're broke."

Shea smiled weakly, fighting back tears. "I tried," she said. "but, I've failed all of you."

Annie came around the desk and put her arms around her boss. "Shea, come now. You didn't fail us. It wasn't your fault. You did everything you could. But, you just can't fight Washington. You can't."

"What do we do?"

"You're going to have to call that attorney from EG."

"No! I won't sell out to them – anyone but them!" cried Shea, pounding her fist on the desk.

Annie just looked at her. "You know that's our only option now. You have to call."

Shea shook her head, but in her heart, she knew Annie was right.

"Get Chow on the line," she instructed.

A few minutes later, Annie returned. "She's on line one."

The image of Chou appeared on Shea's desk. Putting on a good face, Shea smiled as they exchanged pleasantries, but then got right to the point. "We received your letter, dated October 12, and I've had my legal counsel and CFO review it. Of course we deny any infringement on any engine design that EG has in production and you and I both know that. It is also something we could get summarily dismissed out of the courts. So, my attorney tells me you have no case."

Unfazed, Chou calmly answered. "Well, that's for the courts to decide. But, I will say that we have allocated fifty million to prosecute this case. How much do you have to defend yourself and your company?"

Shea was stunned and speechless. "You're bluffing," she said.

"Maybe, but maybe not. We are a one hundred twenty billion-dollar company, so the amount is insignificant to us. However, I assume that fifty million dollars is more meaningful to Lenoir Labs?"

Shea looked at her CFO who was in the room. Annie just shrugged her shoulders in despair.

"What do you want?" Shea asked coldly, the earlier smile having long-past vanished from her face.

"We are willing to offer to buy you out. We are prepared to buy Lenoir Labs," said Chou.

"How much are you offering?"

"One dollar," said Chou with a straight face.

Shea laughed. "That's pretty amusing. No really, how much is EG willing to offer for Lenoir?"

"One dollar."

It took all Shea could muster not to explode. She had been taken advantage of by many during the previous months, but this topped them all. The audacity of someone offering nothing for the company and take over everything Patrick, she and the others at the lab had worked their entire lives to build was more than she could bear.

"I have been insulted before, Ms. Chou. However, I think you take the cake."

"We mean no disrespect or any insult whatsoever, Ms. Disone. It's purely a matter of finance. You see, we've determined that your company is nearly bankrupt. You have no money and it's only a matter of time before you go out of business. Therefore, we could just wait until that happens or we can do it now." Then she paused. "I tell you what … we're prepared to offer you seventy-five thousand dollars for everything. That means you walk away from all your debts and pocket seventy-five thousand."

"Lenoir is worth millions!" said Shea. "Our engine designs alone are worth more than two hundred fifty million if not billions!"

"Not if we challenge that in court."

"You're thieves. That's what you are," Shea responded, with spite in her voice.

"You can call us anything you want, but this is our offer. It's a final offer, so you have five days to decide. I thank you for your call. Goodbye." The image disappeared, and Shea was left staring at Annie's sad and forlorn face.

"What are you going to do?" asked Annie.

"When do we tell everyone?" asked Shea, sullenly.

"Tell them what?" Annie asked.

"What I've decided," Shea said, being intentionally ambiguous.

***

Shea consulted with her human resources manager and together they decided to hold a company-wide meeting that afternoon. A simple electronic message went out only advising everyone of the meeting time and place with the subject matter listed as: *Mandatory Meeting*. It was never easy to deliver bad news to the employees, but when it affected all of them, it was especially difficult.

The clock read 2:55, and Shea walked down the hallway toward the large conference room where they held most of their company meetings. More a small auditorium than a meeting room, Room B-1 was spacious enough to seat over two hundred comfortably. It was where they had demonstrated the SECE engine to prospective investors and reporters those many months earlier when life had been so much easier and promising.

As she neared the door, Shea attempted a smile to everyone who passed in front of her, nodding as she usually did, but not speaking a word. It was unusual for her to have a company-wide meeting; it was often that Patrick would summon the group to announce a breakthrough of a technology or celebrate a new milestone the company had achieved. Walking into the room, Shea looked up at those who were seated in front of her, chatting casually with each other, unaware of the news they were about to receive.

Wishing to start on time and get it over with, Shea tapped the voice monitor on the podium to engage the microphone. "Hello?" she said, testing the volume. "Can you hear me?"

Most in the room nodded, and when others began to quiet and stop their conversations, she began.

"I want to begin by saying that all of you in this room are like family to me. You've all been there for Patrick and me when we struggled with one thing or another within this company, and you're here now. I hope you feel that you are a part of our ... of my family during this difficult time. If Patrick were here he would say the same thing.

"But, right now, I must deliver some news that I've been dreading for some time, but Annie tells me we can no longer avoid talking about it. All of you know that the company has come into difficult times with the tax audits, the cancelation of the patent, the prohibition issued by the Ministry of Fair Trade on permitting us to sell our engines, *etcetera, etcetera*. And, of course, most importantly to me, the disappearance of my husband, Patrick.

"I'm afraid I haven't been myself lately. It's been hard running the company on my own, and harder still trying to defend Lenoir from the arrows shot at us by Washington. But, I'm not going to cry in my soup, as they say. Right now, I have to tell you something that hurts me more than anything else. You all have families – husbands, wives, sons, daughters. Heck, Jonathon here," she said pointing to a young man sitting in the second row in front, "just had a baby girl with his wife, Roslyn, three weeks ago. And, yes, baby Jessica is well and adorable from all the pictures Jonathon has shared with us. Then, there's Jeanie Braxton, in the fourth row over there. Her mother slipped last month and broke her hip. They had to put her in a complete-care facility. God bless her – at 110, she's still got the fighting spirit! But, it's been hard on Jeanie, having to mover her there from an apartment she's lived in for seventy-four years."

Shea's eyes moved once again and this time focused on one of the dock workers who unloaded the trucks that delivered parts for the engines. "And then there's Max. Good 'ole Max." She smiled, a tear breaking loose from the corner of her eye and winding its way down her cheek, before she could swipe it away with her finger. "Max has been with us for twenty-two years. He's seen a lot here at the company, but he's never complained. He's always been a trooper for us – always at work, never late, and never cross. Max, you've been wonderful to work with!"

Then she looked down to compose herself, beginning to sniffle to hold back the emotion. "I ... I have to tell you that we are closing Lenoir Labs."

The shock of those words vibrating off the walls on either sides and behind the employees seated in the auditorium was palpable. Gasps became contagious as everyone looked quickly to the person sitting next to them to see if they were as traumatized as they.

"I know this is coming as a surprise to most of you. You probably sensed that things were not going as well as they had been. I think it's a safe bet that you internalized it, but most probably pushed away those negative thoughts. I know that I have. But it's time to face reality. We cannot survive. Our company -- or rather I -- have not been able to hold things together until we came out the other side of this. God knows I've tried. But, I'm afraid I've let you down. My dearest and best friends in the whole world."

There were several outbursts from the crowd, saying "No you haven't!" and "We love you Shea!"

"Thank you, but I've have – I've let you down and I've let him down," she said, looking up at the ceiling as if talking to her husband. It was an eerie reaction, one that she hadn't planned, but it showed where her thinking was at the time. It was in a dark place.

"Anyway, I wish to thank all of you for your service to our company. We've had a lot of good times here. We've had some great company parties, and wonderful experiences creating an engine that is the envy of the world. It's just too bad our own country couldn't see that in us.

"I will be pursuing an agreement with EG Corp to hire anyone from here who wishes to work for them. There will be no restrictions if you choose to move over to that company. I realize they have been our nemesis for years, but now you should go where you can find work, so I advise you to take it.

"In conclusion, I wish you all the best in whatever you choose to do next. I will be honored to write any of you a wonderful reference letter to help you land something else if you choose not to go to EG. That is the least I can do for you.

"Thanks again, and God bless you."

Shea hurried off the stage and left without saying anything more. She was now sobbing, wiping her eyes with the tissue she had brought with her. She didn't bother to look back to see if the meeting had concluded of whether Annie had kept them to go over details as they'd discussed. All she wanted to do was go back to her office and close the door. She wanted to lock out all the badness and curl up in her room, hoping it would all just go away.

But it wasn't long before there was a line outside her office. It wasn't an angry mob of upset staff members demanding to know why they'd lost their jobs. Instead, it was a group of sympathetic friends who'd come to give her comfort and thank her for giving them the opportunity to work with other great people like herself. One after another they came to give Shea their encouragement and their comfort, as they also understood how hard things had been without Patrick and without knowing where he was or what had happened to him. After they had all gone, Annie came back into her office.

"It's done. We will let people go today. You have enough in your savings to pay them through the end of next week. Is that what you really want to do?"

"Absolutely. That's the least I can do."

Annie began to cry as well, and it was Shea's turn to give her a hug. "It will be alright, Annie. Life will go on. It will. And you and I will look back on this as a great experience. Hopefully, we will stay in touch. We've been friends here at work, and I hope we can be after this too."

"I'd like that," said Annie, offering a weak smile. "I've always admired you, Shea – you and Patrick both. I'd be honored to be in your circle of friends."

"Annie, the honor is all mine," Shea answered.

*****

CH 19 Viral

It started as a simple video, recorded and posted online. It turned into a viral video and a rallying cry.

The reaction from Shea's blog followers was swift. This posting, which started at only a few thousands hits, skyrocketed to 450 thousand within a day, and 1.5 million within two. Picked-up not only in the United States, it caught fire in Europe and those parts of Asia that didn't have government censored blackouts. By the end of the week, the post had seen over 40.2 million hits. A number of underground organizations picked up the story, citing it as evidence of a government out-of-control. The Freedom Party posted several links to the blog and the video as did the few conservative radio hosts that were still broadcasting on frequency hopping channels. Used with a special receiver, listeners could synchronize their radio with the broadcast's as it bounced from one frequency to the next to avoid getting jammed by government censors. The Ministry of Electromagnetic Wavelength Regulation (or MEWR) had outlawed most conservative stations based on the Fairness Doctrine – that they did not also broadcast competing opinions equally during their own broadcast time. Allowing a competing segment right after their slot was rejected by the ministry. By contrast, the ministry did not find that progressive radio broadcasters espoused overly political viewpoints and were exempted from the ruling. But as for Shea, when her blog hit one million subscribers within the week, she got a call – this time from the MEWR, which had discovered her site and told her she had to shut it all down. It violated the Fairness Doctrine, they claimed.

However, the imp was out of the bottle, and it would not go quietly back. The problem quickly became one even the major news organizations were having a hard time ignoring. The story was everywhere, and they weren't covering it. And to add to the frustration, the ministries weren't able to quash it either.

Finally, one station, *Channel 7 News*, mentioned the growing interest in the matter. The segment aired with the same reporter who had aired the initial story.

"Yes, Morgan," said the reporter, standing in front of the MEWR government building in D.C., "we have an update to the story we've been reporting on for the past several weeks. Our original broadcast stated that Lenoir Research Labs had been indicted by several ministries of the government for various violations of federal law. Not only were they accused of stealing hardware and software applications from EG, Incorporated, but they were also being pursued by the Ministry of Taxation and Enforcement for tax violations.

"Earlier this week, an owner of Lenoir Labs, a Ms. Shea Disone, posted a response to our story that purportedly refutes the allegations brought by the government ministries. Her video post also paraded several employees of the company whom she alleges have been hurt badly by the government's actions. None of what the employees said on the tape could be verified as true. This is an on-going story that we will follow as we believe it is warranted. Jake Roberts, *Channel 7 News*."

There was no apology or retraction of any sort. In fact, the presentation only tried to portray Lenoir in an even worse light, hoping that the piling-on approach would have an effect.

The holographic image from the TV suddenly became blurry and then black altogether. It soon returned, but it did not show the broadcast studio. It was another backdrop – a well-lit room with banks of computer servers stacked on racks behind the face and body of the person now addressing the audience. A well-dressed young woman, showing signs of poise and presence, began speaking.

"Good evening. This is Robin Burke with the Greater Organization for Fundamental Liberty in America, otherwise known as GOFLA. We do apologize for interrupting your regularly scheduled program of propaganda, but we feel it is necessary for you to be aware of the facts for once – the real news that you are not getting and have not gotten for many years," she said.

Robin was attractive and very photogenic. Striking in appearance, her long brown hair flowed to her shoulders, and her large, velvety, hazel eyes melted most of the opposite sex. Her makeup was perfect, but in reality she didn't need much. The natural beauty of her face -- the high cheekbones, full lips and long eyelashes – made her an obvious choice to represent another viewpoint on the world's stage.

"As I only have one minute and forty seconds before I am removed from the airwaves, it is important that I quickly outline the truth about Lenoir Research Labs. Unlike what you just heard, here are the facts," she said quickly. Pivoting to another camera, she began listing her points with a summary popping up on the right side of her image, seemingly floating in mid-air.

"One, ..." she began, going down the list. Bullet points appeared, emphasizing the most important parts of her outline. "Lenoir Labs invented the High Efficiency Gasoline Engine or HECE technology twelve years ago. They applied to the Ministry of Technology Assessment for a patent at that time, but were rejected without providing a reason. Repeated submissions during the course of ten years finally led to a patent grant for the HECE. But without informing the company and without cause, the MTA cancelled the HECE patent last month. Two weeks ago, EG submitted its patent request for the *same* engine, and it was approved by the MTA within two days.

"Second, EG, Inc.'s technology for its engine, as submitted, was an *exact* copy of the documents created by Lenoir Research Labs. The only change was the substitution of the company name of EG, instead of Lenoir Research Labs, in the headers.

"Third, Lenoir Research Labs filed all tax returns in accordance with tax law, paying over twelve and a half million dollars in taxes on taxable income of the firm. It is important to understand that even though the company had a profit according to the accounting books, it generated no excess cash to pay taxes. Therefore, the owners were forced to take out bank loans to pay the company's taxes. That's the way the tax system in America works. Neither of the Disones took anything out of the company other than their small salaries – it was all reinvested.

"Four, no deal was ever struck with any foreign government for this technology by Lenoir Research Labs. The MTA denied the company the ability to sell anything within the boundaries of the United States. In fact, there were never any discussions held with anyone outside the United States about buying the technology. By contrast, EG is attempting to sell the technology to many foreign countries, including some of our enemies, such as Iran, Russia, China, North Korea, Iraq, Pakistan, Argentina and Venezuela.

"And finally, the government ministries have done everything in their power to destroy the Lenoir Research Labs and its owners. And they have succeeded. Earlier this month, Shea Disone closed the doors. Over three hundred Americans have lost their jobs. Many are single mothers with young children who can ill afford to be without work. Some of these families have members who are hospitalized and two are on life-support. Although eligible for the massive government handouts offered by social programs, their petitions for help have been, quote, *delayed for technical reasons*. Aid usually granted within days will be held up for months. Under the law, they are entitled to receive Food Stamps, Medicare, Medicaid, Cell Phone or TV Vouchers, USA Entertainment Allowances, and Gasoline Cards, as their earnings fall below the poverty level.

"Therefore, we ask that you give your support to GOFLA to help these families through this hard time. It is unfair and un-American to force them into poverty. But it is even worse to discriminate against them because they worked for a successful, innovative company that was willing to fight back. That is the way tin-pot dictators rule their countries. Is that what we've become?

"Thank you for your attention. It will be difficult to find free airwaves to continue to give you the truth, but we will do so when we can and for as long as we can. Good night, and God bless you all."

The screen went black again, but there was no resurfacing of the *Channel 7 News* team for another five minutes. Finally, the local team came back on the air, showing the anchor clearly frustrated with his technicians' inability to regain control of the broadcast.

"We are truly sorry for what just happened. We don't know how our broadcast was hacked or by whom, but we are diligently investigating that as we speak. This is clearly an act of terrorism, and the perpetrators will be found and justice served." The anchor's words were harsh and filled with contempt.

"Now, with the time remaining in our broadcast, we will turn to our weather and Tom Rios. Tom, go ahead please," said the anchor.

The camera shifted quickly to the weather map before Shea put down her glass of water and told the computer to turn off the telecast.

"Wow!" exclaimed Meghan. "What was that all about?"

Shea sat down, thinking. "I'm not really sure," she answered. "I guess we have more defenders out there than we thought."

"Do you know anything about this GOFLA?" asked Meghan.

"No, but I did get this e-message yesterday from them. It said that they had seen my blog and wanted to promote it everywhere they could. This Robin woman wrote the message. She claimed to be an independent organization that defends the Constitution and the American way of life. I don't know much more than that."

"The only thing I know is what the underground says about them," said Meghan. "I think they say it stands for *Go 'F' Your Liberal Agenda*," she answered, smiling. "At this point, those are my sentiments too."

"Well, I didn't do anything about the message – we've been getting so many. But, I'll reach out to Robin and see what it's all about," said Shea.

Just then, her phone rang. The image of another news network came up on the monitor. Shea hesitated, then answered. "This is Shea Disone. How may I help you?" she asked.

The picture of a well-known news figure appeared. "Ms. Disone?" he asked.

"Yes, how may I help you?" she asked again.

"This is Walter J. Jennings. You may know me from ..."

"Mr. Jennings. Yes, you're from the PBC network."

"Yes, I would have had my producer call, but I thought I'd have better luck calling myself. We have been following the story about your company and ..."

"Mr. Jennings, I apologize for being suspect, but my attorneys have advised that I should get verification of the identity of everyone who calls. We have to be sure you're not an avatar or robotic simulation created by someone else."

The person in the picture did not laugh or smile. "I am not surprised that you would question my authenticity, so I have provided you my DES number, which should show up now."

The DES, or digitally encrypted signature, was government issued – a type of digital passport to which only the user would have access. When sent through the government website, the complex image could be decoded and converted into the name and image of the person to whom it was associated.

Shea received the finger-print like image and entered it into the government system. Sure enough, W.J. Jenning's face and name appeared.

"Okay, Mr. Jennings, so what can I do for you?" Shea asked again.

"I want to do an interview. When are you available?"

*****

CH 20 *Jennings V. Disone*

After receiving calls from several other news organizations, Shea agreed to the interview with Walter Jennings only if it were done live with no cuts or interruptions. Reluctantly, Jennings had agreed.

Shea knew what she was getting into. She knew the slant on the story would be pro-government, anti-business, and, moreover, anti-Lenoir Labs. Yet, there seemed to be the beginnings of a ground-swell, and she hoped that she could make her case, regardless of the spin put on it by W. J. Jennings & Co.

The recording studio was small and cramped, with three camera's to provide holographic imaging and different angles. The backdrop was a green screen, which worried Shea. She was well aware that anything could be superimposed on that while they were talking without her knowledge. The two chairs were basic metal frames, the cushions a bland medium, quilted gray color that matched the low-quality carpet scrap that covered the floor; it too was just large enough to fill the frame when the camera zoomed out.

Shea sat and waited for twenty minutes until the host walked in briskly, his entourage in tow, completing his makeup and hair as he got situated into his chair. He neither said hello to Shea nor made eye contact before he began.

"We're on in three ... two ... one ..." said the producer, using his fingers to count down to the live broadcast.

"Good evening," said Jennings, looking at the camera. "Tonight, we have Shea Disone, former owner of Lenoir Research Labs, a company that has been embroiled in a series of illegal activities and questionable business practices."

Shea was prepared for the onslaught from Jennings, but she didn't expect it so soon.

"Now, Ms. Disone, we'd like to thank you for joining us to discuss the role your business has played in poor image business has in this country. From a recent poll, eight out of ten people believe business is bad for America, and from what is coming out of the ministries, it looks like Lenoir Labs has contributed to that tawdry image."

"Well, Mr. Jennings, with all due respect ..." Shea began. But he cut her off quickly.

"As we all know, capitalism has been the source of greed for the rich and misery for most of the working class of the country. It has exacerbated the problem of class envy as the one-percenters have taunted the poor with their wealth for decades, if not centuries. So, based on that, how did your business contribute to the misery of American society?" asked Jennings, speaking to a virtual audience of millions using the government's SI-net channels. Censors had been lifted temporarily by the Ministry of Electromagnetic Wavelength and Digital Source Regulation to allow the broadcast to go forward. By all accounts, there were 8.3 million viewers when the broadcast started, and 14.5 million by the time it finished.

"Excuse me?" asked Shea in response, startled at the combative approach he'd taken right from the start. "What was the question in all of that?"

"I guess you weren't paying attention or didn't want to hear my question," Jennings shot back. "What I asked was how Lenoir Labs, your company, contributed to the poverty in America and how it enriched those like you at the expense of others who are less fortunate?"

Shea was prepared for battle, but she wasn't prepared for a sniper shot directly to the head on the first salvo. Flustered and agitated, she said, "Well, I guess I would have to disagree with you Mr. Jennings. I don't think that we have done any of those things to society or to those less fortunate."

"But the Ministry of Facts and Statistics just released its annual report on how much businesses like yours actually contribute to the wealth of this nation. It found that during the past year, small businesses *took* more than two and a half percent from the increase in the gross domestic product, while government workers contributed over seven percent to the increase in the nation's output. Now, I know this is hard for you rich people to understand, but what I'm saying is that companies like yours actually suck productivity out of the system – not contribute to it. What do you say to this report's findings?"

"I was an economics major you know, so I do know a little bit about GDP numbers, and what you are saying doesn't make any sense."

"You're questioning the ministry?"

Shea knew it was a criminal offense to question the facts and figures that came out of a ministry. And, on a live feed, it would be suicidal.

"I'm just saying that you must have misunderstood the report's findings," she answered, trying to be diplomatic.

Jennings held up the report in his hand and read the section verbatim, restating what he'd just said to her. "So, I don't think I've misunderstood, Ms. Disone. It sounds like it is you who didn't do very well in your economics classes."

Shea crossed her arms defensively but then caught herself, taking a deep breath and re-engaging. "Or, perhaps, those in the ministry needed to proofread their work more carefully."

Now it was Jennings who was caught without an answer.

"Mr. Jennings, then please explain to me how the government produces anything for public consumption? Is it not the role of the government to establish and administer laws that are to govern the people? How is it that we now count, as goods and services produced in this country, the creation of laws? Is the creation of laws on some assembly line someplace? Perhaps in Washington. But, if left to the independent decision of the consumer, who would pay money for these laws? What would one get for purchasing, say, the Anti-ID Voter Registration Act of 2018. Would I just get a piece of paper? If so, what would I do with something like that? Therefore, under the true definition of gross domestic product or output of this country during a period of time, it must be defined by what the private sector creates and sells in the way of finished goods and services – things that are actually consumed by people domestically and exported to others across the globe. Isn't that what your economics class taught you Mr. Jennings?"

"Let's move on to another topic, shall we," Jennings said, ignoring her and turning the page in his notebook. "Your company has been in violation of federal, state and local laws for some time now when it comes to the development and use of technology. Isn't that right?"

"No," she answered shortly.

"In addition, your company's mistreatment of its labor force – by paying them below the minimum wage of fifty-two dollars an hour and working them forty-three hours per week – is the reason the Ministry of Unions and Labor Control is forcing you to close down. Right?"

"Where are you getting this?" Shea said indignantly.

"This is all coming from the ministries themselves," said Jennings. "So, it's pretty safe to say that Lenoir Labs is the quintessential small business that runs contrary to most laws in this country. In large part, this is why the government has to continually fight to keep the economy going. Wouldn't you agree?"

"No, I don't. The unfortunate truth is that small business generated sixty-five percent of the new jobs in the country, at least up until the Fourier Administration came into power. It has all but shut down small business with its avalanche of regulations and red tape. Big business supports President Fourier because it knows that the administrative burdens of reporting and taxation will wipe out their small-business competition. In addition, most times the GovCo's are exempted from the very laws you put on the books for the rest of us to follow. GovCos have long been in bed with government and officials on the Hill, scratching each other's backs. It's the little person, like me, that takes it in the back of the head – time and time again."

"Ms. Disone. The evidence to support what you're saying just isn't there. Our own Ministry of ..."

"Our Ministry of Facts and Statistics isn't always right," said Shea, being careful with her words. "For real numbers, you need to start using those put out by the Foundation for the Accuracy of Economic Statistics, the FAES. They are the ones providing truth in the numbers."

Ignoring her remark, Jennings continued. "We all know, and have known for a long time, that capitalism is a scourge on society. Your company exemplifies the greed of the rich and the abuse business heaps on the poor workers who slave away day after day at your plants just trying to make enough to put food on the table for their families. You are a union shop, correct?"

"No, but ..."

"So, you refuse to pay what is required by union rules. Isn't that right?"

"My workers make – made – more than union workers – that is, before the government came in. After the payment of union dues and other fees to support the union president's seven figure salary, union workers earned less than my people and were far less happy."

"So, you're answer is no. You currently don't pay as much as what union workers get."

"No, because we're no longer in business!" said Shea, increasingly frustrated with his twisting of her words.

"Now, let's go on to another subject."

"Let me finish what I was saying about ..." she shot back, beginning to stand her ground.

"I'm sorry, Ms. Disone, we really need to go on to the next issue here," said Jennings, cutting her off.

Shea's face grew red with anger. "Listen, Mr. Jennings! Here are the facts. My company employed three hundred thirty-five employees last year. Their average wage was twice what union workers make at the same positions. My employees submitted responses to our annual employee survey, giving us a 9.5 out of 10 as a great place to work. I've lost only two staff persons during the past five years – one moved away when her husband's company transferred him and another retired from us. Our business had been growing every year by over twenty percent. We hadn't lost a single customer in three years and had been able to grow our business through word-of-mouth alone. We made a great product – the HECE engine which was purchased throughout the world. It is a high-efficiency engine that gets over 156 miles to the gallon of gas. It's relatively inexpensive, and the maintenance is the lowest of any engine on the market. Yet, we couldn't sell it here in the United States. It was banned. Why? Because the government wanted to shut down the oil industry and if we had a high efficiency engine, then oil reserves would last longer and gasoline would easily compete with all the alternative energy sources, even with the 326 percent taxes they impose on every gallon. That's why.

"And, as far as my being rich. My husband and I made only fifty-two thousand dollars last year. That's the poverty level. We reinvested everything we earned – putting it back into the company to grow our people and improve our technology. We live in a small home and have two eight-year-old cars. We borrowed from the bank to pay our taxes every year. Now, does that sound like we're rich and that we had a horrible business that mistreated our employees and screwed over our customers?"

Jennings was used to having absolute control over his program and was caught off-guard by the assertiveness Shea threw at him. He tried several times to interrupt, but she would have none of it. Finally, he held up his hand.

"I'm sorry, Ms. Disone, but ..."

"Oh, and by the way, Mr. Jennings. What did you do with the 67.4 million dollars in salary you collected last year from PBC? How much of that did you give to the poor in this country that you so frequently pull up to throw in the faces of us mean, nasty, greedy capitalists?"

"Like I said, it's a shame that your company is going under, but I think it's pretty evident that it's your denial that has brought the calamity upon you and your tragically trusting employees. The government has every right to shut you down, and thank goodness they're doing just that. More companies like yours is the last thing this great progressive experiment called the USA needs."

Jennings turned away from Shea, effectively ending the interview.

"Next week, our show will focus on the productive relationship that government ministries have with large companies, especially in the area of defense and telecommunications. Through this partnership the nation has benefitted mightily, and we will have as our guest, Kilby Thorne, CEO of EG incorporated, who will describe how his company does research to develop new and society-changing technologies and virtually gives these away to the people of this great land. The contributions by EG have gone a long way to bettering the lives of every American – something that has been the bedrock of this greatest nation on this green earth," he said, as the music came to a close.

"This was all crap!" Shea muttered, standing up and walking off the stage. "All of it."

Jennings didn't say anything more to her. He began to motion to his crew to cut the feed before starting to disconnect his mike, but Shea caught him.

"How dare you!" she said to him, before he had a chance to turn things off.

He heard her and turned back to engage. "Go tell it to someone who really gives a damn!" he'd said to her, waving her off. He was visibly angry, equally at himself as with her for stealing his show.

"You're a small man, Mr. Jennings. You're someone who was never anyone until someone else made you someone. You couldn't do it on your own. You don't have any idea about the things you talk on the air, do you? They are just cue-cards that you parrot as you read them. You don't know the first thing about how economics works, how money supplies flow through the system, what impact the minimum wage has on hiring, how small businesses actually do add to the GDP and how they are terribly burdened by the reporting and regulations imposed by government – do you?

"You've never run a business before, have you Mr. Jennings? Have you ever had to make payroll to provide for others who were dependent on your ability to run a company? Have you ever had to make a decision that might either employ another two hundred people or that would put three hundred out of work if things went wrong? Have you ever had to contend with unscrupulous competitors who would use the ministries or the courts to undermine your company? Have you?"

"Those things are irrelevant," Jennings shot back. "What's important in *my* business – hell, what's important at all -- is that we create the narrative for everyone else to follow. We create a message we want people to grab onto. Once we do that, we can sell the story all day long."

"Does it matter at all if it's true or not?" she asked.

"Of course not. Truth is irrelevant. What's important is whether the people will buy into what you're peddling. We have the government ministries behind us to support us in that. Or, I should say, we back the ministries in what they are selling to the masses. Sure, a lot of times we know what they are selling isn't true, but that makes no difference. The ends justify the means. It's always been that way. If we have to lie for them, we will, particularly if it furthers the cause."

"And what is the cause?" asked Shea.

"The cause – the narrative – you know! Things like class warfare sell. They prey on people's inner vices. It's sold for over six hundred years, and it will continue to sell. People drink it up like Cool Aid. Jealousy and envy are deeply engrained in the human character, Ms. Disone. We don't work against these things; we work with them. We bring them to the surface and exploit them because they sell. And, in the end, it lets us keep our jobs and the politicians keep theirs. People dependent on their government is a great thing, don't you see that? We get the people to do what we want them to do; we keep them in their place so they don't disrupt the system; we collect money from you working saps by taxing you to death; and we get to spend that money on ourselves, our friends, and then what's left we sprinkle around a bit to make it *look* like we're really helping those at the bottom of the barrel. That's the way it works, and it works pretty damn well if you ask me."

"Thanks for the confession," said Shea.

"What do you mean?" Jennings asked.

Shea pointed to the microphone he was holding in his hand. "You didn't turn yours off. You just confessed to the millions who watch your show every week. I guess you could say I've been vindicated."

Jennings's face drained white. His eyes darted down to the open mike. She could tell he was panicked, but he tried not to show it. It wasn't until three days later that the news channel said that Mr. Jennings was taking time off to be with his family. Shea read the news with a smile. *Small victories,* she said to herself. *We have to start someplace, and small victories are better than none at all.*

***

Within minutes, the open microphone incident, together with the video from the show, was circling the globe at astounding speeds. Even more watched than her earlier blog, the video drew people in. Everyone was talking about it, and it began to make the White House nervous. But what alarmed Fourier most of all was the formation of what became known as *C-corps*. These weren't military groups; these were unsanctioned civilian militias. Fed-up with the dictatorial ways of the Fourier regime, the C-corps arose online from a singular forum posting where a contributor signed his or her name with the now infamous acronym – GOFLA. Most assumed that it stood for the organization represented by the lovely woman who had interrupted the nightly news cast only days earlier. When asked in the forum what that stood for, the user answered with *'Go F*ck Your Liberal Agenda.'*

Calls for Shea to run for political office began to take off in earnest, and *in absentia*, she was voted online as honorary president of the GOFLA organization, even though neither she nor most anyone knew exactly what this mysterious group was or did.

It was no surprise that president Fourier forced Congress to take up a bill putting strict limitations on what could be put on the SI-net. Sites such as GOFLA were singled out as 'inciting violence' within the United States. Such provocation was, "not in the best interest of the nation at large," according to the legislation.

Yet, the damage had been done. More than half the country had seen the clip before it was yanked from the SI-net and the website closed. And polling data, even by the most liberal of news outlets, showed the president's favorability numbers were falling precipitously. By the end of the month, fewer than 26% believed Fourier was doing a good job in the White House, and talk began about seeking impeachment.

Fourier confided in his Cabinet for the first time since being elected to office, over seven years earlier. They didn't want emotions on the Right to get too far out of hand; yet, at the same time, they didn't want the Left to overstate their case and make Lenoir Labs and Shea Disone become a martyr for their cause. Shea Disone appeared as a very sympathetic witness when she wanted to be. Yet, her ability to defend herself and her company made her dangerous. Too dangerous.

***

The government crackdown on the SI-net and prosecution of those violating the SI-net Safety and Compliance Act, as it became known, went a long way to squelch the unrest. The courts were more than willing to take up the cause against rogue websites on behalf of the Administration to ensure the civility of the populace. And after the little hacking incident with the *Channel 7 Newscast*, members of GOFLA were highest on the FBI most-wanted list. There was a nation-wide manhunt for any known members of GOFLA. Many were arrested even though most people doubted that they even knew about the organization. More often, these things were merely excuses to go against Fourier's political enemies.

An example was the alleged Executive Director of GOFLA, who was arrested in his home. TV cameras were brought in to show him being taken from his home in Bethesda, Maryland, in handcuffs while his wife and three children, all under the age of eight, watched from the front porch of their two-story, red-bricked colonial. The reporter stood at the end of the driveway, stating to his audience that the executive director had violated the SI-net law and was also believed to have had child pornography on his home computer. No proof was ever offered, but the personal attack was successful and his reputation was ruined. Later, the charges were dropped, but that story never hit the e-papers.

Shea had eschewed finding a contact at GOFLA or seeking help from them, not because she didn't believe in the cause, but because she was still working tirelessly to find her husband. Besides that, she was emotionally drained. Every ounce of strength she had went to getting herself out of bed in the morning and forcing herself to make calls to anyone who could help her find Patrick . She was broke but had received some money from anonymous donors who had seen her

Jennings interview. But, her poverty was little different than the millions of regular, every-day Americans who were also growing poorer each day. As the government promises of giving out more benefits rose, the reality of being able to actually receive those benefits shrank. The money was running out for everyone, and the U.S. printing presses – that usually printed trillions each year – were running out of ink. Pressure was building, not only on Shea, but on America itself.

*****

CH 21 Drama Grips a Nation

The headline of the *New York e-Tribune* read:

Doubts Arise over the Louisiana Refinery Explosion

And that's all it took.

The article ran while the editor-in-chief was away on vacation, and when he returned, he was furious. The associate editor was immediately fired, and a retraction issued the next day. However, the article raised serious and lasting concerns about the little-known and even less-reported incident that had occurred in the oil refinery just outside of Baton Rouge, Louisiana more than six months earlier.

> *What is being questioned is the Administration's assertion that the incident was the result of mismanagement at the refinery. This reporter could find no history of safety problems at that refinery – in fact, it had been recognized as one of the safest in the country,* read the article.

The e-paper went on to say,

> *The Fourier Administration contends that there was no explosion – only a minor disruption caused by a broken line in the catalyst section of the plant. The federal investigation stated that it was a massive oil spill caused by 'a flagrant disregard for standard safety practices and a culture of non-compliance at the refinery.'*

> *But, as we have now uncovered, there* was *a gigantic explosion on June 9 that led to the deaths of over 350 employees at the site. Information about the conflagration has been hard to get, but what has been obtained refutes the Administration's claim that it was due to mistakes made by management at the company. Fourier's Environmental Ministry insists that executives at the company were cited by OSHA numerous times for being reckless and uncaring about the welfare of their workforce. Many of these executives were arrested and summarily imprisoned for their gross negligence in the matter.*

> *However, the* **NYeT** *has determined that the oil company, CarbonOne Group, had twelve years without any safety violation or reportable incident. They have one of the best safety records in the business, as one government agency employee told us, off the record.*

> *Records show that the night of the incident, the Ministry of Environmental Protection demanded the refinery allow in four individuals into the plant – unscheduled and unannounced. The plant manager questioned their*

*credentials and refused them admittance; however, audio tapes of phone calls tell the **NYeT** that the Vice-Minister of the EP ordered the company's vice president to allow the four complete and unfettered access throughout the plant.*

The CarbonOne VP, who is no longer with the company and whose whereabouts are unknown, relented. However, this reporter has learned from the logs of the plant that the explosion occurred not more than two hours after the four were admitted. The names of the individuals were not listed on any entry logs, but the names given by the Administration – Jose Gonzales, Manuel Hernandez, Ernesto Emanuel, and Juan Valdez – are so common that no specific identification can be made. One eye-witness told this reporter that the men were white, not Hispanic.

The plant has now been closed permanently, as the ministry has prohibited the company from rebuilding, citing concerns over the company's ability to operate safely.

*Sources that refuse to be identified by name have told the **NYeT** that it is part of the White House's attempts to shut down all fossil fuel companies. One person, high-up in the ministry told the **NYeT** that he was ordered to threaten oil, coal and natural gas companies with stiff fines and their executives with imprisonment if they were found operating after the president's re-election. When told that President Fourier could not run for a third term under rules of the U.S. Constitution, which explicitly prohibits any third term for a sitting president, the official merely shrugged her shoulders and refused further comment.*

The article ignited a powder keg.

The population began to wonder - *If the federal government was lying about something as important as that, then what other things were untrue? And what was the official trying to say about the president running for a third term?*

Those who did not follow the news were oblivious to the implications; however, there were enough of those who did understand that made a difference. They were the ones who would not let go of that story and others. And when the obvious became undeniable, the dam became too porous to plug. It was now Fourier's emergency, and he had to take action quickly.

The GOFLA website mysteriously came back on line; however, it advertised itself as an online channel surfing site, switching to the frequency hopping technology others rogue sites had been using for years. It instructed its followers how to find it, and how to keep up with its changing web addresses. The origin of the websites was concealed -- bounced around all over the globe to hide its source. Many thought it now came from Indonesia; others thought it most likely came from a small office in the northern part of Scotland. However, no one knew, and the government was unable to stop it.

The biggest stories to come from the GOFLA site dug deeper into the refinery incident. And one of the most disturbing was the rumor that the assistant editor at the *NYeT* who was responsible for printing the story was missing. He hadn't been seen since the story broke and the editor-in-chief had returned.

As GOFLA drew more attention to itself, it began a series of other articles as well – those questioning the legitimacy of the information coming from the Ministry of Facts and Statistics. Despite being a criminal offense, questioning the numbers became a regular feature on the GOFLA site. It claimed outright that the statistics given out by the government were fabricated. One example GOFLA presented was the government's alleged fact that the U.S. economy had grown by 2.3 percent during the previous quarter according to the ministry. Its investigation, supported by internal government documents, showed it had been actually contracted, *falling* by 4.3 percent -- showing the country was in a recession. In addition, the inflation rate, based on the CPI or consumer price index, was running at 0.5 percent according to the ministry. This was a true fact, but it was based on the twisted definition of the CPI concocted by the government. That index excluded any product using oil, any transportation costs, healthcare costs, food costs, and other costs deemed 'appropriate' by the ministry. These exclusions were necessary, according to a ministry spokesperson, because these items distorted the results. The fact was, these items made the index *more* accurate, not less. Finally, the unemployment rate cited by the ministry was 4.5 percent. But everyone knew that a lot of people in the country were unemployed. So, to say that 95.5 percent of people capable of working were employed was a joke. The Administration had adjusted this figure too, stating that it reflected those people who: one, were looking for work; two, were qualified to hold down a full time job; three, had interviewed within the last thirty days; four, had been offered a full time job during the last thirty days, and five, had completed the requisite government paperwork to verify they met all of those criteria. The truth was, few bothered with the red tape. Real estimates put the unemployment and underemployment figure at closer to 33 percent, with 67 working to support that 33.

Seeing himself being boxed into a corner, Fourier ordered his internal police – a special division of his FBI -- to purge the ranks of the ministries and find those responsible for the leaks to GOFLA. The president announced that these rogue elements would be identified and punished. However, after months of searching for the offending parties, none were found.

The apogee of GOFLA's flight to prominence came when a primetime news conference was airing on all the government-controlled media channels. The president was having a rare interview and it was being conducted Walter Jennings, the same anchor who was so badly bruised by Shea in their one-on-one earlier that month. Jenning's defense of the Administration won him the right to talk with the most powerful man in the country.

Although intended to be seen far and wide throughout the country, the interview garnered only a paucity of viewers – at least initially.

The backdrop for the interview was the elegant East Room of the White House. Although not as grandiose as most European palaces, the East Room was renovated by Fourier at the cost of more than one hundred million dollars. The twenty-two foot ceiling retained its plaster artisanry with its intricate medallions flanked by swags, acanthus, escutcheons, and scrollwork. The walls were refinished with hand-carved ebony panels, which created a simulated picture frame around each of the silk tapestries that depicted scenes of the Civil War, Martin Luther King, Selma Alabama, and the ascendancy of Barak Obama to the White House in 2008. Fourier had also removed the elaborate parquet floor and installed Brazilian mahogany. The rest of the room glittered with the beauty of its gold-cloth, cut-away drapes, gold-leaf ornamentation adorning the doorways and arches, black marble busts of FDR, Woodrow Wilson, and Barak Obama, and three cut-glass chandeliers, dating back to Theodore Roosevelt's time in office. Started by Thomas Jefferson and completed by Andrew Jackson, the East Room had been host to many events – both highs and lows -- throughout its nearly two hundred twenty-year history. This would be just another.

"President Fourier, I want to thank you for setting aside your valuable time to speak with me and share your thoughts and views about what has been happening in this country during the last few months. I know you have deep concern about the reprobate elements that have been working feverishly to undermine your Administration."

"Quite right, Walter. I worry about the abject lawlessness that is going on in this country. The total disregard for justice and our judicial system. It is a travesty – but not one that cannot be corrected. My Administration is doing everything possible to ascertain the identity of the members of this scofflaw group that has distributed lies about this country and our greatness. It is only seeking to destroy the very foundation that made this country so great. And, I will not allow it," said Fourier.

Sitting on rosewood, Queen Anne's chairs, covered in colorful, floral-pattern, the two men conversed, sitting opposite each other in the middle of the floor with the chandeliers shining brightly overhead.

"You have taken many steps to find and apprehend these people. Are you any closer to identifying who and where they are?"

Then, the interview transmission went dark, and the face of Robin Burke appeared. She sat composed and relaxed as she looked into a camera from behind a news-anchor style desk.

"Good evening, my fellow Americans. I apologize for the interruption, but we at GOFLA believe it is more important that you hear the truth about what is going on in this country, rather than the distortions you will get from watching the original broadcast. As before, I have a limited time to speak with you, so I will make it brief.

"Unknown to most of you, the president and his Administration are planning a *coup d'etat* over the legislative and judicial powers of this country within the next thirty days. He will ensure that he is not only re-elected to an illegal third term, but that his power is permanently established. There can be no shirking or absolving yourselves of your responsibility as a citizen of this country. You owe it to yourself, your community and your children to act. Our time is running out. Once Fourier takes over, there will be no recourse. We will be shackled to a life without our most cherished freedoms – life, liberty and the pursuit of happiness."

But, to the horror of those watching the broadcast, there was a loud crash in the background of the GOFLA studio, and Robin Burke glanced to the side off camera to see what had happened. Shots could be heard, and she covered her mouth with her hands, her eyes as wide as silver dollars.

"My God!" she cried. "Who are you and what are you doing!"

The next shot heard was also seen on-screen, entering Robin's forehead and spraying brain tissue and blood across the back of the green-screen wall behind her. Robin fell backwards in her chair, lifeless.

The picture rotated suddenly on its side, as the cameras were toppled and the rest of the room destroyed. Then, the screen went black again, and the interview with the president continued as if nothing had happened.

"Therefore, Mr. Fourier, we can assume you will take every measure at your disposal to route-out these anarchists and put this country back to where it needs to be?" asked Jennings. "Can we count on that?"

"Absolutely, Walter. It is important that this country be guided with a firm hand. It requires leadership – the kind that doesn't shirk from adversity. I will gain control over this country and the wrongs being perpetrated against it. It is my solemn vow to do everything I can to bring order and fairness to each and every person listening to me tonight. I am your leader. You are my people. I will show you the proper way and you will be grateful."

135

***

"What just happened?" asked a young staffer, shocked at what had just played out on the air.

At the GOFLA headquarters in a remote part of the United States, the members of the secretive organization were stunned. Although the filming had not taken place at their location, they knew all involved and had seen live what had happened to their friends. Finally, after years of fighting the propaganda machine of the Administration, their naïve, protected view of their position had been shattered. They were being hunted. They were in danger.

"They're … they're dead," said another member, sitting down on a ratty, third-hand, brown sofa. She looked over at the GOFLA director bereft of feeling or emotion at that moment.

The director pursed his lips, and shook his head. "I never thought it would come to this," he said. "I knew they were capable of much, but not this. This was cold blooded murder."

There was silence in the room for several minutes as they tried to process what had occurred.

"We have to re-connect with Shea Disone about this government vendetta against her. It puts a face on the issues of the day, not just some bad statistics. No one cares about the numbers anyway. It worked the last time Jonathon was able to create the GOFLA website before the government crackdown. That's what resonated with people. That's what we need," the director said.

But he wasn't addressing what was on the minds of all in the room, and he knew that too.

"Are we safe here?" asked another staffer.

"I don't know," the director answered. "I think we should all leave as soon as possible. It looks like there is no safe place in America these days."

Everyone scrambled to get their things, especially anything with their name on it that would incriminate them if the safe house were discovered and scoured for evidence. Within minutes, all had cleared out, running to their cars and scurrying off into the darkness.

Alone, sitting at his desk, the director peered over the top of his black-rimmed glasses. He'd been around Washington for a long time and thought he knew all the tricks on Capitol Hill. He'd been wrong. He had underestimated the ruthlessness of the regime. It was war now. He knew it and so did millions of other Americans. What he would do about it was another thing altogether.

He pulled out his PCD and opened it. "Call Shea," he said calmly.

The line pulsed her site on the SI-net, but there seemed to be no answer. Then, finally, the image of Shea came up. She was visibly disturbed, shaking as she took her hand to pull back a band of hair and tuck it behind her left ear.

"Shea, how are you doing? I assume you saw what happened to Robin."

Shea choked back tears. She had not known Robin, but somehow she felt partially responsible for what had happened. Fearless and persevering, Robin had been the epitome of a patriot willing to die to save the freedoms of her country.

"Congressman Sumner?"

"Yes. I'm here," said Sumner. "Shea, you need to start calling me JC. I'm not in Congress anymore."

"So you're behind GOFLA," she said, now beginning to understand.

"Yes. I have been for some time, but only recently have we geared things up to take on Washington."

"Are you safe?" Shea asked.

"I'll be fine," he answered. "It's my staff I'm worried about. I'm responsible for them now. I've gotten them into this. I just hope I can get them out of it."

"If there is anyone who can lead them out of this ... lead the country out of this ... it's you, JC," said Shea.

"Sometimes I'm not sure, Shea. Especially on nights like tonight."

"So, what do we do now?" she asked. "How can I help?"

"We'll have to do something sooner rather than later. Our timetable just got moved up. I must admit that I hadn't heard what Robin said tonight on the air – about Fourier planning a *coup d'etat*. She must have gotten that information late in the day or just before she went on. She would have told me about it."

"I didn't know anything about that. Is that true?"

"I don't know. It may have been what got her killed. I just pray she didn't have any of her source information with her. They'll have that too by now."

"If Fourier is planning that, he'll have to do something soon," said Shea. "The election is only a few months away. The two parties have their candidates already and have been campaigning for almost two years. In the meantime, Fourier's said nothing about his plans. If he's going to take control of the government, he'll have to do it before the election. How do you think he'll try to do it?"

"I have my ideas, but none are worth anything unless we get some more information. People aren't talking at all these days, and those who do are either found dead in the Potomac or not found at all," Sumner paused for a moment, and then asked, "Shea, have you thought about running again for office?"

"No JC. I'm just trying to find my husband and keep my sanity."

"Well, I'm afraid the day is coming soon when we'll all need to make hard choices. You may have to find a new vocation. I think politics would suit you."

"Hell no, JC. Not in Washington D.C.."

"Who said anything about Washington, D.C.," Sumner answered.

*****

CH 22 The Angel, the Devil, and the Lawyer

Kilby Thorne was a mercurial man. He had his highs and his lows; yet, lately there had been more lows. He'd fired six staff in the previous two months for minor errors in judgment. However, he claimed that any one of them could have led to the total and utter demise of his company. Some of the tension was understandable – what with his wife's abduction, the extortion, and the matter with the SECE engine, Griffin and Ratner. However, he was not accustomed to the adversity, and it was quickly catching up with him.

With his company's stock price dropping, Thorne' board of directors was troubled by the direction in which the company was headed and where their stock options were going. They had protection from most government officials because of generous gifts to their campaigns over the years, especially to President Fourier. Although they were banned from giving any more than $20,000 at a time, EG had constructed countless super pacs under different names and affiliations to avoid the cap. All this was under the protective arm of the Ministry of Justice and the Federal Election Commission which turned a blind eye to the machinations of such groups as long as the contributions were properly 'qualified,' that is funneled to candidates or incumbents of the People's Party.

But the biggest of his problems was Ratner. His General Counsel, Chou, had failed to buy Lenoir Labs, and he was still without the SECE design specs. He had nothing with which to bargain with Griffin, and at the same time he feared Ratner was working on her own version of the SECE with information she'd stolen from the patent filing.

Thorne had contacted Ratner's office to arrange a meeting to find out what was going on, but had gotten no response. Finally, after weeks, rather than the usual days when she had been a lesser-powered dignitary, he got his answer. *Meet me at the Barrister in Alexandria at eight tomorrow night, AR* read the cryptic note. He jumped on a plane the next day and took a cab from Reagan National airport south to the historic suburb of Washington, D.C., in Alexandria, Virginia. The ride was only twenty minutes from the airport, and he arrived well before the eight o'clock rendezvous time.

Finally, at quarter past eight, Ratner walked into the tavern, carrying a small black bag along with her crimson Hermes purse. It looked like she had dressed to go out on the town later, certainly not wearing the charcoal gray jacket and skirt mandated by the Fourier regime. Rather, she wore a long, high-collared, black evening dress, three strands of natural pearls with matching earrings, a light faux fur shawl together with low-heeled pumps.

"It's nice to see you again, Thorne," said Ratner, coming into the booth and sitting across from him. He glanced outside the window and saw the three, black government-issued SUV's parked outside, complete with secret service stationed at the entrance.

"You too, Angel. You're as beautiful as ever," Thorne said, unabashedly. "You didn't have to dress up for me you know. Looks like you're going someplace tonight. Is there a party nearby?"

"If there is, I certainly won't be taking you," she said snidely. "The president is hosting a party at the National Museum of Women in the Arts building downtown. He's renovated it, you know. It looks magnificent now. The party should be fun. So, Thorne, why do you want to see me? I thought our deal was off."

"You know, Angel, it's been a while," he said, smiling at her, flirtatiously.

The two had been involved in an extra-marital affair on-and-off during the previous four years. However, ever since she had been promoted as Minister of Unity, those trysts had ended. They had used each other for their own advantage, but now that he needed her much more than she him, that relationship was over.

"Yes, it has, hasn't it," she answered, cautiously. "But, I don't have all night, Thorne. Really, what is it that you want?"

"I've got things arranged," he said, returning the mischievous smile.

"I've moved on, as if you hadn't noticed," she answered.

"Always business before pleasure, isn't it Angel."

"I'm afraid so," she replied. "It's got to be that way. I trust you're not wired -- are you Thorne? It would be a mistake if you were." She held up a small, watch-sized device that she turned on, watching the red and green diodes flicker on and off until only green ones were showing.

"Of course not. You didn't need to bring that thing in here to determine that. I've always been straight with you. You know that," Thorne said.

"Not always."

"What's that supposed to mean?"

"Come on, Thorne. I've been watching your stock price. You can't afford much right now. And your personal fortune can't either. It's just too bad you didn't do the deal with me sooner."

"What do you mean?" Thorne asked.

"I mean that the price has gone way up. What was the number we talked about?"

"Thirty million," said Thorne, knowing it was actually higher.

"Like I said, you're never straight with me. It was forty million and you know it. But it doesn't matter now."

"How much are you asking now?"

"Three hundred million," she answered with a straight face.

"What? Are you f*cking kidding me?" shouted Thorne, nearly spewing his martini across the table.

"So, how are you coming up with that kind of money?" she asked him with a devilish smile.

Thorne sat back in the booth and raised his dirty martini to his lips – this time downing what remained.

"I know it's worth a lot to you, Thorne. But you're blowing smoke up my skirt tonight. You and I both know it. You can't bullsh*t me! Not like you used to. I'm far more experienced in the ways of the world and of politics to fall for it. So, again, I ask, what do you want? I sure as hell know you can't buy what I'm selling. I'm way out of your league now."

"You can't get that kind of money for the SECE," Thorne said casually.

"Well, for your information, there is something I've learned recently – that power trumps money every time. You can have all the money in the world, but if I have the power, I can take it all that money away from you. You can slave away and work your ass off for years, decades, to accumulate your wealth. You can scheme and swindle and destroy a lot of people to get the fortune that you have, but in the end, it only takes me a second to sign my name to a piece of paper and have it all transferred over to me. That's what power is about, Thorne. It's trumps money every time."

Thorne winced. He'd never thought of political positioning and power in that way before. In the past, politicians' powers had been governed by the Constitution and the rule of law. This was becoming less and less the case, and the raw ugliness of that reality was beginning to surface in every aspect in Washington. It was becoming the Wild West again, except no one was even bothering to pay for tombstones on Boot Hill.

"So, are we still going to talk money or what?" said Thorne, acting as though what she had said was meaningless.

"Sure, why not," she answered, in an about face. "But let me tell you how this is going to work. This is not a negotiation. You understand that, right? I need your manufacturing capability to produce the engine. You need my blueprints from the patent filing. It's as simple as that."

"You're forgetting one thing," Thorne answered. "You don't have the complete filing, or at least you don't have the complete software protocols."

Ratner stared at him, not amused. "Who told you that?" she asked, coldly.

"It doesn't matter. I know you don't have everything I need. So, if we work together, maybe we can find the missing pieces. Does that sound like a reasonable proposition?"

Ratner, strummed her fingers on the table. "Go on," she said.

"I'm prepared to offer you ten million for the technology that Lenoir sent to you for their patent protection. Since it's an incomplete package, I'm not about to pay any more. At the same time, you will secure finding the rest of the software information we need to make this thing work. I think that's a fair exchange."

"We need to find Patrick Disone," she said directly.

"Patrick Disone? What about him?"

"We need to find him, I said. His chief technology officer is dead, so we need Patrick to come up with the details to make the SECE run," said Ratner.

"But, Disone died several weeks ago. His car was found in the reservoir."

"No, his chief technology officer was in the car – not Disone. No one can find him."

Thorne sat stunned. He had thought Disone had been in the car. *So, there was still a chance to develop the SECE engine,* he thought.

"Yeah, it's too bad it wasn't his wife that they found in that car. Now, I'd give you a few million just to get rid of her," said Ratner spitefully.

"There's another option," said Thorne.

"What's that?"

"Lenoir is filing bankruptcy. You need to seize all of their documents. We can't let them get destroyed or carted off someplace to a remote warehouse. You have to send your people in there."

"I don't have jurisdiction," said Ratner.

"You can find a way. I know you can," Thorne replied.

"You mean using the Ministry of Internal Inquiry," she said using the new name for the FBI.

"Yeah, whatever," he answered. "You can take all your ministry stuff and put it someplace where I don't have to deal with it. You use your men, Angel – the ones in the black suits. They're good at this kind of stuff."

"Okay. So, if I use the federal government to do this, you'll need to come up with more money. I'll need at least fifty million dollars. There are a lot of palms that will need greasing."

"Forty million. That's as high as I can go," said Thorne.

"You can write me the check for forty-five, then," she responded. "I'll need to make a lot of calls, and phone lines are expensive these days. When I get the info, I'll let you know. We'll need to move quickly to setup the SECE plant and begin production before the Chinese rip off the idea by reverse engineering it. But I want the money first. Got it?" she asked aggressively.

"Half now; half later."

"Just get me the money," said Ratner, getting up and walking out. The secret service agent was there to open the door and escort her to her limo. After the door slammed, the entire grouping sped off back toward D.C. and the president's gala event.

Thorne sat alone in the booth. He admired … no, he loved … that woman. She had balls. She was one of the few he had ever met that he couldn't steam-roll. In fact, more often than not, she usually rolled him. He spent the next few hours watching the antiquated, flat-mount TV on the wall – reruns of old *Maybury RFD*, starring Andy Griffith. With his head beginning to spin, he scanned his account card into the table mounted register and to pay the bill. As he was leaving, he got a text and voice-over from her.

Ratner, Incoming Call, the message read ….

"Oh, by the way, you need to pick a better in-house counsel to work for you. It's a shame the talent pool for such people is so limited. You can definitely do better, Thorne.

"But, today is your lucky day. You need to replace Chou. She's run into some difficulty and won't be able to give you any more legal advice."

Thorne responded, voicing his text. *"What do you mean?"* he asked.

"She was just pulled out of the Potomac River this morning with a bullet through her head. It's a pity. She was young too. Oh, well. Life goes on. Talk to you later. AR."

*****

CH 23 Ellen Chou

Thorne had been shocked by Ratner's casual declaration that his General Counsel was dead. He had been upset with Chou over screwing up acquiring the patented software from Lenoir Labs, but he had never imagined it might lead to this.

He sat in his office, mulling things over in his head. It had all gone wrong – from the very start. How could Chou now be dead? How could that have happened, and how did Ratner know? He could contact the police and provide information, but that would implicate him, and with Ratner's power, he dared not raise the issue. No, he would sit this one out. The police would come to him eventually anyway, and he would give them no answers. *It was better this way,* he kept telling himself. *It was better this way.*

It was Chou's family who pressed the police for answers. There was little evidence, they were told. Nothing from the scene suggested foul play.

"But what about the bullet through her head!" her father had screamed, at the top of his lungs. *"How do you explain that!*

"Suicide, sir. Plain and simple. She just killed herself," the police had told him.

Yuan Chou, Ellen's father, categorically rejected the police report's conclusion. He finally quit his job and dedicated his time to find out what had happened to his girl – his precious little girl. Yuan's wife pleaded with him to stop. She told him that nothing good could come from his efforts. She had heard stories about people who had challenged authority, especially those of the police state. Most just disappeared. In rare cases, their bodies were found but then it was usually declared an accident or suicide.

Yuan had gone down to the Chesapeake Bay Bridge many times, looking out across the water that had become a temporary resting place for the body of his daughter after she had allegedly shot herself. This time, the sun was shining brightly even though there was a brisk breeze coming in from the northwest, blowing the crests of the waves toward land.

As he glanced ahead toward the bridge and then to his left, along the shore that led to Sandy Point State Park, he noticed a disheveled man sitting by the water's edge, not far away. Yuan walked over to the man, who initially seemed unaware that he had a visitor.

"Excuse me," asked Yuan, trying not to be too obtrusive, "but do you come here often?"

The man looked up at him in bewilderment. His beard was stringy, but short and misshapen, looking like he trimmed it without a mirror in hand. Weathered and gray, his face had furrows along his temples that were etched dark and deep. With two large, dark-green garbage bags holding all his earthly possessions, he was a sorry sight. Yuan could relate to his despair.

The man squinted into the sun that was low in the sky behind Yuan, making it hard for him to speak without grimacing from the intensity of the glare. "Maybe," was all the man said in reply. "But who wants to know?"

Yuan drew closer, but the man recoiled. "I'm not going to hurt you," said Yuan. "I'm only looking for answers. You see, my daughter's body was found right over there a few weeks ago." Ellen's father began to choke up and bit his lip to check himself. "I was just wondering if you happened to be here. You know. Did you see anything?"

The strange man could see a father in pain. The edges around his eyes softened, and he glanced back at the water without saying anything. The only sound was that of the water lapping up on the rocky shore in front of them and three sea gulls fighting over a piece of bread the man had thrown to them.

Thinking the old man wasn't going to say anything more, Yuan turned to leave.

"I'm sorry for your loss," said the old man, still looking out over the water.

Yuan turned. "So, were you here then?" he asked, gently.

"Yes."

Yuan walked back toward where the man was standing, but was cautious to keep his distance. "Did you see something? I'm guessing you saw or heard something. Did you?" It was a question Yuan had to ask even though he was afraid of the answer.

The old man pointed back up a road that came through the park and ran along the shoreline just under the bridge. "There," he said. "I was sittin' right here, just like I do almost ever' night, lookin' out over the water. It's so damned beautiful here, ya know. I've been comin' here for pretty near twelve years now – ever since my wife passed. But, that night … oh … it must have been about two weeks ago today in fact, there was a roar of two SUV's comin' down the road in a big hurry. They were big, black SUV's, no markin's or anythin' I could see, but it was gettin' dark. Anyway, two men got out of one and one man and a woman got out of the other. She was small, and I couldn't see what she looked like. I heard her say, 'Leave me alone! I haven't done nothin' to you!' or somethin' like that. One of the men threw her on the ground and said, 'You f**king whore!'" The old man stopped, shaking his head. "I'm sorry, I didn't mean to …"

"No, it's Okay. I understand. Go ahead," said Yuan.

"Well, they say somethin' about an engine and some money. What I hear was like 'Our boss doesn't like it when someone f**ks up a $300 million deal!' I remember 'cause the number was so big. Anyway, she screams and tells 'em she's goin' to the police. She is scared; I could tell. Real scared. But then, I is too."

Yuan choked up and found words difficult, but he managed to say, "Then what? What did they do?"

The old man became suddenly quiet. But the look on Yuan's face forced a confession.

"They laughs at her," said the man, feeling guilty at having divulged more.

"Go on," said Yuan, trying to stomach the description. He stiffened his lip and braced himself for the worst of it. "There must be more."

The old man looked back out to the bay. "I … I don' think I should. You're her dad. The rest is too much …"

Yuan knew he was right, but he still had to know. "I insist," he said, his face stern and direct.

"Nah, I can't. Really, I can't."

Yuan's face tighten; his jawbone rigid.

"Okay. Okay. But, I don' think you's ready for it. I don' think any father could be," said the old man. He sighed. "Well, one of da' guys laughs at her and tears off her blouse. The others stand 'round her. She looks so pitiful. Her hair is down to her eyes, but she doesn' push it away. She jus' stares at 'em. She's mad – real mad. Then … sir, I can't. I really can't. All I'll tell you is they takes her – they takes advantage of her. You know what I's sayin'?. That's all I'll say on it."

The fury in Yuan grew. He wanted to kill each and every one of those men. He just had to find them.

"Then they killed her? They killed my little girl?" asked Yuan, his anger building.

"The only thing you needs know is they drugs her over there and there was jus' one shot," said the man, pointing to an area down the shoreline, farther toward the park. "That's it. I knows what they done. The men come back 'round from that point there." His finger was shaking. "The girl ain' with 'em no more. They gets back in their cars and jus' drives off."

Yuan fought his anger and his tears. It was as if someone had thrust a knife into him and had twisted and turned it until there was only mush inside him. He was unable to speak and took a deep breath, trying to calm himself looking at the peaceful calm of the bay. "Did they see you?" he asked the man.

"It don't seem like it. I wasn' gonna' move a muscle, though, that's for sure, or I'd be next. It was like they was so caught up in what they was doin' they missed me. I don' know why – they just did. I guess God has other plans for me. But I sure as hell don' know what they is."

"Could you identify them for the police?"

The old man shook his head. "Sorry, sir. I can' do that."

"Why not? You saw what happened. You saw what they did to my girl!"

"Yeah, I know, but ..."

"But what!" screamed Yuan.

The old man was quiet for a moment. "I jus' don' want to get involved, ya' know. I knows my life ain't worth much, but ... as they say ... it's all I got."

"It was my daughter! They killed my daughter!" Yuan shouted in agony. "You have to help me!" The angst was pronounced. It was a father whose soul was almost dead. He was screaming for a lifeline ... anything that might pull him back from the abyss of his condition.

The man looked into the pained eyes of the father. "Alrigh'. My name is Hank Randolph. I'll be here if you needs me."

Yuan nodded gratefully. "Thanks," he said. "My wife will appreciate it too." He walked away, emotionally drained. He wondered how he would tell his wife.

***

There was a knock at the door. Yuan's wife, Xia, went to answer. She opened it without hesitation. "Yes?" she asked, looking at two men dressed casually who had come to the door.

They barged in and threw her to the floor, one taking out handcuffs and thrusting her hands behind her back.

"What's going on?" she yelled in shock. "Who are you?"

Yuan ran out of a bedroom to see what the commotion was about. "Leave my wife alone!" he bellowed, holding a powder blue towel he'd been using in the bathroom.

"You're both under arrest for violation of the U.S. immigration law," said the older of the two men holding up a gold badge that read simply *Homeland Security.*

"What are you talking about? We're U.S. citizens!" exclaimed Yuan in protest.

"That's where you're wrong my man," said the other, younger man with long hair and a beard. "You never re-applied for citizenship. You're under arrest. You are illegal aliens, and we have warrants for your arrest and deportation. You have the right to remain silent, but we advise against it," said the man.

The young man grabbed Yuan and slammed him up against the wall, pressing his face into the drywall as he applied the handcuffs.

"No one ever said we had to reapply!" shouted Yuan. "There's no law that says we have to!" said Yuan, feeling violated. "You're lying!"

"There *is* a law. But I'm not required to tell you even that. Ignorance, as you know, is no defense. The immigration law passed earlier this year stated that all undocumented workers must apply for citizenship right away or face deportation. However, since you didn't apply, well, we can't help you."

"But, we're not undocumented!" shouted Yuan, trembling at the thought of being kicked out of the country. "We are rightful citizens of this country! We got our citizenship papers back in, well, it must have been 2024 or 2025, I think. I have the documents to show you. I can prove it!"

"Save your breath, man," said the younger man. "You're Asian, right? So, you're undocumented – that's what I think. Isn't that what you think too, Boris?"

"Yep. That's the way it reads in my book too," said his partner.

"You can't do that!"

"It's done. It was approved by the minister herself, this morning. You'll be on a plane back to China by this afternoon."

"But we're not from China!" exclaimed Yuan's wife.

"Show me the papers!" demanded Yuan.

"Okay," said the older man. He reached into his coat jacket and pulled out a folded set of papers. Flattening the packet, he began reading. "... hereby, in accordance with the Immigration and Deportation Statute of 2047, the federal government of the United States of America via the Ministry of Domestic Policing, the Ministry of Citizenship and Immigration Services, the Ministry of Immigration and Customs Enforcement, the Ministry of Customs and Border Protection, the Ministry of Organized Labor, and the Ministry of State, we the state find Yuan and Xia Chou in defiance of the statute, remaining in the country in violation of your visas. Therefore, the state has determined that you shall be deported back to your country of origin at the soonest possible date."

"But ..." Yuan stuttered.

"It's all here. Now let's go!" shouted the younger man, pushing them out the door.

Neither Xia nor Yuan had a any chance to recover anything from their house. They left behind everything, including the dead body of their daughter, which was at the funeral home awaiting services that were planned for the following day. They would never see her again, and would never get the chance to visit her gravesite.

Ellen's body was buried in the gravesite her parents had picked out for her. But, no one was there to attend the services. Her casket was lowered into the ground, alone and quiet. Only the sounds of ropes running through the rings mounted in the coffin's sides could be heard over the murmurings of the grave diggers. Her half of the twenty million dollars would do her no good where she had gone.

*****

CH 24 Business Fairness

Minister Ratner produced a stack of paper nearly two feet high. She had instructed her staff to pile the paper on a special table placed in front of her podium. The reporters gathered there, as ordered by their respective media houses, to listen and note anything newsworthy. In this case, the president was supposed to speak, but had cancelled earlier in the day, asking the minister to present her ministry's findings.

"I'm sorry that the president was unable to meet with you; however, we have some very important things to cover," she began. "We have made important changes to the *Unity Plan*, and the president has already agreed to approve it. It is a monumental achievement, and that is why we've placed it on this table – the one where the British General Howe signed his surrender papers to General Washington at Yorktown in 1782. I will, however, not be taking any questions. You may read the Executive Mandate on your own. My office will, of course, be available to answer any questions later."

Not surprisingly, no one questioned her statement. Ratner's six thousand page tome was written with so many footnotes and references to other laws and statutes that it was indecipherable. And, as expected, no reporter could reach anyone at her ministry later to get any clarification. They were told to *just read it*.

Worse yet, none in the room was educated enough to realize a more obscure, but egregious falsehood espoused. The British General Howe never signed surrender papers at Yorktown, and there had been no special table. In fact, the general was Cornwallis, not Howe, and Cornwallis never showed up for the surrender ceremony, alleging he was ill. Worst of all, the surrender took place in 1781, not 1782. It was all for show, so the facts and details were irrelevant.

"Now, what I do wish to point out are the following. We have renamed the *Unity Plan* the *Fair Business Mandate*. In essence, any owner, officer or senior manager of a company that has not turned over all of their company's assets to the government, will have their personal assets seized. There are no exceptions. This means that not only will their homes and cars be taken, but all of their furniture, china, silverware, books, electronics, bank accounts, investments, pictures, clothes, family heirlooms … *everything*! They are thieves! These business owners steal from the poor, keeping the money for themselves instead of sharing with others." There was mild glee in her voice as she reviewed the pronouncement. "Yes, my friends, the rich will finally get what they deserve. And we shall give them no mercy."

The briefing was just that – short and pointed, skewing the wealthy and describing a vast redistribution scheme to take from those who produce and give to those who don't.

The next day President Fourier signed the mandate with the Ministries of Unity and Taxation and Enforcement standing behind him, smiling and acknowledging their part in the historic moment. Fourier only commented that it was an historic achievement for his Administration, putting it on the road toward rectifying centuries of injustice that had been foisted upon the American citizenry. "It is time," he said, "that America realized its true potential and righted the wrongs of previous generations."

When the news agencies read the entirety of the mandate, there was unease and disquiet. But, believing that they would continue to be exempted from the new order as they had in the past, the heads of the major media outlets cautiously supported the regime in power – that is, until the first shoe dropped a few days later.

"Today, armed paramilitary units from the Ministries of Taxation and Enforcement and Unity stormed the homes of the chief executives of USBC – the U.S. Broadcasting Company – and UBN – the United Broadcasting Network," said a news reporter, looking nervously into the camera.

To the right of her image on the screen was a grainy video taken from one of the millions of surveillance cameras that had been installed on every block throughout the city of New York. In it viewers could see a SWAT team ramming through the front door of a large, modern-looking home someplace in uptown Manhattan. Seconds later, a man wearing dark pajama bottoms and a T-shirt was being dragged out, his wrists cuffed behind his back and his feet scraping the walkway behind him. He was thrown in the back of a van marked Ministry of Unity, which sped away down the street and out of sight.

"The Assistant Deputy Minister of Unity said that these actions were just the start of a wider crackdown on blatant defiance of the new law. The CEO's of these companies are being arrested without bail and will be arraigned in court later this month. This is Erin Morales, reporting from New York City."

After that, more executives were arrested. So, rather than continue to report these arrests, the media went dark for a while. Afraid to air them, yet afraid not to. It wasn't until journalists began to be arrested – those who did not support the Administration – did things change. The media decided it was safer to join the Executive Branch than to fight it. From that point forward, there were no news stories that showed the Administration in a negative light – none. No one dared to challenge the Fourier Administration, which was precisely what Fourier wanted.

Overnight, the fourth branch of government had been emasculated completely, just as the other two had – the Congress and Supreme Court. There was no one to stand in their way now. All had been broken, now servile to a supreme ruler of the land.

As for small business owners and executives, they saw the writing on the wall and scrambled to find ways to get their companies out of the country before all travel visas were cutoff. The countries of Singapore, Japan, and Canada began to accept them in droves, and their economies began to take off. As the only safe-havens left in the world for entrepreneurship, these nations welcomed the newcomers with open arms. And as the brain drain in the U.S. intensified, those in the ministries worried. From where would tax revenue come? Money for social security? Manpower for the military? Knowhow to advance society?

The first reaction of the White House was "good riddance." As one White House aide said, "Let all the fat cats leave and take their greed and corruption with them."

However, soon they realized how much company profits and their government tax revenues were leaving their borders. They had counted on that money coming into the Treasury. But now, those taxes were leaving the country, evaporating before their eyes. So too was their dream of a utopian society where they would be the unquestioned leaders and the people would live in gleeful ignorance and bow down before their secular altar – a wretched trough of government handouts, motivation-killing drugs, and the false hope of winning the next megabillions lotto.

At first, the president contemplated playing along and exempting GovCo's from the mandate. But his defiance and ego got the better of him. Within a month, the president's press minister was at the podium, announcing even more executive mandates. His tie was askew, and it looked as though he hadn't slept in days. The Administration was under siege, scrambling to right a sinking ship. But instead of conciliation and moderation, the rhetoric became only more heated.

"I will not be taking any questions today," said Press Minister Kenneth Biester. "Instead, I want to announce a new executive order that will take place immediately. All travel outside the country must be approved through the Ministry of State. Travel visas will be required for anyone leaving the borders of the country, whether by plane, train, automobile, ship, or tube." The tube was a relatively new mode of transport underground, given the invention of matter liquidation techniques developed to bore through the earth, paving the way for superfast, subterranean bullet trains. "All requests for such visas must first be sent to the Ministry of Unity to ensure the person is an upstanding citizen and has no criminal record or past improprieties."

The reality was only those connected to the People's Party would be able to travel outside the country. All others were deemed a flight risk. Those connected to the party got visas within three days. Those who weren't were interrogated about why they were leaving the country and ultimately denied a visa anyway.

But by the end of the year, violence in the cities only grew worse. The police ranks in all the major cities initially swelled in numbers to deal with the riots and civil unrest. But, oddly, the Ministry of Justice cut funding to the states for their police staff. Instead, the federal government established its own internal police force, known as the Red Shirts. And as the number of jobs in the private sector shrank, jobs in the Red Shirt battalions grew. Applications for these positions overwhelmed the system, as people sought financial security and safety for their families. Once on the force, an officer's family was protected from most of the abuses going on around them.

Beyond growing the police state, the government seemed incapable of much else. It was too big to react quickly, becoming a bloated leviathan, weighed down by feasting on the fortunes of others. Its belly distended; its limbs flaccid from misuse, the creature known as the USA could no longer run, walk or stand on its own. It lay incapacitated by its own excesses, mired in a fetid pool of its own making.

With so little tax money coming in, the president ordered his ministries to do whatever they could to generate more. By the end of the year, Ratner ordered the Ministry of the Government Funds, formerly the Treasury, to print another trillion dollars to make up for the shortfall in tax revenues. This led to inflation rising above 65 percent - a level high enough to be classified as hyperinflation. But for the president, as well as Ratner, it was less about saving the country and more about building a personal army.

Ratner had been asked about the growth of the Red Shirts and the costs involved, and she had replied, "It's a necessity. We have to keep Americans safe, now don't we? It's our obligation as servants of the state to keep our citizens free from harm. There are elements within this country who are trying to destroy us, to undermine the very fabric of our government. They are on a mission to ruin the core of this nation, and we will not let that happen," she'd said.

"Are the Red Shirts intended to replace the police?" asked another reporter.

"Of course not. We will work hand in hand to support and bolster the state and local police departments," she answered. It was a lie. The truth was that the federal government was doing everything they could to dismantle the autonomy of the local and independent police state. Ratner believed it was critical that the police state be under the control of her ministry. Leaving it to the states was not an option if they wanted to bring the nation together. She was already preparing an executive order for the president to sign making it more difficult for these groups to continue operating without significant federal oversight. In her plea she cited irregularities in police policy and, more importantly, numerous violations of civil rights and police brutality, which she would claim were rampant throughout the locally sponsored system. These practices would have to be stopped, and the only way was via Executive Branch management.

In the meantime, Ratner had hired twenty million more Red Shirts in order to supplant the precinct houses and county and state authorities. They were mainly unemployed men and women desperate for a job. Her goal was to phase out the police and setup Red Shirt houses on most every street corner to monitor everything that was going on. To help them, she planned on millions of surveillance cameras to be installed as well as millions of fly-sized drones that would be released into every neighborhood to record the movements of every denizen. Only through this iron-fisted approach could she be assured things were, well, under control.

It was no longer the case that the government was the humble servant of its people; instead, the people had the harsh reality of realizing that they now served their government.

*****

CH 25 Invitation

Congressman Sumner couldn't believe what was happening before his very eyes. Everything he had believed in about his country had been dismantled and replaced with a socialist model of government that took from those who worked and gave to those who didn't. To the uneducated, it sounded wonderful. To the educated, it was a shell game. And to those who believed they were beyond the pathetic cries of the *hoi polloi*, it sounded like a path to power.

However, the socialistic utopian dream was struggling to materialize. But rather than change course, Fourier elected to *double down* with even higher taxes and increased debt. "We just haven't had enough money to fix the things we need to fix," he was heard saying. "We need to increase our spending now, not decrease it."

At this point, most turned to their new messiah, President Fourier, for their salvation. They would begin saying their prayers for him, hoping he would turn things around. Fourier was their new religion – it was the final shift to secularism and the worship of the state as a new-age religion.

As Lenin and Trotsky understood, the citizenry can only worship one god. If that's in the form of religion, then they won't rely on their government for their future. Worshipping their government leaders instead ensured that their place was safe and secure. Indeed, religion was an opiate for the masses, as Marx had said, but Fourier preferred to legalize drugs and give himself control over that dependency. In all respects, churches were considered enemies of the state and needed to be more tightly controlled. Although not expressed openly, religion was for all intents and purposes *verboten*, unless it was for the allegiance to the country and its leadership.

So, Fourier stepped up the attack. He needed money and hated the churches. No longer were churches or synagogues tax exempt. New executive orders were imposed on religious institutions to generate revenue at rates approaching 75 percent. If paid, they could continue to operate; if not, they were closed. A special exemption was granted to mosques, as lawmakers could support a religion that forbade the practice of usury, or charging interest on loans. Still, they chose to ignore the fact that Islam permitted fees to be paid instead – merely a semantic difference.

As for the common man, he felt empty and rudderless. It had been religion and faith that had sustained him over the centuries, enabling him to believe that someday, God would come to the rescue and provide him true salvation. Now, deprived of that last refuge, he had no other place to turn but to those in power

– those who could decide who succeeded and who failed, who became rich and who begged, and who lived and who died.

Sumner had gone through such feelings of hopelessness and despair. He had left Congress a frustrated and broken man, beaten down by the illegal machinations of more radical elements of the People's Party members. He had lost faith in the government and the country. However, it only took one Monday morning to turn him around. It was the viral SI-net video of Shea Disone's interview with Walter Jennings that had ignited new life into him. *Yes,* he thought, *there still was hope in the world.*

***

Despite the tragedy with Robin Burke and her team, Sumner had renewed his faith in the movement – GOFLA. Sumner flew to Boston hoping to persuade Shea to join him at GOFLA, but he knew it would be a tough sell.

They met at a Starbuck's on Beacon Street, not far from where the Battle of Breed's Hill had been fought. Getting their hot beverages – he, a double latte espresso, and she, a decaf cappuccino – they sat down at one of the wooden tables located along the floor-to-ceiling windows. The wind had begun to pick-up outside, and the overcast skies had begun to loosen their grip on their cache of raindrops which had begun to fall, splattering the pavement with dark stains.

"Good thing we got here when we did," said Sumner, smiling kindly at Shea as he got comfortable.

Shea returned the smile, but her face was gaunt and hollow. Life's events had all weighed heavily on her, and it showed. The campaign being waged against her by her government was draining her strength. Yet, her performance had only recharged his. Sumner only hoped he could revitalize her as she had him.

"How are you doing, Shea?" he said gently.

She tried to smile again, but couldn't muster the emotion for it. "JC, I just wanted to thank you for all of your help."

"Aw, Shea. I just wish I had actually done something for you. I tried, of course, but I couldn't get things straightened out like you needed. The system has been stacked against us."

"It's Okay. I'm not sure anyone can help at this point." She paused, taking another sip of her cappuccino and setting the paper cup down. "But, I did want to tell you that we are filing bankruptcy – both the business and me personally. I have no assets left. It's all gone – all used to fight the tax authorities and all the other ministries that have ganged up on me. You know Atlas tried to hold up the heavens for an eternity. Somehow he didn't crumble under the immense weight of it all. I feel like I've had to do the same – but I'm not Atlas. I'm failing, JC. I'm crumbling. I just can't do this anymore." She began to cry, but turned away.

"I'm sorry," said JC sympathetically.

Shea shrugged her shoulders. There were no more tears to be shed over it. She merely glanced outside at the falling rain, watching pedestrians as they jostled to get inside out of the weather.

"Shea, you know I'd love to have you with me at GOFLA. We need someone like you. We need someone who has fire or, at least, has the potential for fire in their belly to change things. I know you have that inside you. You've shown that."

Shea shook her head. "No, I'm not the one you're looking for, JC. I think you're seeing something in me that you wish you saw, but it's not me."

Sumner smiled. "Perhaps I know you better than you know yourself, then," he said. "There's something special in you, Shea. I've seen it, and I don't say that lightly. I've been around a lot of powerful people in my time. Most are empty suits. They put on a mask of intelligence and caring, but it's not real. You can spot it a mile away. No, Shea, you are different. I saw that in the video you did for the company and then again in the interview you did with Jennings."

"I ... I just don't think so," she answered.

Understanding that she was not in a place where she could yet move ahead with her life, JC backed off. "I understand, Shea. You've been through a lot. So, what will you do now?" JC asked.

"I don't know," she said with sorrow in her voice. "But, I'll stay in touch."

JC put his hand gently on her arm. "Well, when you're ready, you can come to Wyoming. I have some work there for you."

"Wyoming?" she asked surprised.

"Yes, we've got a building just north of Cheyenne. There are only five of us right now, but we've got a following as you know. It's been difficult to stay one step ahead of the ministry, trying to broadcast on frequencies that won't get jammed, but we've managed. We've got a lot of very smart supporters out there who are helping us."

Shea smiled. It was a genuine smile this time, and one that seemed to crack a veneer to which she'd held fast for quite some time.

"And what about Robin and the others? Aren't you all in danger now? Does the government know where you've gone?" she asked.

"No. Not yet," responded Sumner. Then, he said, "Shea, you ask if are we in danger? Yes, but don't you see that all of us are? None of us can be safe anymore in this country. I'm no more likely to be taken by the Red Shirts or someone inside one of the ministries than anyone else ... Since Robin's murder, we've minimized our visibility and those of our members. Everything is anonymous. For now, it's the best way for all of us."

Shea thought for a moment, looking down into her half-full cup.

"I think you'd make a great addition to the team," pressed Sumner.

"You know, JC, I'd love to take you up on your offer, but I can't."

"You've said no to similar offers, I know," he answered. "I really can't let you turn this one down. We need you. The country needs you."

"That's flattering, but again, I have to say no. I have to find out what happened to my husband. He's gone, and I need him home."

Sumner patted her hand. "I understand," he said. "I think if it were Maria, I would feel the exact same way. But, the offer is a standing one. It's open to you any time."

Shea grinned. "You're a good friend JC. Thanks. I'll keep it in mind."

She got up and shook his hand. "Thanks again."

"You'd better use my umbrella," he admonished, holding out his as an offering.

"It's Okay. I'll be fine," she said, pulling up the collar of her coat. She left through the door and disappeared down the block and around the corner.

Sumner was disappointed, but not disheartened. *She'll be back,* he thought to himself. *I'll make sure of it.*

*****

CH 26 Unrest Begins

With the growing unrest, Fourier took advantage of the crisis to call out the National Guard and have them dispersed throughout the country, concentrated in the major metropolitan areas. There had been minimal violence, but there had been peaceful protests. Fourier made sure the media covered the protests daily and focused on any incident of violence whether directly or indirectly associated with the uprisings. This only fomented more unrest.

As a result, the president demanded an audience on all networks to be aired at 8PM Easter Standard Time, just three weeks before the scheduled national election.

"Good evening," said the president, standing before most people in a 3-D holographic image. "It is important that I address you this evening to inform all of you of the grave danger we are all in due to anarchist groups at work within our country. As much resources as I have dedicated to ferreting out and apprehending those criminal elements responsible for the current unrest, we have only achieved partial success. There is still much to do.

"As a result, I've directed the Ministry of Justice to work with the Ministry of Internal Inquiry, the FBI, and even the Agency of International Policing or CIA to quash those who wish to do this country harm. We will be using every available means to arrest and convict those who are committing crimes against our families and our children.

"Due to the severity of the situation, I am suspending the general election scheduled for November 3 until we can regain control over the situation. This is part of a broader imposition of martial law throughout the country, including a nation-wide curfew of midnight local time in all major metropolitan cities. Likewise, I am suspending the writ of habeas corpus. These measures are necessary and prudent to ensure that justice and the rule of law will prevail.

"Thank you, and good night."

***

What had prompted the president's startling pronouncement was a peaceful protest that had been held only a week prior to his address. With the federal election fast approaching, the freedom fighters felt they had no choice but to act.

While education in the U.S. was poor with eighty-five percent of college students unable to identify the first president of the original United States, incapable of naming the leader of Nazi Germany during World War II, failing to locate Canada on a world map, and unable to name the three branches government, the country relied more and more on the *intelligentsia* within the country – for good and bad – to sway public opinion. They were influencers on both sides. The Left utilized the universities to espouse their socialist philosophies and brainwash the malleable minds of the youth to perpetuate it. It also had the advantage of a complicit media that could perpetuate their idealism. The Right had been long shut-out of the process, relying on common sense and maturity to help many grow out of their youthful disillusionment. They still dreamed of the day when their principles would be eagerly understood by millions without a struggle. However, they still faced the full force and threat of a president willing to do whatever it took to strip them of this vision.

Generally, the older generations had experienced the failures of a socialist agenda. They did understand. And the intellectuals of the Right – although considered an oxymoron by the Left – were alive, but living in the shadows of subterranean rooms and cellars inhabited by frequency-hopping bloggers. What the Right feared most was a pogrom by the Left to exterminate right-wing leaders and thereby eliminate all resistance forever. It had been done repeatedly throughout history, and it wasn't beyond the realm of possibility with the current regime.

The small protest had started in Cheyenne, a small city and capital of Wyoming. Since the SI-net was government-censored and calls for large group gatherings were prohibited, it was underground communication that brought out over five thousand denizens of a town that usually hosted a population of only ninety-two thousand. The demonstrators hoisted placards and signs reading *Impeach Fourier!* and *Give Us Back Our Freedom! USA – USA!*

As the crowds chanted and marched up Cheyenne's 22nd Street, more seemed to join in. By the time they reached the Wyoming Supreme Court Building on Canam Boulevard, the road was filled with protesters crying: "Down with Fourier!" "Free Us from Prison!" and "Taxation without Representation!"

The cants kept coming – one after another. They became louder and louder, even though the crowd remained well behaved.

It only took thirty minutes before the city police moved in. Cheyenne's finest used their cars to block off access to the court building and began surrounding the crowd. The group didn't push back, but continued to cry out, pulsing their signs up and down as their shouts grew louder.

"You are hereby ordered to disperse!" shouted the police chief, using a megaphone. "If you don't leave the area immediately, you will be arrested!"

But the assembly stayed, undaunted.

"If you do not disperse, we will have to use force! Disperse now!" came the second warning from the captain. However, he was inclined to use force against the crowd. He knew many of them. They were his friends and neighbors, and at his core, he and his men were supporters of freedom, not necessarily Washington, D.C. He'd been raised in the wilds of Wyoming like most of his officers. They wanted order, but they were not willing to harm innocents for a peaceful assemblage.

Several underground organizations, including GOFLA, were there secretly filming the entire scene, streaming the pictures live over the SI-net. The flood of data on the SI-net was too much to handle, overwhelming the blocking protocols and filtering the Ministry of Appropriate Communication had implemented to prevent such anti-American behavior. This time, the images were real and indisputable.

As the protestors stood in front of the county building, one man walked confidently to the front steps and raised his megaphone. "We are here for one reason," said Sumner, who had orchestrated the demonstration. "We are here to demand a return to the Constitution and our freedoms under the Bill of Rights, a proven and once-cherished document. We're talking about the one adopted by the original thirteen states in 1791 – the U.S. Constitution. The one molded and sculpted by our Founding Fathers – Madison, Monroe, Jay, Hamilton, and Henry.

"We are *not* here to advocate violence," reassured Sumner, "or the violent overthrow of the current government. We just want our freedom back! We want what we were guaranteed under the first ten amendments, especially the Tenth. Under that amendment, the powers of the federal government were to be limited! -- limited to only those specifically enumerated by the Constitution. That, my friends, has been subverted! Washington, and even Hamilton, would be horrified by the power grab of today's Administration. Now, there is nothing that is out of the grasp of the federal government – nothing! It has no limitations or governors. It is an unbridled power and a threat that has been loosened on the American people. And if we don't get that feral creature back in its cage now, we may never be able to."

There were shouts and screams, booing their disapproval against Fourier. Meanwhile, the police stood in riot gear, watching and waiting.

"So, where does that leave us? Where does that leave the average American in this country? They say we're too stupid to know what's good for us? Is that true?"

"No!" came the crowd's retort.

"They say they know better how you should live your lives than you do?

"No!"

"They say you just need to shut up, sit down and let them drive this country."

"No!"

"They are the ones driving us – driving us off a cliff!"

There was a tremendous roar of approbation, as the crowd began to chant "JC! JC! JC!"

But at that point, things changed. Loud mechanical noises could be heard in the distance, but they were growing louder. It was like a tidal wave approaching, threatening calamity and destruction. Within minutes, the joyous, ebullient emotions of the scene were replaced with tenseness and fear.

The sounds became louder, and soon it was clear they were military units moving into the area. Down the side streets, protestors could see Nr11 Stryker-class armored personnel carriers rolling in with light M1128c tanks right behind them. As they arrived, the local police got in their cars and sped off, leaving the matter to the hardened forces of the Red Shirts.

Sumner noticed the change and saw the units as they began to take positions around the group. "As I said, we do not advocate violence. We only want reform," he said nervously.

But that didn't stop the rush of Red Shirt personnel, bearing machine guns and completely covered in body armor. They descended quickly on the group, and Sumner had no choice to but tell the group to disperse.

"This protest is over. We will leave peacefully," he said, as urgently as he could without causing a mass panic. In advance of the protest, Sumner had plotted escape routes, and most of the people got out through alleyways and other little-known routes of which only the locals would have been aware.

Although a few were arrested and cuffed, the scattering of people in all directions made corralling them difficult. It was lucky that the Red Shirt commander had hesitated in ordering the troops to open fire; most had managed to get away – to demonstrate another day. It was a Fabian strategy used by George Washington against the redcoats. Washington's forces had been too weak to take on the British head-on, so other tactics were needed. Sumner too knew he was up against the might of the federal government. He was not advocating armed revolution, but he was spiriting the effort to keep up the pressure for reform – a reformation not to a new way, but back to the old ones.

As for the people who were caught, the videos that surfaced showed the relative brutality of the Red Shirts. People across the country watched on their computers as the Red Shirts attacked with their German Shepherds tearing into the flesh of the men and women who had been trapped within the three sides of the military's guarded perimeter. People were bleeding; yet, the Red Shirts kept up their assault. Under orders to stop the protest at any cost, they continue relentlessly, savagely attacking anyone and everyone at the scene.

Fourier's Minister of Justice, Dutch Welbourne, put down the phone. "No worries," he said, talking to his deputy minister sitting in front of him. "The Wyoming state commander just reassured me things were getting back under control. The rebellion is being put down."

"They *will* use every means available to them, right?" asked the deputy minister.

"Absolutely," said Welbourne. "We can assure the president this little matter of insurrection has been quashed, and we are unlikely to see anything more after word gets out about how others will be treated if they try something similar."

In the end, there were fewer than one hundred protesters rounded up and put into paddy wagons. Within a day there was more chatter on the SI-net than ever before on the need to change what was happening in Washington. Yet, according to the domestic media, it wasn't big enough to report. There was no mention of any problem in Cheyenne and certainly no mention of any illicit chatter on the SI-net. It just never happened.

Yet, it had happened, and it had made a difference. It was the beginning.

*****

CH 27 Travel Visa

Shea went home and poured herself a short glass of single-malt scotch – then another, and another. By five-thirty in the afternoon, she could hardly stand up. She picked up the bottle and saw that half of it was gone, but it hadn't made her feel any better. In fact, she felt worse – the guilt of drinking piled on top of the ruinous state of her life.

Instead of staying up, she went to bed, placing her head on top of the three goose--down pillows she'd stacked up against her walnut, beaded headboard. *I'll just rest for a few minutes*, she thought to herself. The next thing she remembered was waking up, staring up at the big, red numbers projected onto her ceiling. It was 2:03 a.m. She'd passed out, and her eyes were blurry as she tried to refocus her mind on the numerals above her.

She flipped over to turn on the white, ceramic lamp next to her bed and then reached for her black reading glasses. On the nightstand was a book that had been resting there for several weeks. It was one her husband had been reading before he disappeared. He liked heavy tomes – classics that had withstood the test of time and had principles that applied to every one of every generation. She read the title twice -- *The Federalist Papers. How ironic*, she thought, as her sorrow returned. Shea missed Patrick dearly. He had been her rock and often times her life preserver. Now, she felt she was drowning in a sea of self-pity and gloom. The sea bottom was miles below her, but she panicked at the thought of how long it would take her metaphoric body to descend before it and her soul were lost forever.

Shea opened the book, and a faded, color picture that had been stuffed between some pages fell to the floor. She reached down to pick it up. Holding it in her hand, she saw it was a photo of him smiling broadly and putting his arms behind others on either side of him – Shea and Sergei. It was the moment that Patrick and Sergei had figured out the precise solution that could increase gas or diesel fuel efficiency by quantum leaps over previous models. In the picture Shea was standing beside him, proud of what they had achieved together and the potential they believed they had ahead of them.

Tears welled up in her eyes, and she quickly wiped away one that had gotten loose and trickled down her cheek. Lenoir Labs had been filled with good times – times she wished she had back again. But, she knew deep down those times were gone. It was over.

It was 3:18 when her PCD rang. *Who could be calling at this time of the morning?* she asked herself. Her head throbbed, a reminder of the lapse she'd had the night before. "Hello?" she answered, making sure the *Show-Image* button was off on her end. But just as she answered it, the line went dead. *Must have been a wrong number*, she thought. Moments later, it rang again, and again the line disconnected when she answered.

Then, it rang – but this time it was different. This time, it was *his* ring -- it was the signature telephone ring for her husband– the first part of the old country song by Willie Nelson, *Always on My Mind.*

She nearly shouted, "Answer phone -- Hello?" she asked anxiously, her heart beating as if she'd just run the one hundred-meter dash. "Patrick!" There was no answer. She asked again, "Hello? Patrick? Is that you?" But again there was no answer. Instead she got a hissing noise that suggested it was a bad connection. "Image On!" she told her computer, asking to see the person on the other end of the line, but it too came up blank. She stayed on the line until it went dead again. "Dial Patrick," she said within seconds of hearing the dial tone. But minutes passed, and she got nothing. She tried several more times, but the phone just rang and rang. Many more minutes passed. "Come on, Patrick! Answer!" she shouted anxiously. Finally, she was about to hang up when a click suggested someone had answered. "Patrick?" she asked excitedly.

"Shea?" was the response.

"Patrick? Is that you?"

"Yeah, I think that's me," said the voice.

It sounded like Patrick, but the line was so bad, she wasn't sure.

"You *think* it's you?" she asked, not sure what to say next.

"Shea ..."

"Yes hon; where are you?" Her heart was beating so fast it felt like she could have an attack at any moment.

"There's a lot to tell you, and very little time ... but," he said haltingly. Then there was a pause. "I have to hang up now."

"No, don't!" Shea exclaimed, almost hysterically.

But the line went dead. She again tried to call him back, but there was no answer.

"No, no, no!" she yelled. "You can't do this to me, Patrick! You can't!"

She broke down into sobs, hitting the pillows and throwing her PCD across the room. "Where are you?" she asked herself, crying. "Where are youuuu?"

It took time to compose herself, and as she lay in bed staring at the ceiling, she thought about every microsecond of the call. She played it over and over in her mind. *There was something there,* she thought, *something happened.*

Then, she realized it. She had heard another sound – a clicking sound in the line. She remembered reading about how wire taps sometimes hung up abruptly. *Patrick had probably heard it too*, she thought. *Is that why he hung up so quickly? Was someone listening in or taping their conversation?*

She tried to contact him for the next several days, but she got nowhere. The clicking noise persisted, yet she continued to make the calls, knowing that someone was listening in.

In frustration, she called her GovCo. SI-net carrier to ask from where the call had originated. It took hours to find a human, but she finally got one. "Ma'am, I'm not sure I can get you that information," said the telephone supervisor. "I may need to ask my superior."

"If you have to, that's fine," Shea answered, "but I don't see that it's really necessary. It's my line that I'm inquiring about. I pay for it. Why do you have to get someone else's approval to give me the information?"

"It seems we always have to get approval for everything now-a-days," the supervisor said. "Legal stuff, I imagine." She was new to the position -- young and gregarious. She had been told by her bosses to be accommodating, but not *too* accommodating.

"Well, I don't see that there's any legal issue in just giving me a location?" Shea asked, trying to soften the request.

"I guess you're right," answered the operator, although still uncertain. "It appears it was from – Belize. Where is that?"

"Belize? Are you sure?" asked Shea dumbfounded.

"That's what it says here on my screen. Is that in Kentucky or Tennessee -- someplace like that?" asked the operator.

"No. I'm afraid not. Thanks for the information," replied Shea, hanging up the phone.

She sat motionless in her armchair. *Belize? How in the hell did he get down to Belize?* she thought. She picked up her large tumbler of scotch and took a swig. It had become a more frequent pastime for her, and one she was no longer enjoying. *How on earth am I going to find him down there?*

Shea booked her airline tickets to fly to Belize City in Belize, Central America. She asked her computer to find the soonest departure for a flight itinerary and got the earliest date available. When the computer asked about her return flight, she hesitated. "Not sure," she answered, settling on a one-way ticket. Finally, the travel-bot with which her computer was communicating asked for her travel visa and passport numbers. She read them off and waited. The screen finally flashed an error message:

> We're sorry, there has been a problem in processing your request. Government records show you are not authorized to leave the country at this time. Please try again at a later time or contact your local travel agent for more information.

"What?" she exclaimed. "That can't be. Everything I have is current!"

Moments later, she got a call on the same line.

"Ms. Disone?" asked a portly, double-chinned lady who wore heavy makeup. The image on the screen was unusually flat – two dimensional, instead of the usual three; however, often times government technology had not been upgraded to the latest standards. "We show you are trying to purchase tickets out of the country. We also show that your travel visa has been suspended. Why do you think you can get tickets out of the country?"

"I don't understand. When did my travel visa get suspended and why?" Shea asked.

"Three months ago. You have to be re-approved by the Ministry of State to get a travel visa to go anywhere outside the country."

Shea was exasperated, but understood that her attitude wouldn't make it easier to secure a travel visa. "Then, what do I have to do?"

"Well, you'll have to ..." the woman stopped and she put her hand up to the wireless earpiece invisibly buried deep in her ear. Listening to some unknown person, she nodded, mumbling, "Okay ... Okay. I understand."

"Is there a problem?" Shea asked, confused with all the distractions happening in the image in front of her.

"No ... no, I guess not. Ms. Disone, I was told that there is an exception to the rigorous requirements of getting a travel visa, but I will have to ask you a few questions," said the woman.

Surprised, Shea asked, "Oh, and who was it that told you this?"

"That was just someone higher up the chain," said the woman, being dismissive. "So, the first question is Are you a citizen?"

"Yes, of course."

"Have you paid your taxes for the past five years?"

"Yes, absolutely!"

"Have you been or are you being investigated for criminal activities?"

"No!"

"It looks like you're planning to go to Belize …" she said, looking into another monitor. "When do you plan to return?"

"Uh, I will return within five days," she said, really not knowing when she would be coming back.

The woman was getting more verbal messages through her earpiece and finally looked back at Shea. "I don't show a return flight, but …" Again, there was more talk in her earpiece. "Yes, you have been approved for a visa. You can pick it up at the airport when you check in at the desk."

"That's it? That's all I have to do?"

"Yes. You're done. Have a good trip."

"Okay. Thanks," said Shea, confused, but happy she could get out of the country and feel like she was actually making some progress in her search.

***

Shea arrived early at the airport, as it would take over four hours to get processed for her flight – even with a travel visa. After checking her bags through the scanners, she stood in line until she was next for the full-body sweep and chemical analysis. After retinal scans confirmed her identity, she was ushered into a small room where she was interrogated prior to her departure.

"Next!" shouted the man inside, waiting for the next passenger to be processed. "Sit!" he commanded, taking Shea's passport and papers. "Where's your travel visa?" he asked, indignantly.

"I was told to pick it up here," said Shea. "I have a confirmation number – A459TYP1087."

"Nope. You don't pick those up here," he snapped.

"If you'd look up the number I was given, I'm sure it is all worked out," she answered.

In his late fifties, the man looked like he'd seen many more birthdays than that. His hair was long, but pulled back tightly in a bun. Gray with residual streaks of black, his mane looked as if it hadn't been washed in days, heavily matted to his head. His voice was rough and deep, as if he'd smoked six packs a day all his life.

Worse yet, he was grossly overweight and out-of-shape. His face was puffy and eyes red, reflecting an unhealthy lifestyle that he, no doubt, had practiced for much of his adult life.

The man grunted. "It's highly unusual for someone to pick-up a travel visa here. Wait here. My speech recognition software isn't working, so I have to go to the back and look it up."

After more than twenty minutes, he returned, huffing and puffing from the short walk. "Yeah, you're good. I still don't understand it, but on occasion we get privileged people like you walk in here and get right on a plane," he said sarcastically. "You get the lucky *Pass Go* card, I guess. It's always you rich people who get to bypass the system. It makes me sick."

Taken aback, Shea leaned forward. "What is the problem?" she asked.

"You're getting special treatment. You uppity ones always do," the man said smugly.

"I really don't know what you're talking about, sir. I just contacted the Ministry of Unity and …"

"Oh, so you know someone there, do you? Typical," he answered.

"I … I … all I want to do is get on that plane. Are my passport and visa good or not?" she asked.

The man snorted at her. "Yeah, you're good. And have a nice trip down in Belize – laying on the beach and sipping umbrella drinks all day long."

Shea held her tongue. She wanted to make that flight and knew he was baiting her.

"Thank you," she answered, smiling disingenuously.

"Flight 82 to Belize City now boarding," blared the loudspeaker. "All ticketed on flight 82 should be aboard or in the boarding area."

Shea ran to the gate and the attendant scanned her electronic pass, motioning her onto the craft before closing the door.

Closing her eyes, Shea let out a deep breath. At last, she was on her way. She didn't know what she would or wouldn't find once she got to Belize. It was a shot in the dark, but it was all she had. She wanted to believe that Patrick would be there. In her dreams, he would be standing in the terminal with a bouquet of flowers, waiting for her. He would be smiling, ready to embrace her and take her back into his life as though nothing had ever happened to them.

Quickly, she fell asleep. The flight was short – a hypersonic trip of only an hour and a half. She thought of nothing as the plane lifted off, its wheels tucking in underneath the hold. Her mind drifted off. What she didn't dream about was her return flight. *It would come when it would come*, she had thought. But, it would be more complicated than she could ever have imagined.

*****

CH 28 EG in Flames

EG was in trouble. With the Unity Plan, all assets of the behemoth company would be seized by the government within days, and its board dismembered, replaced by government bureaucrats. Thorne could smell the blood in the water, and knew his only chance of survival was to get a favor from Ratner.

The Board Room at EG filled quickly as the Executive Committee members came in for an emergency session called by the CEO. Thorne brought in his executive board members to discuss the recent developments and what it would mean for the company.

"Thanks for coming on such short notice," Thorne said opening the meeting. "I just want to reassure you that I am in full support of the president's latest executive orders. It's best for the country, and what's best for the country must be best for all of us." Thorne was covering himself, as all senior executives did, as the session was being recorded and could be later sent to one of the ministries by someone in the room trying to curry favor with a high-ranking government official. "But, I feel it is our fiduciary responsibility to protect the shareholders of this great company and the consumers we serve to the extent we can. Therefore, I'm asking for your help in crafting a strategy to deal with the aftermath of these new regulations."

Marjorie Williams, one of the newer members leaned forward. She was the founder of another company that had gone public several years earlier when such actions were legal. She had made billions on the deal, and now served on various boards to keep herself busy. "I believe we owe it to the people of this country to comply with the Administration's edicts and let them assume the assets of this company. Without a vital and thriving nation, our company can't do well either." It was a hypocritical comment, as she had cashed out of her company and no longer had anything at risk. All of her assets were far out of the reach of Uncle Sam, having been invested on Swiss accounts and real estate overseas. "We have benefited from the expenditures of the federal government for a long time," she continued, "It is time that we give back."

Another board member, Maxwell Perkins, spoke up. "Marjorie, somehow, I knew you'd take their side on this. But, what I have to ask you is what are the government expenditures you're referring to?"

Williams and Perkins had often been at odds in their views, so this dispute was nothing new.

"Who do you think built the roads, the bridges, the tunnels of this country? It wasn't private companies," she answered. "It was all done by the federal government."

"Actually, much of it was built by private companies, Marjorie. Back in the middle of the nineteenth century, the railroads were built almost exclusively by private money. If it wasn't the Central Pacific or Union Pacific in the 1860s building the transcontinental railroad, it was community businesses paving private roads to get to their own business establishment for truck hauling or consumers. Through the centuries, businesses have paid trillions in tax revenue to the government, enabling it to build the roads, bridges and tunnels you refer to. And if the money didn't all come from them, it came from the taxes on the wages they paid hard-working employees."

"But companies profited mightily from money spent by the government to build that infrastructure," quipped Williams. "Take Eisenhower in the 1950s who pushed Congress to build the interstate highway system. That was a huge benefit to this nation and its interstate commerce. You can't deny that!"

"No, I don't," retorted Perkins. "It was a great idea to build such a system. But where did the government get the money for it? The taxpayer. It wasn't a toll road, was it? No, it was a freeway, and freeways are built with government bonds or taxpayer money. Either way, taxpayers have to pay it off."

"You just don't understand things, Maxwell," said Williams, condescendingly. "The government's spending is what creates jobs and keeps the economy going. It's simple. Keynes told us this over a century ago."

"Believe it or not, Marjorie, I did read John Maynard Keynes's 1936 work on demand economics. It's rubbish, and you know it. It has been demonstrated repeatedly not to work – only to create things like the 205 trillion dollars in national debt we now enjoy. And what has it gotten us? Unemployment of over forty percent, inflation at over sixty-five percent, and all the misery that goes with both of them. Hell, nine dollars of every ten in taxes goes to pay the interest on our debt. The rest we need, we have to borrow!"

"If I may," said Thorne, intervening. "It is important that we discuss next steps with regard to the government's action. I'm not here to discuss whether it's good or bad. I'm only here to figure out how to protect our company and shareholders."

Randolph Hershman was next to speak. He had been the CEO of the revitalized American Motors corporation until it was shut down by the fossil fuel ban. "Thorne, I think we need to close our plants here and relocate everything to our Auckland branch in New Zealand. Although there is a movement to socialize this country, I feel we're facing something more than that. It's a hubris in the White House that I feel is unsettling."

It was LaTisha Brown who chimed-in. "I've spent my whole life building up my wealth. I'm sure has hell not going to do anything to bring on the wrath of the ministries. We all know that they monitor everything we do, and they are more than willing to seize our homes, boats, cars; hell, even our bank accounts overseas for God's sake. I'm just not willing to sacrifice all of that just for being on the wrong side of this thing."

"I agree," said Toby Wilson, Vice Chairman of the Board. "I understand we have a responsibility to the company as board members, but there is nothing in the by-laws that says we have to sacrifice everything we own. I'm not willing to do that. I've worked too hard all my life. I say we let things go as they will go. If the government assumes control of the company, then so be it. We'll only be out a few million in stock options. I can live without that. What I can't live with is the loss of my foreign holdings and my relationship with congressmen and senators on the Hill."

The meeting began to degrade into a shouting match between executive members – some for and some against what the government was trying to do. Many times, Thorne tried to intercede but to no avail.

Just as Thorne tried once more to restore order at the meeting, the boardroom doors opened wide. There was an instant hush to those talking, and all turned their heads to see who had entered.

"Good afternoon," said Minister Ratner, briskly walking into the meeting with an escort of three administrators. "I hope I'm interrupting," she added, intentionally offering no apology. "Now, what is it that the EG Committee is discussing?"

Thorne looked over at Ratner with a scowl on his face. He did not appreciate her interruption, but they both understood there was little he could do about it. "Minister, we were just discussing the latest actions by the White House with respect to domestic corporations such as EG. We were going over the impact on our …"

"Yes, yes,' Ratner said dismissively, moving over to the head of the room where Thorne sat. She stood next to him, making him lean forward to stay engaged in the meeting he was chairing.

"I've come here today to ensure that the Executive Committee will act responsibly when it comes to the latest orders from the president. I don't see how there can be much to discuss. I believe the orders are quite clear. However, I am willing to entertain any questions you may have on the subject," she asked.

173

Her stare was penetrating; her face rigid and lips tight and pursed. She did not expect any questions, and that was the whole point of her coming – to discourage resistance. If she could subdue EG, then other companies would be much easier to bring into line.

"I see. Well, I guess there's nothing more to debate, is there," she said coldly.

It was Thorne who pushed himself back from the table. "I do have some questions, minister," he said as respectfully as he could muster.

"Yes," she answered him, swiveling her body to face him in his leather chair. Their relationship was over, and there was no longer any attempt to show warmth. Ratner's glance toward him was distant and detached.

The other people in the room held their breath, not knowing what Thorne might say and how Ratner may react to whatever it would be. Thorne was treading on dangerous ground, and he knew he had to be careful.

"So, who will be overseeing the operations of EG? If your ministry is the one involved, will we get someone who has an understanding of what the company does?" asked Thorne.

"Of course," said Ratner. "I will assign one of my deputies to your company. They will review your company filings and read-up on your business. They will be more than capable of running things at that point. It's not as difficult as running a multi-trillion dollar government after all. We're only talking about several hundred billion dollars, aren't we?"

"Yes, it is much smaller than the government's purse, but there are many aspects that will require specific attention. How do you see your deputy minister working with our company's senior staff and myself?"

"You will report to my deputy ministry, of course. My ministry will set production goals for you based on our knowledge of all companies in your industry. It will be rolled into our first Five-Year Plan. That's the beauty of having the government run your business. We know what everyone else is planning so we can optimize the entire economy. We no longer have to worry about the inefficiencies of competition. We won't have any. It will be much better when we collaborate and work together rather than working against each other. We can achieve … we will achieve so much in the coming years."

"I see," said Thorne. "So we will get production quotas from your ministry?"

"Yes."

"And you will work with us to make sure we can meet your quotas?"

"No, you will work with my ministry to make sure you do. You have no choice. In order to get this economy back on track, each of us must to our part. You can't fail. You *must* meet your quotas!"

"And if we can't?" asked Thorne.

Ratner got red in the face, but exhaled to calm herself. "You will," she said flatly.

Ratner turned to walk out of the room. "I guess that's all I have time for. It's been nice talking with you about this most important matter. If you have any questions, please take them up with my deputy and my ministry. Good day." And with that, she pivoted on her heels and left, leaving the double doors open behind her.

Thorne had no emotion on his face. He banged his gavel after she'd left and said, "I believe there is no more business to discuss. I formally order this meeting adjourned." Then, almost whispering under his breath, he added, "... perhaps forever."

***

Two days later, Ratner issued an order from her ministry seizing all assets of EG, including the patents and drawings for their version of the SECE engine. Not only had she gotten forty million dollars in cash by emptying the accounts of Chou and Muntz and was waiting on half of the forty-five million from Thorne, but now she had the capability and software detail to do it all by herself – to develop the SECE under her name -- free.

EG, along with all other companies, both large and small, were taken over almost overnight – privatized under the control of the government ministries. Ratner, as Minister of Unity, now controlled vast resources – nearly all of the U.S. economy that once generated over 65 trillion in value from goods and services. Even though that economy had fallen to twenty-fourth in the world, behind Nigeria. It now created less than 9.6 trillion in value, half of the 19.4 trillion it had generated thirty years earlier, in 2018.

EG shuttered most of its operations worldwide under the oppressing oversight of the Ministry of Unity. Thorne was replaced as CEO by the deputy minister, who had no experience running a business, let alone one as large as EG. Within a year, many operations were terminated, and as losses mounted, the government was reticent to offer anyone a bailout. It too had no money.

But the death of EG was not the only casualty. Also consigned to the graveyard of industry were the patents and designs of the SECE and HECE engines. The blueprints and prototypes were left in an old government warehouse, not far from the now-closed Lenoir Lab headquarters in Boston. There they gathered dust –

abandoned diamonds that had immense value to the outside world – one more and more starved for resources and a revitalized economy.

Thorne had never been able to get his fingers on the SECE, as hard as he'd tried. It was Ratner who had seized it when Lenoir Labs had folded. However, with the collapse of the fossil fuel industry at the hands of the Fourier Administration, there was little point in pursuing its development. It was true that there was a huge market for the SECE elsewhere in the world, but finding a favorable government and economy to produce the engine was increasingly difficult. Most were either Islamic states or deeply socialistic and, therefore, were as much against fossil fuel as was the United States. No, Ratner had given up on that mission, but she had only begun her quest for a more lucrative post – one that would bring her both money and power.

*****

CH 29 Belize

The trip to Belize was only a short plane ride south, especially with the hypersonic technology that had grown popular during the last decade. After leaving the Belize City airport, Shea took a taxi to her hotel, dropping off her bags before venturing out into the urban jungle. Formerly, British Honduras, the country of Belize had become a melting pot for *Kriols*, previous slaves and slave owner descendants, the *Garinagu*, from Central Africa, the *Mestizos* or those with Spanish-Mayan ancestry, and a few Englishmen. Both Spanish and English languages were common, but most spoke Spanish or a mix called Belizean Creole.

Walking around the city, she saw the highlights and lowlights of Belizean culture. With the slow decay of the U.S., more entrepreneurs had moved south to Costa Rica and Belize as warm havens to expand their businesses. As technology was increasingly portable, they could setup shop almost anywhere and transmit their products electronically all over the world. To that end, these young business moguls had built shiny, new buildings, employing thousands to develop software and cutting-edge technology. It was the type of environment for which Shea had longed when Patrick and she had started Lenoir.

But there was also the seedy side of the city, where prostitutes, drugs and filth were in full view. Shea had been warned to be careful in that part of town, and she was vigilant as she walked along muddy, trash-strewn roads. It was along one such road that she found a bar called the Tropico de Paraiso. The bamboo hut-like building looked as if it might fall over if a gust of wind hit it in the wrong spot. The three ceiling fans turned slowly overhead – just fast enough to keep the flies from landing on their dusty, brown paddles. Dried grass lined the bar like a skirt on a Hula dancer, and the wooden counter hugged three of the four walls on the inside. There were only ten or so patrons sitting at the bar, drink in hand, chatting away with others whom they appeared to know well. It was a small, local watering hole, where the men went after work to get drunk before they went home to their disapproving wives. Those who didn't work, just hung out at the bar all day, collecting a government subsistence check whether they worked or not.

Shea pulled out a stool and sat down. The weather was warm, nearly 36 degrees Celsius, with a mild breeze that made the palm tree fronds rustle outside and the cheap, white paper napkins dance off the tabletops and onto the dirty wood-planked floor.

"*¿Qué te gustaría beber?*" asked the bartender, speaking pure Spanish.

It had been years since Shea had taken Spanish, and she sheepishly asked, "Do you speak English?"

"Certainly," replied the young, bearded man behind the counter. "What can I get you?"

"I'll have a margarita," answered Shea, digging through her purse for some Belizean dollars. "How much do I owe you?" she asked.

Even though the U.S. dollar was not as valuable as it used to be, it was still more than the Belizean one.

"That'll be twenty-three fifty," said the man.

Shea handed him thirty and leaned in to sip her umbrella-festooned drink. She had made some calls before coming down and had found someone who said he could help. He was referred to her by a friend of a friend of a friend or something like that. It was circuitous, but it was all she had to go on. He was to meet her there at the Tropico de Paraiso , but she was an hour early.

Around her sat an interesting array of characters, from a jewelry shop owner, dressed in a Ralph Lauren Polo shirt, gold chain necklace, khaki Bermuda shorts and Dolce and Gabanna flip-flops, to a small man with a heavily weathered face and straw hat who sat at the end of the bar, merely watching the others and sipping his beer. She had chatted with those at the bar on and off during the course of the hour, as they were more than eager to talk with such an attractive lady as she, particularly an American.

However, there was another gentleman, a handsome bloke, sitting at a table in the corner, who seemed out of place. Alone and wearing a dark sport coat, he looked more apropos in a New York City café than a Belizean bar. He wore dark glasses and lace-up tan shoes, albeit without socks. Occasionally, he would glance over at Shea but would nonchalantly resume sipping his drink and reviewing his PCD. She had gone over to him when she'd first arrived to ask whether he was her intended appointment, but he had only shaken his head and looked back at his PCD.

After a while, he stood up. Shea was sure he would come over to talk to her; however, he only left the bar for a short while, probably to relieve himself in the men's bathroom, before coming back to resume his post at the back corner table.

At four-thirty, another man entered the bar. His stature and features matched those of the person she expected to meet there. She rose and looked over at him to catch his attention. He immediately smiled and came to the bar to join her.

"You must be Shea," he said, extending his hand.

"Yes, Miguel?"

"Yes, yes. Miguel de Tavera. I am the one and the only," he said in slightly broken English, laughing at his own joke.

"Thank you for meeting me here. I understand that you've seen my husband down here? Is that true?"

"Yes, madam. I see your husband. His name is Patrick, right?"

"Yeah, that's right. We discussed this on the phone. You said you saw him about a week ago or so. What can you tell me? Where did you see him? What was he doing?"

"Oh, I make delivery to market on Neals Pen Road and see somebody working there. He look exactly like picture of your husband. He go by Ricardo."

"Ricardo? Why would he be working at a market? He's got a PhD in engineering."

"I dunno, ma'am. This is what I see."

Shea took a sip of her margarita as she thought. "So, where can I find him? Where is this market?"

The man smiled. He was missing a tooth on the lower part of his jaw, and an upper one that had a partial gold filling. He held out his hand. "Eight thousand," he said.

"Eight thousand what?" Shea asked naively.

"Eight thousand American."

Suddenly, Shea realized he was asking for money, and it wasn't discounted 50% as it would have been in Belizean dollars. "Eight thousand U.S. dollars? Are you crazy?"

"I see him over in market, ma'am. If you want to find husband, you have to pay. That is the way it is in Belize." He pushed his hand out closer to her.

Shea hesitated. "But I don't even know whether you really saw him or not. Why would I pay you all of this when you could just leave and I never see you again?"

"I am honorable man, miss. I will make good on my promise. I take you to him. I will do this tomorrow."

Shea was desperate for information, so she reached into her purse. She hadn't brought that much in U.S. currency. Instead, she pulled out several bills and laid them out on the table. They were in various U.S. notes, from the one hundred dollar bill with the updated image of FDR on it to the five hundred denomination with Obama's portrait on the front. "I'll give you half now and half when I see my husband," she answered.

"Oh. I don't do that. How do I know that you not stiff me when you see him," Miguel said.

"I am an honorable woman," said Shea as a retort.

He smiled again. "I tell you what," he said, showing his broken smile, "you give me six thousand now and I trust you for the other two tomorrow. Okay?"

Shea started to reach back into her purse when a stiletto knife, some nine inches in length, slammed down into the thick lacquer surface of the bar, pinning down the money she'd already placed there. It also fell just beyond the outstretched hand of Miguel, missing his middle finger by less than an inch. Miguel recoiled in surprise, drawing back his arm for fear of another attack.

"Back away, amigo," said a voice coming from behind them.

Shea turned around. It was the man in the dark sport coat from the corner table, still wearing the black sunglasses that hid his eyes from the world around him.

The look on Miguel's face was one of surprise but not shock. It was clear to Shea that Miguel knew this man. He pulled back his stool and ran out of the bar as fast as he could, not turning to see if anyone was following him.

Shea looked over at the young man who had so violently interrupted their meeting. "And who the hell are you?" she asked him, more shocked at the crudeness of the act than fearful of the man himself.

The young man took off his sunglasses. His eyes were a light blue, soft and inviting. "I'm Hank Fannon," he said, extending his hand. "I'm sorry to be so rude in my introduction, but you don't want to get wrapped up with Miguel there. He's a con artist. He makes a living taking people's money."

"And how do you know about him?"

"I work for the U.S. State Ministry. We work closely with what we used to call the CIA down here. We keep a watch on the low-lifes in town only to get information on terrorists who operate down here. This city is teaming with them, although you wouldn't know it from the looks of things. Miguel there gives me information when I pay him. I keep him straight, as he knows I can find him anytime I want if he doesn't play by the rules. He's no terrorist, but he's no angel either."

"I see," said Shea, suspiciously. Now she wasn't so sure she was in any better hands now than she had been moments earlier.

"Yeah, he'll steal you blind – take everything you own if you let him."

"What makes me think you won't?"

"Ma'am?"

"Well, I'm from America too, and I don't have any contacts in this city or this country. I was trying to find someone who could help me find my husband down here. I've been looking for him for almost a year. He disappeared from our home, and I've received just one call from him – it came from Belize City. I'm down here to find him. Is there anyone at the embassy down here that you know who could help me find him?"

"What's his name?"

"Patrick. Patrick Disone."

The young man shook his head. "No, I haven't heard that name around the city."

He was hard not to appreciate. She felt attracted to his low-key manner and smooth ways. His hair was dark brown, combed straight back and gelled. Although his sideburns were longer than she liked, there were few other things to which she could honestly say she objected.

She took a picture of her husband out of her purse and put it next to the knife the young man had planted into the bar top. "Have you seen him?"

The young man picked up the picture and studied it. "I'm not sure. The face does look familiar. The only thing I know for sure is that he's not on our top ten most wanted down here."

Shea laughed. "That's a good thing," she answered. "But you haven't seen him anywhere?"

"No, I don't think so."

Shea put the picture back in her purse.

"Do you mind if I ..." he began to ask, pointing to the empty stool next to her.

"Oh, no. Go right ahead. Please, I insist," she answered. "What did you say your name was?" she asked.

"Hank. But my real name is Henry. You can call me Hank, though."

Hank motioned to the bartender who came over after cleaning out an empty beer glass left behind moments earlier. He nodded, inviting Hank's beverage request.

"I'll take another Red Stripe, and the lady will have another ..." He hesitated, waiting for Shea to claim whatever drink she was having.

"A margarita," she said.

Hank looked at her, puzzled. "A margarita? In Belize? Really?"

"Why? What's wrong with that?" she asked.

"You're not in Mexico, you know. We drink rum down here, not tequila. If you want a great drink, I suggest mango rum or maybe something with a little pineapple thrown in."

Shea giggled. "Fine. Fix me up," she said.

The bartender brought over the two drinks and plopped them down in front of them. Shea took a sip and smiled. "Good," she said, licking her lips.

"I thought you'd think that," Hank said.

Shea took another sip. "How long have you been down here?"

"Oh, I've been here for the last year and a half. It looks like a great place – no worries about cold weather or snow – but after a while, it wears on you. I miss the usual American things – you know, hamburgers, fries and all that. I have to say that a Big Mac sounds really good about now."

Shea laughed. "I don't think I've had one of those in years." Then, she asked, "So, could you ask around about my husband? See if anyone has seen him or anyone at your department has heard about him? I'll give you a copy of his picture." She handed him an extra that she kept to distribute while she was down there.

"Sure, no problem," he answered. "But you can just sync it with my PCD if you have it that way."

"Of course," she said.

"No, we're not as backward as you might think. We do have running water and electricity here, you know."

They talked for another hour about life in Belize and what she and her family had gone through. He found her story hard to believe but was kind and empathetic.

There were two more rounds of drinks, and after each, Shea found herself more and more relaxed. She hadn't felt as fun-loving and care-free in years. Hank smiled, told her some jokes, and she giggled and laughed like a school girl. She listened to his tales about other crimes going on in the city and how he had been instrumental in helping local police. Shea suspected he was exaggerating his importance but by then she didn't care. He was a piece of art, and the warm, red glow of the setting sun over the mountains behind them, combined with the wet, pulsing breezes that wafted through the bar, made things even more irresistible.

Hank put his soft fingers on her leg, and as they continued to banter back and forth he moved his hand higher up her thigh. She felt the erotic connection with him from the start, and she welcomed his intrusion into her private place.

Without being asked, the bartender brought two more drinks, and although Shea had already had more than she'd had in ages, she accepted them without protest. She sipped and laughed, as her new-found partner began messaging her inner thigh, moving up and down, and finding its way to her very sanctum, where lust and logic no longer coexisted. Prurience and sex were the only elixir her mind could grasp. Hank took her by the hand, steadying her with his arm, and together they left the bar. Her mind was in a euphoric fog as she willingly left with someone she barely knew.

It was only a short cab ride and up a flight of stairs into what she could tell was some renovated, but gray, stucco building. The only thing on which Shea could focus was the apartment number - 218; it was the same as her birthday.

The apartment was dark, but light from an outside streetlight streamed in through the front window, where the curtains parted. Hank shut the front door softly and locked it behind him, throwing the keys onto a small, square table next to the couch. It was a moment that made Shea uneasy, realizing she was now a prisoner inside a stranger's home.

But his smile melted away any anxiety she had, and he approached her slowly, gliding across the room like a knight on a white horse. She suddenly felt safe, and she could hardly wait for that warm touch to embrace her again.

Shea's head began to spin, and all she could remember was Hank unbuttoning her blouse, twisting each button slowly, trying to heighten her feelings of want and desire. The evening was erotic and passionate. They writhed on each other's bodies, undulating and caressing. It was a night of ecstasy and drunken euphoria, living for the moment in an ephemeral world that could not last forever, as much as Shea would have wanted it.

***

The sun's rays sliced through the thin draperies that framed the double windows in the bedroom, just as the street lights had through the front window the night before. Shea rolled over, putting her arm over her head to shield her face from the invasive, prying eyes of the morning. Her head throbbed, and she rubbed her temple to no avail. Rolling over, she reached for her night's companion but found the sheets empty and cold.

"Hank?" she whispered, groggily. She looked around the apartment and listened intently for an utterance or a sound. Yet, she heard nothing. "Hank?"

The rapture of the previous evening was still radiating through her body, even though her head was sending her a very different message. Pain and nausea dominated her upper senses, overwhelming the calm and satiation of those from her lower ones. But one sense that dominated both was guilt.

Shea clumsily rolled out of bed, her breasts tender from all the attention they'd received. She walked to the bathroom where she climbed in the shower. She needed it, subconsciously trying to re-purify her soul. The hot water eventually came on, but only momentarily, giving her brief warmth that soon left her just as had her partner. After she put on her clothes, she opened the bathroom door, adjusting her hair by clipping it with a braid and letting it fall down her back.

"Hello gorgeous," said Hank, standing in the bathroom doorway.

Shea stepped back, surprised to find he was there. "I ... I thought you'd left," she stammered.

"Leave? And leave behind someone as beautiful as you? What sense would that make?"

She laughed, just as she had at the bar the night before.

"I had a little bit too much to drink last night," she said, trying to make an excuse for what had happened.

"Yeah, so," was his reply. "It's kind of obvious." He pulled his hand from behind his back and held up a bag. "I thought I'd go get some of these for us."

He had a brown paper bag in one hand and a knife in the other.

"What is it?" asked Shea nervously, nudging past him in the doorway and going back into the bedroom.

"Bagels! You don't find bagels down here very easily! After about six months, I found this little bakery about three blocks from here. They made a fresh batch of six one morning, and I bought them all. I think they believed it was a new fad catching on in town, because the next time I went, they had two more in the wicker bin."

"And you only bought two?" she asked.

"Hell no! I bought two dozen! I didn't know if they would make any more after that."

"And did they?"

"Next time I went they had three dozen out. And no, I didn't buy all three dozen. Two is my limit."

They had a good laugh, and Hank took her by the arm and gave her a kiss on the cheek. "I had a good time last night," he said, his light blue eyes twinkling at her.

Shea didn't answer. She only grinned and picked up one of the bagels. "Where's that knife?"

Together, they had breakfast out on his balcony. It was narrow, and the small gauge iron table and chairs filled what little space there was. The cool morning breeze blew steadily, letting the seagulls swoop down to pillage some of the bagel morsels Shea had left for them as a treat.

"Hank," Shea asked, picking up a teabag and plunging it into the hot water he had poured in her white, ceramic cup, "are you really a CIA agent?"

"No," he answered, taking a sip of his own tea. "I'm with the Ministry of State, like I told you."

"I could have sworn you said you were with the CIA."

"Nope, just the State Ministry."

Hank got up and opened the sliding glass window to the inside. He came back within a few minutes holding out his wallet with Ministry of State credentials and a silver badge that read *Ministry of State Marshall* on it.

"I guess you're legit, then," she said. "Perhaps I was a little looped by the time I'd asked you," she added.

"So, how do I know that you're some lone widow down here in Belize?" Hank asked.

"What?"

"I said, how do I know that *you're* legit?"

It had never occurred to her that he would question her the same way she questioned him. "I'm not a widow, first of all, and second of all, why would you question who I am?"

"Sorry, Shea, but I've met a lot of people down here who are not who they attest to be. It's just my nature to be skeptical, that's all."

"I'm looking for my husband. I'm not a widow," she answered, agitated at his accusation.

"Okay, I understand," he answered

There was a moment of awkward silence before Shea said, "Patrick, my husband, and I had this business ..."

"Yes, I know," said Hank. "You told me all about it last night."

Shea blushed. "Oh, yeah. I probably did. But, I'm just down here trying to find him. That's all."

"It's not going to be easy ... to find him, that is," said Hank, taking a sip of the tea. "People come here for a lot of reasons. Many are down here just so they aren't found."

"That may be true, but I'm going to find him. I know he's here!"

"You know this because the phone company told you that a call *may* have come from down here?"

"It did come from here," Shea declared.

"Alright, let's say it did. How are you going to track down your husband in a city with a population of seventy-thousand people?"

"There you go again," Shea said, exasperated. She was not in the mood to be told how she was wasting her time there.

She got up and put down her cup of tea. "I've had a very nice time, but I think it's time to go. Thank you Hank. It's been nice to meet you."

Hank stood up. "I'm sorry, Shea. I didn't mean to upset you. Please, stay a while longer."

"No, I think it's time I go."

Shea walked to the door, which Hank unlocked for her. As she opened it, he caught her arm. "Shea. I will look around for your husband. I believe you are who you say you are. You just can't be too careful down here, you know?"

Shea nodded and bit her lip. Then she said, "That would be nice. Thanks. If you find out anything, please call the Royal Palm Hotel. I'll be there until at least next Thursday." She hesitated and then added, "But Hank. We can't do this again. Do you understand? I'm married."

"So am I," Hank said, giving her a wink.

For the next three days Shea talked to store owners, government officials, police officers, beach-front lifeguards, garbage collectors, food stall owners and anyone else she could find, showing them pictures of Patrick. However, none said they had seen him. But also during that time, Hank didn't call her either. She thought for sure he would, either following up on the good time they had or finding something from his inquiries about Patrick.

Days passed, and still there was no more information. She was at a dead-end. Frustrated and dejected, she booked her flight back to the states. Again, it was a one-way ticket, and she felt that in many ways it would represent the end of her long journey seeking closure.

It was only a few hours before her flight was to leave for Boston. The two leads she'd been given had proved false – one, an American working in a real estate office who'd just been hired and was doing analytical work for the owner. He resembled Patrick, but when Shea went to see if it were he, she could tell immediately from the back of his head that it wasn't. The second lead came from the bartender at the Tropico de Paraiso where she'd gone when she'd first arrived in Belize City. He told her that a customer said he'd seen a man resembling Patrick about a month earlier. He'd seemed lost and confused. The bartender didn't know the customer well, so couldn't vouch for him. The man had been seen just outside a vegetable market – a central hub where the natives went to buy their fruits and vegetables from local vendors. She had stopped by several times, but hadn't seen anyone, and no one there had noticed anyone resembling Patrick.

The white taxi pulled up to the Royal Palm Hotel, and the front desk phoned Shea to notify her. Just as she closed her suitcase to go downstairs, her room phone rang again but the caller's image was blocked.

"Hello?" she answered.

"Shea?"

"Yes."

"This is Hank. Remember? We had the …"

"Yes, yes," she answered quickly to avoid the trip down memory lane. "Hi, Hank. How are you?"

"Shea, I can't talk over the phone, but you need to meet me at my apartment. Come as soon as you can. I think I've got some news for you."

"About Patrick?" she said, initially with enthusiasm.

"Just come as quickly as you can," answered Hank, "there isn't much time."

Shea paused. "I … I don't think I can, Hank. Just tell me what you have and I'll …" It was then that she heard a crashing noise in the background. "Hank? Hank?" she asked urgently.

Am I being played or is this real? she asked herself, frozen with indecision. "Hank?" she asked once more, but the call became disconnected. *Don't trust anyone here,* she thought, remembering what Hank had told her when she'd first arrived.

Dismissing the call, Shea took the elevator down to the mezzanine floor and floated across the Florentine marble floors and past the silk tapestries that hung on the walls. She checked out at the front desk before picking up her bags heading toward the thick, brass-framed front door. Outside she saw the taxi that had been patiently waiting for her, but as soon as she made her move toward it, it pulled away. She started to run after it, but the porter outside just smiled and said in rough English, "D'ere be a'nudder. No worries. One be by soon."

However, another did not appear for another twenty minutes, even though the porter had been on the phone the entire time trying to get one to stop by.

"I sorry, madam," he said. "I don' understand why so long. I guess lot's of people leavin' paradise today, eh?"

Finally, one zipped up to the hotel, screeching to a halt in front of Shea. She tipped the porter and climbed into the back of the red taxi as the driver slung her luggage in the trunk.

"*¿Dónde?*" asked the driver, turning around toward her.

"The airport," she replied.

The cab sped off toward the airport under overcast skies. There was a storm blowing in, and the black undercarriage of the clouds portended a downpour ready to strike. But as the drops began to fall on the windshield, traffic ground to a halt with red brake lights marking their path into the hazy distance. Shea looked at her PCD – she only had thirty minutes to make her flight.

"I've changed my mind," she said, getting the driver's attention. "Turn around. Let's go to … 425 Allenby Street."

"*No problemo,*" said the man, gladly whipping his steering wheel into a one-eighty and heading back the other way.

Although the address was across town, the cabbie took no time to maneuver the streets and backstreets to get her there quickly. They pulled up in front of the familiar apartment complex, and Shea got out paying the driver and getting her bag before he raced off down the road. She knew she' be missing her flight anyway, and she just couldn't let go of a nagging feeling she had about that call from Hank. What if he'd really been in trouble? What if he really did have some information on Patrick for her? Anyway, she could catch another flight the next day or the day after if any information Hank had proved promising. Even if he didn't have anything substantial, a part of her wanted to see him again. She knew she shouldn't feel that way, but she did just the same. Whether it would lead to another romp in the bedroom, well, she couldn't predict the future.

Shea knocked on the apartment door, but there was no sound inside. The apartment was dark, and the curtains in the front window were closed, no longer showing the gap she'd seen that one enchanted evening.

"Hank? Are you home?" she barked, knocking loudly on the door.

She listened, but there was no answer.

"Hank? It's Shea. Can you let me in?"

Shea held her palms to the corners of her eyes like blinders and peered inside through a side window, unfettered by any coverings. There she found pure chaos – furniture overturned and broken, sofa cushions ripped open and strewn across the floor, and books pulled off the shelf and scattered throughout the apartment.

Shea pounded this time, rather than knocking. "Hank! Hank!"

Then she pushed on the door. To her surprise, it moved effortlessly – unlocked and unlatched. The apartment was destroyed, and there was no Hank.

"Hank?" she asked one more time, not expecting an answer. Stepping through the debris, she looked around, afraid of the possibility that she might find Hank, or what might be left of him. She continued through the apartment but found little that was undisturbed. At least there was no Hank – no body, anyway.

Shea went to the bedroom where they'd had their tryst. She managed a grin as she relived the ecstasy of that night, the explosion of emotions she had felt as Hank had kissed and caressed her entire body, starting at her toes and working his way up. He had passion and had been able to bring out that same passion in her. She hesitated for a moment, running her hand over the now-broken bed frame, but then walked back into the front room to pickup her suitcase and head out the door. Just as she reached for the door knob, she noticed a folded piece of paper wedged just behind the hinge. *Odd?* she thought. Plucking it from its hiding place, she unfolded it.

> Dear Shea,
>
> If you find this message it will be a miracle, but if you do – I want you to know this. I've been taken. I've only heard about others recently, but it may happen to me as well. The ministry will tell you that I've been reassigned, but that would be a lie. Don't try to find me. It will likely be impossible. You've got enough on your hands trying to find your husband. You are special, Shea Disone. Don't let anyone tell you differently. But if I'm gone, you need to pursue what I'm telling you below.
>
> I told you I'd contact you if I learned anything about Patrick. Well, this morning I did. Ironically, that con man you met with that night at the bar was telling you the truth about one thing. He said he'd seen someone resembling your husband in a market on Neals Pen Road. That's all I can say. Others may find this message, and that wouldn't be good for you.
>
> I can't tell you if this is true or not, but it's all I have.

Good luck,

Hank

Shea refolded the note and stuck it in her purse. A new rush of excitement hit her, but this time it wasn't the erotic emotions she had experienced in his apartment. It was deeper. The possibility of seeing Patrick again after all the months brought a fresh outlook on life and a renewed spirit. She hurried down the stairs and waited until an empty taxi approached.

"Neals Pen Road," Shea said to the driver. "Go to the market there."

"Señora," said the driver, "which market? They many there. Which?"

"I don't know. Let's just drive. I'll show you when we get there." Shea had no idea where she needed to go. She only knew she had to go back to the market she'd visited a few days earlier and hope she'd find something – see something. If not, she hoped it would be the only market on Neals Pen Road.

The old, red cab made several turns with the driver deciding to floor the accelerator after every stop light. For the cabby, as well as for other drivers, the stop signs made little difference. Most simply regarded them as *'suggestions'*. Shea simply held on to the black, plastic hand strap that was securely bolted to the car just above the rear passenger window.

They passed one store front after another, and Shea watched intently as each passed by. *Just in case,* she thought, *I want to make sure I don't miss him on the street someplace along the way.* Finally, they drove past a run-down market with a wooden sign nailed out front alongside the entrance door. It read Unzio - Mercado Fresco or Fresh Market of Unzio.

"Stop!" she shouted, tapping the driver on the shoulder and pointing to the market. "Wait for me," she added.

The driver slammed on the breaks and then pulled to the curb. Shea grabbed her bag and jumped out, running inside. The place was decrepit. Filled with so much dirt on the white linoleum tile floor, it looked like it hadn't seen a customer in years. Yet, there were half-filled bins of ripe fruits and vegetables sitting on wooden tables peeling with white paint. The old lady behind the desk looked on, not caring who was in the store but tasked with guarding the 1960s style cash register.

Shea took the picture of Patrick out of her purse and held it up for the old lady to see. "Have you seen this man?" she asked.

The old woman only shrugged. She had no idea what Shea was saying and didn't much care.

"*Esté hombre*," Shea said in as much Spanish as she could remember, "*¿Lo has visto?*"

The lady shook her head. Shea wasn't sure she believed her. She spotted another door off to the side and went through it, hoping to get to the back to find the workers.

"*¡No! ¡No! ¡No puedes ir alla!*" the old woman screamed, telling her she couldn't go back there.

Shea ignored the woman and quickly surveyed the area where dozens of workers were laboring, offloading vegetables and fruits from old, barely-running trucks. The men were all in their forties and fifties, she reckoned; all had seen hard times from the looks of things.

"*¿Lo has visto?*" she asked, holding up Patrick's photo.

The men stopped only for a moment, but they too just shook their heads before going back to work.

Their supervisor came over and glared at her. He was a large man with a double jowl, big ears and a bulbous nose. His dark brown eyes narrowed their fix on her, making her feel vulnerable and exposed.

"*¿Qué quieres?*" he asked angrily.

"*¿Lo has visto?*" she asked, again holding up Patrick's photo.

"*¡Vete!*" yelled the man, waving his arms, telling her to get out.

Not seeing Patrick, Shea left, discouraged, but not defeated. She hopped back into the taxi which had waited for her, and they sped down the street in search of the next promising market along the way. They slowed passing two other markets but they were small with few, if any workers. Yet, undeterred, they turned around and went back to the first market where she'd been chased away. This time, she went down an alleyway to the back of the market where she found the loading docks. There she found workers stacking wooden pallets and breaking down cardboard boxes. The big, bad supervisor was nowhere in sight.

Once again, she asked if anyone had seen her husband, holding his picture. But this time, one of the men's eyes lit up. "*Sí*," he answered.

"*¿Dondé?*" she asked, excitedly.

"*Es uno de nosotros. Trabaja con nosotros*," the man answered, telling her he worked with them.

"Is he here?" she asked. "*¿Él está aquí?*"

"*No. Él no trabaja hoy*," said the man, saying he hadn't worked that day.

Another man standing nearby asked, *"¿Qué es?"*

"¿Trabaja aquí?" she asked, showing him the picture too.

"Si …. Uh, no," he answered, seeming to change his mind. *"Solía trabajar aquí, pero ya no. Alguien quien le entregó una nota ayer por la mañana. Lo leyó y dijo que había que salir. No he oído nada más de él."*

Shea didn't understand. *"Mi Español no es bueno, No entiendo."*

The man glanced at the first man and then back at Shea. "I speak little English," he said. "But, this man," he said, pointing to the picture, "he no work today. Dunno if he come back. But I know where he live."

"Where does he live?" she asked.

"Oh, I know," said the second man smiling.

"Okay, so, yes," she repeated. "Where does he live?"

The man looked at her.

"¿Dónde esta?" she repeated in Spanish.

"I know," he said again. "But …" he held out his hand, palm up.

Shea knew exactly what that meant. It seemed like she was right back to where she'd started when she'd come down, only a week earlier. "Money? You want money to tell me?" she asked.

Money was a word both men understood, and they grinned as they reached out for whatever she was willing to give them.

A whistle blew, and many of the men ran back into the market to get back to work. Shea feared another visit from the supervisor, so she quickly left, retracing her steps down the same alley she'd taken to find the market's dock area. Shea made sure the sup wasn't out front waiting for her before she dashed for the cab, opening the back door and jumping inside.

"¿Dónde, ma'am?" asked the driver.

"Home," said Shea, dejectedly. "It's the only place I have left."

"What?" the driver asked again, not understanding.

"El aeropuerto. Take me to the airport," she said, collapsing in the backseat.

The driver put the car in gear and pushed on the accelerator. The airport wasn't far away, yet to Shea it seemed very far.

*****

CH 30 Hate Speech

Profit was a term that had seen its usage carom between lionized and pejorative descriptions for centuries. However, it had been decades since the positive connotation had held true. From the date of the president's second inaugural address, Fourier had branded money-making as evil. And only a year later, Congress passed the Hate Speech Act, banning the word *profit* and another 2,657 words from use – whether verbal, visual, or electronic. The *P*-word and the other terms were branded offensive to the public, and if used, posed a clear and present danger to those who might be exposed – translation: they were a danger only to the standing government. That Act also authorized the formation of the Ministry of Prose and Language, a new ministry that would regulate which words were appropriate and acceptable in government, business, military and even personal communications.

The first words it struck from America's vernacular were those that had long-since been eliminated for their vulgarity against ethnic groups – particularly against African Americans, Hispanics, Muslims and others considered oppressed minorities. Yet, they were only a handful compared with the mountain of additional terms added, including: *illegal alien, union thug, Islamic extremist or terrorist, and Islamic intolerance.* Even words with no previous negative connotation were stricken because of a fear that the less-educated masses may misinterpret their meaning. Listed in this group were *niggardly* (meaning frugal), *tar baby* (describing a sticky situation), *water buffalo* (or raucous crowd), *ghetto, black sheep, black racist, Founding Fathers* (exclusionary to women) and *black coffee.* Another group of banned words were subject to their context. Those that conveyed a positive meaning to words like *profit, entrepreneur, capitalism, self-made,* and *independent* were not permitted, although negative references were acceptable. Likewise, language that vilified words or phrases such as *misandrist* (mistreatment of men – which could not exist according to feminists), *global warming* (which was still pending a resurgence according to NASA climatologists), *left-wing, progressive,* and *socialism.*

"But why?" asked Cassandra Livingston, a young reporter for the *Boston Gazette*.

"'Cause you can't say that!" screamed Bull, her editor. "It's against the law now! And it's okay by me, actually. I think it's time we rein in the crap that people write about. Journalism isn't about objectivism! It's about something bigger. It's always been about something bigger – bigger than you or me. It's about the big issues of today – things that people need to get onboard with. It's about changing a broken system. We have to convince them. That's what journalists do. Don't you see that? From Henrik Ibsen to Fredrick Douglas, Harriet Beecher Stowe and Upton Sinclair.

They've all changed the way we look at certain things. *That's* what Pulitzer-class journalism is about, deary. That's what *we're* about!"

"But what I wrote is the truth!" she exclaimed. "The story is about the inner city and families who live on government subsidies."

"Yes, that's right," said the editor. "That's what I approved before you started it."

"But, what I found was that there were a lot of people who really don't need it. They're using the system – manipulating it – like taking a play from an old playbook. They know people who know people who tell them how to do it! It's passed down from generation to generation, almost as if it were an Aztec myth when there was no written language. It could only be transferred by word of mouth. It's really disturbing how much corruption and theft is going on in the system! They're stealing millions – no *billions* – of dollars and the hard-working stiffs out there who have jobs are paying for it with their taxes. No, I stand corrected," she added, "the business owners and the more wealthy are paying for it with taxes at a rate of seventy-five percent. In fact, they pay over ninety percent of all taxes in this country!"

"They can afford it," said the editor. "Anyway, that's not my problem. My objective is to tell a story that fits what I think people need to be told. It has to move the people to action! We're promoting things that change society, not report the news. If you want to be a news reporter, then be a librarian. Maybe that's a better place for you."

Cassie shook her head. "I'm confused. I've been working on this story for a long time – almost two years. So, all along, there was only one way to report on it? Is that what you're saying?"

"Yes. You're young, Cassie. I understand that. You're pretty too. That's really important to me," he said raising his eyebrows.

Cassie had put up with the sexual harassment from Bull for a long time. His real name was Robert Bulstrom, but people just called him Bull. He was about as tall as he was wide. In his early forties and scheduled for a heart attack at any moment. He threw his weight around all the time. Not unattractive, he'd been an all-star football linebacker in college, playing for Tulane University, and had a short stint playing the Baltimore Colts team. Wearing nice but faded khakis and the same elbow-patched, plaid sport coat every day, Bull had carved out his niche in the media world. People looked up to him for his outspoken positions on social injustice and his Robin Hood-approach to wealth distribution.

Cassie rolled her eyes, but Bull was used to that too. *"Oooo,* please!" she answered, turning her head.

"Come on baby!" he said, half serious – half jesting.

"No!" she said, dramatically. "And about the story. I only talked about the *black pepper* that was on the table as I interviewed a single mother of four who's sixth generation welfare. It's not a problem taking it out, that's not the issue. The issue is that I *have* to take it out. The government is telling me I can't say black pepper anymore! I thought we had the First Amendment! I thought we were free to speak our mind as long as we aren't intentionally trying to start or incite a riot."

"But you are."

"What!"

"You are. By saying anything that's on the banned word list you *are* trying to incite a riot."

"No, I'm not!" she replied. "You don't seriously believe that saying anything about pepper is racist? It's just pepper, for God's sake!"

"People look at things through their own prisms. They judge things based on their own life experiences. You learned that in journalism school. That's J101."

"That's true, but it has to be viewed through the eyes of a reasonable man," she said.

"Person," said Bull, correcting her.

"Man – person – hermaphrodite – undecided – whatever!" she said, frustrated with the political correctness. "You're missing my point! It has to be seen through sensibility, not insanity!"

"There are too many viewpoints that we have to be sensitive to these days, I realize. But it would be insensitive *not* to acknowledge them. We are a civilized people – not some group of crass heathens who run amok over everyone and their feelings. We've evolved into better people – at least I have," he said smugly.

"I'm not changing it!" Cassie said, adamantly.

"You will," countered her editor. "Now, bring it back to me with all of the changes, and we'll assess whether it goes into print."

Cassie stared at him. Then she said, "So, you want me to lie about what is really going on with these families – their dependencies on everything else but themselves. They're dependent on government programs, dependent on scamming the system to get more than they're entitled to, dependent on taking everything and anything that's made available to them for free, and dependent on liquor, drugs, and sex."

"Shut up!" shouted Bull. "You're disgusting! How can you say such things?"

"It's the truth!" she said. "Yes, there are the exceptions, and my story covers that aspect as well. But to suggest that all of them are desperately poor, starving, diseased, and barely surviving is false! Patently a lie!"

"Your truth is not the truth we need to tell. It's our truth — my truth — that matters!" said Bull.

"The real truth," Cassie shouted back, "you just don't want to hear it!"

Bull glared at her.

"Anyway, they didn't teach me in college that there were many different kinds of truth. But they did teach me that there were people who lie!" she said.

"Get out of my office!" said Bull, pointing to the door.

Cassie left and sat in her office pod, gazing passed at the panels that surrounded her -- live monitors broadcasting nonstop news from around the nation and the world. Thinking about how hard it would be to find a job when unemployment was actually close to 20 percent, she thought better about throwing it all away. It wasn't so much about changing a few words in a story; it was about spinning the story into pure fiction because it painted an altruistic picture of those less fortunate — showing them as the victims of a repressive society, dominated by greedy capitalists. Demanding accountability and self-responsibility were never an acceptable part of the discussion.

Cassie spent the next several hours rewriting her piece, and when she'd finished she hit the *Send* button. It would be in her editor's hands within seconds. *There,* she thought. *It's done.*

But what she wasn't so sure about was whether she could to continue to manufacture the stories that her boss wanted her to produce. She'd never thought of her company as a manufacturing plant and her position as simply an assembly line worker putting pieces of a pre-designed product together. However, it was becoming more and more clear that it was just that. *Ironic,* she thought, *they demonize mindless production work that enslaves the worker to the whims and demands of the shop owner — yet, that's exactly the kind of world they, themselves, created in their own house.*

*****

PART III – CHANGE IS GOOD

CH 31 USSA

The series of executive orders released from Fourier's desk during the many months leading up to the election had pushed the ministries to the breaking point. The new regulations had been dramatic and earthshaking. Those on the Left heralded the changes as revolutionary and the ultimate solution to pushing the country to a better place – a more humane place. Those on the Right just tried to get their voices heard.

Fourier was late in his second term, and by law his time was running out. It was already 2048, an election year, and his dream of completely transforming the country into the Marxian utopia was still unfulfilled. Unfortunately, it was that pesky matter of the Twenty-second Amendment to the Constitution restricting an elected president to just two terms that troubled him. Ratified in 1951 after the four elections of FDR, the Amendment had been in place to prevent someone from becoming president in perpetuity. The fear was of a dictatorship. But, even the most well-crafted legislation was no match for a bright, articulate, charismatic politician who lacked all morals and whose narcissism reigned unchecked.

It had only been a week since the president's declaration that martial law was necessary to quell the uprisings around the country. He had manifestly stated that he would remove such law and reinstate the election as soon as he had suppressed the violence. Later press releases from the White House clarified that President Fourier 'was concerned about the safety of the American people as they would venture out to the polls. He could not protect all of the polling places and didn't want an incident where someone was injured or killed.'

However, that did not mollify the public, which was growing more uneasy with every new pronouncement. Even the media was becoming queasy about the imposition of martial law and the suspension of the election – something never done before in the history of the Union.

That made the president's emergency call for a press conference all the more ominous. It was lapped up immediately by the major news organizations, as it was rare that such opportunities were afforded to them anymore. Promised the chance to ask the president questions directly, instead of through surrogates, was too good to pass up. So, the conference was blanketed on every frequency, channel and prominent site on Si-net.

An hour late, Fourier strode out to the podium in front of the news media, the dark blue curtains waving behind him. Oddly, there was no presidential seal or American flag stationed on the podium with him.

Reading his pre-prepared script as it was flashed onto his contact lenses, Fourier made it appear that he'd memorized the entire speech – all fifty minutes of it. Yet, he had practiced his delivery, making it all seamless.

"Good afternoon," Fourier began. "I'm here today to reveal the next phase in the ongoing evolution of our democracy. Since the time of the Athenians in the sixth century BCE, the democratic state has undergone tweaking and adjustment. The Romans improved upon the idea just before Caesar was pronounced Emperor. It wasn't until the eighteenth century, when this country resurrected the idea in its ratification of the U.S. Constitution, that democracy re-emerged. Other European countries followed suit, and before long, most of the developed world gravitated toward democracy as their ultimate salvation.

"However, the world was wrong. Democracy was *not* the answer, and we have since discovered that very hard fact. A better way was illuminated two hundred years ago by Hegel, Marx, and Bauer. Communism was a bad word back in the twentieth century, but it was misunderstood and poorly implemented by Lenin in Russia and Mao in China. Its essence is social justice and fairness for all. To care about those less fortunate; to provide for those who cannot provide for themselves; to ensure our children will grow up in a society -- a community -- that joins hands to hold each other up and support each other. For those who are Christians, it is the philosophy they would say Jesus came up with 2000 years ago, that is, 'Take care of thy neighbor.'

"So, today I am proud to announce fundamental changes in our government that further the improvements made in political and economic philosophy during the past three hundred years. No longer must we be saddled with antiquated ways and views. No longer do we have to feel the weight of Stone-Age thinking. We are two hundred years behind the forward thinking of Enlightened Age philosophers who pushed their progressive, socialistic views into society. We are saddled with a constitution that drags us down with democratic ideals. Such antiquated thought must be changed if we are to achieve our own enlightened era.

"To drive us toward the highest level of society, I have mandated that, henceforth, the United States of America will be known as the United Socialist States of America – the USSA. And with this change, we will adopt a new foundational document that is more in alignment with the ideals of Marx and Hegel. I call it *Constitution 2.0*. It will bring this country into the modern era."

There was a gasp in the reporting gallery. But that didn't stop the Fourier.

"Beside me, here, is General Williams, Shontal Williams, my chairperson of the joint chiefs of staff, who has categorically declared her support and that of the USSA military for this action. I also have a mandate from the American people to make fundamental changes to this country -- to make it work again. They want change. And I have vowed to give it to them."

Fearful for expressing their opinions openly, the reporters cowered. It was a feeble and cowardly reaction, but there were no longer any spines in the media regiments. Those with fortitude had long abandoned their journalistic posts. So, it made little difference that they knew nothing of the mobilization of the Red Shirts. Minister Ratner had put them on high alert and moved them into positions at all federal government buildings throughout the country. Armed with M-18 fully automatic rifles, M-2A4 tanks, and M5 Bradley fighting vehicles, the Red Shirts locked down the country. At open stadiums and major downtown areas, the latest Golden Eagle II attack helicopters were called in to dissuade discontent. Armed with shock pulse guns that could shatter eardrums, they were intimidating resources that could easily quell any temptation of rebellion.

"Therefore," continued Fourier inside the press room, "I will be sending before Congress the new *Constitution 2.0* for ratification, which I expect without issue. I have already gotten confirmation from the Supreme Court that it meets their standards for acceptance, and it will not be challenged.

"This historic document and its principles will be widely circulated after the Congress ratifies it. In addition, in keeping with the transformative nature of the new Constitution, I hereby declare that the Office of the President of the United States of America should be more accessible to the people of this country. Their leader should be *of* the people which he serves, not some position on a pedestal. As a result, henceforth, I will be known as the First Citizen Fourier, *not* Mr. President. And the office itself will be referred to as the Office of the First Citizen. The elitist term of 'president' shall no longer be used in connection with me or my office. Is that clear? That's all I have to say today. Thank you."

There was one voice in the group, Cassie Livingston, who was banished to the meaningless post of covering the White House, that broke the silence. "First Citizen Fourier, do you not follow the current Constitution that is in force which specifically requires ratification by the states or a constitutional convention to modify or replace the Constitution?"

Other press members let out a gasp and urgently distanced themselves from Cassie, who was standing with a computer tablet to record the session. Fourier, turned and scowled, but then, just as quickly, replaced the contortion in his face with a faux serenity that looked nearly as unsettling as the first.

"And you are?" he asked insincerely.

"Cassie Livingston from the *Boston Gazette*," she answered bravely.

"Ah, Ms. Livingston. What was it in my press conference that you failed to hear or understand? I thought I was very clear in the need for the actions being taken."

"Perhaps, sir. However, you still haven't explained why and how you are able to circumvent the requirements as outlined within the current document we have called the U.S. Constitution."

Anger rose up in the First Citizen, and his face flushed with a ruddy hue. In an even-keeled voice, he replied, "The current document is failing this country. We need a new set of guidelines that is up-to-date with modern thinking, not something that was thought appropriate in the eighteenth century. Do you not know your history, Ms. Livingston? Do you not know that in 1787, when discussions were held on the drafting of that document that our Founding Forbearers lived in crude and disgusting conditions? They did not have an indoor toilet in the White House until Thomas Jefferson installed two in 1801 or running water until 1833 with Andrew Jackson. Electricity wasn't brought to my home on Pennsylvania Avenue until 1891 with Rutherford B. Hayes. Horses shit in the streets of Washington all the time, and when it rained, Constitution Avenue became a cesspool. That is the era from which such thinking sprung that created the original Constitution, my dear. It is a far distant place from where we have evolved today."

Cassie smiled, "First Citizen Fourier, yes, I do know my history – apparently better than you. Rutherford Hayes was the president after Grant, from 1877 to 1881, not 1891. It was Benjamin Harrison in the White House in 1891. And, by the way, there were no horses and mud on Constitution Avenue. B Street was renamed Constitution Avenue in 1930, well after horses trotted down the streets of D.C."

Fourier exploded. "You're so stupid you just don't see the bigger picture, do you?" he shot back. "This isn't about horse shit! This is about what is good for this country! What I am doing will save this country. I, First Citizen John F Fourier, will be known throughout history as the man who saved America. That's right! John F Fourier! I will make America a truly great nation that all around the world will love. Everyone will want to become just like us. Just like the future of the United Socialist States of America. They will come to me for advice and counsel. *That's* what the future will be, Ms. Livingston – with or without detractors like you!"

Fourier stormed out of the meeting and never looked back.

Cassie closed her computer pad and stuffed everything into her bag. She left the White House, walking through Lafayette Park and toward K Street where her corporate headquarters lay. Once out of sight from the White House grounds, a

D.C. police car pulled up beside her, and the window on the passenger's side dissolved to show the face of an officer, gun drawn. "Get in," he demanded.

"Why? I haven't done anything?" she answered, shocked at the suddenness and boldness of the move so soon after the press conference.

"Get in!" said the policeman again, pushing the button on his gun to charge the electrode.

Cassie thought about running, but then thought better of it. It would only make things worse. She got in the back of the car, and it sped off in the direction of Red Shirt headquarters.

"You can't do this you know," she said from the backseat. There was no answer from the front seat, where two officers sat silently.

The squad car pulled up to the newly built, two billion dollar facility built by the Ministry of Domestic Policing. It was originally estimated to cost 200 million dollars and take two years; however, six years later and at a cost of 2.3 billion dollars, it was still unfinished.

"Get out," said one of the officers, opening the door and holding a set of clear-plastic handcuffs.

Cassie submitted to the order and walked into the building holding her satchel with both handcuffed hands clasped together. "I get a phone call," she said as soon as they got to the processing area.

"Five minutes. That's it," said the lady behind the desk, working to shape and color her fingernails.

Cassie contacted her boss who grudgingly made some calls. She was out on bond within the hour, but Bull put her on probation. He didn't want to fire her unless he had to, as government rules required he pay her an extensive severance and all benefits. No, he would try to let things blow over and, perhaps, give her just one last chance to save herself and her job.

"You're on probation, Cassie. And, when you get back – you'll do the beat – downtown Boston, parks and recreation. That's it! You can't screw that up! If you report anything but cold streams, green grass and blue skies, I'll personally kick your ass from here to Cheyenne!"

"Yes, sir," Cassie had answered, grateful to have one more chance. It was hard for her, though. She was a rebel at heart, and muzzling her only made that rebellious spirit want freedom that much more.

Fourier had left the podium with a grin on his face. He knew there would be no more challenges. He had the Red Shirts, the USSA military, his own party in power on the Hill, and loyal ministers who would do whatever he asked to keep their powerful jobs. For those on the fence, he had directed the Bureau of Internal Policing to dig up everything they could that could be used as blackmail. His files were stuffed full of incriminating evidence that assured his enemies and those who were undecided would toe the line.

But, even with the meticulous planning, it was an old, now-deeply underground blog that brought details to light about what Fourier really had planned for America. Details about *Constitution 2.0* were leaked, and the information set-off a firestorm, going viral in minutes. Those who could get the website did, and those who were blocked got it from those who weren't.

DrudgeUnderground

> *OpEd:*
>
> *The Fourier Administration just declared the end of the United States of America. It has replaced the USA with the United Socialist States of America – the USSA ... In connection with that change, it is pushing a new constitution on all of us called Constitution 2.0. We can only imagine what it will say, perhaps:*
>
> > *We the People of the United Socialist States, in Order to form a perfect dictatorship, establish Justice for some, insure Domestic Tranquility for all including illegal alien criminals, provide for the Government's defense at all costs, promote Welfare for as many as possible, and Secure Liberty for those worthy of such distinction, do ordain and establish this Constitution of the United Socialist States of America ...*
>
> *We can only assume that if there is a Bill of Rights (the first ten Amendments) that there will be notable differences. What was formerly known as the First Amendment will most likely omit all reference to religion, even though many doubt that freedom of the press or assembly has existed for some time. The Second Amendment will most assuredly be gone, opening the door to the confiscation of citizenry arms.*
>
> *More troubling would be the omission of the fourth, fifth and sixth amendments, protecting us from unreasonable search and seizure, self-incrimination and a jury of our peers. Yet, we can't imagine they would eliminate the Tenth Amendment, which gave all powers not enumerated for the federal government to the states. Even that change would be too far reaching for even this government. Wouldn't it?*

But, something must be done! If we don't fight this, there is no hope for this country. As Fourier has stated, we are no longer the United States of America; we are now the USSA – the Useless Sorry State of America. E Pluribus Unum could not have been more prescient than it is today.

By Publius the Resurrected

*****

CH 32 Shining City on a Hill

Congress quickly ratified the First Citizen's proposed *Constitution 2.0*, violating in every way the mandates setup under the first constitution for how any change to that document could be legally made. Instead, the original 1791 U.S. Constitution, as amended, was eviscerated in its entirety.

In its place was a document unrecognizable as compared with those principles upon which the country was founded. Most damning was the Tenth Amendment.

As most feared by the *DrudgeUnderground*, the Tenth Amendment was the most far-reaching of all others.

AMENDMENT X.

All other powers not specifically enumerated within this constitution are hereby granted to the executive branch, the Directorate. All rights formerly left to the states are hereby superseded and subordinated to the federal government. Any laws of any state that conflicts with that of the Union shall be null and void. All laws, both state and municipal, must be congruent to those of the federal government in meaning and spirit.

That amendment alone shook the country. It essentially emasculated the states, taking away any vestige of states' rights. Although not dissolved, the states no longer had any ability to function independently of Washington. And, if ministries were needed to ensure this, there were plenty of them being created to monitor each and every one of them.

Sumner's old party fought the ratification, but without any meaningful representation on Capitol Hill, it was a moot point. The People's Party was the only party now. It could do as it wanted, when it wanted. Some would refer to it as a dictatorial party, but others shied from that characteristic, favoring instead the phrase, "the dominant party." Once adopted, the new constitutional measures were quickly implemented. New ministries were formed within days to deal with the stricter regulations and the usurpation of power from the states. Federalism was no more. Overnight, the fifty states imploded into one – the new, USSA.

As for Minister Ratner, she was placed on an inner circle committee, called the Sixth Column. It was in reference to the Fifth Column, a term that was used widely in Spain to describe a group working on the inside against a government that was dominating them. The Sixth Column represented a cut above this Fifth Column, suggesting dominance over anyone who dared challenge the mandates of the First Citizen.

The Sixth Column had supreme power over the changes and would be challenged only by the express authority of Number One – First Citizen Fourier. What he approved or disapproved was the final word on virtually everything. There was no other – only him.

The shock waves roiled the country, but were suppressed. Anyone who criticized Fourier was subject to immediate arrest and imprisonment. Most would be sent off to sanitariums for a mental evaluation, as it was believed that one must be insane to object to what the First Citizen was doing for the good of the country. To enforce this, the states' National Guard units were converted into Red Shirts. These units added to the swelling numbers of Red Shirts already on the payroll. These new brigades were deployed in every neighborhood across the country to keep the peace. In reality, they were thugs, recruited for their ability to be brutal and show force quickly to suppress resistance. Local police were subordinated to them or eliminated entirely. In many ways, this group was more powerful than the USSA military, which had been starved of resources for years and was no longer able to project power anywhere in the world.

The Red Shirts were the new Stasi. They were the unchallenged police force of the Fourier Administration.

***

"Tonight we begin the news with a story about a mother who finally got what she's been looking for after twenty years," said the news anchor on a seldom-watched government news station. Dan Redolencia was the aging, yet familiar voice on the nightly broadcast. His stories were usually light and colorful, void of any hard hitting edge that used to characterize the evening's national news broadcasts. Now, the less controversy, the better.

"Martina Vazquez and her nine children have always wondered what happened to their father. As for the children, they are all grown -- each with at least four or five children of their own. Martina sits in her government-provided apartment searching for answers as to where her husband went those many years ago."

The story dragged on for another twelve minutes, taking up much of the news broadcast air time. "Finally," added Dan, "Martina search ended late last week when the government informed her that her husband was, in fact, a hero. He had enlisted in the army and had served his country with distinction. He had been killed nearly twenty years earlier during an act of workplace violence that claimed his and sixteen other lives. He was gunned down at his military base by a fellow soldier who was not authorized to carry a gun on the base. This is just another example of how guns kill," said the anchorman, emphasizing the point.

In reality, Martina's husband had been a deadbeat dad who had abandoned his family when he was sought by the police for not paying child support. He had escaped detection at an army recruitment office and signed up to hide from authorities for a while. Fully planning on deserting his post when things cooled down, he worked on a military base in the accounting department. There he was mercilessly gunned down by an Islamic terrorist. The terrorist had murdered five other soldiers at the same time before turning the gun on himself. This, then, was the new definition of a *national hero*.

The real news of the day was buried. It was the massive protests going on in many cities around the country. People were upset about the power grab by the White House and the dissolution of all the rights they had ever enjoyed – virtually overnight. Tanks had been rolled into these cities, directed by the Red Shirts, and many people had been shot. The casualty figures rose into the hundreds, then the thousands, before the government was able to get things under control. There was no need to publicize the embarrassment, and the news media obediently complied. Softened by years of sycophantism, the pool of reporters covering the White House no longer had the stomach to fight a losing battle. Instead, they chose to join the other side. It was easier that way, and there were fewer casualties. Reporters slept better at night, and so did their families. It was a matter of survival, and everyone knew it. So, no news was good news.

Sumner turned off the broadcast in disgust. He only tuned in occasionally to see how pusillanimous the news had become. He was fully aware of the outbursts arising across the country, and he wanted to see how deeply the news media would bury it. In this case, it was worse than even he thought possible. There was *no* mention of any unrest – none at all.

Even though Sumner's body was nearly healed from his harrowing experience in D.C., his psyche was becoming increasingly traumatized by the bold, unapologetic usurpation of raw power at the federal level. He was in his sixties, and by the charts, he could expect to live another sixty years. But, he wondered whether it would be a life worth living and bemoaned, not his own fate, but those of his children, grandchildren and especially his great grandchildren. Certainly, he knew, it would not be the same land of plenty – the land of opportunity – that he and his ancestors had enjoyed.

"What's wrong, dear?" asked Maria, coming into the room. "Is there anything I can get you?"

"A new government," Sumner responded.

Maria patted him on the shoulder. "I know. It isn't what we thought we would have when we were young, is it?"

"No."

She sat down next to him and placed her hand on his knee. "When you were in high school, what did you think this country would be like in forty years?"

It had been a long time since he had thought about that. Those were memories that he had stored away, deep in the recesses of his mind, not thinking that he would ever have to pull them out again.

"Wow, that's, uh, well," he stammered. "I guess I ... I guess I haven't really thought about it in a long, long time."

"Sure you have," answered his wife. "Maybe not consciously, but unconsciously."

"You're probably right, Maria. Well, then, I'd have to say that I thought it wouldn't be that much different than when we grew up. You never really expect things to change for the worse. Perhaps it was that viral disease of American optimism that I had. I always thought we'd all be living like the old *Jetson's* cartoon of the 1960s – you know – space age. Everything would be perfect, clean, and orderly. And that was supposed to be only twenty years from now. Reagan even talked about it in one of his acceptance speeches at his party's nominating convention. He called America's future the Shining City on a Hill. Obviously, it was altruistic, but when you're eighteen, the world *can* be anything you want it to be, I guess." He paused for moment and then asked, "What about you? What did you think?"

Maria looked away wistfully. "You'll laugh."

"No I won't. Tell me."

"I was actually really worried about other countries at the time, like China. I thought they would spread their communism far and wide by now and that we'd be fighting a world war against them."

"Boy, that was certainly deep thinking for an eighteen-year-old," said Sumner. "You were worried about the Red Menace way back then?"

"Yeah. I thought that with a couple billion people, you could afford to put up a huge army against us, and even if they lost millions, they would still have plenty left over to keep fighting. That was the way their regime ran – they didn't really care how many they had to sacrifice."

"That's why I married you," said Sumner, smiling. "I always knew who had the brains in this family." He laughed.

"You better believe it!" she said, giving him a big, fat kiss on the lips. "And that's why I married you."

"Why? Because I'm a deep thinker?"

"No, because you humor me every once in a while, JC." She too was grinning and kissed him again. "I'm going upstairs. Do you feel like making love tonight?" she asked him.

"With a request like that, how can I turn you down." He took her hand, and together she helped him up the wide staircase to their bedroom.

Once inside, Maria closed the door behind her. The night was bliss as they rekindled their love. Their passion had never really left them, but it had taken a holiday while he was in Congress and while he had begun his quest to build GOFLA. His close call in D.C. had been a wake-up call. Maria meant more to Sumner than anything else in his life. This night, Maria and he would revel in their feelings for each other. It would be glorious. But it would end, and daybreak would come. It was just the way of the world.

*****

CH 33 The Little Red Book

Until after Congress passed *Constitution 2.0*, no one leaked its contents. It was kept secret with the ominous threat of imprisonment for anyone who breathed a syllable of it. There was no debate of the measure in committee or when it was sent to the floor of either the House or Senate, as the motion was pushed through quickly from start to finish.

Once passed, the First Citizen signed it into existence. Many hailed it as the most far-reaching and monumental document since the Magna Carta. Eventually, its provisions were made public, and these, then, would be the new laws by which all Americans would have to live.

But rather than having an extravagant premier to showcase the new constitution to American society, the White House opted for a low-key approach. Not wanting to rile the public any more than they already were, the Administration hatched a scheme to post the document in bits and pieces, one section at a time, during the course of two weeks.

The first SI-net post read:

> *The U.S.S. Constitution 2.0 hereby replaces the U.S. Constitution of 1790, as amended. As such, the First Citizen has ordered all copies of the old Constitution to be burned. Our National Archives has already destroyed the original U.S. Constitution and replaced it with the new one, signed by our First Citizen and every member of Congress. It now resides in the glass vault in the National Archives in Washington, D.C. for all to see.*

> *By Executive Decree, the U.S.S. Constitution 2.0 shall have the full force and effect of law and cannot be overturned or countermanded by either the Legislative or the Judicial Branch without unanimous consent of each membership.*

> *The following is the first post in a series that will inform the populace of its   mandates.*

U.S.S.A. CONSTITUTION

> ***"Be it Known to All in the Land:*** *We, the multiethnic people of the United Socialist States of America, united by a common fate on our land, establishing human rights and freedoms, civic peace and accord, preserving the historically established state unity, proceeding from the universally recognized principles of equality and self-determination of peoples, revering the memory of ancestors who have conveyed to us the*

love for the Motherland, belief in the good and justice, reviving the sovereign statehood of America and asserting the firmness of its democracy, striving to ensure the well-being and prosperity of the country, proceeding from the responsibility for our Motherland before the present and future generations, recognizing ourselves as part of the world community, adopt the CONSTITUTION OF THE UNITED SOCIALIST STATES OF AMERICA.

"Article 1. The UNITED SOCIALIST STATES OF AMERICA is a socialist state under the people's democratic leadership led by the working class and based on the alliance of workers, the disadvantaged, and the poor. The socialist system is the basic system of the nation. Sabotage of the socialist system by any organization or individual is prohibited.

Article 2. All power in the UNITED SOCIALIST STATES OF AMERICA belongs to the People. The organs through which the People exercise state power are the National People's Congress and the local people's congresses at different levels. The People administer state affairs and manage economic, cultural and social affairs through various channels and in various ways in accordance with the law.

Article 3. The state organs of the UNITED SOCIALIST STATES OF AMERICA apply the principle of democratic centralism. The National People's Congress and the local people's congresses at different levels are instituted through democratic election. They are responsible to the People and subject to their supervision. All administrative, judicial and procuratorial organs of the State are created by the people's congresses to which they are responsible and under whose supervision they operate. The division of functions and powers between the central and local state organs is guided by the principle of giving full play to the initiative and enthusiasm of the local authorities under the unified leadership of the central authorities."

The posting ran on for hundreds of pages before ending. There were ten postings in all, eventually disclosing the contents of over five thousand pages of laws and statutes to be obeyed. Unlike the original document, this constitution went far beyond providing a general framework. Similar to most other legislation of the time, it was wrapped in arcane and intentionally confusing language that made it difficult to decipher.

However, the most important aspects of the proclamation were:

First, the Socialist State of the federal government consisted of an executive branch, renamed the *Directorate*, with the power to pass and execute laws of the land. The First Citizen was responsible for ensuring that all laws would be consistent with the new Constitution and that the laws were fairly imposed on all segments of society, regardless of race, gender, religion, age, ethnicity, or any other heterogeneous characteristic of the constituent. There was no longer be a vice president, or Second Citizen. Instead, succession would be based on the priority of each ministry and its minister.

The Legislative Branch was reduced to a single chamber, to be known as the National People's Congress or NPC. It would be determined by the people through supposedly free and open elections, held every ten years. The NPC would then duly select the First Citizen to the Directorate. The NPC would be the prime advisory body that counseled the First Citizen on matters of domestic and foreign policy and would work with the First Citizen to craft appropriate legislation to carry-out the needs and wishes of the people.

The Judicial Branch was renamed the Supreme People's Court or SPC. Its membership was reduced from nine to three-members and appointed for ten-year terms by the First Citizen. The SPC would consider any challenges to laws not deemed consistent with the new constitution and merely advise the First Citizen of incongruities. It had no power to overturn law.

As a check and balance on the First Citizen, the Constitution 2.0 provided for the NPC and SPC to have the power to remove with First Citizen with their unanimous consent, together with that of the Central Military Commission or CMC, which was overseen by the First Citizen. Of course, this provision had intentionally been made weak.

Second, all property would be owned by the people. However, as the people's representative, the State would act as custodian for all such property, which included real estate, mineral rights, buildings and structures, transportation facilities and conveyances, such as rail, air, ground, and shipping. As custodian, the State would manage the ecological, economic, and social needs of the nation and its people. Most importantly, the State would take ownership of all intellectual property created within the country. It was believed that these assets should be owned collectively, not individually.

Third. A progressive tax would be implemented to redistribute the wealth of the country. This section of the document ran on and on, detailing all of the new taxes to be imposed. At the end, it added a final nail in the coffin of bequeathing wealth from generation to generation, stating that "tax law should ensure equality amongst the people." It proclaimed a wealth tax on individuals and any entity created to avoid this tax, whereby any net worth exceeding one hundred thousand dollars would be taxed at 99 percent. Thereby, it read, "wealth created on the backs of others shall be reallocated to those in greater need."

Fourth. As unions were deemed "a critical component of balance to equalize the power of management with the powerless laborer," and every industry and company would be required to have a union presence. Henceforth, all labor would be required to belong to a formal labor union and be forced to pay union dues. Such dues would be divided between union leaders and the current-ruling party in power – the People's Party.

Fifth. All citizens would submit to a recordation chip. The implanted device was 'intended only for the protection of our citizens and would make location by federal authorities easier should one require rescue from a serious threat.' However, there was no provision made for an agency to act as a central monitoring station if any SOS signals were to be issued by the chips.

Sixth. All commercial businesses not already absorbed by the State would be nationalized. Only those under two employees would be exempt.

Seventh. Government control of all servers and nodes pertaining to the SuperInternt, or SI-net, would be strengthened. Going forward, all broadcast frequencies, airwaves, and web sites on SI-net, including frequency hopping devices and websites, would be controlled by the State. Information would be regulated by the Ministry of Electromagnetic Wavelength and Digital Sources and approved by the ministry prior to release. This was done to ensure 'the content was appropriate and not offensive to anyone in our society.' Political correctness was paramount and the government said it did not want the release of anything that might "cause emotional and psychological damage to one of our citizens."

Eighth. Because of the complexity of the issues of the day and to reduce the cost of elections, the people's voices would be heard decennially, or once every ten years, in the year a new census was taken. The people would vote on the members of the NPC but that all candidates would be vetted through the Ministry of Federal Elections to ensure they were qualified.

Ninth. The definition of citizenry had become blurred during the previous decades, and as such, the government believed it was no longer necessary to distinguish between people living within the country. This, after all, had been discriminatory against those who were not citizens. As a result, anyone living within the country would be considered citizens, with full rights and privileges. Even foreign tourists entering the country on holiday could, hypothetically, vote and even collect government food stamps or welfare checks if they registered and stayed long enough.

Tenth. States' Rights. Most dramatically, the new constitution drastically reduced the power of the states. There were no longer any areas excluded from federal law or reach. Education, elections, motor vehicles, and many other areas now came under the authority of Washington. Thereafter, any state or local law that did not comply with a federal law passed on the subject was deemed null and void.

The details of the new constitution with its volumes of interpretations were eventually disseminated far and wide. Even though a gigantic mass of pages and words, the entire abomination was referred to as Chairman Fourier's *Little* Red Book. It was irony at its best.

Intentionally, Fourier had made the entire document very convoluted. But with its ambiguity came opportunity.

***

Ratner left the White House after a meeting with the First Citizen to brief him on the success of the new Constitution's roll-out. She had never felt better in her entire life. It was the penultimate point in her career, playing out just as she'd planned. Yes, things were good for the minister. She was now Number Three on the succession list – with Bailey Griffin, head of taxation, as Number Two.

That night, Ratner had a dinner appointment. She summoned her driver, who pulled up outside her lavish Georgetown townhouse at exactly 7:03.

"What the hell is wrong with you?" she screamed at her driver, Winston, an older gentleman who had worked for six administrations. He was used to abuse, but being Minister Ratner's driver had been a near death-sentence for him. He was frail and becoming increasingly so. Yet, he needed his job, as Medicare and Social Security programs had run out of money long ago, leaving nothing for those of whom they had promised to take care.

In his kind and gentle voice, he said, "Good evening, Minister Ratner. And where are we off to tonight, ma'am?"

She looked back at him with a scowl on her face and said gruffly, "You're late! You were supposed to be here three minutes ago!" She waited for him to get the door for her, and she hopped in, pulling in her fifty thousand dollar, black designer gown, made by the old firm of Armani. "And if you're ever late again, you're fired!" she added.

"Yes, ma'am," he said, without emotion. Winston continued to smile even though he feared that someday she would carry out her threat. She was unpleasant and mean – ungrateful at best. He worked hard for her – being there to pick her up at seven-thirty even though she rarely appeared before eight-fifteen. Usually having to go without lunch, he waited for her at night after running her personal errands all day. Then, he would drive her home, sometimes as late as eleven o'clock. She never let him put in for overtime, as that would look bad on her budget. It was illegal too, but she didn't care. No one would challenge her. At Thanksgiving, she made it up to him by sending his family a four-pound ham. A nice gesture, but they were Kosher Jewish.

The ride to the five-star, Italian restaurant in Bethesda was short, but he would have to park the limo and wait for her to finish – usually two or more hours. He often wondered where she got all of her money to do the things and buy the things she did. Government salaries were high, but not in the millions. She spent money like it came from a spout in her kitchen. He just didn't know, but then again, he wasn't sure he wanted to.

At midnight, she sent him a message to pick her up outside the restaurant. He pulled to the curb outside the café, and she climbed into the black limo, moving over so that the woman she was with could hop in next to her.

"Where to, ma'am?" he asked.

"Home, James," Ratner said. She was drunk, and by the looks of it, so was the other woman. In the backseat, they giggled like school girls, but he couldn't understand a thing they said.

Winston steered the limo over to the curb in front of her townhouse and jumped out to open their door. Both got out, and the woman staggered up to the double walnut door that elegantly guarded the entrance to the minister's home.

"Will there be anything else, ma'am?" he asked.

"Yes, Winston. I need you to drop this letter off with Minister Griffin," she said, handing him a paper envelope. It was unusual using paper in an age when everything was sent via computer. "You need to do this tonight. But you also need to pick me up tomorrow morning at six. I have to go to the gym to work-out after what I ate tonight. Be here then."

"But, tomorrow is Saturday, minister. I had plans with my grandson to …"

Ratner shot him another look that could have melted the steel off the Memorial Bridge. "I told you to be here. So be here!" she shouted. She slammed the door and ran up behind her friend, pinching her on the butt.

Winston traipsed back to the driver's side and opened his door. He pulled out his aging version of a PCD and pushed some buttons. The phone on the other end rang, but an answering service came on -- " ... and leave your message at the beep," it said.

"Martha, it's Winston. I know you're probably in bed, but something's come up. I won't be able to take Zack to the game tomorrow for his birthday. I'm really sorry. I'll call you when I can. I love you and tell Zack I promise to make it up to him."

Winston hung up the phone. He sighed. He was unsure how much longer he could do this. His personal battery was low, and at his age it was difficult to recharge it. *I'll make it up to him,* he thought. *But then, who was he kidding?* The minister would not give him a few hours to himself, let alone an entire day. She had become his master, and he her servant. This was not the way it was supposed to be.

*****

CH 34 Riotous Reaction

The public reaction to the Constitution 2.0 was inexplicably divided. Approximately 52 percent of the people cheered it. Thrilled with the prospect of being equal with the 'haves' against whom they'd fought for years and hated for their wealth and comfort, the Takers of society could hardly contain themselves. *Finally, we will be rich too – just like the one percenters,* was their thinking. *Social justice is finally ours!* This was just what they had wanted all these years.

That left the other 48 percent, who were self-made Americans. They believed in themselves, not the government, to create their own opportunities. And, they were the ones who would feel the pain. They would be the ones paying for the free lunch enjoyed by the other 52, and they were resentful. In addition, all of their accumulated wealth would be gone – ripped from them by their own government, like a mob shakedown of the 1930s.

At first, the 48 sat on their hands, fuming and irate. They usually held their anger when they had much to fear and so much to lose from defying the government. Defiance had become a traitorous act, and they risked losing everything – their jobs, their possessions, and even their families – if they had engaged in it. Now, they had – lost it all. The government had become all powerful – everything *would* be taken away. There was no longer an *if* or a *when*. There was little left to fear, except the possibility of having their lives taken away as well.

However, as the economy collapsed from the Unity Plan and *Constitution 2.0*, more people were thrown out of work, and the lines for government benefits lengthened. Waiting times for the handouts grew longer as patience grew shorter. Even the 52 began to rethink their support. Healthcare had plunged to new depths of deprivation. An opening for an appointment with a government doctor, if one could get one at all, was on average a year to eighteen months away.

But even as people lost their jobs and the mortality rate climbed, the labor statistics continued to show a robust economy. It was miraculous that the Ministry of Facts and Statistics persisted in its claim that only 2.3 percent of the population was unemployed. The number, according to FAES, had grown to 32 percent and was climbing rapidly. Many who worked could only find part-time jobs, as their hours had been cut as a result of the Unity Plan. Equal pay for all meant those who produced less, worked less. Instead of the usual forty hours, they were now cut to just eight or sixteen. Not only had their pay rate not gone up as promised by the Unity Plan, but their hours had fallen dramatically, leaving them far less than they had before. They had turned to government benefits for the bailout, and many had quit work entirely, cashing in on more benefits than they would get if they continued to work part-time. But eventually, the gravy train was running out of fuel. Tax revenues were drying up, even though the tax rates were nearly 80% on average. Fourier's policies of equalizing the rich and poor was coming to fruition. Everyone was – or was becoming -- poor.

The pot was boiling with the lid on. It was only a matter of time before the lid would come off.

***

On April 19, it boiled over. It took place merely ninety miles from Boston, in Springfield, where rebellion had a long history. Illegally armed with guns and clubs, a group of over two hundred amassed in front of the USSA District Courthouse. Just down from where another rebellion had taken place at the Armory nearly three hundred years earlier, the courthouse was an aging building, constructed earlier in the century when funds were more abundant.

Although the Red Shirts arrived quickly in their armored military personnel carriers (APCs), initiators of the protest had notified more than half the town of the spontaneous assembly via social media. Nearly as fast as the Red Shirts could begin mobilizing paddy wagons to haul off the criminals, more people showed up. Within thirty minutes, the crowd had grown to over five hundred.

"We need more backup!" shouted the Red Shirt Brigade (RSB) commander, speaking into his army-com PCD. Dressed in the RSB uniform – a blood red shirt with the RSB insignia on the front pocket, skinny black tie, and a single-silver commander bar on each shoulder. "I need at least fifty wagons and another company of members," he said, referring to about a hundred more RSB recruits.

"Roger that," came the reply.

But the backup never came. Instead, the commander had to make do with the small company of men he had with him. With orders from the White House to subdue and disperse crowds that were unruly, the RSB generally used rubber bullets that were seldom lethal. However, many platoon members had begun to bring their own lead bullets in case they felt threatened – at least that was the reasoning they used. But in fact, members of the RSB were barely vetted or not vetted at all before being given a badge and power, and they weren't afraid to use them. These were known as the "punks" – ill-tempered recruits, undisciplined and itching for a fight anyplace they could find one. Ratner had wanted a million Red Shirts in her army, and they only way to get them was to hire anyone who applied. Pressuring Fourier, she had gotten him to clear-out the prisons. It had been a good excuse to purge federal corrections facilities of their crushing overpopulation and champion the rights of those less privileged at the same time. Everyone won – everyone except the public, that is.

"Damn it!" yelled the commander, watching the crowd carefully for any sign of violence or anything he deemed 'could lead to violence.' "We have to deal with these traitors!" he exclaimed nervously, his eyes shifting back-and-forth across the scene.

As the APCs began circling around the courthouse building, blocking off State Street and other key avenues to and from the area, the protestors began chanting: "Down with Fourier!" and "Give us back our freedom!"

Unlike the supporting rallies organized by the White House, this group held up signs that were crude and had been quickly assembled. Some had obvious misspellings and others were coming apart as they were pumped up and down and swung sideways to get the attention of passersby.

To the commander's chagrin, it was the media vans and not RSB backup that rolled up to see what was going on. At first, the reporters had been directed to the scene hoping for a violent outburst by those gathered. This could be used to show the truly dangerous nature of the people who were protesting Washington. Made to look like crazed, unprincipled thugs, the rebels could be marginalized and labeled outcasts – people to be demonized, not emulated. However, try as the RSB might to provoke the crowd, they couldn't ignite an explosive incident.

Directed by their corporate overseers to leave, most of the journalists departed, putting their vans in reverse and driving back up the same roads from which they'd come. *There is no story there,* they were told. *Let's not waste our time.* But shockingly, a few reporters stayed in defiance of what their bosses were ordering them to do. And, they let their cameras roll. These journalists knew their careers could be over because of what they were doing, but they had become just as incensed as the other 48 at what was happening. They were the true journalists at heart – wanting to report the real story, instead of being mere propaganda mouthpieces. They were in the minority, but they were determined to stay at their posts to cover whatever happened. *If not then, then when? If not them, then who?* they were heard saying later from their prison cells.

The energy of the protestors was also growing. Spurred on by a loudspeaker, the group listened to the words spoken by their *de facto* leader, Thomas Dorr.

"We are here only to make our voices heard," Dorr said. "We have *not* come to disturb the peace or clash with police. Ours is a peaceful demonstration. But what we have to say must be heard by the White House. American society was born out of revolution, yet it was necessary at the time because King George would not listen to his subjects. The same is true today ... King Fourier will not listen to us! Yet, there are huge differences between then and now. Fourier is *not* our king and we are *not* Fourier's subjects! He does not rule, but for the will of the people. It is not Fourier who bestows the rights of men, it is God. Our inalienable rights do not come at the whim of a first, second or a last citizen ... they come from the Almighty."

The screaming became more vociferous, and the faces of other men and women who came to join the confrontation looked strained and reddened with anger as they listened.

"Fourier's a murderer!" shouted one woman, raising a wooden pole with Fourier's picture on a poster – marked through with red ink.

"We demand our rights!" yelled another. "Our Founders would roll over in their graves!"

Dorr tried to settle them. "We do not call for revolution or armed rebellion. We only ask for free and fair elections to be held and that the original U.S. Constitution be restored. What has happened has been illegal and the American people have the right to take back their country. We were given that right by our Founders – those brave men who were willing to give up their lives for freedom; by our ancestors who died in the two great wars defending our liberties and those around the world; by those earlier in this century who were willing to fight against radical Islamic darkness, which has taken over vast amounts of the world and its population. We are still fighting for our rights after nearly three hundred years!"

"Get ready to open fire," said the RSB commander showing no emotion. He had heard the singular word *fighting* and had decided that was all he needed to declare the gathering a threat to the government. Borderline sociopathic, he cared little for others – more interested in his ability to control others and bend them to his will than reconcile with them.

The APCs were brought around all sides of the courthouse and the turrets trained on the unruly mass in front of them. The guns ranged between the standard 12.7mm Mauser machine gun to the larger 25mm Bushmaster Model 4, but their capability of more than twenty thousand rounds per minute was more than enough to shred everything in their path with devastating effect.

The RSB commander believed that the mere presence of his APCs should have been enough warning to anyone protesting. *There is little need,* he thought, *to announce my intentions. They deserve what's coming.* "On my count, fire on anything that moves."

Then, he gave the order. "Fire!"

At first, only a few APCs began their lethal barrage of lead on the unsuspecting group. Then, after their commander threatened the rest with execution if they didn't fire, they joined the onslaught. It only lasted a few minutes, but that was enough time. When the members of the Red Brigade peered through the smoky haze around them, even they were in shock.

There was a sea of blood and body parts scattered all over what had been a carpet of green grass around the district building only moments earlier. Hundreds lay dead. Hundreds more lay wounded. Many were unrecognizable as human beings – their arms, legs, and even heads ripped from their owners and either disintegrated by the hail of shells or splattered over the pavement and nearby shrubbery.

Anyone who could run from the carnage did so. They ran like hell was nipping at their heels – and it was. Those who could hobble did the best they could, and those who could only crawl, tried to claw their way as far as they could from the barbarians sitting inside their heavily protected military machinery.

And, it was all captured on digital recorders.

Those journalists who had stayed sat in shock. Never before had they witnessed a mass execution like what had just happened. Several reporters who had been interviewing protesters when the shots rang out were also killed, their mikes on and their cameras rolling up to the point that a shell ended their live feed.

Fearing for their lives, the other journalists packed up quickly and left before the guns were trained on them. Although some were trying to stream their coverage live, the feeds were shut down immediately once the assault began. Unfortunately, those same roads that had offered them free passage in, were now blocked by the Red Shirts. They were to make sure no one left, especially anyone with incriminating evidence. In fact, no one was allowed in or out. The area around the courthouse was roped off within a two-square mile radius and a synthetic canopy was suspended overhead to prevent satellite or drone surveillance from spying on the activities below.

The Red Shirts made quick dispatch of the remaining protestors who had not fled, but did not kill the reporters who stood, huddled by their news wagons, trembling and terrified that the guns would be leveled at them next. Instead, they were herded into prison buses and driven off to some undisclosed location.

However, there was one reporter who defied the odds. When her camera crew had been obliterated by a spray of BushMaster lead, she had pulled the digital tape from the dead cameraman's equipment and run off with it down the street, hiding inside an abandoned storage facility. Three days, she had waited while dogs had sniffed around the building and the Red Shirts had searched every structure, looking for anyone who was still hiding. Once the paramilitary crews had left, she had gotten out, catching a bus to a friend's apartment that was on the outskirts of town.

Cassie Livingston knew her life was in danger, and soon learned that the images on the tape she carried were invaluable. She listened to the media reports, but the only word about what happened in Springfield Mass was that there had been a warehouse explosion that had killed many people who had gathered for a town celebration at the district courthouse nearby. The blame was squarely cast on the owners of the warehouse, who were summarily arrested. It would be weeks before the young reporter was able to return to her own home in Boston.

Cassie took secondary streets to get back to her two-story brownstone, a place she had rented for more than four years while she worked at the news agency. She didn't have much inside. Sparse of furniture and anything else of value, the place had merely been a place to sleep from one AM to five AM when she would have to return to work. The hours were hellish, but until recently, the work had been gratifying. Being reassigned to parks and recreation had been a banishment worse than death for her. Violating her parameters for reporting, she had seen the notices about the gathering in Springfield from her heavy involvement on social media outlets. She had convinced some camera crew friends to join her – *It will be fun*, she had said. Now, she was grief-stricken at the thought that it was her fault that her friends were dead.

After stuffing clothes into her backpack and stashing some money credits she had put aside as savings, Cassie hurried toward the front door of the house. It was then that she could hear the squealing of tires outside as the patrol cars began surrounding the house.

"Come out!" shouted a policewoman. "We know you have information we want. We will not hurt you if you come out now and give us the tape. You have our word."

"Bull sh*t!" Cassie muttered under her breath, clutching the small disc in her fingers.

The brownstone had been renovated many times and had stood defiantly against the wrecking ball several more times through the years as different developers had wanted to tear it down to make room for a new entertainment arcade or shopping mall. Initially constructed at the time of the Civil War, it had been intended as a safe house to protect slaves that had escaped bondage from the south and traveled north via Harriet Tubman's underground railroad. As a result, it had corridors leading to-and-fro through the underground pathways that had linked the house to various orchards, waterways, groves and other areas that had provided cover for its occupants when needed. Most of the surrounding orchards and groves were long gone, but the passageways remained, and some still offered an escape elsewhere in a neighboring community.

Cassie slipped out through one of the tunnels, climbing up and into an abandoned water shed not far from the house. It was dark, and she feared using anything that would create a light to draw attention to herself in case they were canvassing the entire area. Although the reception was not good, she opened her PCD. "Make a call," she commanded. She knew that she risked being instantly traced, but she had to find help. Everyone she knew had either been killed, arrested or she didn't trust.

The number that she highlighted on her PCD was one she had never before contacted. It had been in her list for years, and she'd never used it as a reporter or for any other reason. She had heard things about the person, and only based on that, she dialed.

The line rang three, four, five times. Then finally, a voice …

"Hello?"

"Hello? Is this Congressman Sumner?" she asked frantically.

"Yes, this is he. Who is this?"

"I'm Cassie Livingston, a reporter for the *Boston Gazette* …"

"I'm sorry, but …" said Sumner.

"No! Don't hang up! Please!"

"Okay, but I don't talk to reporters," he said patiently.

"This is not about a story … well it is … but it's not what you think," she said, stumbling over her words. "I need to talk to you right away. I was in Springfield, Mass. Do you know what happened there?"

There were a series of clicking noises on the line, audible to both parties.

"I can't talk right now. I'll have to call you back," said Cassie, panicked.

"Ms. Livingston, how will I be able to reach you?" asked Sumner, sensing their line was being recorded.

"You can't. I'll call you." Cassie hung up. She knew they would be able to triangulate her call within minutes. She had to run, and run fast. If she didn't, there would be no point to her risking all she had known to get the information out to the public. It would all die and most likely die with her.

*****

222

CH 35 Springfield Leak

Sumner began to worry. He hadn't heard from Ms. Livingston, as he referred to her, for several days. He had looked into the Springfield incident, but all he could find were stories on the warehouse and the explosion. There were pictures included, but Sumner could see that they were pictures of different burning buildings – they didn't match the surroundings of other pictures of the area taken before the fire. Even the fire trucks in view had the names of fire departments from Detroit or Providence, Rhode Island, rather than any trucks from Massachusetts.

"She'll call," said Maria, his wife. "Have faith."

"I hope you're right. I've looked into the case, and there is a lot of misinformation out there. There are many things that don't make sense."

"And what about this Cassie Livingston – is there anything on her?" asked Maria, bringing over two cups of green tea for them.

"Yeah, there's quite a bit on her as well. She was a graduate of the Columbia School of Journalism – graduated with honors, actually. She was hired at the *Worcester Daily News* where she did excellent work by all accounts and then transferred to the *Springfield Times*. But, she wasn't there long when, apparently, someone from the *Boston Gazette* picked her up. She was there for several years but one blog said she allegedly had a falling out with her new editor. Nothing tells me what it was over. However, she was recently put on parks and recreational types of things."

"Sounds like she was demoted," said Maria.

"Yeah. Her career's been totally torpedoed. Going from covering the pressing social issues of our time in Boston, like drug abuse, family unit dysfunction, crime, gang violence, and all of that, to writing about what the Boston library was planning for its fall fund raising event."

It was later that day when Sumner's PCD buzzed, but it was a cryptic message. GOFLA HQ 0821 0800.

"What do you make of this?" he asked his wife, showing her the readout.

"Looks like someone wants to meet you at your headquarters on August 21 at eight in the morning," she said quickly, without even thinking. "But you can't risk it, JC. You've been down this road before and look what happened to you – you took a bullet. You can't go."

"But it wasn't an ambush then. It was someone who had information – something important about an incident that had happened at a refinery and was being covered up. Maybe this is the same type of thing?"

"Even if it is, you can't just walk in there without protection or at least finding out more."

Sumner sent a message back. *What's this about?* he asked.

It took a few seconds, but the answer came. *It's CL. Pls come.*

Sumner felt he had failed this test before with the incident in Louisiana, and he was not about to fail it again. It all pointed to another cover-up. But this time, he was determined to get to the truth – whatever it was. And, more importantly, he would get it out to the American people who needed to know.

***

Sumner glanced at his watch. It was 8:24. *Is she coming?* he asked himself. He was more worried than impatient. What if they had misunderstood the message? What if something had happened to her? What if this was just all a setup to get him arrested? All of these thoughts ran through his head at the same time.

Eight-thirty came and went, and so did nine and nine-thirty.

He called Maria and asked if she had gotten any messages or signs, and she hadn't. "I'll wait until noon," he told her. "If she's not here by then, I'm headed back home."

At just before eleven-thirty, there were noises coming from the creaking stairs outside. GOFLA had gone deep underground, renting an old, two-room office out of an abandoned manufacturing plant just outside of Washington. Rats were the only other occupants of the sprawling, but empty building. The cold water, but not the hot, worked in the two, rust-stained bathrooms of yellow and black tile. Avoiding the areas where light fixtures hung with exposed wires from the ceilings, drywall lay in broken pieces in the hallways, and dead bugs and dirt created a mat-like carpet on top of the gray, cracked linoleum, the small GOFLA staff of five had managed.

"Who's there?" asked Sumner, standing up from his wobbly, steel desk.

"Hello?" came the sheepish reply.

"Yes, hello? Is that Miss Livingston?" Sumner asked again.

Opening the office door and peeking in was the youthful but gaunt face of Cassie.

"Congressman Sumner?"

"Yes, and you must be Miss Livingston. I was worried about you," he said, reaching out his hand.

She took his hand and gripped it tightly. "I'm so glad to finally be able to meet with you. You really have no idea what is going on in the world right now. It's all being kept from us. It's all a lie."

"I know more than you think, Miss Livingston," Sumner said. "But you are right about the fact that there's a lot going on out there."

"Call me Cassie."

"Alright, Cassie, and you should call me JC. Now, what do you have for me?"

Cassie dropped her satchel on the desk and pulled out several red folders. She arranged them in front of Sumner. Then, she reached into her pocket and withdrew a disc. "Here," she said. "This is what you need to see. This is what the people of this country need to see. They murdered hundreds in Springfield last week."

"They? Who is they?"

"The government. They killed innocent people by the scores – mowing them down with machine gun fire like they were cardboard cutouts. Blood flowed in the streets that day, JC. I was there. I know."

"You're referring to the warehouse explosion?"

"No. There was no warehouse explosion. That was a fraud. People were protesting in the streets against the Little Red Book and the Unity Plan and everything else that's going on. People were fed-up; they'd had enough. So, they started gathering outside the district courthouse in Springfield. It was a peaceful protest. Of course they had their signs and chants – who doesn't these days. But it was peaceful – no threats, no violence, nothing. Then, it started."

"What exactly?"

"The Red Shirts. They started rolling in with the tanks and guns. They seemed like they were itching for a fight. There were a lot more protestors than militia, and I think they felt outnumbered. More and more people came. Even with all of those people everything was orderly. Eventually, there were probably, oh, I'd say a thousand people or more. That's when it happened. The first shots were fired. The Red Shirt commander order the tanks to fire on the people. It was ... it was horrible."

Sumner put his hand on her arm. "It's okay. Take your time," he said trying to comfort her. He handed her a tissue, and she wiped her eyes of the shiny droplets of tears that were forming in the corners.

Cassie went on to describe the barbarous act that followed, the senseless act of brutality. The protestors were cut down on the lawn – men, women, old, young, it didn't matter. The more she talked, the more Sumner was drawn in, the concern and shock growing deeper in the furrows of his aging face.

Sumner shuddered. He looked down at the disc she had provided him.

"It's all captured there," Cassie said pointing to the storage device. "It's right there – unadulterated. You can see for yourself."

Sumner didn't want to look at it, but he knew he had to. It was not unlike the feeling he'd had when he was in Congress and he sat on the Intelligence Committee. They had been forced to watch videos of beheadings of Americans by the still-looming threat of Islamic radical terrorists.

"I will look at it," he answered her, "but I believe you." He took the disc and put it in his pocket. "I'll make a copy and give this back to you."

"No. I don't want it!" she answered him. "Anyone who has that is in danger. You are in danger, and I'm sorry to put you in that position. But ..."

"I know. Someone has to do it, right?"

"Well, yes, but someone who *can* make a difference. You see, I can't, but you can," she said.

"That's where you're wrong, Cassie. Each of us can make a difference – just in a different way."

She thought about what he'd said. "Maybe," she answered. Then, she added, "Okay, so maybe you should make a copy and give that one back to me. If we both have copies, it will be harder to bury this. They *will* try to bury it, you know."

"Yes. I know. I've been down this path, Cassie. I know how they play the game, and believe me, they play hard."

"They play to the death, JC."

"Yes, they do."

"So, what do we do now?" she asked, looking at him with her puffy, red eyes.

"We broadcast this," he said holding up the chip. "We use every outlet known to man. We flood the SI-net. GOFLA has the technology to evade the government's blockers – at least for a time. Then we'll have to go off the air again, maybe for quite a while. But in the meantime, we can do this for you."

"For us ... for all of us," she corrected him.

226

"Give me two days. That's all I need. I'll also have to find other places for GOFLA to hide. We'll probably have to move every day while we're broadcasting."

"Thanks, JC," said Cassie, getting ready to leave.

"Here, take this. It's a private-line PCD. The codes haven't been discovered or broken yet by the ministry. Use it to contact me. And, Cassie ..."

"Yes?"

"Go out the back door. You'll have to watch for the rats scurrying about in the dark, but it's safer than the front."

Cassie left through the docking area door, and Sumner watched as she walked down the street away from the building. No one seemed to be following her – not yet anyway.

Sumner took the chip out of his pocket again and stared at it. *This could either kill me or free this country,* he thought. *Could the stakes be any higher?*

***

By the following night, the team at GOFLA had succeeded in finding over seventy outlets for the video. Broadcast from an anonymous source, the images were graphic, disturbing and impactful. To say they went viral was an understatement – they were the secret talk of the nation, of the world, for the following weeks and months. The Fourier Administration was livid. "How could those videos have escaped them? Heads will roll!" the First Citizen had screamed.

The immediate response from the Ministry of Domestic Policing and the Ministry of Electromagnetic Frequency and Digital Source Control was that the images were manipulated. Using sophisticated digital techniques, the people who produced the footage were traitors to the Motherland and were inciting anarchy and a revolt against the People's government. They would be found and imprisoned, said the government communication, not giving any suggestion of a trial. It had concluded with a reward for information leading to the arrest of the perpetrators – a whopping fifty million dollars.

Few believed the government would ever pay such an amount. Like everything, it was a lie. The government was broke, and much like the old insurance industry, it would find every way possible not to pay the amount promised.

All protests had stopped for a while due to the infiltration of protest groups by the Red Shirts and the brutal torture and imprisonment of those who had escaped the Massachusetts massacre. But the images of that event lingered. The damage had been done. The government's careful bottling of anarchical emotions within the country was going to come under more pressure, which meant more extreme measures of containment might be necessary.

*****

CH 36 Passport Control

The plane landed, but it was some two hours later than that scheduled. To make matters worse, ahead was a long line to get through various checkpoints within the airport. Miami International was not unlike every other large airport in America. But after the takeover of all property and businesses within the nation, the situation had only deteriorated. Still, with fewer people allowed to get travel documents in the first place, it was assumed that travel for the rest would be easier, not worse. But, because of more terrorist threats at airports, even stricter measures were put in place, mainly to protect the politicians or people with wealth and connections who were the only ones traveling anymore.

As a result of falling employment, First Citizen Fourier instructed the Ministry of Domestic Policing to setup a more elaborate system of checkpoints and document reviews at all seaports, airports, crossing points, and train stations. Even local bus and commuter rail systems implemented the system. The result was a marvelous improvement in employment – a staffing level nine-fold larger than what it had been -- while at the same time increasing wait times several hours. All in all – security was no better and costs skyrocketed.

Shea had counted the airport checkpoints when she had caught her initial flight to Belize. The first person had checked her identification before she could get into the airport building itself. The second had handed her a card of some sort that had the airport name and logo on it. A third person had examined the card and stamped it. At that point, she had been permitted into the airport terminal building by the fourth person. Inside, a fifth person had again asked to see her card and passport, writing her name and passport number on the card.

There had been eleven more points of review, examination and scrutiny before she had gotten to her gate, excluding the two last checkers who had made sure she was on the right flight and hadn't opened her luggage. A total of nineteen people was required to ensure she got on the flight 'safely.' Ironically, since the new system had gone into effect, there had been three more terrorist incidents at airports across the country, with the perpetrators never being apprehended. Most believed it had been maintenance personnel, but the ministry had been unable to come up with answers. So, instead, they had added more checkpoints to show people they were doing something.

However, returning from Belize, Shea found the story quite different. After getting off the plane, there were no checkpoints. Shea merely got into a long, winding line that moved slowly passed a sign that read *Passport Control*. It branched off into two lines after that point – one for USSA passport holders and one for foreigners. The process was straightforward. Shea saw that most people simply inserted their travel chip, which contained their passport and travel authorization permit, into the computer slot for reading and analysis. It took only a few seconds before they received a blinking green light and the robotic words "Entry approved. Please proceed to customs."

Eventually, Shea got to the front of the line, standing just behind a yellow mark on the carpet and a placard that read *Stay Behind Line Until Called. All USSA citizens are subject to search and seizure.* Ironically, there was no such sign for the non-USSA citizens.

Next in line was the command that flashed onto a blue screen in front of her. There was a red arrow and the words *Station 41* that pointed her in the direction she needed to go. Shea picked up her bag and walked to the station where the computer beckoned. *Insert Travel Credentials*, it read on the screen. She pushed the small fob into the slot and waited for the next instruction. Several seconds went by, but there was no response. Shea was about to summon an agent when the screen began flashing red with the words *See Ministry Agent.*

Surprised, Shea looked around and saw an agent walking briskly toward her. Perhaps I put my fob in the wrong way, she thought, and she reinserted it just to be sure. However, that set-off the computer, which began sounding an alarm. It wasn't loud, but rather a dull, vibrating sensation that shook the floor and was followed by a low, pulsing -- almost throbbing -- noise.

The agent quickened his pace. "Stop right there, miss!" he yelled. "Don't move."

"What have I done?" Shea asked, bewildered. "I don't understand."

"You'll have to come with me, miss," said the man, taking her by the arm.

He pushed her along, passed the other passengers who stood with their mouths agape, as they believed she must have been some terrorist that the agent had successfully apprehended. Forced into a backroom, Shea now stood in front of another agent who sat behind bullet-proof glass in a booth raised about two feet off the floor. The woman was obese with a triple chin and extra skin flapping from her upper arms. "Push your face into the machine," she said dryly.

It was a retina scan and facial recognition system designed to single-out those on the criminal watch list who were deemed threats against the government. The process took only seconds, and Shea waited nervously, watching the woman in the booth to see if there was still a problem.

"Ma'am, you have to push your face into the machine for it to work!" said the passport woman, now showing a nasty attitude.

Shea pushed her face farther into the machine and watched as a line of brilliant green light passed across her face.

"Now, hold your eyes open," barked the woman in the booth above her.

This time a red light blinked on and off three times before stopping.

"Please wait," ordered the woman, shutting off the speaker to the outside world and talking into her government-issue PCD.

Soon, the woman finished the call and pushed the open mike button on her console. "Ma'am, you'll have to stand over there." She pointed to a roped-off area where two guards stood with M-16C fully-automatic rifles.

"Is there a problem?" Shea asked.

"Please, just stand over there," said the woman, not revealing anything.

Shea felt sick to her stomach as she walked to the guarded area and set down her purse and carry-on. Something was obviously wrong. She wanted to go back to the lady in the booth and ask why she was being detained, but she thought better of it. Defying authority and instructions at this point would only make things worse.

Time passed. She looked at her watch. It had been forty-five minutes, and no one had come for her. She was really worried now. Her hands were cold and clammy and she was perspiring. Not only that, but she really needed to go to the bathroom.

Finally, after an hour, another official from the ministry approached her. He looked rough and stern. Not quite as large as the other woman, he was also rotund. However, he was much older, with a receding hairline that was still parted in the middle as when he was younger. Wearing two silver bars on each of his broad shoulders, she figured he was a ranking officer for the group.

"Shea Disone?" the man asked, without a modicum of sympathy.

"Yes."

"Come with me."

"Is there a problem?" she asked.

"Just come with me, ma'am."

Shea followed the man, escorted by one of the armed guards who walked behind them carrying her military rifle. After taking an elevator down to the basement level, they entered a small, gray room, dimly lit by a single, energy-efficient, florescent bulb.

"Sit down, Ms. Disone," said the officer, less than politely.

Shea followed instructions, sitting on a hard-plastic, orange chair with a cracked backside.

"We seem to have a problem here," he started, looking at his computer terminal. "Your passport and travel documents are no longer valid."

Shea looked at him with stunned silence. Then she took out her Travel Chip to check the expiration date.

"We'll be needing that," said the man, snatching it out of her hand.

"But, it hasn't expired," she said. "I don't understand. I just got these last week."

"It's been revoked, ma'am."

"What? Revoked? How could that be?"

"I don't have any particulars, but we can't let you back in the country, ma'am."

"You've got to be kidding me!" exclaimed Shea, the shock of not being able to return suddenly hitting her.

"No, ma'am. I'm afraid not. You'll have to take the next flight back to Belize. We can't help you with that, but you can't get past Passport Control. You may call someone to help you. By law, you have four hours to make the arrangements. You may only make two calls."

"What happens after that?" she asked.

"We'll have to take you down to Extradition. You'll spend time in a cell until we can get you sent back out."

"I'm being thrown in prison?"

"No, not if you can get out of the country within the next four hours."

The man got up and left the office, leaving the guard to stand by the door, not letting her out until she could show she had passage back to Belize.

What the hell do I do now? she thought. She called her attorney, Emery Lawson, but he only told her she'd have to do as the authorities told her and fly back to Belize. "There's nothing I can do," he'd said to her. "All I can do is look into it for you." She hadn't been able to pay him in months, so it didn't come as a surprise.

Next, she called Sumner. It was his old private line, and she hoped he still had it. The line rang and rang. But, there was no answer.

"Crap!" she said.

Shea spent the last of her savings and booked her return flight to Belize. The flight wouldn't leave for another three hours, so all she could do was wait.

The hours passed slowly, as she could do nothing but check the time every ten minutes or so. It was like staring at a kettle of water, waiting for it to boil. Yet, as much as she wanted to explode on someone and let the kettle boil over, she contained her anger. Someone was doing this to her and she could guess who. But again, it was a force she couldn't fight.

The plane lifted off from Miami airport, and below her were the brilliant and colorful lights of downtown and of the nightlife scene along Miami beach. Reflecting off the Atlantic, the lights blended together into a canvass fitting of a Renoir or Monet painting. It was beautiful.

Shea choked up, and tears ran freely down her cheeks. *It may be the last time I ever see my country,* she thought. *I may never be able to go home.*

Sobbing quietly, she eventually fell asleep, her head pushed up against the oval window and her feet tucked in under the seat in front of her. There were few on their way back to Central America. Indeed, the flight was as empty as her heart felt at that moment.

***

The sudden jarring of the plane as it touched down awakened her. It was still dark outside, but she had arrived back in Belize City. Unable to find a place to stay so late at night, she found a park bench not far from the airport. She was exhausted, smelly, and hungry. It was all she could do to stuff her purse under her head before she quickly fell asleep.

An hour or so later, someone kicked her in the leg. *"¡Levántate!"* yelled the voice.

She opened her eyes. Standing over her was a man in a uniform, carrying a hard, wooden baton. "I say, get up!" he said again, threateningly.

"No, hablo español," she answered, rubbing her eyes.

"You can' sleep here. Get up and move on," he said in broken English.

"But I have no place to stay," she answered.

"Not my problem," said the officer.

Shea started to pick-up her things. "Where can I go?" she asked, about ready to break down.

The officer's demeanor changed, and he grinned, revealing a grill that was missing two of his front teeth. "Oh, senorita, you stay at my place. I no charge you," he said.

Shea recoiled. She knew what he intended, and it made her sick to think about it.

"No," she answered flatly.

"I could arrest you, you know," the officer said again, menacingly.

Shea put out her wrists. "Go ahead," she answered. "Arrest me, then."

The officer looked away. He hadn't expected her to call his bluff. "Give me money," he said, holding out his hand.

"What? Give you money?"

"Give me money," he said again, shaking his open-palmed hand.

Shea hardly had enough for a hotel and a meal for the day. "But …"

"Give me money," he said one more time. "I won' ask again."

Shea pulled out her wallet. She only had two hundred Belizean dollars left. "This is …"

The officer ripped it out of her hand. "You can sleep over there," he said, pointing toward a group of trees where she'd be better hidden. Then he disappeared. It was an expensive bribe, but at least she wouldn't be bothered the rest of the night.

The next morning, she rose. Her mind was clear, but her situation wasn't. *What am I going to do?* she thought. Despair was a now an ever-present phantom, hovering close-by. She continued to fight it off, but its minacious image was growing by the day.

She had no money, nowhere to stay, and nowhere to go. She had gone from having everything – a loving husband, a great company with staff who adored her, millions awaiting her from the hard work she and Patrick had put into their dream – to being penniless, homeless, and broken.

Then, she remembered that she did have a place to stay -- Hank's apartment. She hoped it would still be vacant. She thumbed a ride to the apartment complex and climbed the stairs she had scaled only two days earlier. Once at the door, she could tell it was in the same shape as she'd left it -- a ruin of broken furniture and belongings strewn everywhere. Yet, it was still a place to stay, at least temporarily.

She closed and locked the door, lowering the blinds in all the windows and going into the kitchen to see if Hank had left anything in the refrigerator. There were only eight bottles of beer, a dozen eggs, assorted condiments, salt-free butter, some moldy papaya, and a half-drunk, clear bottle of orange juice. In the cupboards she also found two boxes of wafer crackers, a bag of white rice, a quarter loaf of whole-wheat bread that still looked edible, four cans of tomato sauce, two of whole corn, and six each of low-sodium vegetable and beef barley soup. *Thank you Hank!* she thought. *At least I can survive the week!*

Shea opened the crackers and devoured several before putting back the package. Grabbing one of the vegetable soups, she found an old-fashioned, wing-crank opener and creased the round seam in the top of the can and dumped it into a pan. It didn't take long before it was bubbling on the stove. At that moment, that and a cold beer tasted as good as any three-star Michelin restaurant.

Later, she sorted through the mess on the floor, picking up the broken pieces and putting them in a corner so she wouldn't step on them in the middle of the night. Rummaging through Hank's desk, she found his bottle of Cristal Parrot Rum hidden away in a lower drawer. She smiled and poured herself a glass while she looked through the rest of his things. Inside the desk she found mostly old papers and some unpaid bills. Inside another drawer were two small cardboard boxes – the size in which old check stock used to come. She opened the first one. "All be damned," she said out loud. Inside was about B$2000 – not a lot, but enough. *I'm shocked they missed this when they were ripping apart his apartment,* she thought. Then, she lay back into the ugly sofa that had been stripped nearly bare of foam, pushing enough pillows together to soften the pointed ends of the loose springs sticking out of it. The rum went down fast and smooth, and before long she was floating in a sea without pain.

Mustering some energy, Shea got up and wobbled over to the closet where she pulled down several clear-plastic storage containers. The contents inside were a jumbled collage of pictures and bits and pieces of paper, some folded, others torn. She dug through all of it, finding old photos of family members and one that was probably of his wife and a daughter of about three years old. *So he did have a family,* she thought. *I guess he was telling me the truth about that too.*

Below the photos were several old three-by-five cards with names and numbers written on them. She flipped through them, but most meant nothing to her. Finally, she turned over several in a row that read: U.S. Embassy, followed by a name and number. Some had titles of the people; others did not. *This may be my only way out of here,* she reckoned, putting the cards in a pile next to her PCD.

She was getting sleepy, so she put away her bottle and glass in the kitchen and went back into the bedroom to crash. Throwing herself onto the mattress, she felt pain in her foot as she'd hit something hard at the base of the bed. *"Ouch!"* she cried, doubling over and rubbing the top of her arch. *What the hell could have done that?*

She crawled down to the base of the mattress where she found something rigid in the otherwise foam padding. Grabbing some scissors from the drawer, she slit open the mattress and reached in, feeling around for whatever had caused her the pain. She took out two thin, flat pieces of wood wrapped with a rubber band. The band snapped as soon as she pulled on it, sending pieces in different directions. But when she lifted one of the wooden pieces she found an envelope. The packet had several folded papers inside, which she dumped on the bed sheet in front of her. *Why would he keep something like this in his mattress?* she wondered, as she unfolded the papers.

The reason was quickly apparent. At the top of the first page was the letterhead for the Ministry of Internal Policing.

The page had the words **TOP SECRET** at the top and was dated 5 December 2048.

MEMORANDUM TO: Colonel H. J. Young

Subject: Liquidation of Belizean Assets

1. Liquidation of Belizean Assets will take place no later than 3 May 2049
2. Extreme prejudice should be used to execute mission and all efforts are to be made to remain undetected throughout the mission.
3. If conditions change, the scheduled date and circumstances may be altered.
4. Additional resources will not be available to you.
5. If you are discovered, you will be a *persona non grata* and *without portfolio* with the USSA government. All travel documents will be revoked.
6. Destroy this communiqué once read.

L Chin
Lancaster Chin
Minister of Domestic Policing

"Holy crap!" Shea said aloud. "Hank was an assassin?" *Jesus,* she thought, *and I was with him in this very room!* A chill went up her spine. Now she really wondered why he had so suddenly disappeared and what had happened when he was making that phone call to her. *Had the Belizean police found him out? Had his cover been blown? Did the ministry whisk him out of the country before the police could get to him or had they gotten to him and put him away in some deep, dark prison someplace where he'd never be heard from again?* She shuddered at the thought of what he might be going through at that moment.

There was a second page attached to the first. This one was from the Ministry of Unity. In part, it read:

... there is something else the ministry needs from you. You will call the following number in America 01-8572-555-9090 within two days of this notice. The script is enclosed. Also enclosed is the voice emulator you will use. You will speak with a woman, Shea Disone. Her bio is part of this packet.

Shortly after your call, we expect Ms. Disone to make arrangements to come to Belize City in search of her husband. All you need to do is ensure she arrives and keep her busy for at least two days. Once she is out of the country, we will be able to take care of things on our end.

Regards,

A Ratner

Minister Ratner
Ministry of Unity

***

The sun rose early, but Shea was already up. She couldn't sleep. All she could think about was how evil a person could be to willfully destroy her life. It had all been a setup. She'd been tricked to leave the country, so that she'd have chance of ever returning. *Who could be that wicked?* she thought, but then she already knew the answer.

There was nothing more she could do about it, but what she could do was contact those embassy names she'd found in Hank's belongings. First, she wanted to try someone else – at least one more time.

The line rang and was answered this time on the first ring.

"Shea?"

"Yes, JC? It's me. Thank goodness I got through to you."

"Where are you, Shea? My phone says you're calling from Belize? Really?"

"It's a long story JC. Right now, I need to know if you have anyone who can hack into the Ministry of Domestic Policing's data center?"

"The MDP's data center? Are you mad?" he asked, incredulously. "That's almost impossible to get into. Why do you need that?"

"I can't get back into the country. They've banned me – rescinded my passport and travel docs. I need someone to get in and restore them."

There was a sigh on the other end of the line. "I'm not in Congress anymore, Shea. You know that. I'm just a regular citizen now – don't have the access I used to."

"Don't you know anyone who can do this? Please JC, I'm begging you!"

"Alright, let me see what I can do. You'll have to give me a day. I'll call you back."

A day passed, and then another. But her PCD did ring and it was Sumner on the other end. "It's fixed. Now what are you going to do?"

"I've got some numbers here to call. Wish me luck."

Shea pulled out the first 3x5 card and spoke the number into her phone.

"Hello," she asked after the receptionist at the embassy answered the line.

"Yes, to whom do you wish to speak?" asked the woman on the other end.

There was no video calling in Belize, as the government had outlawed it due to privacy rights. If both parties had the same carrier and had opted for the video and audio feed, then both would see each other on the line. In this case, and in particular with a foreign embassy, such calls were never permitted.

"Hello," Shea said again, nervously. "Yes, I'm calling to talk with … Julia Novak. Is she in?"

Shea had started with the most senior person she could find in the deck. She was listed as the Senior Field Officer for USSA Citizenship and Immigration.

"With whom am I speaking, and what is the nature of your call?" asked the receptionist.

"Uh, I'm Shea Disone, and I'm a friend of Hank Fannon's. He asked that I call." Shea held her breath. She figured he probably used the same alias with everyone, but it was only a stab in the dark.

"One moment."

It took only a few moments before another voice came on the line.

"This is Julia Novak. To whom am I speaking?" she asked very formally and somewhat stiffly.

"Ms. Novak, you don't know me, but I'm a friend of Hank Fannon's. I know that you and he …"

"Excuse me a moment, miss. I really don't know how you got my number, but my relationship with Mr. Fannon was purely professional."

Shea could tell immediately that she was lying. The woman's defensiveness was overt, and her willingness to 'clarify' their relationship so quickly was telling. But, that was just the information she needed.

"Oh, no. I wasn't suggesting anything other than that, Ms. Novak. Mr. Fannon always had the utmost respect for you and your staff at the embassy. I wasn't privy to the nature of his dealings with you, as he was only someone to whom I turned to help me find my husband down here in Belize City."

The word *husband* was key, and it worked. Julia Novak's guard quickly dropped, and she became much more receptive to giving assistance, even to someone she didn't know. "Oh, I see," said Novak. "Well, again, how is it that I can help you?"

"I have been down here in Belize City searching for my husband who's been missing for over a year. We believed he was kidnapped in America – taken from our home on August 5th -- but we've heard nothing from him since then. I received a call from him about three weeks ago, and I traced the call down here."

"Perhaps he wanted to disappear down here," said Novak. "A lot of people do, you know."

"Maybe, but he told me that he was trying to find a way home when we got disconnected. I could never reach him again after that, so I came down here looking for him. Hank tried to help, but he was reassigned somewhere. You don't happen to know where he is do you?"

"No, I'm afraid not. I've been wondering where he is too. I haven't heard from him in several days now."

Days? thought Shea, *not weeks or even months – but days?*

But Shea continued. "I tried to go back to the states, but there's apparently a problem with my travel documents. I assume there's just been a mess-up in the processing. I got them just before I came down here, so I can't imagine there is any issue."

"Oh, I'm sorry to hear about that," Novak said. "Is there anything I can do?"

"I hate to trouble you with it, but I'm down to my last dollars and need to get back to the rest of my family. Is it possible for you to look into it for me?"

"I'll have to do a background check and then look into the travel visa records. If there's something there, I can let you know."

"That would be great. Thanks," said Shea.

She gave Novak all of her pertinent information and the number where she could be reached. Assuming it would take several days or even weeks, Shea planned out how she would survive on Hank's rations while Julia looked into her situation. But it didn't take that long. The next day, Shea got a call.

"Hello?" Shea answered.

"Yes, Shea, this is Julia Novak from the USSA Embassy. Have you heard from Hank?"

"No, unfortunately, I haven't. I'm assuming you haven't either. I'm worried about what's happened to him."

"I as well," said Novak. "I've contacted officials at the Ministry of State to see what they know. So far nothing."

"I'm sure he's fine. He'll call you once he's settled into his new role, I'm sure," Shea said, feeling uncomfortable lying.

"Yes. Well, I also looked into your situation. It appears that you have a clean record. There was no reason that I could find why you would be denied admittance back into the country. I've contacted everyone I know here and at the Ministry of State in Washington and based on the people I talked to, they can't find any reason why that happened. You should be good to go back home. I'm sorry for the inconvenience."

Shea was stunned. Could it really be that easy? she thought. "Oh, that is wonderful news," she replied. "Thank you so much for your help. You've really been a God's-send."

"You're very welcome. And if you hear from Hank, please have him call me," Novak said, with a delicate sweetness in her voice.

"I certainly will," Shea answered.

Shea was on the next flight to Boston. She approached Passport Control just as she had the week before and her body trembled again. *Well, they'll either let me pass or arrest me. It's going to be one or the other this time,* she thought, *forcing her body forward.*

*****

CH 37 The Puppet Master

The number was staggering, but it was real. She couldn't help but look at the balance on her bank statement and pinch herself back to reality. She, Angel Ratner, a woman who grew up with nothing, was rich.

The 22.5 million dollars – half the 45 million Ratner had demanded -- that Thorne systematically wired to her Swiss Account before EG's takeover by the feds, plus the forty million from Chou's and Munt's accounts had been mere drop-in-the-bucket additions to her overall net worth. Once she was made third in line to the top job, her leverage grew exponentially, and so did her ability to extort money from every deal her ministry handled.

In addition, she had shorted the U.S. dollar just before the new constitution was announced. Selling the dollar when it was strong and buying it back after it was severely devaluated, she was able to score profits in the billions. The conversion from the U.S. dollar to the new U.S.S.A. *United Coin* had also been a boon.

As a result, her stash totaled 32 million UnitedCoins – what 55.3 billion devalued dollars had been worth earlier in the year. Insiders, wealthy patrons of First Citizen Fourier, were flooding her with suggestions on where to park her money – like in commodities, such as gold, titanium and manganese. Of course, they were also looking for return favors. So, as Lady Luck continued to stand by, Ratner watched as her holdings grew even larger.

By any measure, she was rich.

Ratner knew she didn't need to work anymore; however, she had gotten something else during her claw toward greatness – something as alluring and corrupting as money: *Power.*

"Dutch, it's Angel Ratner. How are you?" she asked the attorney general, pressing the phone receiver against her cheek. "I was wondering how you were doing in prosecuting those bastards that protested in Cheyenne. I trust you were able to put most of them away for a long time … you know, traitors against the Motherland, and all of that sh*t."

Dutch Welbourne was known to bend the truth and even more famous for targeting enemies of Fourier for investigation and torment. However, his ruthlessness was always directed toward the benefit of one person – himself. He understood where power lay and how to pander to the one who had the most. He took scraps of influence when it fell to the floor and had become astute at preserving his chits, rather than squandering them on misguided vendettas or personal grudges that got him nothing in return. He was every match for Ratner, and she did not underestimate him. To do so would have been foolish.

241

"Minister, it is good to hear from you. Well, I have to say that we've had to let most of them go. The judge out there is a Right-wing nut. He let almost all of them off on technicalities, as far as I'm concerned. Anyway, I'm looking into other possible outbursts of rebellion right now. I'll keep you in the loop."

"No, Dutch. You don't understand. We were to make an example of these people. They can't just get off without being punished. How is that going to look? It will encourage others to do the same thing. No, we have to act on this. We have to string them up by their balls!"

"I understand what you're saying, minister. But, the judge is acting within his legal right to ..."

"I don't give a damn what some loony judge is doing. I want those people locked away or even shot! I want them down on their knees crying for mercy! They need to feel the pain so they aren't advocates for this sort of miscreant behavior going forward."

There was silence on the other end of the line for a moment. Dutch knew what she was saying, but he wasn't willing to sacrifice his reputation in a confrontation with a low-level federal judge. "Alright, then what do you want Justice to do?" he asked, just trying to placate her.

"I want scalps."

"Scalps?"

"Yeah. I want a pound of flesh from each one of them. That's what I want."

"I'll have to clear this through the First Citizen."

"Dutch, I'm not asking you to do this. I'm telling you."

"But you don't have the authority to do that, minister. With all due respect, there is a chain of command. We both report to the same person – First Citizen Fourier."

"No, I don't think you understand, Dutch," she answered. "I will send you a file. Please look at it. If you still feel the same way, let me know." She hung up.

Dutch waited patiently. He didn't get riled easily, but she had pushed his buttons. Even though she was number three and he number four in line, she wasn't supposed to talk to him that way.

Then he heard a bell *ding*, signaling an electronic message. It was from some source he didn't recognize, presumably bounced around the globe several times to conceal its origin. The email was encrypted, so he applied the Executive Branch decryption algorithm and opened the file.

MX 45
RE: Matter
To: Dutch Welbourne

Attached are photos you may find interesting.

That was all it said. MX 45 was obviously an alias, and the message was cryptic. It was the attachment that worried him.

He hesitated, but clicked on the attachment anyway. A holographic file opened.

Dutch's mouth dropped open. He couldn't believe what he was seeing. It was a series of pictures of him with another man in a hotel room. The pictures were dated earlier that year. The dates coincided with when he had been staying at the St. Regis Hotel in New York City. A plush, five-star accommodation, the St. Regis was one of the priciest, most exclusive hotels in the city.

The pictures were pornographic in their unrestrained depiction of graphic private moments. Two men having sex, with clear elements of cocaine on the table, it was a scandal that would rock the Administration and the White House, not to mention the Justice Ministry. The suggestion of the head of Justice involved in such activity was too ripe for even the most stalwart and supportive news outlets to ignore.

Dutch sat in stone silence, fuming.

He picked up the phone and dialed. "These are fabricated and you know it," he said. "It will be easy for a lab to show they've been doctored. You having nothing here."

"I think you'll find they are quite authentic, Dutch. You see, there is technology out there that not even you are aware of – technology that can make these images very real. In addition, I have the man in the film willing and able to swear the whole thing happened. I've even got the people in the hotel on my side. It's all wrapped up in a nice little bow for you. There are no loose ends. I've managed to tie everything up quite nicely! Now, will you play ball or not?"

As minister of the most powerful organization in the government and access to virtually every other ministry's resources, she held the upper hand, and he knew it. And, knowing what she was capable of, he realized he could take no chances that she was not telling the truth. "What do you want?" he asked.

"I want you to arrest JC Sumner. In fact, pick up his wife Maria too. I want them both in prison. They are the instigators behind all of this. They're fomenting the unrest and rebellion in this country and must be stopped."

"But I don't have any evidence that they're breaking any laws."

"Make it up," she answered coldly. "You've done it plenty of times before. This is not new to you, for God's sake!"

"But ..."

"Listen, Dutch. I really don't give a flying f**k how you do it, just make it happen!" She hung up on him again.

Dutch commanded his PCD to make a call and waited for a greeting on the other end of the line.

"This is Jack Marburg."

"Jack, it's Dutch. You need to arrest JC and Maria Sumner. I need it done as soon as possible."

"Minister, I understand, but we have to have grounds. What have they done? I can't arrest them without cause."

"Treason of course," Dutch said, answering his long-time friend, Jack Waters, who was the Laramie County Sheriff in Wyoming. "Jack, I'm not asking. I'm telling you. We've got to arrest them. Find something – anything. I want them behind bars."

"But ..."

"I don't want to hear it, Jack. If you can't do this, I'll find someone who can?"

"Whatever it is, I don't see how we can get them on a treason charge. I'm not aware of anything that ..."

"I will make a few calls. We'll get them on treason charges, even if I have to plant evidence. You worry about arresting them."

Dutch hung up the phone, shaking. The shoe was now on the other foot. Rather than being the jailer, he was seeing that he was quickly becoming the jailed. This new movement of socialism in America was not starting out the way he had thought. He had fully expected to be the number two behind Fourier in the pecking order. Now, he was fourth. His power had shrunk with the new constitution, not expanded, as he was promised when he helped Fourier draft it. No, he realized that anyone could suddenly go from being the one in charge, throwing out the food scraps for others to grovel over, to one of the pieces of scrap, ready to be devoured by another too eager to serve his real master.

*****

244

CH 38 Seized

Next in line flashed onto the now familiar blue screen in front of her, with the red arrow and the words *Station 33* pointing in the direction it wanted her to go. Shea walked to the station where she read the computer commanding her with the message *Insert Travel Credentials.* Her hand trembled, and she could feel her heart racing. She felt as if she were having a coronary, but she tried to calm her emotions. *They will only get me in trouble*, she thought.

Shea pushed her travel fob into the slot and waited for the next instruction. Several seconds passed. *What is taking so long now?* she thought. Then, she became panicked. *Oh my God; it's happening again!* She looked around, shaking. *Should I run? Should I escape?*

Then, the screen changed. Turning green, it read: *Approved. Please proceed to Customs.*

Finally, she took a breath. Relief poured out of her from all pores. She closed her eyes. *There is a God,* she thought.

But, passing by Customs, Shea caught the attention of an officer standing next to an exit door.

"Documents," asked the officer, reaching out her hand.

Shea pulled out her fob again and handed it to the Customs agent. The agent pushed it into her computer and read the data. "Uh, what did you say your name is?" asked the officer.

"Shea Disone."

"Do you have a middle initial?"

"R as in Randolph," she answered.

"Date of birth?"

"August 18, 1992," she said.

"Place of birth?"

"Milwaukee, Wisconsin."

The officer still did not look up.

Shea's heart began to pound one more time. She thought she had been home free – safe. *What was this?* She felt the blood draining from her head. Light and dizzy, she began to feel nauseous, almost like she would get sick right there and then.

Hurry up! she said to herself. *Let me through before I do get sick and throw-up all over the carpeting here.*

"Is there a problem?" she asked, hoping to get an answer.

"It says here that you were denied access to come back into the country."

Shea could feel a cold sweat creep over her forehead. Her hands grew clammy and the room started to spin. She took a slow, deep breath, hoping the officer wouldn't notice, but she kept silent.

"But, it looks like ..."

"What?" she asked.

"It looks like the restriction was lifted yesterday. So, I guess you're good to go. Thank you Ms. Disone, and welcome home," said the officer.

Shea smiled and took another slow, deep breath. "Yes, thanks," she replied, and hurried through the line toward the baggage retrieval area. When her bags came, she grabbed them and walked as fast as she could past the sign that read *Exit*. Outside in the terminal she sat down on one of the cold, metal benches and put her head between her knees. She could feel the blood rush back to her brain and her senses start to return. *That was close,* she thought. *But, it was over now, and it was time to get home for real.*

***

Shea stayed overnight in Miami before finding another plane home to Boston the next day. The taxi ride from Logan was also a nightmare, as the traffic was snarled with cars trying to get home from a busy day. City streets without potholes and asphalt riffs were few and far between, having been ignored and abandoned due to a lack of repair funds. As a result, roads that were once smooth now required a four-wheel drive to traverse.

Pulling up the house, Shea felt a sense of relief. *Finally,* she thought, *I'm home.* She paid the driver and wheeled her bags up to the door. She pressed her thumb into the biometric reader and expected to hear the locks click open – but nothing happened. She tried again, and again nothing happened.

Biometric fingerprint readers were notoriously unreliable as a result of outdoor weather conditions, dust, and other factors. Her backup was the old method – a key card. Rummaging around in her purse, she finally found the house key and pressed it into the slot in the handle; however, it wouldn't work. *What is going on now?* she asked herself.

It was then that she noticed a piece of paper taped to the window next to the door.

SEIZED

By Order of the Ministry of Taxation Compliance.

The Ministry of Taxation Compliance hereby seizes this property for nonpayment of all taxes and penalties due. Occupants are hereby evicted and all property within and without the structure are hereby confiscated by the federal government under MTC Code Section 145071 – B2.498.897, subsection (c4)(iii).

The document went on to cite the exact wording of the Code and its corresponding regulatory explanations and interpretations.

Shea grabbed the door handle, madly twisting and turning it to reclaim her house – her home. To try to get back some small piece of something she once held dear, she continued. But it was all in vain. Emotions were welling up inside her, and as she kicked the immobile door, she dropped to the gray, wooden planks that supported her front porch. She sobbed, putting her hands to her face, and let the tears flow freely. It was the last straw. It was something that finally crushed her spirit.

"Why?" she cried out, looking up into the heavens. "Why me?"

She was a pitiful sight, sprawled out on a porch that had once been a scene of happiness. Thirty years earlier, Patrick and she had reveled in opening the front door to their brand new home. They had just been married, and the home was something neither had dreamed they would ever own. It was large, but needed finishing, and although Patrick had promised he would get to it after the business was built, those projects never materialized. Shea had learned to live with it, and, in fact, the Spartan interior made her feel comfortable and free – unencumbered by the materiality of things that sometimes possessed their owner.

Ironically, she was now free of such ownership, but it was not real freedom. It was another forfeiture of her rights – a seizure of liberty and property. It seemed that it, as with everything else, was beyond her control. There was little she could do about it.

In the original drafting of the Declaration of Independence, the Founding Fathers had considered all citizens to have natural rights -- the right to life, liberty and *property*, rather than the pursuit of happiness. Property had been the third element that John Locke and to a lesser degree, Algernon Sidney, Francois-Marie d'Arouet (Voltaire), Renee Rousseau and other political philosophers of the century believed were essential to a free society. In the end, the Declaration of Independence was prepared with the phrase ... life, liberty, and the pursuit of happiness. It had been left to the constitution to clarify the ownership rights of the citizenry. But those were concepts of another age and, it seemed, another world.

Shea couldn't help but think that the right to property was just another casualty of a war on freedoms. The government was eroding the natural rights of people for years, including that of property ownership. Now it was gone, and what would be next? What was left? *Was the right to life the next freedom to fall?* She shuddered to think. It had occurred in many other dictatorships and banana republics. *Had the country fallen this far?* She had not seen the video of the Springfield massacre, or she would have already known the answer.

However, such thoughts were fleeting. It seemed that she was back to square one again – almost as if she'd fallen through a wormhole from the park bench in Belize City to now. She was still without anything and quickly running out of hope.

She dialed a familiar number, hoping someone would answer.

"Yes?" was the answer.

Shea had expected someone else. Instead, she got a woman's voice who seemed distracted or even rude.

"Hello?" Shea asked. There was discouragement in her voice.

"Yes, I said," came the response from a brusque voice. "Is there something I can help you with?"

"Is Congressman Sumner there?" she asked.

"Just a moment."

It only took a moment, and a deeper, man's voice answered. "Hello?"

"JC? This is Shea Disone," she said, her voice trembling. "I'm sorry to trouble you. I know I've been asking a lot lately, but …"

"Shea? Is everything alright?" It was Sumner. "As I'm sure you know, we were able to help you with your problem. Are you back in the country?"

"Yes, JC. And thanks for that. You certainly have been a gods-send for me these past few days. But, now I'm in Boston, and … Oh, JC. I … I have no home. I have nothing left. I'm … They've taken everything."

"Where are you Shea? Are you at your house?"

She started sobbing, tears rolling off her cheeks and onto the phone.

"Shea, Shea? Are you there?"

"Yes, JC. I'm here. I'm at home – or what was my home. I don't know what to do now."

"I'll send a car to pick you up," he said finally. "Sit tight. It should be there within the hour."

"Where am I going? I have no place to go, JC."

"You're coming here. Maria and I want you to stay with us for a while – at least until you get on your feet again."

Shea wiped the tears from her face.

"I don't know how to thank you," she answered, not wanting to take help, but not knowing where else to turn.

"You can thank me by showing up on my doorstep tomorrow morning. I'll see you then."

*****

CH 39 Wyoming Style

Wyoming was a large expanse of plain, with many more prairie dogs than cows, and certainly more cows than people. With a population of less than six hundred thousand and enough square miles to contain nearly sixty-seven Rhode Islands within its borders, it was one of the ten largest states and the least densely populated of the states in the Union.

It was not easy getting Shea out to the Equal Rights state. She was worried about getting stuck at an airport. It was only via maglev or magnetic levitated rail that she felt safe to find her way west of the Mississippi River. Although the computer networks for air travel were updated on a regular basis, those at the rail terminals were still woefully antiquated, and it was safer to purchase a ticket from Boston to Cheyenne without trepidation that those in the Ministry of State would change their minds. As for bus travel, it had been scrapped decades earlier.

The trip by the high-speed train took two days even though the train traveled at over two hundred miles per hour; this was due largely to the many stops made along the way. The national rail system had been unprofitable for years and had eventually been absorbed into the Ministry of Transportation. It still ran at a tremendous loss, but it produced government jobs and was useful during election years when candidates could tout the good they were doing for their constituents.

Arriving in Cheyenne, Shea was both physically and mentally drained. Sumner and his wife, Maria, were there to greet her as she stepped off the train platform and walked toward the exit.

"How are ya?" asked Sumner, upbeat and smiling. He put his arm around her and gave her a friendly squeeze. Although only ten years older than she, he had that avuncular way about him. Everyone liked him, and it was easy to feel comfortable around him. Since his days in Congress, he had hardened and softened at the same time. He felt it was important that he be viewed as a leader now, head of the GOFLA organization and, possibly, a broader movement. He had to be decisive and resolute in the course he was taking for the benefit of the greater good. Yet, he had become more empathic of the plight of those who really were working hard to make a living and feed their families. An avuncular patriarch, he often called himself – it was a fitting description.

"I'll make it," she answered weakly.

"You will indeed," Sumner answered, still grinning. He picked up her luggage and threw it in the back of his black SUV. Then, he activated the car with its autopilot. The vehicle went through its checklist, scanning its panoramic auto cameras to ensure no one was around before pulling out of the terminal parking garage.

Shea didn't know where they were going, but she finally felt safe. They chatted for an hour or so about the incidents in Springfield and Cheyenne and what had happened to her in Belize. They had much to catch up on, and Sumner, Shea and Maria talked about the state of the Union and the pieces of it that still remained. But eventually, the turbulence of the last few weeks caught up with her, and she soon dozed off in the backseat. It wasn't until they turned off onto a gravel road and hit a few deep ruts that she woke up. Rubbing her eyes, she peered out the passenger window. "Where are we?" she asked.

Maria turned around with a smile on her face. "You're going home – to our home, Shea. You can stay there as long as you like. We have a guest house in back and plenty of firewood."

The SUV traveled down the windy road jumping and bumping along, taking all the jolts in stride. Finally, in the distance, Shea could see a rustic cabin and several other buildings surrounded by a split-log fence. She couldn't tell how big the property was, but the fence continued on for what seemed forever, vanishing over the horizon into a series of wheat-colored hills – one an exact clone of the other. Their SUV split the two, square stone pillars more than ten feet high that supported a mighty timber hewn from a large cedar tree that joined the two posts. Bolted into the wood and hanging from hooks was a shiny, copper sign that read **J Galt Ranch**.

"What's the J Galt Ranch?" Shea asked as the sign flew overhead.

"It's a question with many answers. Perhaps you'll find the answer that best suits you once you've been here a while. But for now, we want to get you to your room so you can relax a bit," said Sumner.

After pulling up to the main house, Shea saw that it was more than just a small, rustic cabin. It was more like a lodge with wings on both ends. The timbers laid as the main support beams were nearly two feet in diameter and soared over twenty feet above them. In the front was the quintessential wrap-around porch, complete with rockers and swinging benches. The ebony shutters complemented the natural-wood exterior. Flower boxes on the lower and upper level windows were empty, as it had been many weeks since their annuals had blessed the home with their rich rainbow of color and pageantry.

"Here, we'll get these for ya," said Sumner, fetching her luggage. He waved at a young man with a blue, chambray shirt, jeans and cowboy boots to come over, asking him to take the bags to the guest house.

"You'll be staying over there," said Maria, pointing to a smaller cabin some fifty yards away. It was near another large building that Shea could only think was a barn for the horses. "Don't worry. Your cabin has a full kitchen, bath, and all. It's not at all like the barn." She laughed. "You'll be comfortable."

"I can't thank you enough," Shea answered. "I really am appreciative of all that you've done. You've both been too kind."

"You can't be too kind," said Sumner, smiling. "That's the problem with you eastern folk. You look at people funny when they're nice to you. You're not used to that, are you?"

"No, we're not," Shea said, a bit embarrassed. "I didn't mean to sound like …"

"Oh, don't worry about it. JC was just giving you a hard time. Now, come inside. Let's get something for you to eat. You must be starved," said Maria.

After a light snack, Maria took Shea out to her cabin and got her straightened away. From the guest house, they could see the entire back side of the main lodge. The back was one full level lower than the front, which meant that the lower level opened directly to the outside. There Shea could see the enormous flagstone patio complete with two large fire pits and a cooking area. Fire wood was stacked high in preparation for the winter which was fast approaching.

"It's supposed to get cold tonight – probably down to freezing or below – so you'll need some extra blankets and a comforter. The fireplace is stocked with wood over in the corner there. Just help yourself. Make sure you open the flue first; I don't want to have to send someone to rescue you," said Maria, chuckling. "Especially when it's going to be so cold!"

"I got that," said Shea, smiling.

Maria had a sarcastic wit about her, but she didn't have a mean bone in her body. That was just her way.

"Now, tonight we're having a barbeque, right out there on the back patio. We scheduled it some time ago, so we really couldn't cancel. You're welcome to join us if you're up for it. In fact, we'd love to have you."

"I appreciate that. Thanks," Shea answered. "About what time does it start?"

"Oh, it starts when people show up, honey," said Maria. "That's the way it works out here. But usually, we get things going by seven or so. It gets dark here by five this time of year."

***

It was early in the afternoon, about three, when Shea heard activity outside her cabin. She had been resting and had propped-up her head, reading from her tablet the 1776 classic of Thomas Paine's *Common Sense*. She had read it before, but there was something about it now that made her seek it out – to reread it and understand it in a new way. It was about the destiny of a people to want freedom and independence from a tyrannical government that wished to control them. It was about the citizenry resisting King George III and his attempt to suppress the will and freedom of a people yearning for the same.

She rolled out of bed and went to the window, pulling back the pale cream curtains that Maria had drawn together tightly before she'd left to go back up to the lodge. Some yards from her cabin, but still near the stone patio that encircled the back of the main lodge, was a crew assembling another, larger fire pit just beyond where the other two lay. They were stacking wood in a crossing pattern, piling it high to allow the air to circulate freely and keep the embers of the fire alive. Next to the pit was a golf cart with a bundle wrapped in black, plastic. It took the crew some time to get the fire started and even more time for it to die down enough for them to begin preparing the main feast for the evening.

Although she had already guessed the contents of the black plastic, it was quite another thing to watch them unwrap the hog from its iced packing and set it on the pit skewer. It had already been partially-cooked to seal in flavor and accelerate the cooking process; otherwise, they would have needed another day to slow-cook the animal to get it ready for the night's festivities. Soon the smoke from the pit was roiling around the meat, creating that unique and wonderful flavor that only comes from an open-pit BBQ.

Sumner stopped by later that afternoon and asked whether Shea was up for a tour of the ranch. Hopping onto the cold, gray all-terrain buggy, he pushed his foot to the floor, throwing Shea's head back against the headrest.

"Hang on!" he warned in jest. "I'm not licensed to drive this thing, ya know."

"Really," Shea asked, rubbing her head. "I couldn't have guessed."

Sumner only laughed, slapping his knee with his hand. "Good one," he said.

The rest of the afternoon was spent touring the grounds and examining the prize Black Angus Sumner had been raising for years. Maria and he had over two hundred head. It had taken time to grow the herd, as well as luck. Too often, droughts or disease would decimate the herd, forcing them to restart the line. They hadn't had any calamities recently, so their animals were large and strong.

"That's Bessie over there," said Sumner pointing out a huge heifer that was out grazing in the field. "She's been with me for a while. I've never had the heart to take her to the butcher. She's, well, part of the family now."

"What about the others?" asked Shea, sympathetic to the animals.

"What about them?" answered Sumner. "I care for them, sure. But, I also realize that God put us at the top of the pecking order for a reason. Other carnivores hunt and kill; that's what they do. If every species had been created as herbivores, then maybe that would be wrong. But, God didn't do that; did He? He created carnivores, herbivores, and omnivores. It's pretty obvious He intended for animals to hunt for their own survival. It's Nature way. I didn't create it that way. He did." Then he added, "Say, you're not a vegan or anything like that, are you?"

Again, Shea couldn't tell if he was kidding her. "No, I'm not a vegan. I tend to be a vegetarian, although I eat meat occasionally, so I can't really claim to be that either."

"It's Okay if you're either of those or anything else you want to be. It's a free country ... or, well, it used to be, anyway. So, as far as I'm concerned you can eat whatever you want."

"What about armadillo, bison and some of that other stuff I hear about going on out here?" she asked him.

"Those are fine. They're actually pretty good, if they're cooked right. I just don't think people should eat dogs, horses, and things like that. I guess they do over in China, but that's up to them. It's all about what your customs are, I think."

It was getting late, and the sun was already setting in the west. Sumner pulled the buggy up next to her cabin to let her out. "We'll eat about eight. Guests should be arriving at about seven, but you may come when you like. Dress is casual, of course, although boots are mandatory," he said, chuckling, "... that is, if you have them. And lastly, come with an appetite. I'm sure you noticed the hog we're roasting in your honor. We'll see you later then."

"In my honor? What do you mean?" asked Shea, apprehensively, but it was too late. Sumner had already stomped on the pedal and zoomed off down the short trail to the main lodge. *Crap!* she thought. *Maybe I really don't want to go to this thing if they're going to mention me!*

At about six-thirty, people began arriving. The trucks and SUV's started streaming up the long, twisted road that led to the ranch. It was clear that most had money, but it was also evident that these were practical people. There were no low-slung sports cars like Porsches, Lamborghinis or Ferraris. Instead, there was a plethora of Land Rover Range Rovers, Hummers, Cadillac Escalades, G-Class Mercedes Cruisers and the ubiquitous Porsche Cayennes.

Outside, Sumner had hired his ranch hands as valets to handle the pricey vehicles when they arrived. Stepping out of their Hummers in their ostrich and crocodile boots, both men and women showed up for a good time. In the back of the lodge, the featured band was already setting up their gear on stage. It was not some fly-by-night group, but one that had been in the top ten on the still-popular country music hit charts for the previous two years. Country music had come and go over the years. More recently, it was approved for broadcast in the Plains and Mountain states, but could not be aired on the East or West Coasts. Thought to be hick-ish and backward, country music was to be contained by the Ministry of Culture so it wouldn't *infect* more people. When asked about the lyrics of other music being crude and explicit on sex, violence, brutality, and licentiousness, the Minister of Culture said that it was perfectly fine for people to express themselves in any way they wished. When asked about country music, all the minister said was "Well, if you call it music, *that's* another matter completely."

Shea joined the hundreds of guests who had gathered on the lawn, mingling freely with them and talking about whatever topic they wished. Caterers were busy serving hors d' oeuvres, and there was an abundance of beer and wine in glasses the size of brandy snifters. Beluga caviar, Camembert and pecan wafers, morel mushroom fricassee, Alaskan king crab, white truffle flambé, and abalone tartar also made the rounds as the guests laughed and palavered, catching up on each other's lives and escapades.

"Ah, there you are," said Maria coming over to engage Shea, who was munching on a crab-stuffed mushroom. "I knew you wouldn't be able to resist our appetizers. JC has this caterer that he's known for years. They do wonderful things with food. Here, try one of these," Maria said, thrusting toward her a small, grayish mound on a wafer.

Up for anything, Shea just opened her mouth and took the wafer in whole. She bit down and began chewing. "Wow," she exclaimed, rolling her eyes in delight. "Where did you get these?"

"Those are Olympia oysters ..." Maria said, adding, "... cultivated, of course. The natural ones are protected by law. Good, aren't they?"

Shea only had time to nod her approval before Maria was whisking her off to see others.

"Come on," said Maria. "Let me introduce you to a few of our neighbors." She grabbed a couple drinks off a tray that was passing by and handed one to her guest. Coming over to a group already deep in conversation, Maria interrupted politely, "Sorry to interrupt, but I'd like to introduce a friend of mine. This is Shea Disone. She's from Boston."

The couple closest to them were young, European Americans but seemed just as hip as many others in the group. She wore skin-tight, faded blue jeans with tan, rattlesnake boots. Short and petite, she wore her jeans low on her hips, enough to show some skin from her well-tanned, but taut stomach. The jade necklace around her neck plunged down the front of her blouse, splitting her ample breasts. Yet, she smiled sincerely, expressing more beauty from that one act than all the makeup that donned her face. Brown-eyed with chestnut hair, she had a calm demeanor – one of quiet confidence and self-assurance.

"Howdy," she said with a marked twang in her voice, unusual for Wyoming which was so much farther north than the southern accent she bore. "I'm Sunny James, and this is my husband, Desmond. We're glad to finally meet you. You know you're a bit of a celebrity around these parts!"

Shea was surprised both at her accent and her accolades. She returned the compliment with a smile, shaking the woman's hand and that of her husband. "I … I'm very glad to meet you too," Shea answered, timidly.

Sunny's husband, Desmond, had been a middle-linebacker for the now-defunct NFL pro-football league. It had only been five years since Congress had ruled the game illegal due to its violence and the harm it caused young people. Its detractors also contended that it promoted rage and bullying at school. *It was a gladiator sport, a blood sport,* they had said, *and it had to be abolished*. And so it was. But Desmond had moved on, reinventing himself in business, and he had been very successful in that as well. Broad-shouldered and thick-bodied, Desmond was a natural athlete. His neck was the size of a tree trunk, and his hair was short, virtually shaved around the ears, like an old marine cut. His facial features were striking, with angular traits similar to those chiseled sculptures of the ancient Roman gods. His large and imposing presence was a sharp contrast to his diminutive wife.

"Hi, Ms. Disone. We really do believe you are the inspiration of this movement." He glanced quickly at Maria, and added, "Of course, we still believe JC is the one who will lead us to the promise land."

Shea laughed. "I thought that was Moses, not Jesus Christ!" she said, referring to JC's initials.

Desmond chuckled, as did Maria. "We often kid JC about that," she said. "But that's a good one. I'll tell him he's not Jesus – only Moses. He's always complaining to me about never having seen a burning bush."

They all had a good laugh.

"And this is Frank and Latoya Black," said Maria, introducing the other couple. He was tall and handsome, his face, a dark bronze that was cold and hard. He wore a ashen gray Stetson with a brown leather band and a small, black-and-white speckled feather tucked into the side. Dressed in a heavy, brown leather coat with fringe that dangled from his sleeves and blew in the wind, he stood with his arm around his wife, as if the two of them were on their honeymoon.

She too was striking. Almost as tall as her companion, she was thin and modelesque. Her large, gold hoop earrings dangled from her ears, and lay only partially covered by her shoulder-length blonde hair. Like her husband, she dressed western-style – cowgirl boots in pink ostrich, tight to the calves, and a short, black jacket with rhinestones on the shoulders.

"Glad to meet ya'," said Frank, giving Shea a firm handshake.

"Yes, my wife and I were just talkin' about you the other day," said Frank, piping in. "We really admire what you've done, and, to some extent, we understand what you've been through. You see, both of us had a similar experience with the ministries. LaToya and I owned a successful venture capital firm out of Dallas. At one point we had over $230 billion that the firm managed with all of our teams and analysts. I guess you could say we were lucky. My father was into tribology and invented a PTFE nanomotor that's used in a lot of medical device systems. After his company went public, he reinvested his billions in other start-ups. Some succeeded, and some didn't. We made millions on some and lost everything on others. It was high-risk but offered the potential for high-returns if we did our homework and guessed right once in a while."

"You look familiar?" asked Shea, looking at LaToya. "I've seen you or a relative of yours somewhere, but I can't place it."

"Well, my maiden name was Randolph," LaToya said.

"Randolph! Of course! Your father discovered triberium, which is a superconductor, and when used to coat something creates an almost frictionless surface. It paved the way for our HECE - high efficiency engine. The triberium makes the interaction of parts of our engine slide without almost any friction to slow them down." Shea stopped. "It is a small world after all," she added. Then, she asked, "So, what happened? What did the ministries do to both of you?"

"If you remember," Frank said, "about three years ago, Congress passed a finance reform law making it illegal for private companies to provide money for other private businesses. The minister of the Bursars said it was his job and solely that of the government to provide capital to businesses because 'only the government knew what the long-term best interest of the country lay.' He said his ministry was unrivaled at picking companies that were what the economy needed." Frank coughed loudly, almost choking. "As you know, that's a joke. The government has almost never picked companies that are viable in the short or the long term. Most of their investments go bankrupt within months if not years. However, profit is not – has never been – the point."

257

"Yeah," said LaToya, "the bureaucrats have yet to make the connection between making money and being able to sustain a business. It's a concept that's just too foreign to them."

"I remember a time when the White House said that private businesses 'Didn't Build That,' referring to the businesses of the entrepreneurs," said Shea. "The Administration claimed that all the wonders of the modern world came from government funding of research labs and scientific projects. The Fourier Administration single-handedly snuffed out the private equity business, saying they were *ripping off* small, struggling business owners by taking over their companies and giving them very little in return."

"That's right," said Desmond. "I remember they got the media to run all kinds of negative stories on small business owners that had supposedly gotten ripped off by rich, greedy business tycoons preying on their naiveté and inexperience. They cited one example after another of small business owners getting the shaft and being left with nothing – one in particular who sold 90 percent of his business to a banking group. When they went public, the man only got about 2 percent of the proceeds when he had created the thing in the first place. Fourier said it was an example of what was wrong with the system."

"Oh, yes. I do remember that," said Shea.

Frank stood, shaking his head. "The problem with the story is that it wasn't true."

"What?" asked Shea.

"It wasn't true," said LaToya, his wife. "The basic story was true, but the numbers were fabricated. The venture company was our company. We didn't buy 90 percent; we bought a 15 percent stake in the company for 13 million, making the company's value, in our eyes, worth about 86 million. After three years, we had put another 13 million into the company to build a prototype to prove the product's viability. We hired a management team to sell the technology to the major robotics manufacturers, and we developed a marketing program. It took another 40 million dollars to build a plant and the tools and dies we needed to make the human-touch robotic hand, called SoftTouch, in a mass-production environment. So, all told, we had 66 million invested. It is true that we got 100 million from the sale, but after the 66 million invested, the initial gain was 34 million. Not bad, I know. The original owners did Okay too. I personally wrote them a check for 660 million dollars."

"That's a far cry from nothing," said Shea.

"Well, in the end, we all got fleeced," said Frank.

"Fleeced? By whom? How did that happen?" asked Shea.

"The government took 90 percent in taxes. So, yeah, they were right – the inventor didn't get all that was coming to him. He got to keep 66 million – still really good. As for us, we ended up netting only 3.4 million after having invested the 66 and three years into the project. We paid Uncle Sam over 30 million in taxes. I know, you shouldn't cry for us, but is that fair? There were many other deals we did where we invested millions and lost it all. We took the risk, and our reward was very little," he said.

"Then how did they come up with that story about the inventor and his wife living on the streets?" Maria asked.

"They made it up – lock, stock and barrel, and neither the media nor the public ever questioned it. It fit their narrative to a *T*, and that's all that mattered to them," said LaToya.

"You're right. That doesn't seem fair," said Shea.

"It isn't. But you can't tell them that. You see, we are the rich, greedy bastards who shouldn't make money from the hard-work and labor of others. We, who risk substantial amounts by placing our money with people we don't know and situations that aren't totally guaranteed – well, we don't deserve anything. In fact, we get what's coming to us if we do lose it all. And, that's basically what ultimately happened. We were losing millions in the end. Finally, we gave up -- threw in the towel -- while we still had some money stored away for retirement."

"A similar thing happened to us," said Desmond, interjecting. His voice was melodic and deep. His teeth gleamed in the flares of the fire pit. "I started my own chain of grocery stores. We were living in Baltimore at the time. My father had started the first store and had saved to send me away to college. He was proud when I graduated – top of my class at Georgetown. But he was even prouder when I decided to come home to the family business. Growing the business took guts. We were lucky enough to get favorable terms for loans from the banks. We took that money and picked another location on the south side of the city to start our second store. Within eight years, we had fifteen stores throughout the city. Things were good. We'd repaid our loans and were starting to make some money. It was in the ninth year when things started to close in on us. The Ministry of Eco-Agriculture took control of the country's food chain, declaring it was too important to be left in the hands of the private sector. They also claimed their mandate under the principle of national security. Congress dithered, so Fourier authorized it through Executive Order 16302 . *'It is too critical for the safety of the citizenry and the security of the country,'* read his order, *'not to control every aspect of the food supply within the borders of America. Therefore, we must act to secure this so that every American has confidence in the food he or she eats every day.'*

"There were some undercurrents of resistance in Congress over the issuance of the order even when the media remained quiet, not wanting to alienate the president. The public began clamoring about it, riled up by the food associations. Fourier found that he was losing the argument of public opinion. People were worried about the government taking over food production and distribution. Government never had a good track record of running any business or, for that matter, directing one. So, given the history of inefficiency and corruption in the systems the government already controlled, the people pushed back – calling their Congressman and complaining. But by then, Congress was too entrenched with the Administration, and they feared retribution."

"What happened?" asked Shea.

"The CDC and the Ministry of Food Inspection and Control issued a joint warning of disease being discovered in lettuce and other produce in grocery stores. The ministry claimed at first that thirty people had died from an outbreak in Los Angeles, and then progressively upped the numbers each day. By the end of the first week, they claimed there had been over two thousand fatalities from contaminated lettuce crops. The government directed grocery stores all over the country to pull all of their lettuce off the shelves."

"I thought it was milk?" asked LaToya, standing next to Frank.

Desmond nodded. "That was the next week. The media reported then that there was a second epidemic – problems with the milk supply. Hundreds of children were dead and thousands more were sick as a result of bad milk. Then it became the chicken farmers who had permitted their birds to contract the *Ionovicvirus*, which was found to be transferrable to humans. This continued for six straight weeks, until Fourier issued another executive decree requiring *all* foodstuffs be inspected by the federal government -- from growing it on the farms to selling it off the shelves in the store. Thousands of government workers -- loyalists to the People's party who were never trained and had no experience -- were hired and sent out to inspect the food that was to be sold to the public. Problems surfaced almost immediately. Massive delays and holdups in inspections caused product to rot at the source or on the shipping docks. Diseased product wasn't caught until it was at the grocery stores, where it was trashed. Losses mounted for everyone and the stores began to run out of basic staples. Shelves were empty of vegetables, poultry, fruits, bread, and dairy. There were outcries all over the country. The Ministry said it was the farmers who were producing bad food, but that was a lie."

"I remember all of that!" said Frank.

"Things quickly got out of control," continued Desmond, "and after the Administration blamed private companies for interfering, Congress passed the

260

Collective Farm Act, requiring all private businesses that grow, produce, package or distribute food items be nationalized and turned into collectives that could be controlled the government. It was like the *eminent domain* provision for property, as the government took over everything from the farms to the grocery stores. Owners got virtually nothing for their businesses."

"But what about Archer Williams and other conglomerate food producers?" asked Shea. "They were still in business and were doing fine. It is only recently that they've come under the thumb of Washington, right?"

"Congress initially exempted them. If they were large enough, they weren't taken-over because the Act said *large businesses had the means to ensure their products were safe*. They were a GovCo. It was all b*ll sh*t!" he said with force in his voice. "They just paid Congress off. That's all."

"So, what happened to your grocery stores then?" asked Maria.

Desmond answered with invective in his voice, "We had to close them. My father said he'd rather die poor, than sell out to the extortionists in government."

"We didn't hear anything about that on the news," said Shea. "The only thing I heard was that small grocery stores weren't doing well in the economy and they needed government help. Fourier said the government would rescue them, give them something for their failing businesses – at least enough for them to live on."

"That's actually true," said Desmond. "They gave them just enough to live on – but nothing more. But, the media was afraid it would happen to them too, if they squawked. At least, that's what I think. So, they said very little about it. What they did say, they made sure it fit their model of capitalistic greed! *It was those greedy business people. They brought it all on themselves – causing the diseases in the food supply just to make a buck.* That's what they did talk about." He stopped and then added, nearly whispering, "You know those capitalistic pigs are the bane of the nation."

"And mankind," said Maria.

No one laughed, but sadly nodded in agreement. All understood, as all had suffered similar consequences from having high ambitions.

"All I heard was capitalistic pigs," said Sumner coming up and stepping into the conversation. "I guess you're talking about me again." This time, they all did laugh.

"We were just talking about what happened to Frank and Latoya, JC." said Maria.

Sumner frowned, his demeanor changing. "Yep, it could have been anyone. And yet, it has been. Nearly all of us. You know that while they impose thousands of laws on us, Congress almost always exempts itself from those same laws. Why I know personally, senators and congressman who came to Washington as middle class Americans and within four to six years amassed millions. For years there were no laws prohibiting insider trading by congressmen. And, when they finally put the measure in place, there were plenty of exclusions added. Sure, they're supposed to keep their investments out of anything that might even smack of impropriety, but they don't. They buy and sell on inside testimony and information they get all the time. They also buy and sell property -- either buying land and forcing a federally-funded state program to build next to their property with all the roads and infrastructure needed to make it a thriving-busy intersection or doing it for friends who gratefully *repay* the congressman after the deal is done. Either way, they make a fortune. I've been there. I know."

"It's not illegal?" asked Shea.

"It doesn't matter. They protect their own. There was once a congressman from New York who had millions of unpaid taxes. He was a crook. He cheated the government every way he could, yet his constituents kept re-electing him because they were stupid. But honestly, it's gone on so long, there's mud on both sides of the aisle -- the Constitution Party and the People's Party. Both are corrupt. It's the establishment parties that are the problem – not one or the other. They've been in power too long and they'll do everything and anything they can to stay there."

As the night wore on, Shea met person after person who'd come to Wyoming to try to escape from the shenanigans and the cheats. And, she learned something else. The former state of Wyoming was becoming known as the *Freedom Islands* of the USSA. But, what did that mean? To more and more, it meant independence from the tyranny of Washington. People could build businesses and live their lives knowing that the state government would protect them – at least when it had been considered a state under the old constitution. Wyoming led the country in being the least cooperative state in implementing federal programs and assisting with inquiries and investigations. It had decided not to take federal money for anything and had become more and more delinquent in sending its hard-earned tax dollars to the D.C. coffers. Wyoming was self-sufficient. When pushed by the ministries for some action or response, the state governor generally answered with, "We'll look into it." But he never did.

The Administration eventually threatened federal action if the state didn't cooperate, but at that point, D.C. had little leverage. The state took virtually nothing from the feds. The only thing left to Washington was military intervention – something to which even the Fourier Administration wouldn't even be willing to resort.

The other people Shea spoke to included a husband and wife doctor team who had quit practicing medicine, forced out by the National Health Care Act. The NHCA required all doctors to submit patient diagnoses to a National Board for a second opinion. The National Board then took its time to review everything and prioritize the treatments. That took time – a lot of time -- and patients died. Doctors were fed up. Many left the practice and even fewer wanted to get in. The doctor shortage was more acute than any epidemic of a serious illness could have been. So without doctors and with a crumbling healthcare system, the Ministry of Health and Human Dignity created a group of *para-doctors*, like physicians' assistants but with the authority of a full medical doctor. They had completed up to two years of medical school, but were otherwise not licensed. These para-doctors filled the treatment gap even though malpractice was wide-spread with this group.   But these para-doctors were granted complete immunity from prosecution by the government ministry.

Another couple had sought refuge in Wyoming after developing an extensive catering business with branches in many of the major cities. A gay worker filed a discrimination lawsuit against them when he wasn't promoted to shift manager. The Equal Employment Ministry filed a lawsuit on behalf of the employee. The couple had elected to fight it; yet, after staggering amounts of legal costs, they lost the case and were forced to turn over their entire business to the worker as restitution. The couple said they had an older son who lived with them who was gay, but none of that had mattered.

Another woman, young and single, had taken over her family business of seventy-five years before a uniquely-owned company started up and took all of her business. She had tried to compete as a woman-owned business, but the federal mandate for GovCo's requiring them to spend a minimum of 25 percent with disadvantaged vendors (known as set-asides), in this case with transgendered, physically-impaired, minority persons, had forced many of her GovCo customers to drop her company and use the competitor. She had provided better products and services and even better pricing, but it didn't matter. Cutting her prices even more, far below those of the competing business, also made no difference. She went out of business, as did hundreds of others. But for that one transgendered, physically-impaired, minority person, it was winning the lottery – worth hundreds of millions. The woman had learned later that the uniquely-owned business had performed poorly, but had been given grants from the federal government to keep it in business. Such was the way the world now worked.

Shea learned of other stories too – one just as egregious and tragic as the next. The irony for all was that for a government so bent on *fairness*, it had a created a system completely antithetical to that premise. Those who were deserving based on their hard work were punished, and those who were either part of the crony class or were in positions to take advantage of the system, did just that. *It was evident who the losers were,* Shea wondered, *but in the end, who were the real winners?*

By the end of the evening, Sumner came over and put his arm around Shea. "I'd like to show you one more thing," he said. "Come with me."

Shea followed him up the log stairs, through the double French doors at the back of the house and down the hall to his study.

"So this is where the real work is done," she said smiling. "Nice office."

The study was large and paneled with knotty Pine. Two thick trusses girded the sides of the roofline , and an alcove surrounding the ceiling offered a place for abundant wildlife trophies, ranging from red foxes to badgers. In the back of the room were mounted heads of bison, bighorn sheep, and a tremendous fourteen-point elk that dominated the room.

"Did you shoot all of these?" asked Shea, looking at each specimen.

"Oh, hell no," answered Sumner, "although I wish I could say I did. No, the law doesn't allow you to hunt these anymore. These were all bagged by my great grandfather and my great, great grandfather. I guess you could say they're heirlooms." He laughed.

Sumner grabbed a beautiful, lead-crystal decanter that sat on the credenza behind his rough-hewn desk. He poured healthy portions of some of his reserved McCallen scotch-whisky straight into two short, cocktail glasses nearby. "This is how we do it in Wyoming," he said with a grin, handing her a glass. He took a quick sip and put it down. "You don't have to drink it if you don't want to."

Shea could only think of Patrick. She would sometimes have a nightcap with him before they went up to bed. It was usually a single malt scotch, but never as good as the one she was sipping.

"Nice," she said, taking a drop of the ultra-smooth scotch on her tongue.

"Yeah, I quite like it," answered Sumner. "But this is what I want to show you." He walked over to a dresser where there was a cherry humidor and an antique, hand-wound clock. The clock had been his great-great-grandmother's, dating back to the 1800s. It ran by a spring that had to be wound at least once per week. Weights would drop as the second hand clicked through its paces, making the complete orbit around the clock face.

Sumner pushed two hidden buttons on each side of the dresser, and a secret drawer that looked to be part of the dresser frame popped forward from its moorings. It was a clandestine drawer – one that someone might find in a spy novel or suspense thriller. Inside the drawer was a black, leather case double-tied with a thick, red cord. Sumner untied the binding and opened the case, moving with the care of someone deactivating an explosive device. He proceeded to lift out a short stack of paper and set it in front of her.

"This is what is going on here," said Sumner, pointing to the top page. "This is why we're here."

The page read,

Declaration of Secession

Shea looked up at him with astonishment. "You can't be serious," she remarked.

"Oh, we're very serious. We've all sat around and been the victims of a government that is out of control and has become our ruler and master. This is not what made this country great. America is but a shell of what it used to be. We must change that," said Sumner. "Read on …"

Shea diverted her eyes back to the page, intrigued by the document she held in her hands.

Here now, in accordance with the laws and statutes presented within the framework of the state constitution, as originally ratified and subsequently amended, we, the people of the great state of Wyoming, do hereby approve and endorse this declaration of secession from the federal union of states, known as the United States of America (USA). As this state does not, nor has it ever, recognize its admission into the conglomerate of states now known as the United Socialist States of America (USSA), no declaration of succession from this body is required.

Forthwith, we assert that the state of Wyoming is no longer part of the USA, as this legal body was formally dissolved when the USSA was established. Furthermore, the inherent contract between the federal government and the states is breached, and that which was enumerated within the ratified 1790 Constitution of the United States of America (US Constitution) is no longer binding.

The inherent provisions and, thereby, the covenant of the US Constitution with the American people are null and void with the ratification of the USSA Constitution. Specifically violated are the following articles and amendments.

1. Article 1, Section 8. The responsibility of the federal government is to protect its people; that responsibility has been abrogated. The U.S. military, established by Congress, has been replaced by a domestic, federal police force , conscribed without the consent of the states or the Legislative Branch. The formation of a domestic military unit to enforce unilateral orders and proclamations of the Executive Branch of government is against the provisions of Article 1, Section 8 and Article 2, Section 2 of the US Constitution. The power to establish an army lies only with the Legislative Branch of government, explicitly to prevent the leader of the Executive Branch from usurping power from the people whom he / she is sworn to serve.

2. Article 10. The nullification of the rights of states to elect and assemble representatives of their own people is in direct conflict with the provisions granted and protected by Article 10 of the US Constitution. The rights of states in a federal system was an essential concept to the ratification of the original constitution in 1790. Without such rights, the will of the people is trampled and the rule of law becomes – and has become – subject to the vagaries of those who legislate from their ivory tower in Washington, D.C.

3. Amendment 16. Taxation of the states and their citizenry has reached usury levels at which the rights of the individual taxpayer have been peculated and replaced with a system of welfare that supports a majority who are able to sustain themselves but choose to live from the

266

bounty of others. Such a system cannot continue without detrimental ramifications to the rest of society. Such action was never intended by the Sixteenth Amendment to the US Constitution, which was established to reduce tariffs which were crippling the economy. Modest taxes of two percent enabled the nation to build a military force capable of defending the country from foreign aggression.

4. ...

In total, there were sixteen pages of complaints filed with the secession declaration. And, on the final page, the last paragraph read,

This declaration is hereby ratified by this state convention, duly formed and constituted for the purpose of determining the future of the region and its people, this day, April 15, in the year of our Lord 2049.

The closing paragraph was one of immense irony. Only months earlier, the federal government had outlawed the use of the words God, Lord, Christ, Apostle, Disciple, and other Judeo-Christian religious references. However, an exclusion was made for the words Allah and Mohammad.

Shea took a deep swig of her scotch, paused and looked at the remaining tea-colored liquid at the bottom of her glass.

"Go ahead ... finish it. There's more," said Sumner.

Shea knocked back the glass and put it down on the desk. "No, I think that will do," she answered.

"Is something wrong?" asked Sumner, watching her.

"How could things not be wrong?" she responded. "But I guess I really never expected things to come to this. I mean, you read about the Civil War and all ... about South Carolina's first move to secede in 1860 ... but you never expect the country would ever devolve back to that point again. Will this lead to another civil war?"

"I don't know," said Sumner. "I truly hope not. We'd like to think that Washington has enough problems domestically and internationally not to press the case against us. They are bankrupt and wouldn't be able to raise much in funding to rebuild an army."

"Okay, then what's next?"

"As you know, I've cut all of my ties with Congress. And the friends that you met here tonight have been working with Maria and me for the past two years to get the necessary signatures in Wyoming to move this declaration through to the legislature. The governor has approved the language, as have both houses of the statehouse. It will be passed next April, if not sooner."

Shea stared at her friend, shaking her head solemnly. There was terror on her face. "But what if they do take action? Do you realize what they will do to you – to all of you?"

Sumner looked at her, perplexed. "You say *they*. Who do you mean when you say *they*?"

"Of course I mean the federal government. I don't think they'll let you do this, regardless of how distracted you think they are. If it does come to a civil war, what can come of it but tens of thousands … hell hundreds of thousands … killed or injured. Four years of fighting between 1861 and 1864 left over six hundred thousand dead. Is that what you really want?"

"No. But at some point the people of this country have to stand up to tyranny! That's what our Founding Fathers did during the Revolutionary War. They stood up to the British and King George III. They didn't back down and go quietly into the night. We here in Wyoming are a different breed than others, I guess. We don't put up with this crap. We're a lot like those Texans down there. We're fiercely independent, and we want to stay that way. If the government won't represent us any more, we'll represent ourselves."

"If you do, you're inviting the tanks," said Shea, "just like the Soviet Union when it moved into Hungary in 1956." But then she stopped suddenly. She looked at Sumner and tilted her head to one side, almost imperceptibly. "But, you don't think they will do that do you?" she asked, seeing the calmness and resoluteness in Sumner's demeanor.

"Again, we don't know," said Sumner without flinching. "We must be fully prepared for it, just like John C. Calhoun and South Carolina. The big difference is that we aren't fighting about the injustices of slavery – something everyone agrees on and have for two hundred years. No, we're seceding over the violation of the basic premise embedded within the Declaration of Independence – that our natural rights as citizens are being and have been taken by the very government we elected to safeguard them."

"So you're prepared to fight in the streets if necessary? Fight the tanks? Fight the convoys and bombers? Fight your own countrymen?"

"As you say, they had to make that choice in April 1775. This regime is the face of tyranny. We believe it will only grow worse, especially since there are no constraints on them with the new constitution. There is nothing keeping them from exerting total and utter control over all of us. You've read Orwell's *1984*? Well, it just took sixty-five years longer than he thought it would."

"Isn't there another way, though, JC? There must be another way – something other than this?" said Shea.

"We've tried. We've played by the rules and look where we are. Now we can only elect our congress once every ten years, and even then, they will choose the first citizen. You and I both know those elections won't be free and fair – they haven't been since the dismantling of our borders and the granting of amnesty to anyone who walks across the Rio Grande. No, Shea. The only hint at change came from your broadcast interview with Jennings. That is what brought us together here tonight in Wyoming -- to celebrate the drafting this document. We saw in you what we, ourselves, had been unable to do. Challenge the *status quo* and confront the Geryon of the Administration. There is no question that this Secession Declaration will smack them in the face and, likely, they will not tolerate it. No leader would want to see the Union dissolved on their watch. Lincoln didn't, and I'm sure Fourier doesn't."

"You're right about that," said Shea. "I'm just worried about the aftermath here in Wyoming. It could be devastating – especially after what we've seen in Cheyenne and Springfield."

Sumner just shrugged. "We will prepare as best we can. That's all I can say."

"Is this a secret? Is the secession document something you've been able to keep from people on the outside?" asked Shea. "I would think you'd have leaks."

"We haven't tried to keep it a secret, but at the same time we haven't made any announcements. It's well known throughout the state. We had to advise the state legislature, of course. To our benefit, the news media has ignored the story. It's too damaging to the Fourier. One of the local news outlets tried to run a story, but it was silenced. They were threatened with their license being pulled, so they shut it down before it hit the airwaves."

"What about the foreign press? Why haven't they picked up the story?"

"There's too much foreign aid coming out of Washington these days. They don't want to disturb the gravy train. Billions are spent overseas every year by this government. Much of it goes in the pockets of foreign dictators or national officials. Even governments in the former countries of Britain, France and Germany get paid off. Everyone is in on it. It's a way they can all cash in. An official of what government sends his tax money to another country as foreign aid. That country sends him their tax money as aid. Both deposit the other country's aid into their own pocket. It's a *quid pro quo*."

"What do you mean?" Patrick asked.

"You've heard the saying 'You scratch my back and I'll scratch yours?'"

"Yeah."

"Well, it's great for them. The problem is, it's not their money. Essentially, they steal it from their own citizens who pay it in taxes."

"When will the Wyoming governor sign this?"

"Oh, the governor doesn't have to sign anything. We're holding a state convention. The delegates of the legislature – statehouse and senate -- will assemble to vote for its adoption. We have the votes too. Mark my words."

Sumner put the document back in its leather case and locked the drawer. "I have my shotgun locked and loaded. We're ready for a fight out here, and we won't shrink from it."

They left the study and headed back outside. As they walked, Sumner continued to press Shea. "So, what do you think? Are you with us?"

"I'm not sure, JC."

"I was hoping we could count on you to be here and support us. We need a spokesperson like you. We need a face for this revolution."

"Revolution? You're calling this a revolution now?" asked Shea, now agitated. "It sounds more like the Nicaraguan Contras of the 1980s or the Castro rebels of the 1950s than the voice of reason now."

Sumner stopped and turned toward her. "Really? You think this is all about a violent overthrow?"

"I don't know. I'm afraid it could lead to that."

"Maybe it will, but we're all hoping it won't. We don't want violence, even though the other side has already brought out the guns."

"You're right, JC," said Shea. "My comments were a little strong. I didn't mean to suggest that you were fomenting a violent overthrow."

"All we are trying to do is separate and form an independent, sovereign nation that will protect the rights and liberties of the individual – the way America used to be. We are just rebelling against the oppressions of a regime that threatens our way of life. It threatens what we have known about this country since we were young. They have been deconstructing America for a very long time and have finally brought her to her knees. It's a sad ending for the once great experiment they used to call the United States of America."

"And you think the sacrifice of thousands of Americans is going to make it right? There is no way you can go up against the military might of the USSA, regardless of how depleted it has become. Wyoming doesn't have 1 percent of the resources of the federal government."

"What if others joined us?"

"Who?" asked Shea.

"Other states."

"Have others expressed interest?"

"I have heard from the governors, or should I say former governors, of many states. That is all I can say on the subject."

"Have they started their own secession process?" Shea asked.

"I'm hopeful that they will jump on the train as they see it leaving the station," said Sumner. "But we need someone who can articulate the message as you've done."

"Your problem is you have the wrong message."

"Perhaps," said Sumner. "Then, what would you say?"

She thought a moment. "We are challenging those who seek to turn our country from one of opportunity to one of dependency. We are rejecting the ideology of a political aristocracy ruling us under the chains of a secular divine right. We, the people of that more perfect Union, categorically reject any allegiance to a government that is not of the people, by the people or for the people of this great nation."

Sumner smiled. There was a twinkle in his eye, and he extended his hand toward Shea. "As in ancient mythology, Atlas struggled to hold up the heavens, just as we have. But, we will no longer suffer under the weight of it. As of now, Atlas is in revolt," he said. "Welcome aboard."

*****

CH 40 Officer Vasquez

The BBQ at the Sumner's had been uplifting, showing Shea that there were many in the country, or at least in Wyoming, who supported the need for change — something more radical than those with which conservatives were normally comfortable. Moreover, she found that she was not the only one who had suffered at the hands of the Administration's ministries. Hers was not an isolated incident. It was one of many, and it was one of many more that were most assuredly to come.

The next morning, she heard the rooster crowing outside her window, just beyond the grill pits that had offered the luscious feast from the previous night. Maria had mentioned they usually had breakfast on the porch around seven o'clock, and Shea's PCD told her she had plenty of time to ready herself.

The air was crisp and cold as Shea marched the short distance toward the lodge. The sun cast long, distinct shadows all around her, and a brilliant blue sky shown overhead. It was a day that oozed with new possibilities.

"Good morning," Shea said spiritedly, as she approached the patio where Sumner and Maria sat at a large, antique oval table that had been in the family for generations.

"We waited for you," said Sumner, putting down his computer tablet and placing the white, cotton napkin on his lap.

Maria came in with the coffee and poured a cup of black Joe for everyone.

"What did you think of last night?" she asked, setting the floral, ceramic pot down on the table.

"Inspiring," Shea said.

It was then that Sumner noticed a change in her. Her mood was upbeat – no longer the down-and-out melancholy that he'd seen in her during the previous months.

"Good," Sumner responded. "That's exactly what we hoped for."

"So what are you going to do now?" asked Maria.

"I'm not sure. I haven't thought that far ahead. But, I guess I'll go back to Boston and figure out what to do." Deep down, she knew that wasn't an option. She knew she couldn't return to Boston. There was nothing there for her anymore. Her home had been confiscated by the government as had all the rest of her personal property. She was homeless. She was spouse-less. She was penniless. But she was not friendless. She was finding that friends were, in fact, plentiful.

"You should stay here with us until you figure it all out," said Maria.

Shea smiled graciously. "I appreciate that, but I couldn't."

"Yes, you can. And you will," said Sumner, not taking no for an answer. "You can find someplace in Cheyenne and eventually move then. You'll have a job at GOFLA, and … well … that's it. That's all there is to it."

"But …."

"No buts, Shea. I insist," said Sumner. "You'll stay with us. We need you."

"Thanks," answered Shea, embarrassed by the flattery. "But only until I find a place. And it won't take me long."

"Stay as long as you like. We haven't scheduled anyone else in your cabin for at least a few days," Maria said, laughing.

"And JC, I'm not going to sign-on with GOFLA. I admire what you're trying to do, but I just don't think it's the right thing right now. I'm worried about the potential for violence."

"I understand. Well, you can still stay with us. I'll see what I can do to help you find something nearby. I know a lot of people in Wyoming, as you can tell. It shouldn't take me long."

Sumner made a few calls on her behalf and set her up with a long-time friend of his from Laramie. Winton Castello owned a large software engineering firm that specialized in writing programs for the Ministry of International Security. He was a billionaire who made his money in developing sophisticated targeting and evading software for military weapons systems. Since then, he had retired and spent his time with a new software firm, which had received National Security Administration grants for top-secret projects. Prior to becoming an entrepreneur, he had been a full colonel in the Marine Corps, retiring with full honors. However, his affiliation with Sumner had tarnished his reputation on Capitol Hill and his grants had largely dried up. Now, his business relied on what he could get working with foreign governments, although he was careful not to offer them anything that would harm the defenses of the U.S. He still did odd-job projects here and there, when a ministry couldn't find anyone else that could solve their problem or create what they needed. Castello's firm was unquestionably the best in the business.

Shea didn't even have to interview, other than a brief phone call from Castello who told her that anyone Sumner recommended was as "good as gold" for him. "You can start on Monday," he had said to her.

But, it was before her first day that she received a call while she was still staying at the Sumners' place. She had found a place in Laramie and was expecting to move the following week, after she'd started with Castello's firm.

Hello?" she answered.

"Hello, may I speak with Shea Disone?" It was a nondescript man's voice, one probably in his late thirties or early forties.

"Speaking," she said casually.

"This is Officer Vasquez. I'm with the Belizean Foreign Ministry in Belize City. How are you today?"

The call sent a cold chill up her spine. Her Belize adventure had been one she had wanted to forget, and this was an unwelcome reminder of that unfortunate event in her life.

It was an odd introduction for such a call. It was as if he were a long-lost friend just calling to see how she was or whether she would contribute to the local police gala event.

"Uh, fine," she muttered, nervously. "Can I help you with something, Officer Vasquez?"

"Yes, Ms. Disone. We received some information about a missing person. I believe his name is Hank Fannon. Do you know him?"

"Uh, no. I can't say that I do," she said, knowingly lying.

"Ms. Disone, our immigration ministry has a record of your visiting Belize only a few weeks ago, perhaps even more recently. Our sources tell us that you were looking for your husband, Patrick Disone, while you were down here. Is that true?"

"Go on," she said, without answering.

"Well, we also know that you were having an affair with Mr. Fannon while you were here."

Shea's heart began to beat faster. "I don't know what you're talking about," she said. "You must have the wrong person."

"You're fingerprints are all over his apartment, Ms. Disone."

"I don't think so. You have the wrong person," she said preparing to hang up.

"Do you know a Julia Novak?"

Shea could hardly breathe. "What do you want?"

"Mr. Fannon was found beaten to death in a swamp not far from Belize City. What do you know about that?"

"I told you. I don't know anything about ..."

"Ms. Disone, you will need to come down to answer questions about Mr. Fannon. You need to be on the first flight out. If you do not comply, we are working through our embassy in Washington to have you arrested and extradited down here. Do you understand that?" said the officer gruffly.

Shea didn't know how to answer. Her head was spinning as she sat down to think. "Uh, well. I'll have to contact the authorities here and see about getting my travel documents."

"You do that Ms. Disone. And, we understand too that you're staying with Congressman Sumner in Wyoming – yes, we know about that too. We know where you are and where you'll be Ms. Disone."

"But ..."

"If you keep us informed of where they are, it will help your case as well. They are co-conspirators now that you've involved them in this matter. It's too bad you had to get your friends wrapped up in this, though. Are they in the house now?"

"Uh, well, yes. I think so," she answered.

"Good. That's a very good start, Ms. Disone. We will be contacting you again later today. You need to be available to answer your phone. We want to make sure you make that flight down here to Belize tomorrow, now don't we." The line went dead.

Shea sat in stunned silence. *How did they know all that?* She asked herself. *They have me. I didn't do anything, but my fingerprints were all over the apartment and if Hank was murdered it was logical they would come looking for me.*

She spent the next hour trying to reach someone in the Belizean ministry, but no one had any answers for her, and they couldn't confirm any information she'd given them.

Beeeeep. Beeeeep.

It was her PCD, and the image of Sumner popped up on her screen. He looked worried.

"Hello, JC? I was just about ready to call you," she began. "I just got a call from the Belizean Foreign Ministry. They say they have information on me being in Belize City, and they're accusing me of killing someone I met down there who was helping me find Patrick. He threatened if I don't cooperate that he'd have me arrested and extradited. What am I supposed to do?" she said in a panic.

"I'm not sure," Sumner answered. "I just don't have a good feeling about it. Did you verify what they were telling you? Did you call the ministry down there?"

"Actually, I did."

"What did they tell you?"

"I reached someone in the documents area of the ministry. They said they can't discuss the particulars of any on-going investigation or program in which they're involved."

"That doesn't make sense."

"Listen, JC, it looks like I have to go down. I'll be leaving here this afternoon."

"Shea, why don't you wait a day or so? Let me make some calls and see what I can find out. What was the name of the person who contacted you?"

"Officer Vasquez. He's with the Foreign Ministry there in Belize City."

"Vasquez?"

"Yes, why?"

"Did he ask about us – Maria and me?"

"Actually, I was going to mention that too. He said I had put you at risk too and that he knew where we all were. He asked if you and Maria were here today."

Shea could see the look on Sumner's face turn to alarm.

"Is Maria at the house?" he said urgently.

"Yes. I thought both of you were here," said Shea.

"Get out of the house now! Get Maria too. You both have to leave!" Sumner shouted at her. "I don't have time to explain other than to tell you that Vasquez isn't who he says he is. He's not from Belize, he works for Ratner. I just got a call from a deputy down at the Laramie County police department. I know him well. He told me Vasquez and the sheriff are taking orders from the Minister of Unity and were told to wait until they had all of us here at the ranch. Ratner was pissed that you got back into the country and now wants all of us put away before we can cause any more harm. You and Maria have to get out of there!"

Shea clicked off the line and raced downstairs. "Maria! Maria!" she shouted. But she didn't hear a sound. She went to the back of the lodge and looked out the panoramic back window which normally framed the beauty of the rugged terrain surrounding the ranch. There, not far away was Maria calmly brushing down one of the stallions, just outside the stables.

The shattering of glass was deafening, and shards from the window sliced into Shea's her face and chest. The pain was so intense, it sent shockwaves through her system, overwhelming her brain and her emotions. She staggered back, clutching her breasts. Within seconds, another shot ripped through the window, taking out the rest of the glass and shattering a ceramic platter on the windowsill. Shea fell to the floor, her mind spinning as if caught in an epileptic seizure. She could only whisper weakly "Call JC" into the phone, and the device connected her.

"Shea! What's going on?" came the shouts from JC over her small hand-held receiver.

"JC, I'm being shot at!" she yelled back. "Maria's out back. I can't get to her!"

"Get out of there!" he told her. "Crawl down to the basement and go out through the tunnel." He had shown her the elaborate maze of tunnels one day when he'd gone down to get a bottle of wine from the wine cellar.

She hung up and hobbled toward to the door as another two shots came blasting through the kitchen. One spray of bullets lodged into the cabinets across from the window; the second struck her in the right shoulder just as she reached the stairway going downstairs.

"She must be in here!" she heard coming from outside as she limped down the wood-planked stairs. She slumped forward, struggling to get to the basement. At the bottom of the stairs, she stopped, panting heavily, her body numb from shock. She leaned back against the doorframe, wondering if she could go on.

Blood ran down the side of her chest, soaking her powder blue blouse and beginning to stain the top of her plaid skirt. It hurt every time she took a breath, so she kept her gulps for air shallow and fast. She dropped to the floor and crawled as best she could, pulling herself along the mauve and green carpet and leaving a trail of bright red on the carpeting behind her. There was no way to hide her trail, and she didn't try. All she could do was make it to the tunnel and lock herself in.

Just as she reached the doorway, hidden behind a row of shelves containing Maria's canned goods, the lights went off. Shea pushed open the heavy, spring-latched door and rolled her body through, collapsing just around the corner from a large, reinforcing steel beam that was meant to fall into place at a moment's notice should an urgency arise. She slammed the door shut and released the latch, letting the steel beam fall into place.

The blood was flowing steadily now, and she felt light-headed. Although the pain was severe, she could feel her body growing cold and realized she was starting to go into deep shock. She feared she was bleeding internally, and if the bullet grazed a vital organ she would have very little time left. She sat gathering her strength and slowing her breathing. *All I have to do is get up and move down this tunnel,* she thought. *Safety is just down the way.*

Then, there was a squeaking noise, and she could hear loud voices coming closer, only a few feet away on the other side of the door. Moments later, she made out the sound of footsteps clomping down the stairs to the basement.

"She's behind the door. Get the battering ram. If that doesn't work, we'll use explosives," said a low, gruff voice.

Shea could feel air coming in from the other end of the tunnel. It was dark, but there was an emergency flashlight next to the door. *Thank you, JC,* she said to herself.

She grabbed the flashlight. "On," she said, and the wooden timbers of the tunnel appeared before her, reflecting the glow from the yellow, plastic lantern she held in her hand. She staggered toward the other end of the tunnel, not knowing where it would lead her. The only thing she knew was that it offered her a chance at survival. Her hands shook as they felt along the cold, hard, grainy earth on both sides of the tunnel, and every few yards they would run into a large, angular post that kept the structure from collapsing onto itself. She was weak, but she pressed on, smelling fresh air gently blowing onto her face.

She was only twenty yards from door when there was a sudden blast from behind her, sending a roar of debris and dust that knocked her flat on her face, blowing past her and choking off the air she had been chasing. She coughed, trying to free her throat and lungs from the dirt that threatened her freedom. Shea covered her mouth with her sleeve and kept pushing ahead.

There was another explosion behind her, and she listened to the creaking of the beams around her. Within seconds, a rumbling noise could be heard as the tunnel began caving in back by the door. It would only be a matter of time before the whole structure collapsed. Hacking and gagging, Shea lurched on until she saw the light, brown boards that signaled the tunnel's end. It felt like she had walked a mile, but she knew it couldn't have been that far.

Where is the opening? she thought, shining the light upwards. *It had to be above, but where?* There was no ladder or rope that she could see. But Sumner wouldn't have left the tunnel with no way out. *Think!* she said to herself. She tried climbing the walls, but there was no place to get a firm grip and with her gunshots, she was in no condition to scale a vertical wall.

Boom! A third explosion rocked the tunnel, and this time, she heard voices clearly at the other end of the shaft — but this time inside the door. *They've broken through!* she realized.

Furiously, she looked for a way out, but she found nothing. *What if she'd been walking uphill in the tunnel?* she thought suddenly. It hadn't felt that way, but there had been many ups and downs during the trek through the dim channel. She glanced again at the wooden wall beside her. She put her good shoulder against the wall and pushed as hard as her body would allow. The wall moved, but only an inch. Hearing voices growing louder down into the blackness behind her, she pushed with all her might. The wall swung open.

Light streamed in through the opening, and she found herself in the old visitor's cabin where she'd stayed the first night she'd been there. The opening came into the backroom and a closet tucked away in the corner. She shut the door behind her and staggered over to the window where she looked out. She could see the back of the lodge clearly as well as the stables. But that's when she saw it.

Shea covered her mouth and began to cry. She could see the body of Maria lying only a few feet from the barn doors, face down and hands outstretched. There were men dressed all in black surrounding the lodge, and she realized it would only be a matter of time before they found her in the guest house.

She left out the back door and limped toward the county road that lay just beyond the fence-line behind the cabin. There she acted as normally as she could and stuck out her thumb to catch a ride into town. A trucker came by and asked if she needed a lift. She nodded, and he'd told her to get in. But instead, she hopped in the truck bed and she ducked down low to ensure no one saw her as they passed the ranch.

Shea remembered little after that, except for waking up at a hospital in town. The trucker had apparently dropped her off at the emergency room when he found her bleeding and unconscious in the back of his truck. He hadn't stayed, probably thinking it were better if he wasn't involved so they wouldn't think he had done something to harm her.

"Shea! Shea, wake up!" said a voice hovering over her.

She tried to open her eyes, but they would not obey.

"Shea!"

Once again, she tried to respond.

"Shea, come on. Wake up!" the voice pleaded.

This time her eyes complied, her eyelids slowly lifting to reveal the beautiful blue irises beneath.

"Ah, there's my girl," said the voice. It was familiar, yet from another time or place. Her mind was still in a fog, and she was having trouble placing it.

"Don't try to talk, Shea. I'm here for you. You're going to be Okay. The doctors said you'll be fine."

Gradually, the more the voice spoke, the clearer the speech became.

"I … I … I don't know where I am," she mumbled, groggy from the sedatives.

"Shea, I said, you don't have to talk right now. I'm just relieved that you've come back to us. You're going to be Okay."

Like her other senses, her vision was also slow to return. The blurred images around her began to sharpen, and the face in front of her began to come into focus.

"Patrick? Is that really you?" she partly mumbled and partly mouthed without any sound coming from her mouth.

"Yes, honey. It's me. You need to get some rest. I'll check on you later. Go back to sleep. You've had a long few weeks. I'll see you again when you wake up."

Shea's eyes closed again, the sedatives kicking in, forcing her back to sleep against her will. *Patrick, are you there?* she thought. *Stay with me! Don't leave! I'll be waking soon, and we'll be together again.* Those thoughts swirled in a chaotic whirlpool of dreams, emotions, and memories. Her mind was in a place where fantasy and reality co-existed, sharing the same space at the same time, confused and surreal. It was hope and agony blended together, and she couldn't discern the two.

*****

CH 41 The Vote

It was Sumner who came into the hospital room carrying a bouquet of flowers. Shea was still heavily sedated, and she could hardly move.

"You've suffered some pretty serious gunshot wounds, young lady," said Sumner, smiling benevolently at her.

She opened her eyes. This time it wasn't the image of Patrick that she saw, but it was her very good friend. But, just as suddenly, feelings of guilt came over her. "Oh … oh, JC. I am so sorry," she said, grabbing his hand.

Tears welled up in Sumner's eyes. "It's Okay. She's in a good place," said Sumner, referring to Maria. "She didn't feel a thing. It was one shot, and it was over. She's with God now."

"I wish I could have saved her, but I couldn't," said Shea.

"I know. There was nothing you could have done, Shea. You shouldn't feel guilty. There is nothing anyone could have done. Maria was the love of my life. She's gone. I guess she's just another casualty of war," said Sumner.

"What are you doing here, then?" she asked, trying to sit up. "You're in danger."

"We're all marked, now," said Sumner with a sigh. "It was lucky that the truck driver dropped you off here at St. Elizabeth's Hospital. It is a stronghold for us citizens of Wyoming. They told the police that they have no record of a Shea Disone here. But, I don't know how long they can keep that up. It's against the law to lie to them, but they're doing it for me. I can only stay for a few minutes. I don't want to make things any more difficult than they already are."

"What are you going to do now?" Shea asked, concern written all over her face.

"We've moved up the vote. The state house is voting on secession tomorrow. We can't wait any longer or they will destroy all of us before that happens. We have to act now."

"It's not safe! JC, you can't go through with it. They will kill you this time!"

"Perhaps. But, we have the police on our side now. Vasquez and the sheriff were run out of town yesterday. We've taken back our police department. We should be Okay, at least for the moment. We'll have the state's National Guard surrounding the capitol building, so we don't expect any trouble."

"I don't know," said Shea. "Be careful."

"We will. You just take care of yourself. I'll call you later and let you know what's happening," said Sumner. "You won't be able to reach me for a while. I'll be out of contact, but I will get a hold of you once we have things worked out."

"Promise?"

Sumner smiled. "Of course," he answered.

***

Into the statehouse in Cheyenne filed the delegates, passing the two statues outside – one of Esther Morris, a women's suffrage advocate, and the other of Chief Washakie of the Shoshone tribe, known as a fierce warrior and diplomat. The state representatives' chamber was where the session was to be held, and it had a balcony overlooking the room where visitors could gather in the gallery.

As the delegates filed in, they had neither a look of delight, nor one of despair. There was a seriousness in the air that was oppressive – a gravity that felt uncomfortable. Any alacrity had been stripped from them long before. Most were stern and measured, but others showed signs of outright fear – a fear of what action the feds might take against them regardless of how they voted, just for being a part of the entire event.

The first vote was supposed to take place after the introductory speeches and an open floor debate. However, as much of the debate had already taken place, all that remained were the grandiose speeches by some of the more well-known and influential delegates. It was a time for venting by those few in opposition, grandstanding by those who were opportunists, and reason by those who were the actual architects of a new order.

From the balcony, many from the Wyoming ranch clan watched the proceedings. They were proud to be part of history – this time a good history that they fully embraced and supported. After so many years, positive change was coming and none too soon. Sumner was in the balcony looking on. He was happy that the event was finally being realized but was sad at the same time. Beside him was an empty seat. He missed Maria terribly, and he knew she would be very excited and proud of this moment as well. He only hoped she was seeing it all unfold from her place in heaven above him.

"I call on the representative from District 45, Matthew Singletary, from the People's Party, to offer that party's closing arguments *against* passing Resolution 671," the House Speaker said from his position behind the dais.

The state legislator came to the podium. He knew there was little he could do to prevent the declaration's passage, but at this point he was only trying to establish his party's position for the official record. At best he thought it was a mistake to vote for secession; at worst, it was treasonous. His belief was that in the end, his party would be vindicated, if only by historians years later.

"I can't tell you how strongly I oppose passage of this resolution. It is a mistake to opt out of the federal union, and it is a travesty that the Freedom Party is trying to railroad this through the citizens of this great state of Wyoming. It is betraying them and the nation. If you really believe that the nation has gone off track, then we need to do things in accordance with our constitutional rights. Every few years, our citizens go to the ballot box and elect USSA representatives who can steady the rudder or move it in the direction we want the country to go. We don't just quit and check out of the game! We don't just say 'To hell with all of you! We're going to do it our way, despite what the Constitution 2.0 says.' You're all cowards! You can't stomach following the law to make things right! You have to make up your own rules.

"You and your Freedom Party are so sanctimonious! You spout off about how great the old constitution was, yet you choose not to obey even that! You don't agree with the new constitution of the USSA, and you won't abide by the old one. How do you justify that? You can't just vote your way out of the Union! Even the old constitution wouldn't allow you to do that! That's called anarchy! That's what it is! It's an illegal revolt against our government – a government that was given to us by the Founders whom you so adoringly worship. Well, I hate to break it to you, but they aren't the Founders anymore – they *were* the Founders! That's it. And they weren't perfect, as you seem to believe. They didn't have all the answers. They made mistakes – yes, I said it. They made a lot of mistakes, creating an imperfect Union as a result. We're in the process of fixing that now after nearly three centuries!

"So, what you continue to worship is old and outdated. It's necromancy. Those dead, white guys don't live in our world today. What they had to say is meaningless in today's society. Our world is like living on Mars compared with what life was like in 1776. We needed a new constitution and a new way of thinking! That's why we have the People's Party. We are the ones who keep the process going. We are the ones who make sure the laws are current with our evolving technology and changing society. We can't live in the past. We must live for the future!"

He was earnest and passionate, but nearly everyone there had already made up their minds – one way or the other. His rhetoric was just that, filled with platitudes of Mother and Apple Pie. It was an art, well-practiced by both the People's Party and the Constitution Party, to say things that could not possibly be challenged. It seemed that only the newly-minted Freedom Party was willing to kneel before the alter of truth and hold it in reverence.

Unfortunately, the problems facing the state and the nation were created because for too long platitudes had usually won elections. Speeches were made, sounding grandiose and inspiring, yet saying virtually nothing. The uninformed voter was left to choose between the outright charlatan who reeked of self-interest and narcissism or the other candidate, every bit the mountebank as the other, only with faux sincerity and more charisma. It was a lose-lose proposition.

Beyond that, there were other practices intended to create smoke to obscure reality for the voter. "Free and open elections" were anything but – often stacked against the party challenging the incumbent. By outlawing photo identification, granting citizenry to anyone who came into the country illegally, issuing cell phone cards to the poor and illiterate as payment for voting for *their* candidate, shuttling the homeless from precinct to precinct to vote multiple times, counting dead-voters' ballots without checking, ignoring unfavorable absentee ballots from servicemen overseas, manipulating the software in electronic voting machines, and encouraging the "accidental" loss or destruction of ballots not to their liking. These hurdles had become insurmountable. With all of these dirty tricks, the system had become hopelessly rigged, and as a result, Wyoming was doing what could not be entrusted to the voting booth.

The state's House Speaker retook the podium and gathered his thoughts. "Mr. President," he said, referring to the president of the convention, "it is time we cast our ballots on the resolution as presented before this convention. I now turn the convention over to you."

As the House Speaker stepped aside, allowing the convention chairperson to come to the podium, the entire building shook violently. Then, within seconds there were several more tremors, followed by a horrific explosion within the chamber itself. To those on the floor of the state house, it appeared to have come from the upper balcony, where stone, plaster, and pieces of wood pummeled the participants down on the house floor below. Huge clouds of white dust billowed from the upper mezzanine choking those in the balcony and blocking them from view from anyone on the floor. No more than ten seconds later, there was another explosion that sent a volley of shrapnel loaded with nails and ball bearings throughout the floor of the convention where all the delegates had gathered. The deadly metal shards sliced through the air, carving a path into everything they touched. Delegates were struck in the head, neck and chest, and many fell face-first onto their tables where they had been seated. Blood splattered everywhere as did pieces of flesh, as people were ripped to shreds by the brutality inflicted on them. It was a gruesome scene, as the remaining attendees staggered to the exits, coughing in stunned silence.

But the quiet was torn as viciously as the bodies of the victims, with people beginning to scream from their wounds. The air thickened with smoke and debris, making it impossible to see much more than a few inches in any direction, and the delegates frantically pushed and shoved each other to get out, turning over tables and chairs to clear a pathway to safety. All dignity was lost. The fight or flight response overtook almost all of them. They were only trying to survive.

But it was the convention chairperson struggled to his feet. "Order! Order! Please exit the hall as quickly as possible, but we insist you do it in an orderly manner!"

The admonition calmed the crowd, but only for a moment, as a third blast erupted from behind him, ripping through the right wing of the chamber floor, sending fragments of desks, chairs and the chairperson's broken body flying through the air. At that point, pandemonium broke out, and those still remaining on the floor began fighting each other, clawing their way out of the room. Some convulsed from the thick smoke and dust and fell, lapsing into a coma. Others covered their mouths with handkerchiefs or pieces of clothing, coughing violently and gasping for air.

It took several more minutes, but finally armed guards swarmed the chamber, helping many get out before another explosion could take more lives. Over the speaker system, the head of security asked everyone to remain calm and exit the building as quickly as possible. Hundreds were led outside and onto the lawn as emergency crews arrived. Fire trucks, squad cars and ambulances from all over the city converged on the capitol building to help. Police sealed off the entire downtown area, preventing anyone from coming in or going out. Identification and credentials were checked and everyone detained as they canvassed the area for possible suspects.

The bomb squad attempted to go into the building but were called off.

"But we have to get the people out of there, chief?" asked the first fire lieutenant.

"Not until we get the Okay from the structural engineers. They said the damage was severe," said the chief, cautiously.

The lieutenant stood anxiously, watching the fires rage inside the building and flames leap from the broken, glass windows of the upper levels.

More than twenty minutes passed before the head of engineering came over to the chief, taking him aside and speaking quickly and quietly. The chief nodded, and the man left without saying another word.

"Well?" asked the lieutenant. "When can we go in? There are people dying in there. We have to get in there to save them!"

The chief just shook his head. "Sorry, lieutenant. Orders are to stand down. All we can do is try to contain the flames as best we can. The dome may collapse at any moment. We can't have you in there with your men. We just can't risk it."

The lieutenant fought the need to disobey orders. He looked at the building and knew the chief was right. It was nearly all consumed by flame. It would only be a matter of time before the entire structure imploded in on itself, killing anyone inside. Anyone who wasn't already dead, soon would be.

An hour passed, and the rescue crews pleaded with the fire chief to go inside to help the wounded. The chief hesitated, wondering if he had made the right decision in keeping his boys back. But then it happened. It looked like a scene from an apocalyptic movie. First the thick black smoke seemed to double in volume, rising over the remnants of the capitol, obscuring all but the golden dome. Then, groans from the building could be heard as the beams and stones began to weaken. The creaking of wood became more pronounced until the spine-chilling vibrations of splintering timbers and crumbling stones sounded the death knell of the capitol's glorious vaulted roof, which had graced the building since its consecration. The ribs of the arches snapped like dry twigs, and the exquisite gold-leaf panels with scenes depicting the grand history of the state of Wyoming crumbled and collapsed inside. Within seconds, the rest of the center collapsed, the walls falling inward and pulling the rest of the building with them.

The fire chief and his lieutenant looked on as the calamity reached its final coda. It was over.

Shocked by the sight, onlookers gasped as the iconic building, which had stood in the center of the city since 1890, vanished. Only the east and west wings were left partially standing, like guard towers of an army redoubt that had long since been abandoned.

Although the story seized headlines within Wyoming, there was little mention of it in the outside world. The only references in the news nationwide were that "an incident" had occurred in Cheyenne. The media noted that an explosion had gone off at the capitol and there had been casualties. One news anchor even commented that there were "suspicions that some rightwing radical group may have been involved in the bombing that took place late today," and that "Police are looking into it with the help of the Federal Bureau of Domestic Inquiry, the FBDI."

The Rightwing involvement had been purely accidental, but Fourier loved it. They immediately grabbed that slant and pushed all the networks to use it. "It's the only logical explanation for such a devastating and beastly act," was what Fourier was quoted later as saying. "It was probably the work of some deranged Freedom Party advocate."

When they began to get traction with the story, the White House ordered all stations to peddle it. They were getting mileage out of it when it was needed most.

It was fanning the anti-rebellion flames, which was just what they wanted ... what they had to have to control the protests that were growing daily.

"Early today," said Walter Jennings, the Fourier-sympathizing, news anchor, "First Citizen Fourier issued a statement through Justice Minister Welbourne that every and all measures would be taken to track down the Right-wing group responsible for the destruction of the statehouse in Cheyenne and the murder of over two hundred servants of the people of Wyoming. Fourier said, quote 'We will not rest until these criminals are brought to justice and face the stiffest penalty for what they have done' end quote. This is a story that we will continue to cover as it unfolds," said Jennings.

A real investigation was started by the Wyoming state police but was stopped after threats by the FBDI, which told them it was federal jurisdiction and the state was to cease immediately. But based on the state's preliminary findings, the explosive devices had been planted inside the walls of the statehouse several days before the event. Such access would have required insider help. They were also planted strategically in other locations throughout the building, next to support piers and beams, to bring down the entire structure -- a level of sophistication and access that would have been difficult for any private group. It all looked like whoever was responsible got intelligence and resources from both inside the statehouse and from outside the state. Execution of the plan was both professional and well timed.

Once the FBDI took over, the investigation went nowhere. No group or person was ever identified, and the investigation was suspended after three months – long enough for the common man to forget it had ever happened. *Other priorities had come up,* the White House had announced when asked later how the investigation was proceeding. "But you can rest assured we are continuing to investigate this matter vigorously," said Minister Welbourne. Of course, it was all a lie.

The news that Sumner and nearly two hundred others were presumed dead was buried on page thirty-four of Cheyenne's *Wyoming Tribune* – presumably due to pressure by Washington. But also buried within the story were other indisputable facts. The first bomb had been planted under a seat in the balcony, where Sumner and his wife were originally intended to sit. However, instead, Sumner was moved to the other side of the chamber after several other people requested seats in the area. The second bomb had been planted under one of the house representative's desks on the floor of the chamber. He had been an ardent supporter and co-writer of the secession document. The third device had been placed in a wall behind the podium, ensuring those leaders on stage would be killed. Other charges strapped to key support pillars throughout the building had been triggered simultaneously after the third charge had gone off. All had been detonated by a PCD. In addition to the over two hundred dead, another seven hundred were injured, many in critical condition.

Fourier smiled in the Oval Office. "I think we've done it," he said cheerfully. "I think we've killed off the revolution. Even King Chuck couldn't accomplish that back in 1776!"

*****

CH 42 Madness in Control

"I think we've had a very good week. Don't you think?" asked Fourier, sipping an Armagnac brandy with his feet up on his desk in the Oval Office.

"Yes, sir," said Ratner. "I think you've had a very good week, if I may say so."

"Yes, yes. I think we've finally shut the door on the entire sordid affair with the F-U Party, I mean the Freedom Party," he said with a loud laugh. "Well F-U to them is what I have to say!"

"It's good to have some peace of mind, First Citizen Fourier. It's been a long time coming."

"Now we can get back to our plans for a new America," he said, looking out at the cranes that surrounded the Washington Monument. "When will they be finished dismantling that ugly monolith, anyway?" he asked.

"I think the Washington Monument is due to be taken down completely within the next few weeks. We've cut up the Jefferson and sold the marble. We're only waiting on the cranes to come in and rip down the Lincoln Memorial. That shouldn't take much time," said Ratner.

"And my monument? When does my statue go up – there in the center of the Mall where Washington's used to be?"

"I believe they said it would be finished by the end of the year, First Citizen. "

"And it will be three times the size of Obama's statue, right? I can't imagine it being smaller than his."

"Yes, of course. His was bigger than King's, and yours is to be larger yet. Congress appropriated the funds for it. It will be bigger than life, for sure."

"Good," said her boss. "And nothing but gabbro granite – you know, the best black stuff there is."

"Of course, sir. That's what is spec'd in the plans," said Ratner. Then, trying to segue the conversation to more urgent matters, she asked, "Speaking of plans, sir. I was wondering what you want to do about the holdouts – you know, the small pockets of resistance we still see protesting against our authority … your authority from time to time?" She was quick to correct herself before she drew the ire of Fourier. "Do we need to use the military to intervene?"

"It's not necessary," said Fourier. "We've crushed them. It's over. They won't continue to fight. They know now that they can't win. We will just grind them into the dirt, like the insects they are. There's no reason to pursue any other options -- they won't be needed."

But Ratner wasn't so sure. She feared the resurgence of the Right, and felt contingency plans were needed.

"I understand, sir. But just in case there is ..."

"I said nothing else is needed," Fourier snarled back, not liking to be questioned.

"Yes, sir," said Ratner. She also didn't like the idea of being obsequious to someone else. Yet, she done so for years, and could wait a little while longer. She was patient.

But, the matter of the renegade conservatives did not go away. Small rebellions in cities popped up as quickly as those in other towns were suppressed by the local police. The news of these flare-ups did not filter their way up the chain to Fourier, even though there were those in the White House who were well aware.

Those in the ministries knew that action by Fourier against the rebels would suggest he had failed in his ability to quash them. Therefore, no one wanted to tell the emperor about his clothes. The First Citizen did have forces available to his command, but with the huge deficits and the shortage of international credit, the readiness of his troops was lacking. Combined with the fact that he had cut the nation's defenses to the bone – less than a quarter of what it had been before he had taken office – Fourier was in a weakened position to keep maintain any semblance of order within the states – other than through the Red Brigade.

To build-up the Red Brigade, drastic cuts were made to the rest of the military. Fourier had wanted his own internal police to keep the order – his order. Consequently, he had slashed the Navy from nine battle groups to two, with eight aircraft carriers mothballed prematurely. Army divisions were reduced to three from ten, and the Air Force emasculated, dropping to only one active air strike force. The USSA Marines were even more devastated, being reduced from three divisions to less than a brigade. Nearly 90 percent of funding for weapons projects had been shut off, citing no need to funnel money into programs that would never be used. As a result, there were no manned fighter jets or bombers in service and no new ones on the drawing boards. Sole reliance was on drones, which had grown in sophistication, but still could not read the minds of those in command. Research continued on a robotic army, but it was still years away. China and Russia already were deploying robotic troops, but they were led by humans. At the same time, each country had bragged about having completely independent, robotic battalions ready by 2050.

Eventually, the domestic unrest grew to the point it could no longer be kept from Fourier and he called a meeting of his czars and ministers to address it. "I want them destroyed!" he had yelled. In the end, his greatest weapon was the million-man Red Brigade, and all Fourier needed was an excuse. That excuse came quickly. Only months after the Wyoming incident, there was an outburst in Texas – one ripe for the picking.

Using old M1-A Abrams tanks from the *Ghosts* of the 1st Cavalry Division, 4th Brigade and a few APC's used in the Middle East war of 2021, Fourier directed the Red Brigade forces from his own office in Washington, not trusting his Homeland Generals to do the task. The event started as a planned rally in Fort Worth, Texas. Fiercely independent, the Lone Star state had a reputation, like Wyoming, for not being easily tamed. Having been under Mexican rule after the country separated from Spain in 1821, Texas fought the repressions of Santa Anna's dictatorial rule over Mexico until it won its independence in 1836. It was officially its own Republic until 1845 when it joined the Union as the twenty-eighth state.

After the devastation in Cheyenne, Texans took notice. Armed with rifles and shotguns, the citizens of Ft. Worth took to the streets downtown to protest the "thuggery" of the Fourier Administration. Chanting "Fourier is the new Santa Anna!" they walked from the Convention Center to Trinity Park, along the Trinity River. Fourier received information about the protest in advance and flew-in armaments to suppress it. However, unlike the other unarmed, peaceful protest of the civilians in Cheyenne, those of Ft. Worth fought back. By the thousands, they defended their positions and forced Fourier's troops to retreat, shooting back at the soldiers who were firing on them. It was a humiliating defeat for a federal government, and one Fourier wanted buried as quickly as possible.

Even the media had a difficult time handling the defeat. Initially reporting it as a test affront against what they characterized as home-grown Libertarian terrorists, the news organizations claimed the Administration's actions were "successful in curtailing those anarchist elements within the country." But further mishandling by the homeland ministry made the whole attack an embarrassment. Inexperienced in military matters, the Minister of Domestic Policing had intervened in the planning of the operation and confused the commanders on the ground. To make matters worse, they had miscued the coordination of backup resources, support infantry and light mortars, which hadn't arrived in time. The result had been a complete and utter failure.

When the news of the failure began to leak out, the White House put out its best tourniquet to stop the bleeding: "Due to the sophistication and organization of the protest in Ft. Worth," said Minister Ratner, "we have investigated and found that these incidents are the result of *foreign* interference. It is not that the citizens of the USSA are upset with what is happening in the country. This is a falsehood. People are *very* happy with the actions taken by the First Citizen. No, these acts of violence and anarchy are the work of foreign countries who wish nothing but the destruction of the USSA and its society.

"We have direct, irrefutable evidence that the Axis of Evil has been involved in manufacturing the terrorism we've seen in this country as of late. That evil, of course, is from Australia and Canada. Their interference in the affairs of the USSA is not acceptable and will not be tolerated. Effective immediately, we are imposing sanctions on both countries and blocking all travel to and from those nations. Unless their involvement ceases and we are issued expressed apologies, we will be breaking diplomatic relations with them and withdrawing our embassy personnel. Our troops will be put on heightened alert all along the three-thousand-mile border with Canada, and a fence will be erected to keep them out. We will also be revoking all passport entry into this country from those countries and bar all travel to those countries by our citizens."

When asked why a fence would be installed when, after two hundred years, there was still no fence along the southern border with Mexico, Ratner explained, "Because the Canadians are a threat to this country, that's why!"

Of course, it was all a lie; but, it no longer mattered. What did matter, however, was that those in power were beginning to believe their own stories. Madness was creeping into their minds, and they so fervently needed to believe their own fabrications that they became self-actualizing. Soon, no longer were they saying these things to convince others, but they were saying them because they believed them to be true. No amount of facts or figures would change them.

*****

CH 43 Shea's Rebellion

Shea had been steadily regaining her strength, and although she had lost a lot of blood, she had managed to survive. One of the bullets had barely missed her liver and surrounding vital arteries. She had been lucky.

"Shea, how are we today?" her doctor asked her, coming in and poking his finger at the computer screen which displayed her vitals and chart.

Shea turned down the volume on the media system overhead and pulled herself up higher in the bed. "Fine, doctor. Much better every day."

Not taking his eyes off her read-outs, the doctor said, "I think we're going to be able to release you here – probably tomorrow."

"Really?" she asked, excitedly.

The doctor glanced up, but his eyes didn't look at Shea. Instead, they were distracted by the 3-D image in the room projected from the media unit.

"What is it?" Shea asked, believing it was something on her chart that suddenly concerned the doctor.

"Oh, I'm sorry. I just noticed the special report on the explosions at the statehouse today," he answered, her brow furrowed with concern.

"Volume up," said Shea, finally seeing what her physician was viewing.

> "... we continue to ask questions about what happened here in Cheyenne. This is a tragedy that this city, this state, has never seen before. Behind me you see the rubble from what was once our beloved state capitol building. Beneath it that lie hundreds or more who were attending the conference when the bombs went off. We still do not know who was responsible, although the FBDI is doing everything it can to find out. A spokesperson for the Bureau reiterated that the perpetrators, which he said were clearly Right-wing terrorists, will be found and brought to justice. But, as for the bodies buried beneath the ruins behind me, we have been waiting for over a day to find out when anyone will be allowed in to begin unearthing the remains and clean up from this disaster. This is Derrick Linden, YBS, Channel 9 News, Cheyenne."

"Why won't they let anyone in to find the bodies?" Shea asked, shaking her head.

"I don't know," answered the doctor. "But, they must have their reasons." He turned back to Shea, putting back her chart. "You just go back to sleep. It's better that you get some rest right now." He left the room, walking down the hall toward the nurses' station, his heels clicking like a metronome on the linoleum floor.

Shea was stunned. *Sumner and all his friends had been there. Were they all killed?* she thought, her mind racing with all the horrific possibilities. There was an ache in her stomach, and she felt dizzy and disoriented.

"Call Sumner," she said. Her PCD dialed the number, but it rang several times without answer. "Sh*t!" she said. *It just can't be! It just can't! With Maria just being murdered, it can't happen that her husband is killed a few days later.* "Redial!" she commanded. But she only got the same result. No answer.

She looked back at the TV image. "Find Cheyenne explosion story," she said. The computer complied and switched channels to another that was carrying the tragedy with wall-to-wall coverage.

> *"This story will continue to get our full attention. But as more information is known, the picture doesn't seem to get any clearer. Earlier today, we learned that the purpose of the convention was to ratify a new state constitution. Although many in the state have been very vocal against the act, it appeared that the new constitution would have been ratified. For months, we here at the Wyoming Global News Network have been warning our viewers to get involved in the process and write or call their state representatives to stop the changes being proposed. It appears now that the more radical elements of the Right were involved in that effort and in bringing down the capitol building," said the local news anchor, dressed smartly in a brown-plaid blazer, starched white shirt and yellow and peach bow tie. "In a related story, the Justice Ministry remarked that the bombs that exploded could have been small nuclear devices. Minister Welbourne said if that were true, he would have no choice but to have the entire area cemented over with concrete to prevent the spread of radioactive decay that could harm local residents. He said his ministry was working feverishly to determine whether this was the case and had cement trucks stationed nearby to begin the pouring."*

Shea found the news report chilling. Any hope of uncovering the truth about what had happened and who had perpetrated the crime would be sealed forever once the cement trucks rolled in. It was easy to believe that covering the truth was exactly what Fourier wanted to do. Worse yet, for her and many others, they would never know what happened to those they cared for – would never see their bodies or be able to have closure. It would be whitewashed, just like everything else.

Upset and rudderless, Shea called other people she had met from the BBQ, but no one answered. No one.

The next day, Shea was granted her release, and the middle-aged nurse who had taken care of her wheeled her down to the elevator. "So, you're finally going home," she said in her usual cheerful tone.

"Yeah, I guess," answered Shea with uncertainty.

"What do you mean, 'you guess'?" asked the nurse.

"I mean, I really don't have a home anymore. My home in Boston is gone and now that of my friends is gone too. I'm just going to find a hotel for a while until I get things straightened out in my head."

The elevator LEDs showed they were going down and that the Mezzanine floor was next. "Shea, you can room with me if you wish. I have a big house – it's nothing fancy, but it's an old ranch house that me and my husband bought thirty years ago. He passed about eight years ago, I guess. It's been pretty quiet out there since then. You're more than welcome." She smiled and waited for the doors to open before pushing Shea out and into the lobby.

"That's really kind of you, but I need to regroup on my own. I've been through a lot these past months, and I'm only going to be a burden to anyone I'm around."

"Nonsense," replied the nurse. "You wouldn't be any trouble a'tall."

Shea tried to be diplomatic. She really didn't want to be around anyone. She'd lost her husband, her business, and most recently her two best friends, JC and Maria. She needed time to grieve and to forget. If she were lucky, she would also figure out what she was going to do with the rest of her life. In the meantime, solitude would be her new best friend.

"Perhaps later," said Shea. "For now, I'll just catch a ride to the hotel."

A bright yellow cab pulled up outside the hotel emergency room exit. The robotic driver didn't get out of the car to help with the luggage, but instead just pushed a button on the inside to relieve the trunk latch. Shea struggled to get up from the wheelchair while another hospital attendant placed her bag in the back of the cab. Shea plopped herself into the black, cushioned rear seat.

"Where to?" asked the auto-driver.

"Just find me a hotel downtown," said Shea. "Anyone will do."

Just as the taxi began to pull out, a hand reached in through the driver's window and grabbed its shoulder. "Not so fast," said a voice.

"What?" asked Shea, startled by the interruption.

"Take her to the J Galt Ranch, if you please," said the voice.

Shea looked out through her passenger window. It was Sumner.

With gleeful shock on her face, she exclaimed, "JC! ... Where ... how ... when?" she stammered.

"I've been here in this hospital too," he said. "I was just released this morning and saw on the board that you were being released as well. I just hung around here until I saw your wheelchair roll down to curbside."

"But ... but, I thought you were dead? Everyone thought you were dead?"

"Yeah, I hoped they would. I've been keeping a low profile. I gave them a false name here so it couldn't leak out. No one knows that I'm alive, except you, Shea."

Shea nodded. She understood how important it was to keep things a secret. There were too many people who wanted him dead and too many spies who would report where he was back to Washington.

"You're coming with me, Shea," he said, jumping into the backseat with her.

"I don't think the ranch is safe, JC."

"It's as safe as anyplace else," he answered.

"You're probably right about that."

They took the taxi to the ranch. Sumner had not been there since his wife's murder, and Shea could tell it bothered him as they drove up the long, dirt road to the log cabin-style lodge.

It was only five in the afternoon, but it was winter, and things got dark quickly on the prairie at that time of year. Shea got situated downstairs in the master bedroom while Sumner took one of the five upstairs guest rooms. He couldn't bring himself to go back to the master bedroom suite. There were too many memories.

"Do you think you'll want anything to eat tonight?" he asked. "You know you need to keep up your strength."

"I know, but I don't think so. I'd rather just sleep. Thanks anyway," Shea answered. She watched as Sumner left her room. It had only been less than a week since she had last seen him; yet, he had aged years during that time. She noticed he was more stooped than before, his shoulders rounded and his gate slower and without the usual bounce.

The next morning came early, and the muted crow of the rooster outside caused only a fluttering of eyelids at the crack of dawn. Instead, it was the sun's badgering rays that eventually hit the right angle to pry open the recalcitrant eyeballs of Sumner who had fallen asleep on the couch downstairs. Groggy, he went to check on Shea and see if she were already up.

Although he could cook, Sumner hadn't cracked an egg in years, and the kitchen looked like a tornado had ripped through it by the time he had finished cooking breakfast. But it was his usual morning feast that he prepared -- three eggs over easy with deer sausage links, whole wheat toast with peach jam, grits, and hash browns with ketchup. Sumner like his coffee thick and black, but he put out cream and sugar for Shea.

"So, tell me what happened," she asked, sipping her coffee from a white, Texas-sized mug.

"It's still a blur to me," said Sumner. "All I remember is sitting in the balcony, watching the opening remarks and the limited debate. Then, my eardrums seemed to explode, and I felt pain in my right arm. At that point, I must have blacked out for a few minutes. When I came to, it was as if I was caught-up in a swirling sandstorm in the middle of the Gobi Desert. Dust was everywhere, and I couldn't see a thing. People were screaming and bumping into each other. I got up and staggered over rows of seat behind me – lifting my leg over one row at a time, until I got to the upper level where I got out. The stairs going down were jammed with people, but there was a back elevator – you know for maintenance, the ones that you're *not* supposed to use in case of emergencies, but I had no choice. That elevator was still working, and I made it out. I knew they were after us at that point. The best thing I could do was hide."

"Where did you go?" Shea asked.

"I thought about coming back to the ranch, but I didn't make it. My lungs gave out from the dust and debris. I must have been picked up by a patrol car and taken to that hospital. That's where I ended up. They just released me yesterday."

"Who did it?" Shea asked bluntly. "Who planted the bombs?"

"It's easy to point fingers, but I really don't know. All I know is it's someone who obviously didn't want us to pass that Secession Proclamation – and there are a lot of people who didn't. I feel certain it all ties back to Washington, but we'll never be able to prove anything. It's all going to be buried under tons of concrete soon."

Shea took another slurp from her mug and stared out over the plain. Haunting memories of seeing Maria's body outside the barn flooded her mind, and she shook her head.

"What's wrong?" asked Sumner.

"There's just too much here to forget, you know."

"Yes. I know. It's hard for me too. I can't imagine how it was for you. The house is still a wreck. There's a lot of clean-up to do. At least, the assassins had someone clean up all the blood and destroy all the evidence."

"I'm surprised they didn't burn this place to the ground," said Shea.

"They tried. I saw where they burned part of the east wing of the lodge, but they must have left thinking the rest would go up with it. It didn't."

"And Maria?"

Sumner began to choke-up. Tears welled up in his eyes and he looked away from Shea. "I don't know," he answered. "Her body wasn't here. It was part of their clean-up I guess. We'll never find her."

"I'm sorry," she answered.

Sumner said nothing in response. There was a lengthy moment of silence between them, but it wasn't awkward. It just seemed right.

"So, what's next?" asked Shea. "JC, we can't let it go. Too many of your friends died in Cheyenne. You and I both know we can't let them die in vain."

"You're right. I lost a lot, but so did others. I just don't think we can beat them. We just don't have the resources."

"That's what they told George Washington."

"Maybe. But things are different now," said Sumner.

"I don't think so. I think it's all in the way you look at it."

Sumner paused, looking out the back window. It was still broken from the bullets that had riddled it during the assault, and Sumner had taped plastic over the gaping hole to keep out the cold. However, it was an unusually nice day for winter, and they didn't mind too much that the relatively warm breeze still blew freely through the bullet holes in the side of the lodge. The view was still awe-inspiring with the snow-capped mountains in the background, a blue sky marked only by puffs of white clouds, the cream-colored grasses bowing gently to the wind, and the few sprigs of lonely ash and red cedar trees dotting the landscape as if God had missed them while shaving the rest of the earth around them.

"You're right," said Sumner, reflecting. "We can't let all we've done evaporate without a fight. We can't let it all be for naught, can we?"

"It's not who I thought you were," said Shea, knowing her words might hurt. "I didn't think you would be willing to let them all die in vain."

It was a poignant moment, and Shea could tell it was tearing Sumner apart.

"Shea, freedom doesn't come cheaply, does it?" Sumner asked, already knowing the answer.

"Threats to our liberties have claimed many more than two hundred lives throughout the ages, JC. It's cost millions, if not hundreds of millions."

He turned toward her and took her hands.

"We will act, Shea. We have no other choice," Sumner said resolutely.

***

Sumner convened a meeting of those who had survived the Cheyenne attack. The meeting was grim and emotional. They were thankful that they had been spared, but each wondered why they had been chosen to live and others had not. But it was Sumner's responsibility, his duty, to channel the energy in the room toward something productive rather than pity and mourning. He began by bringing the meeting to order and calling on everyone to find their sense of optimism and fighting spirit.

"We are up against something that has the potential to destroy us all," Sumner began. "It may believe that it has already succeeded in killing our spirit and our willingness to fight on for our freedom – something that generations of Americans have fought and died for during the past three hundred years." He paused, gathering himself and choosing his words carefully. "I know all of this has been hard. But, I'm not going to stand here and candy coat what lies ahead. I could tell you it will be easy. I could lie and tell you nobody else will die. But I won't. You as well as I know the truth – that it will only get harder. I've been through war. I've been through battles where I've lost my best friend – cut down by machine gun fire. I remember taking shelter behind some rocks on a cliff in eastern Afghanistan while the bullets pelted the stones around me, sending sharp disks of rock everywhere that sliced into my head, neck and eyes. They were like surgical scalpels, cutting my flesh, body and mind.

"My best friend, Bert Hawkins, had been by my side through each of the two hundred twenty days we'd been in that wretched country. We'd smoked together, drunk together, fought together. Bert had even told me about the lust he'd once had for his brother's wife. He'd never acted on it, but it was something he wasn't proud of either. We were brothers – in body and spirit. But then, one day, all of that changed. Our squad got caught in a crevasse between two sheer mountain cliffs, pinned down by gunfire, coming from the Taliban fighters from a local town who were perched up on an adjoining hill. Bert and I had moved over behind a large boulder to fire back and provide cover so the other five guys in our group could get through the pass and find positions where they could stage a counterattack. The Taliban sprayed us with gunfire so thick, I thought they'd shatter the entire rock before we'd be able to fire back. Then, a mortar exploded behind me. It knocked me on my ass, and my left ear went deaf. When I looked behind me to see where Bert was, I saw him not far away -- part of him, anyway.

His upper torso was hanging from the lower branches of a scrub tree; the lower half was lying not far away – a shattered, bloody mess. Bert's eyes were still open but lifeless. He never knew what hit him. I wondered then, as I wonder now – why me? Why didn't I catch that mortar? Why did he have to die? I don't have any more answers now than I had then.

"Yes, I've been to hell and back, and I'm not afraid to go there again. It will be hell," he began, his jaw stiff and his eyes stern. "We've come this far, and I'm not willing to give an inch of hard-fought battle ground back to the enemy. But, I ask you the same question … are you? Are you willing to see it through? Are you willing to go the distance? Are you willing to do what it takes … what's necessary?"

Sumner paused for a moment, searching for his next words.

"You already know that if you go down this path with me, you may not come back. Some of us … hell, many of us … will probably not live to see it through to the end – whatever end that may be. But that's what patriots do, at least those who believe in a right and just cause. We don't claim to be heroes. However, we do claim to be passionate about freedom."

Sumner sat down quietly, waiting to see what the reaction would be from those he'd summoned to attend.

It was Shea who stood up next. In some way, she felt obligated to support Sumner, but now there was something else welling up inside her. She was beginning to see that there was something more than her life, her husband's life and the company they had built together. *Perhaps,* she had thought, *just perhaps there is something bigger than all of that.*

"I don't speak as eloquently as Congressman Sumner. But I do speak with passion about freedom," she began.

"We all feared this day would come. In fact, we wished it never had to come, yet it is here. It is the day when we must decide whether we want freedom or not. It is the proverbial fork in the road or the road less traveled, but whatever you call it – it's a path filled with frightening shadows and phantoms. But, if there is evil and darkness in our future, there must be goodness and light as well. For one cannot create a shadow without light, is this not true?

"What we must do is look beyond the shadows and keep in mind that there is always a source of light. That light must guide us forward. If you believe in God, then let it be that light; if you don't, then let it be the light of truth and goodness. I, for one, believe in God. I do not believe that the wonders of the world could have happened spontaneously out of nothingness as some physicists think. The core, the essence of man is seeded by some higher power, and that power has always wanted us to be free.

300

"When man is free, he creates wondrous things. Even after the Golden Age of the Renaissance Period, we have faced dark times. The Black Death wiped out nearly two hundred million people or 50 percent of Europe's population between 1346 and 1353. In the 1930s and 40s, the evil of Germany and the Soviet Union murdered up to fifty million within the span of a few decades.

"No, the evil within the USSA has not risen to these levels of depravity – not by a long shot. But, neither the peoples of Germany in 1933 or those of the Soviet Union in 1918 could have believed the atrocities that lay before them. They, as did the French in 1789, cheered when their revolutions came. They naively trusted that their new leaders had their best interest at heart … that they would be delivered from the darkness and into the light. Promises were easily made and were just as easily broken.

"But those revolutions were quite different from ours. It is true that we cry out for freedom for the people, just as they did. It is true that we face abusive and oppressive leaders, just as they did. It is also true that they were desperate for change, just as we are. However, those revolutions were based on false hopes and false ideas that centered around a single person thought to be a savior of mankind. No, our cause is steeped in a history and tradition that has been proven, regardless of the charisma one charlatan exudes to all others. True democracy worked for the Greeks over two millennia ago, and it worked for the USA for over two centuries. It was the combination of democracy with capitalism that created the greatest nation the world had ever witnessed.

"Of course, we aren't saying there should be unbridled capitalism. But a harmonic balance is required. The concepts of democracy and capitalism are essential in designing a system that permits man to pursue his dreams and passions, yet offers safeguards against the base, animalistic instincts that are also a part of man. Unleashed in a raw, unfettered form, capitalism will fail us, just as has socialism. However, guided by a light hand, it can be tamed to avoid the predatory human vices of avarice, envy, vanity and anger. Our Founding Fathers came very close to establishing a framework that addressed those concerns, and yet offered every man the opportunity to reach as high on the ladder of success as he dared. No system is perfect, and one that we may create won't be either. But as human beings, it is also in our very nature to fight and strive for something better every single day. That is what we must do.

"Friends, we must continue our struggle. We must try. We owe it to our children and to the rest in this country who hunger for … no, who are desperate for leadership. We must provide it. We must be the light for others. We must use this fire within us to forge a new republic and try again. Eventually," she said with a smile, "we may even get it right." *****

CH 44 The Privileged Few

In the inner cities, fires burned. But it wasn't from people looting and burning neighborhood businesses – no, it was from the lack of heat. Most of the unemployed were not getting their government subsidies for their energy bills for a variety of reason. The official word from the Ministry of Residential Equality was the "checks were in the mail" or "payments were delayed due to technical difficulties that would be remedied soon." The real reason was the lack of money.

For those who worked and had money, threats were made against raising their thermostats above 62 degrees; if caught, they would face stiff fines and even imprisonment. It was a wide-spread problem caused by the dismantling of fossil fuel power plants. There were not enough solar panels, hydroelectric plants, biomass facilities, and wind turbines to generate the power needed to meet the national demand. Oil and gas plants had been demolished due to their hydrocarbon emissions – environmentalists convincing everyone that the "end was near" due to anthropomorphically-generated greenhouse gases. Even though China, Russia and the new Islamic states had ignored the warnings for decades and had continued to build their industries regardless of the emissions, there had been a steady decline in average temperatures around the globe, rather than an increase. Objective scientists were aware of this phenomenon – a recurring solar event known as the Maunder Minimum. Environmental activists had tried to manipulate the data to discredit the findings, but the results had become too stark. Finally, in desperation, they had turned to a new theory they called The Minigravis Maximum. They argued that although the overall temperature was declining, the calefaction in certain critical regions of the earth were causing inordinate long-term devastation, and once the Maunder Minimum was over, temperatures would soar, destroying all of mankind.

Despite the ban on heating buildings above 62 degrees, the White House enjoyed the comfort of 72 degrees on its dial. This was justified due to Mrs. Fourier's rare and unidentified skin condition. But they had many other luxuries the rest of the country was no longer able or permitted to own. A special filtration system ensured their water was always clean, while power outages in other parts of the nation required frequent boiling of water for cooking or drinking. The White House's own electric generating station made sure that power was always available and that the electric cars were always charged and available for use. While clean air was not yet a problem, the bounty of food was another matter. Once the Bread Basket of the world, the Plain States had been converted into the Dust Bowl of the 1930s through federal requirements on farmers to cease using herbicides and fertilizers and stop the use of genetically altered plants (hybrids). By demanding that all foods be natural and organic, harvests had been cut in half within a few years. Blights, disease, insect infestations, and other calamities brought devastation to the heartland of America. Small farmers cease to exist, and the only ones left were GovCo's who got significant government subsidies whether or not they planted anything. In its central planning role, the Ministry of Eco-Agriculture had often guessed wrong when instructing the GovCo's whether to plant a crop or leave a field fallow. The end result was food shortages.

But as money and wealth drained from the grain-sacks of the average person, it burgeoned for people in power. No longer were government employees underpaid relative to the commercial markets during the nineteenth and early twentieth centuries. Now, they were the barons, earls and dukes of wealth.

Seizure of corporate wealth under the Unity Plan had funneled trillions of dollars into the Washington coffers. Much of it never made it into the public domain. Even small percentages that were siphoned off for "management and other fees" were enough to enable thousands in the upper levels of the ministries to live in opulence -- in particular, the ministers themselves. Having entered the government as humble servants worth next to nothing, most were now multi-billionaires.

An example of such big paydays was found in the defense industry. The joint government-private sector military machine had been replaced by just a government military machine, ever since private contractors were forced to convert to government ownership. It had happened almost overnight. The table had been set during one of the State of the Union addresses given by First Citizen Fourier. In it, he said, "There has been a collapse of confidence in how commercial companies supply our military with its armaments. Many times recently we have seen unprecedented failures in systems and prototypes. Billions have been spent and wasted on projects due to the incompetence of the private sector."

The truth was that these failures were largely due to military officials arguing over frequent and onerous change orders. Simple systems became monstrous, complex behemoths that had no chance of success. A new mortar design, soon morphed into a complete anti-ballistic missile system after Congress and the Pentagon had gotten involved. Congressmen, eager to create jobs in their districts, expanded the scope of the work to build more plants and facilities in their own home neighborhoods. Generals from each of the service branches fought over which would have the superior technology or, if forced into a joint project, would encumber the system with so many personal requirements that the prototype would cease any resemblance to its original, intended purpose. And, it would end up failing on all accounts.

But Fourier's State address continued. "Why should we permit companies that sell products to our enemies also sell systems to our military that your sons and daughters depend on for their very lives! These are the very companies whose self-declared purpose is to make money over any allegiance to our country. They would gladly give up your daughter's life to make one more dollar for their shareholders; one more dollar for their directors; and one more dollar for themselves! This is a matter of national defense," he had said. "It is imperative that we can no longer depend on the private sector to support our military needs. We can only rely on the federal government to keep our classified information secret and our most vital military systems out of the hands of our foes."

Bellowing his concerns from the podium on the floor of the House of Representatives, Fourier had warned that unless those defense companies were brought under control of the Ministry of International Policing, all the secrets of the military would be exposed to foreign agents and enemy governments, all of which would like nothing more than to destroy the USSA. Little did the people of America realize at the time, but the man at the podium had already bargained away many of his most sophisticated weapons systems to questionable players around the world in exchange for badly-needed hard currency and assets. Gold was delivered from the Jihadist Shiite State of Iran for sensitive telemetry systems; the Southern Union of Islamic States paid 44.5 billion in the new global currency, the Terrant, for advanced decryption capabilities, and the New People's Dynasty of China paid 15 trillion Yuan for stealth and rocketry technology. There had also been a widely-circulated story that Fourier had sold parts of Alaska and its northern oil fields back to the Russians for gold bullion.

Within weeks, Fourier had issued an executive order, known as the Defense of America Order. Overnight, large defense contractors were stripped of their publicly-owned status, and the Ministry of the Bursars offered them eight cents on the dollar for the company shares. This was not an option – shareholders of these companies had to comply or face penalties and jail time. Consequently, the government not only ran the health care, automobile, education, welfare, energy sector, utilities, food supply, consumer products, media, technology and other segments of the economy, but now managed manufacturing and procurement for the military. The federal government controlled virtually all aspects of the USSA economy.

Trying to cash-in, Congressmen stormed the White House for shares in the defense companies; however, they were turned away. All shares went to the Minister of International Policing and the First Citizen. The price tags for military systems, which had historically been high, became even worse under government supervision. The new price tags made the 600-dollar toilet seat of the 1980s look tame by comparison. In fact, that same toilet seat now cost 600,000 dollars, and every dime came from *The 48* – those forty-eight percent of Americans who paid all of the taxes in America.

Although those changes got little attention, there was something that did receive notice – at least initially. There were reports of two buildings to be built in or near Washington. With money in short supply, it was inconceivable that billions would be spent on such endeavors – yet, nothing, it seemed, was inconceivable.

One was an immense building, larger than that of the Pentagon, located south of D.C, along the Potomac River. Like the Pentagon, it too was pentagonal in shape, and took up as much land area. Above ground, the new building was only four stories high and had as many inner sections as had the Pentagon. However, this building had been dug deep into the earth, with some twenty floors *below* ground. Its volume was five times that of the Pentagon's 6.5 million square feet, and its very existence was classified. Reports suggested it was capturing and collecting *all* data generated by the country and its inhabitants. Others said it captured data worldwide. Either way, the capacity for storage was staggering – more than ten yottabytes every year – an order of magnitude unfathomable only a few years earlier, with one yottabyte equal to one thousand trillion movie downloads. The data center was also fed by surveillance camera systems that blanketed all parts of the country, from highway cams, building cams, and satellite images. Everyone was photographed coming and going, every day, all day. Rumors were that it even dwarfed the aging data center established in the 2010s in Nevada that was seen as a mysterious and frightening threat to privacy at the time.

The other building being constructed was the new retreat for the First Citizen. Camp David, the retreat for presidents since FDR had it built in 1942, had become an antiquated symbol of the old ways -- the old republic. Fourier had decided that a new image was needed. Tucked away in the mountains of Appalachia, the new residence was named Camp Gagra, after the resort town in Georgia where Soviet leaders had their dachas during the twentieth century. Camp Gagra was one hundred square miles of spectacular valley and hill top views that had been seized by the government under the provisions of *eminent domain*. More luxurious than the best resorts on the planet, the chateaux and grounds rivaled some of the finest palaces in the world, with gold leaf, silver, and marble used throughout. Crystal chandeliers worth millions decorated long, royal hallways, and sophisticated electronics and technology could create holographic backgrounds to create whatever scenes were wanted in every room in the building.

Guarding the grounds was a full battalion of the armed forces' finest combat soldiers. They were supported by M3 Bradley Fighting Vehicles, M113 Armored Personnel Carriers, and AH-66 Apache Attack and UH-62 Blackhawk helicopters. The new retreat was better secured than the NORAD ballistic missile silos that had once operated in Colorado and North Dakota.

Billions were spent on both complexes – all the while the American people suffered – without jobs, without direction, without heat, and without hope. *****

CH 45 Co-conspirators

It was true that Angel Ratner had already cemented her retirement security with her payoffs from Lenoir Labs' SECE program. Still only in her early forties, she had also secured her place near the top in her career. She had risen through the ranks of government like a hot flare shooting into the night's sky. But her aspirations were not so easy satiated. Her power and influence bore no boundaries except those placed on her by her boss – First Citizen Fourier. And that chafed her. Worth billions, she had all the comforts anyone could ask, but it was not enough. It was never enough for her. Hers was an unquenchable thirst for more … more power, more money, more respect. Having forty billion United Coins was not as good as having four hundred billion. Fourier and many of his crony business friends had reaped that and more. She had control of 34 percent of the government's spending authority and 55 percent of the overall USSA economy, but that was not as good as having all of it. It was that way with her, and it would always be that way. Having an itch that could not be scratched was like being Tantalus in Hades thirsting for water but only able to watch it evaporate before he could drink. Ratner felt the same way.

"Where the hell is my water?" Ratner screamed for one of her many administrative assistants. None had been able to do the job the way she'd demanded. So, she'd have them fired and hire another. She had been through twelve assistants in eight months, and it was getting harder to find anyone even willing to take the job – regardless of what she was paying. "Where's my water?" she shouted again. Still, no one came into her office. "Shontalya? Where are you?" Ratner said once more. "Shontalya!"

Ratner huffed and rose from her chair to see where her assistant was. Once she got to the anteroom she saw the empty desk with all of Shontalya's personal effects gone. *Apparently, her twelfth hadn't worked out either,* she thought.

"Sh*t!" she said under her breath. "What the f**k is wrong with people?" She turned to the second cubicle where her second assistant usually sat. Veronica's seat was also vacant. "Where the hell is everyone?" she asked. Tonya, her newest assistant still on training wheels came out from behind the third desk cubicle. Sheepishly, she said, "Minister Ratner, I think they left."

"Where did they go?" Ratner snarled.

"I don't know, your Ladyship," Veronica said, inadvertently.

"What did you call me?"

"Your Grace, I mean, Minister?" Veronica said, flustered, but trying to recover.

Your Grace wasn't much better.

"Just get me Griffin on the line," said the minister before going back into her office and slamming the door, making the wall vibrate.

Veronica placed the call to the Minister of Taxation's office, but the image that came up was that of a grumpy old woman with a twenty-year-old hairdo, cut short all around like a bowl. "I'm sorry, but he's tied up in a meeting," she said, unenthusiastically. "He asked if he can call her back as soon as he's out."

Veronica was going to call Minister Ratner and ask, but she already knew the answer. "No, it is important that ..."

It was obvious that the woman on the other end was also used to the routine, and she rolled her eyes. "Yes, yes. It's always a matter of life and death," she said. "I'll try to see if I can pull him out."

The screen went blank, and although it was only a few seconds, Veronica became nervous, knowing her boss would come out yelling if she hadn't accomplished the task quickly. Finally, Griffin's face appeared on the screen.

"Minister Ratner?" he asked, before realizing he was talking to an assistant.

"One moment, sir. I'll get her on the line," said Veronica, before buzzing her boss. "Ma'am? It's the Minister."

Ratner picked up the line in her office, and Griffin's face came on, smiling and unruffled. "Angel, I'm sorry, but I was in a meeting with the Treasury Minister from Canada," he said, "but he can wait. What is it that you need?" He knew the power she wielded; it wasn't much more than his, but he, like others, feared her cunning ways and never wanted to get on the wrong side of her.

"Well, I was just calling to see what you thought of my offer."

"What offer?" he asked.

Many days earlier, Ratner had instructed her driver, Winston to deliver a letter to him at his home. She had been afraid it would get lost in the bureaucracy at his ministry. But, the uniqueness of a letter wasn't enough. It was specially constructed to dissolve within sixty seconds of opening so that nothing was traceable. The paper would melt into a liquid, leaving nothing behind. But the delay in disintegration was long enough to enable the message to be read, but not to be copied or forwarded.

"Bailey, you know what I'm referring to. We've hinted around about it since the drafting of the new constitution ... I tell you what, why don't you meet me at the usual place tomorrow afternoon. Let's say two o'clock?"

"Fine. I'll see you there, Angel."

Ratner hung up, certain that she'd revealed nothing on the phone. They had talked off-and-on about various matters, but had often referred to their current states as "holding patterns." She knew that he would be there the next day to continue their discussion.

It was now Thursday, and Ratner waited patiently in the hotel room. She looked at her cell phone, which showed 2:14, and huffed. *Where the hell is he?* she thought to herself, impatiently. She was about ready to leave, when she heard a click at the door, the lock turned over. "It's about time," Ratner said, as the door opened.

Griffin entered the room, looking around suspiciously. "Have you swept it?" he asked, looking concerned.

"Of course. Do you think I'm stupid?"

"No, you're too damned smart to be stupid," he answered, smiling.

Ratner laughed. "You know, that's one of the funniest things I've ever heard you say."

Griffin chuckled. "Yeah, kind of a Yogi Berra-ism, I guess." He pulled the drapes closed and turned to a minister with whom he'd been having relations on-and-off for years. She sat on the bed, wearing a short-black dress, black-patterned hose and black heals. "You didn't need to dress up for me," he said moving closer to her.

"What makes you think I did it for you?" she asked.

He hesitated. Then she laughed, almost mocking him. "Oh, baby, of course I did. Did you ever doubt me?" she asked, looking at him from her position on the corner of the bed. She was smiling, knowing full well what was in his mind.

Griffin came over and pushed her back into the depths of the down comforter. Her eyes met his, sensing seduction and excitement. She wanted the sex he had to offer, and she wouldn't conceal it.

"How long has it been?" he asked her, unbuttoning her black, silk blouse.

"Too long," she answered, giving him an evil grin.

"I knew you'd say that," he answered. "Now, come to papa."

They had only been able to have each other once or twice during the previous year. He'd been overseas representing the First Citizen at various global financial functions, and she had been flying around the country taking the pulse of local leaders to see what could be done about the growing rebellions rising up in large, urban areas. From the G-20 meeting in Brussels to the World Bank conference on hyperinflation where he gave the keynote address, he had kept a very busy schedule. But now, she pulled him tight to her, feeling him get aroused. His lips pressed against hers, and she opened her mouth to feel the strength of his tongue inside her. Passionately, he kissed her, caressing her breasts and gently stroking her nipples to vault her senses toward ecstasy.

Their love-making was purely physical. He lusted for her, and she for him. It was something that grew within each of them when they were apart and only got released when they were back together – if only for an hour. Aside from that, their relationship was strangely detached. He too was ambitious, but he also had a strong sense for self-preservation. He knew a tiger when he saw one, and Ratner was not one with whom he wanted to tangle.

Although they both would have liked to have stayed in bed together for hours longer, they knew it could only be a short tryst. Ratner lay back in bed, blowing out the smoke she'd inhaled from her cigarette. She only smoked after sex. It was a ritual and a way to get out any remaining tension within her body.

Griffin stood above her, buttoning his shirt and tucking the tail into his pants. "It's been fun," he said, buckling his belt.

"Can't you stay a little bit longer?" she cooed.

Griffin looked at his watch. "I've got an extra five minutes. I suppose so," he answered smiling. "What's on your mind?"

"It's about the note I left you. Have you had time to open it?"

"The note? I got the envelope you gave me, but there was nothing inside it – just some yellow goo."

"If you didn't open it right away, it wasn't going to hang around for you," she said, laughing.

"So, what was this mysterious note?"

Ratner blew out another puff of smoke. She'd been careful to tape over the smoke alarms before he'd arrived, so that wouldn't cause any problem. "I'd like to promote you to number one. What do you think of that?" she said enigmatically.

"Number one?"

"Yes, number one. According to the new constitution I'm three and you're two. It's quite simple. No multivariate calculus needed for that," she said snidely. "With my plan, you'd become number one and I'd move to number two."

"You mean, First Citizen?"

"I would assume you would give me a lot more power than I have now. It would almost be a power-sharing arrangement, but I know how much you've wanted to be First Citizen. Just think … First Citizen Griffin. Sounds nice, yes?"

"Whoa, *offing* the First Citizen? Is that what you're saying?"

She didn't answer. Only a look of mild amusement passed her expression.

"I don't think we can pull it off," he said.

The look on Ratner's face soured. "Of course we can pull it off. I have a brilliant plan. It is untraceable and painless. No one will ever realize what happened. And it certainly could never be pinned back to us."

"Maybe, but it's too damn risky. If we get caught, we're dead. Both of us."

"You know you've always wanted the position, right?"

"Of course."

"So, what's stopping us?"

"He's got his people everywhere – looking at everything. There is no stone unturned when it comes to him. You know that, right?"

"Bailey. We can do this! We can!" The look on her face showed a strange duality -- both earnest and Machiavellian.

He looked back at her without expression. "So, you want to kill Fourier?"

"Yes. And so do you."

Griffin turned around and opened the blinds on the window to look out. The traffic below was a sea of red taillights snaking along the narrow street behind the hotel. The dark clouds overhead began to release their loads, and droplets began falling on the window pane outside, making splattering noises and streaking the glass.

"When?"

"Next Monday night. Fourier is hosting a state dinner, a white-tie affair with the president of Uzbekistan. Why, I don't know. I'm sure this is the first time the man has ever seen a white tie, and most certainly doesn't own a tux with tails."

"Angel, come on. That's a bit harsh."

"So what. It's time. We can handle this. I have my asset who's available. He has access to the kitchen in the White House. He will get inside and make sure that the poison is delivered directly to Fourier."

"He's got taste testers."

"You're right, but certain poisons only act with certain reactants. That's the key."

"I don't understand. How is he going to deliver the poison to Fourier?"

"It really doesn't matter if everyone gets the poison. It's not lethal unless another agent is administered. Together, the two compounds are lethal. If one is in the blood stream when the other is introduced, the two combine into a toxin that kills rather quickly. And, it's not traceable. Within one hour of combination, the substance degrades quickly, leaving no trace."

"So, we have to give him the initial agent to ingest, but won't the toxin machines pick it up before it gets to the First Citizen's table?"

"No! It won't be toxic then. It only becomes toxic later when the First Citizen takes the second agent."

"And what is that?"

"Apple," said Ratner. "Fourier always retires around midnight. But, before he does, he always has a snifter of brandy. Together with the first agent, they will make a very nice mixture for the evening. By morning, his body will be blue and stiff, and an autopsy will show that he had an allergic reaction to something – although unclear."

"But, brandy is made from grapes – like wine, except distilled longer. So, really anyone who has wine that night will die too," said Griffin, now concerned.

"Ah, that's the rub, isn't it." Ratner was grinning with self-adulation. "It's not grape brandy."

"No? Then what is it? I've known Jack for a long time. I always thought his nighttime drink was just regular brandy? Not just any brandy, of course. I thought it was some special, expensive brand that he never shared with anybody."

"Well, you're right about the exclusivity of it. But, it's an apple-based brandy, called *Calvados*. It's actually really good. But, the apple plus the alcohol produced by the fermentation are unique and bond to the agent we're going to use. After he takes the brandy, the toxin will be created and he'll be dead within four hours."

"So, he'll die in his sleep?" asked Griffin, rhetorically.

"Yeah. That's right," said Ratner. "You're so smart."

Griffin stood pondering the possibilities. He walked back over to the window. The rain was coming down harder now, gathering in pools outside the room. "I think that might work after all. What do we need to do?"

"You need to make sure that the black tea they serve is extra-strong that night. You have to give the kitchen your personal request. The strong taste will mask the agent we'll be using."

"What's the agent?" asked Griffin. "I assume you'll be the one getting that for us?"

Angel laughed. "Of course, but if I told you what it was, I'd have to kill you too."

"Really, you'd do that?" asked Griffin, jokingly.

"Only if you piss me off," she answered with a grin.

*****

CH 46 Patriots

The emotional meeting at Sumner's place had re-energized the Freedom Party's base. All attending had agreed that a stand had to be made, and it was they who had to make it.

The first meeting of the New Continental Congress, as they called themselves, would take place back in Cheyenne. Sumner had wanted to meet again at the ranch but understood it would be too dangerous to have another gathering there. Instead, he chose the old Union Pacific Railroad Depot, only a few blocks south of where the capitol once stood. Built back in the 1880s, the depot was a major rail station for those traveling to the West. Its graceful, steeple-like tower and still-functioning clocks were the only aspects of the building that held any similarity to the famed Independence Hall in Philadelphia; yet, it was the only edifice in town that did.

Although most of the state's legislators had died in the capitol explosions, Sumner called on others from across Wyoming to join him in carrying on the torch of freedom. They came with different backgrounds, career interests, and experiences, but they all had one thing in common — the love of their state and their country. Now, with the death of their friends, their own lives took on a different meaning. There was a greater good, a greater cause, and they wanted to be part of a story they hoped would save Wyoming, if not the country. They owed it to their martyred friends and to their children to try.

Rising from the rustic, timber hewn cedar table Sumner had moved from his ranch to the rail station's grand central room, Sumner addressed the gathering of nearly one hundred who had accepted his invitation. They were movers and shakers in the early days, and, he hoped, they would be again.

Sumner held in his hands a large, leather-bound Bible and began by saying, "I'd like to welcome all of you and thank you for coming." He seemed comfortable and sure of himself, talking before such a large and once-influential group within the state of Wyoming. Most were friends, but they were also highly respected members of society. Many were previous members of the state legislature, board members of leading corporations, philanthropists, and clergy, including the bishop of the Cheyenne diocese covering Wyoming and parts of Montana and Idaho, and Rabbi Levine from the largest synagogue in the city. Also present were the governor, Lester Kincaid, several professional athletes from the NBA basketball and MLB baseball leagues, and conservative writers Jack Conway and Jessica Simpson, who wrote articles for the *E-Daily Standard*. But more importantly, were the alternate delegates to the original convention who could not be dissuaded from being there. They had not gone to the secession meeting at the capitol, electing instead to watch the proceedings from close-circuit monitors in a legislative building next door.

"The first thing I'd like to do is have Father Pasquinelli lead us in a prayer. This Bible that I hold in my hands was brought over in a steamer trunk onboard an ocean liner, the *RMS Oceanic* from Liverpool England in 1879. It's dated to 1848 and has been in my family since the early days of its publishing. Father, would you lead us ..." he said, handing the book over to the priest.

The bishop came forward without the signature staff and miter, but dressed in black with the traditional white band collar around his neck. He was an older gentleman, having been through the trying times when the Church battled with the Administration over everything from taxation to the right of Catholicism as a religion to exist at all. The years had not been kind to him. Gray-haired with large ears that draped both sides of his face, he squinted through puffy eyelids and bags that had accumulated below his sockets. His face was rounded and dominated by a triple chin that bulged over his stiff, white collar. Imitating his overall rotundity were his thick, chubby fingers which grasped the black-cover of the holy book handed to him.

The priest took the Bible from Sumner and lifted it in one hand while raising the other with his forefinger and middle finger outstretched, pointing upward, to give his blessing. "Let us pray," he began. "Oh Lord, we come together this day for You to give us the strength to carry forth Your will and help set this state upon the path of Righteousness in Your name. You are the Creator of all Heaven and Earth. You put us here to be good stewards of this realm, but it seems we have failed you. We have let this nation fall into disfavor with You as we've permitted those in power to pursue their own ambitions instead of following the course You intended. Therefore, Almighty Father, we ask Your blessing and guidance as we pursue the course we believe that You want us to take. We ask for Your protection against the dark forces that threaten to take away our liberties and freedoms. Finally, Lord, we ask that You comfort the families of those who died in the Cheyenne tragedy only two months ago. We pray that You have taken in the souls of those who lost their lives that day and have given them peace. We ask this in Your name. Amen."

The Father crossed himself and handed the Bible back to Sumner.

"We all know what has to be done," Sumner began. "Doing it is the hard part. We must have the will and fortitude to see this through. But, we also need to lead others so that they have the confidence to join us and our cause. We must be able to connect with others – both those who already believe in democratic freedom and in an open, capitalist economy and those who have yet to be persuaded. Are you among those who can change the hearts and minds of others? You have to ask yourself that question. Are you ready to take on the opposition? Are you willing to sacrifice as so many before us have?"

"Yes," most said reservedly, nodding their heads and smiling cordially at each other. It was less enthusiastic than Sumner had sought from the group. He needed more.

"I see," he answered them, looking down at his notes in dismay. "This is not what I had hoped. It isn't the energy that we need to find success." He peered out the old, arched glass windows of the rail station. Down the street was the spire of St. Mark's Episcopal Church. It, the state capitol building and the rail station had all been built around the same time in the 1880s. They were beautiful, historic monuments, testaments to an age when rugged individualism defined men and when men and women fought for their families and defended their honor and integrity.

"You know, it was men and women of incredible bravery and fortitude who were willing to risk their lives and everything they loved and held dear to ensure that their freedom and that of their progeny would never be taken away. There are those who are well known, like Nathaniel Hale, and those who are less so, like Virginia Roush.

"As you recall, Nathaniel Hale was hanged as a spy by the British during the Revolutionary War. Enlisting in the Connecticut militia in 1775, he was the only one who volunteered when General Washington requested that someone go behind enemy lines and secure information on how the British would invade Manhattan Island. The island was being defended by Colonel Charles Webb of the 7th Connecticut Regiment. Washington worried about Webb's forces being able to protect the island from almost certain invasion by British naval forces, which were the mightiest in the world at that time. Hale provided information to the Colonists, but was identified by Loyalists in a New York tavern. He was thrown in prison, where he asked for a Bible and clergy. The British denied his requests. The next morning, he was hanged. He was twenty-one. His famous quote says much about his character and courage. He said, "My only regret is that I have but one life to give for my country.

"Then, there was little known Virginia Roush. Born in St. Petersburg, Florida in 1910, she married a Frenchmen and helped the French Underground during World War II. It was her job to question pilots seeking protection to ensure they were not German spies sent to expose their operation and destroy their safe house. She had to be thorough, vigilant and confident when identifying a potential German spy. Her decision meant life or death, as spies were executed by the French Resistance. However, one day before D-day in June 1944, she was arrested by the German Gestapo as she made her way out of Paris. She was tortured to give up the names of people she worked with, but she never cracked. She was then transported to the Ravensbruck concentration camp, and when it was liberated in 1945, she weighed just seventy-six pounds. She never lost faith in herself or her country. It is true that her involvement was with Vichy France, not America. But her bravery saved perhaps thousands of American, British and Canadian lives.

"These were great Americans – willing to risk their lives and those of their families to help liberate a nation and a people. They believed in their cause. They believed in a higher Being who would come to judge all of us in our final moment of life."

The crowd was silent. They understood what they were being asked. The impact of his speech hit home, and they thought about their colleagues who had also sacrificed their lives and, in some cases, members of their family, for a cause that was bigger than they were.

"For me," said Sumner, "there is no other choice. I will not stand here and let others seize the power that is rightfully that of the people. I do not want to face my children or their grandchildren in twenty years when their houses are broken into by state police, perhaps kidnapping a husband or raping a teenage daughter, or perhaps breaking in just *because* – without any reason whatsoever. I don't want to attend the funeral of one of my grandchildren who was killed by a state militia captain for not having sex with him. I don't want my children to live in fear that a neighbor or friend could someday tell the authorities some lie about them because they didn't like the color they painted their house. How horrible would it be to watch from behind window shades as your spouse is hauled off to prison or executed before your eyes for some trumped-up charge of treason. I don't want to be muzzled and told what I can and can't say and what is or is not acceptable in society based on someone else's opinion. Under the old constitution freedom of speech was protected, not politically-correct speech. Under that document I could pray to my own god instead of the god of another religion the state considers more favorable and acceptable than my own. We could also meet, as we are now, in peaceful assembly without fear of being arrested or blow-up. I cannot -- I will not -- accept these conditions in my lifetime, and I will not go to my grave regretting that I could have made a difference and, instead, stood-by and did nothing!" Sumner's big voice boomed throughout the hall, echoing off the walls and shaking the chairs sitting in front of him.

The crowd came to life, this time, roaring its approval, clapping and cheering.

He let the applause die down before continuing. "We all know what we have to do. We have to finish what was started by our patriots in Cheyenne. We have to put ourselves out there – to go beyond our comfort zone – to be fighters of the freedom we once had and will once more secure for ourselves. So, I ask that the alternate delegates to the original, duly empowered Secession Convention, please step forward."

Without further prompting, nearly one hundred people came to the front of the cavernous hall, just in front of the sandstone-framed windows, and formed a choir-like presence before the group. When they were all assembled, there were seven rows of sixteen people standing dutifully at the ready.

"As the new Chairman of this Reconstituted Convention, it is my duty to swear all of you in as duly selected delegates to this constitutional convention. Therefore, if you agree with the following declarations, respond with 'I do':

"I swear and affirm that I have read the 1789 Constitution of the United States of America and the 1889 Constitution of the state of Wyoming and fully understand the ramifications of any action taken to secede from the Union.

"I do," replied the group in unison.

"I also understand that my votes as cast during the proceedings and under the rules of this Secession Convention shall hereafter have profound and lasting consequences for the people of the state of Wyoming and their families."

"I do."

"Furthermore, I understand that after casting my vote, I may not rescind it during these proceedings. All votes cast are final and definitive."

"I do," they chanted.

"And finally, no one here – once duly sworn-in as a delegate to this convention – may leave until all business has been concluded. In the event of an emergency, the delegates, as a whole, will vote to discharge the delegate from his or her official responsibility. However, there will be no substitutions or replacements permitted. Each delegate must be present and vote directly for any and all resolutions put forth. Do you understand this requirement as it has been presented to you?"

"I do."

"You are now duly appointed as full, delegates to this convention," said Sumner, smiling. "Let's proceed with the roll call and the debate over the secession resolution presented this day and before this convention body."

Sumner turned the roll call over to Shea who read the names of all ninety-one newly, sworn-in delegates. After that was completed, he retook the podium and read the Secession Proclamation as it had been written and presented in the House Chamber of the state capitol. Essentially, it was unchanged from earlier versions, calling for the separation of the state of Wyoming from the United Socialist States of America.

The debate went long into the afternoon with each delegate getting three minutes to speak, if they chose. Sumner had not chosen all the delegates who would agree with the proclamation; rather, he selected a cross-section of people with diverse views that represented the people at large. Although most were in favor of separation, there were those who had reservations. In particular, they worried whether the consequence of their decision would be another bloody civil war.

"How can you vote for secession?" asked Emma Skinner, a community activist from Laramie. "The Administration has made mistakes – that is true. However, has it really come to this? For the first time in generations, we have control over commerce and business in this country. No longer are we manipulated and used as serfs by big corporations like our grandparents were. We have finally tamed them! They now answer to the people of this nation, as it should be. No longer do we have to dance to the tunes played by corporate boards of directors. We are human beings, and we need to be treated that way!

"And as for the poor, we are finally helping those in need. For too long they have been ignored. For too long, the rich of this country have turned their backs on those who can't get three square meals a day. It's the rich who are finally being made to atone for their sins and to give back to those who have less.

"I don't understand why you people think this is all so bad? It's the way things should be! *The meek shall inherit the earth* – remember that? Well, that's all First Citizen is trying to do – make things so that the meek shall get a bigger piece of the pie.

"But more than that, I fear we are making a decision the will divide this country, just as it did in 1860. I think it's a bad decision and one we will regret for the rest of our lives. Many may die as a result of what we do here in this hall, and it's because you on the Right think you have all the answers. You've become sanctimonious and arrogant – believing in your own potions and snake oil. You think that going back to the old ways when people starved because they couldn't earn enough to live on and others were discriminated against because they didn't agree with you were the glory days. Well, you're wrong. You live in your multi-billion dollar mansions and sip Champaign while the rest of us suffer. That's not what this country was about. It's about fairness for all. It's about equality for all. And, it's about political correctness for all.

"Thank you, Mr. Chairman. I now yield the floor."

Sumner retook the podium. "Thank you, Ms. Skinner. Now, does anyone else have anything to say?" asked Sumner. "Anyone?"

Sumner looked around the group, but no one volunteered. Then, he turned to Shea, who was standing beside him. "Shea, you haven't said anything. Do you wish to address the floor?"

Shea was caught off guard. "I ... I think it's all been said, JC. I don't think there is anything I can add at this point."

"You were a philosophy and history major in school, yes?"

"Why, yes, but that was a long time ago," she answered.

"I still hear several people concerned about the recreation of a Civil War conflict. What do you say about that?"

She looked at Sumner and saw in his eyes that he needed her to say something. Even though he felt there were enough votes to pass the resolution on the first ballot, a failure to reach a supermajority would cause people to doubt, and doubt might unravel everything for which they'd worked to that point.

Shea made her way up to the front of the room. "This is all new to me," she began. "I'm not used to speaking before a large group."

Sumner handed her his Bible and said, "Here you go. This might help." And with that, he left her in front of the hundred people who had become quiet, curiously wondering what she would say that would be different from all the others.

With the Book in her hands, she collected her thoughts and took a few deep breaths. "I must admit I'm totally unprepared to be up here right now," she exclaimed, her words trailing off as she looked beseechingly at Sumner. But there was little he could or would do for her. It was hers at that point. It was her moment.

"But it looks like either I say something or JC will have the coyotes picking at my bones on the prairie later this evening." She smiled, and the crowd chuckled with the humor.

"I am truly honored to be up here talking to you. This is a very august group. However, if you're looking for scintillating comments from me, you may go away disappointed. But I will do my best. I will share with you some thoughts I've had during the last several months.

"I've had a lot of time to think, and I keep coming back to our country's heroes, who signed a single piece of paper in 1776 that they knew would rile King George and his prime minister, Lord Frederick North. When the Founding Fathers met in Philadelphia for the first time in 1774 to protest Britain's Intolerable Acts, which were retaliatory actions for the Boston Tea Party, they were taking the first step toward liberation. When their boycott of British goods had little effect, they met

319

again in 1775 – this time to ignite a revolution. The Declaration of Independence was drafted and ratified on July 4 the following year and formally signed by all thirteen states by August 2.

"But I hear some in this group comparing what we're trying to do today, not to that seminal moment in 1776, but to that of South Carolina in 1860 when it broke from the Union. Of course, we all know that these two things are completely different. One involved the intolerable oppression of an unchecked authority, which often leads to totalitarianism; the other, the practice of slavery, was a cruel, inhumane scourge that needed to be vanquished from the face of the earth. The Colonists' reasons to separate as independent states from Britain were quite different from those of the Confederates. Both evils – that of unchecked power and the other of slavery -- were sirens of the same song and could have ended with the same coda – the dissolution of someone's liberty.

"Today, we are up against a dictatorship that uses other names to disguise their dismantling of our liberty. They say they are fighting for the poor, for the handicapped, for those who are discriminated against, for those who were left behind, and for those who are outcasts from a system of their own creation. The truth is they are for none of those things. They are for themselves and their own power. It's a populist refrain that has been sung throughout the ages, and when there is a compliant, illiterate public, it works every time.

"I've listened to those here who say we conservatives are the bad guys – that we are the ones who only care about ourselves. Well, if fighting for the freedom of all Americans is selfish, then call me selfish. We *are* fighting for freedom -- freedom to say, do, or think what we wish to say, do or think, without fear of some federal authority or power locking us away. At the same time, we, as citizens, have a responsibility that comes with that freedom.

"Yet, you may ask 'What is my responsibility?'; that is rather vague, isn't it? It's been the topic of philosophy for centuries. From Edmund Burke to John Stuart Mill to Max Webber. In my opinion, freedom and responsibility go hand-and-glove together. Freedom without responsibility becomes anarchy. For those fighting authority or slavery, the lack of personal responsibility only creates chaos and opens the door to something worse. We cannot advocate bloodshed to achieve our goals. We cannot support the violent overthrow of the government, as the Bolsheviks did by a bloody revolution in 1918. We must choose a different path. And as passive protests have resulted in the brutal crackdown we have seen in Cheyenne and Springfield, we must look to other alternatives.

"So, where does that leave us? In the eyes of the Left, responsibility is helping others by handing out free goods and services to everyone they deem needy. *Need*, of course, is in the eye of the beholder. There are those who, by any

320

measure, need the help of others – those who are physically or mentally incapable of caring for themselves. For those, no one quibbles about giving. It *is* our responsibility, as a civilized society, to do so. For the rest, the vast majority of those receiving government handouts, both they and the government believe they too need ... no, *deserve*, the help. For them, it is a *right* – their right – to take from others who have more than they do. Again, it's about fairness, and they believe it is unfair that someone else should have more than they. These are the people who are pleased with the current state of America – a nation at war, a class war pitting those who have against those who want. It has opened a Pandora's golden box of promises to make wealthy those who aren't willing to work for their success by letting them believe they can dip their hands freely into that coffer of money and pull out anything they want – as much as they want for as long as they want. It's a wonderful free ride.

"But there are demons that lurk within that golden box. It is a container filled with pyrite or fool's gold. These phantasms that are being released into our society are masked well. *The 52* see them as advocates, helping them 'screw' the system and secure for them money for booze, gambling or drugs, undermining the very foundation of our country. For *The 48*, the devil released from the box is their enslavement – strapped to a gurney and bled for their money, their energy, and their capability. None of these resources is in enough supply to ever satiate the beast of Pandora.

"The Right also believes in taking care of the truly needy, but as for the rest, it understands that government handouts are not the way to solve the country's ills. As the Declaration of Independence states, we have the right to life, liberty and *the pursuit* of happiness – the pursuit of, *not* a guarantee of. Creating opportunities for those less fortunate is the essence of mankind's benevolence to mankind. Along with it come dignity, a sense of self worth, and the most dreaded of them all – a feeling of independence. Yes, it is true that this concept can be difficult to understand, even for *The 52*. It takes a monosyllabic word – *free* – and turns it into a disyllabic word – *freedom*. Like the parable about giving fish to the hungry or teaching them to fish. Merely giving things away may provide people a single meal; teaching them how to work and how to feed themselves will offer them food for a lifetime.

"But that's the difference between socialism and capitalism. Teaching people to fish is what capitalism is all about -- giving people the opportunity to make something of themselves. They can either embrace it and work for it, or they can decline and hope others will offer them charity. But there is a difference between the charity of individuals and the forced transfer of the government. The former distributes over 87 percent of the gifts to those who need them; the latter, after government bureaucracies and inefficiencies, distributes less than 10 percent, of which 8 percent ends up with those who scam the system.

"But capitalism is not all a bed of roses either. It is true that capitalism lifts all boats; however, it also acts as a net, separating those who really want to work for it from those who don't. It separates those with ambition from those who are lazy. It separates those who want to better themselves from those who want to be taken care of. And, it separates the doers from the takers. Sure, there are those few people who get really rich when capitalism works, but there are many, many others that are also enriched. Capitalism is a system that challenges each of us to be the very best we can be. The better we are, the more successful we become. Men have created unimaginable wealth – only to lose it by the hands of the Fates, arrogance, ignorance, or worse. The entrepreneur understands the odds. There are no guarantees in the world of capitalism. It is a destructive-creative force – but that is how the nation, heck the world, grows stronger. It evolves from this force – ushering in a better world for all of us. So, it is true that capitalism is a tide that lifts all boats.

"But high rewards come with high risk. For every entrepreneur who strikes it rich, two hundred fail. Nothing in the capitalistic system is assured, and it shouldn't be. When someone fails, they either pick themselves up and try again or they give up. When someone succeeds, they may get rich, but they provide opportunity for others – generating thousands of well-paying jobs. When Bill Gates and Paul Allen created a little, computer operating system called *BASIC* and then another, *Windows*, they launched a multi-billion-dollar business that eventually hired over one hundred thousand people worldwide. Steve Jobs and Steve Wozniak did the same with Apple Computer back in the 1970s. They risked everything to push their ideas about a new personal computer. But computers weren't the only job creators. Through the years, Edison, Bell, Birdseye, Schick, Land and other inventors created companies that provided valuable goods and services to customers and paved the way to employing hundreds of thousands of people. They were the ones who created an empire – not only for their own company, but one that fueled the development of the greatest nation the world had ever known -- the United States of America.

"During the nineteenth century, the much-vilified industrialists, demonized today by just about everyone, created billions in wealth for themselves and for their companies. Were they really that bad? The answer is yes and no. It depends on how you look at it. Take John D. Rockefeller. He was smart and visionary – someone who could see the unique strategic relationship between his oil refineries and the railroad industry. Each needed the other. Oil needed cheap transportation, and the railroads needed more payload to be efficient. Was he ruthless in his acquisition of competitors? Yes. But the refining industry at the time was in freefall. Prices were being cut by producers so far that no one could survive financially. Without him, the oil industry would have remained fragmented and not able to achieve the efficiencies it has today. Were his practices predatory? Perhaps, and that is why the Sherman and Clayton Antitrust Acts were necessary. Promoting competition should be a primary tenant of any government that seeks a robust economy.

"Likewise, Andrew Carnegie found the link among railroads, steam lines, and ironworks. By horizontally integrating these lines of business, he created a highly efficient organism that created jobs and helped industrialize America.

"But of course, critics today would tell us that these were money-grubbing, evil men, bent on destroying their competitors and creating their own monopolies – which they succeeded in doing, until Teddy Roosevelt came along. Of course, they are right to an extent. *Laissez faire* capitalism was the rule of the day back in the nineteenth century, and that led us to dangerous and deplorable working conditions, unconscionable working hours, the employment of minors for hazardous jobs, unthinkable filth, and threats against any attempts at a remedy. The first part of the twentieth century was about fixing those things and improving the work environment. Likewise, it was a time when unions were helping the worker and giving them leverage with their employers. However, during the middle of the twentieth century, the government gave unions the upper hand, forcing an imbalance. In the sixties, the same happened with minorities, creating an imbalance that ended with both unions and minorities holding trump cards over their employers. Any grievance, any complaint, any discontent, resulted in lawsuits that quickly threatened the existence of their employer. Either their demands were met, increasing their wages or benefits, or the employer faced a total shut-down of their business. There was no longer any good-faith representation involved from labor.

"When the Left realized they could garner solid, unwavering votes from the unions and minorities, they took advantage, passing a plethora of legislation from Congress to buy their votes. The more they gave away, the more votes they got. It was a win-win for the People's Party – all disguised to show their ersatz sympathy and support for those less-well-off. But the growing imbalance made it more and more difficult to do business in this country and compete globally. Ultimately, we began taking all we could from who had money -- businesses and the upper-upper class -- and giving it to those who didn't want to work. When we couldn't get enough money to buy votes from them, we began taking it from the middle-upper class and giving that away. When that wasn't enough, we took from the lower-upper class. Next it was from those who were upper middle class, doing better than most. Now, it's the entire middle class – those who have jobs and make a living. Unfortunately, it still isn't enough money to give away for votes. We call that Socialism."

"That's why unrestrained capitalism isn't such a good thing. And, unrestrained government isn't such a good thing. There must be a balance. Both government and business, without governors, can and will create monsters of their own making. Human nature is human nature. We are animals at the core, and there will always be those who will exploit and prey on those less able to stand up for themselves. When business gets out of control, government may step in to level the playing field. But when government gets too big and oppressive, there is no one there to stop it if the people don't. It requires a willingness of the people to vote that government out of power. But what if the government changes the rules of the game where it can't be replaced? Where it takes away the power and authority of its people to be heard? What is the recourse? I fear there are three choices: peaceful resistance, which, as I've said earlier, has failed us; overthrow of the government by the people, which may very well lead to bloodshed and civil war; or peaceful secession, without violence or anarchy.

"A properly balanced democracy married with capitalism produced the Greatest Generation of Americans from the 1900s through the 1950s, despite the failed experiments of FDR during the 1930s. That Greatest Generation arose within the United States of America -- a generation that created the greatest superpower that has ever existed on Earth. And, most amazingly, it was benevolent. For the first time in the history of mankind, the greatest power on the globe did not seek hegemony over its neighbors. Instead, it sought to spread freedom and liberty to others thirsting for the same. The USA was charitable around the globe with its aid and support of other developing economies and fledgling democracies. It won two World Wars, and won a third – the Cold War – an existential threat that imperiled the survival of hundreds of millions.

"Europe long ago bowed-out of the super power club. Their economies collapsed in shambles, and they were forced to genuflect to the Middle-eastern powers of Iran, Saudi Arabia and Iraq, which unleashed their Islamic fury from London to Istanbul. At one point, Britain controlled 23 percent of the world's landmass and 20 percent of the world's population. Now, they are a Sunni theocracy – part of the Northern Union of Islamic States – as are most other countries in Western Europe. Their economies have regressed back to levels not seen since the 1950s. In Eastern Europe, Russia flexed its muscle when the U.S. failed to support its European and NATO allies, retaking all the satellites that were once under the Soviet Union. China captured all of Asia and conquered Japan, something it had not done in three thousand years. Neither Russia nor China were challenged, as there was no one left to offer any tangible resistance. The United Nations had long been a eunuch on the world's stage, and America was in full retreat, not wishing to be seen as imperialistic and therefore, not wanting to *offend* anyone.

"Today, we are faced with the same menace -- a government that no longer represents its people, and is no longer able to defend its country. We no longer have a constitution. Instead, we have a totalitarian regime that has usurped power from the other branches of government. We no longer have any separation of powers. We have a First Citizen, rather than a president, and no representation in Congress or in the People's courts. We have been forced into redistributing wealth and now privately held land and property have been expropriated by our government. Yet, the poor get poorer and the cronies of the political elite get richer. We have solved nothing.

"Our state and local governments have been disbanded; our rights and freedoms abridged. It is only a matter of time before we will fear for our very lives and those of our children. Can we not see the day coming when we're herded into labor camps and forced to produce for the state?" Shea shook her head. "No, we must take a stand now. If not for us, for those who come after us. Although our generation won't be the only one blamed for what has happened, it will be condemned for being the last one that could have stopped it. Our generation can't let this once-great country crumble and fall as did the Romans, Persians, Babylonians, Mongols and other great civilizations before it.

"Tonight, we must have courage to take a stand. We must fight for our freedoms – both for our democratic liberties and for our economic rights as a free and civilized society. This is what our forefathers envisioned for us – not a gulag archipelago of labor camp where we are whipped into producing for the state's five-year plan.

"Jefferson, Madison, Monroe, Jay, Hamilton, and others believed in God. They believed that God bestowed man with inalienable rights. These were fundamental elements that no other man could take from him. Yet, we are close to that happening. If we don't push for change, our rights will be taken from us. Our freedom to speak, assemble, worship, and conduct commerce is no longer something we can take for granted. If we look around, we see that each day we are able to do less and less – like mice placed in a box that gets divided and subdivided, repeatedly shrinking our area of freedom until there is no room left to move. Eventually, the mice are climbing on top of each other, struggling for air to breathe. Those on the bottom are smothered with only a few at the top managing to survive – but just barely. We are being shut into a shrinking box with less and less air to breathe. And, if we don't do something, most of us will be smothered.

"Tonight, I ask that you vote your conscience. But understand that whichever way you vote, you will be changing the course of history forever."

Shea stopped. She hadn't planned on talking at all, let alone for almost fifteen minutes. But when she'd finished there was silence in the audience. She didn't know if that was a good sign or a bad one. She just looked back at Sumner and gestured. "I guess I've said enough. Sumner, I'm sorry I took up so much time."

Sumner stood before her, smiling. "Shea, well said," was all that he could muster. Then, he added, "Let's vote, shall we? I turn the voting back over to you, Shea. We will call the roll. Please speak loudly so we may capture your ballot."

Shea stepped back before the microphone. "As I call your name, either affirm the proclamation by voting *Aye* or dissent by voting *Nay*," Shea said. "If you have determined that you will neither vote for nor against the proclamation, then you must vote *Present.*" She looked down at the thick black binder that Sumner had given her and opened it to a pre-selected section.

"Abercrombie ..." she yelled.

"Aye."

"Barclay."

"Aye."

"Butan ..."

"Present."

"Cauldfield."

"Aye."

The vote continued until the final name was read.

"Williams."

"Aye."

Shea reviewed her tallies and then spoke to a tired audience. A red tinge formed at the horizon's edge to the west, harkening the advent of nightfall. But strangely, although the darkness began to settle in among them, the streetlights that encircled the street in front of them flashed on, bathing the building in a sea of brilliance. It was an odd dichotomy of light and darkness – showing two realms, that of endless possibility and that of danger. Each had equal power over all who were present.

Shea, acting as the official recorder, handed Sumner the count sheet, and he put on his reading glasses to decipher the markings. "The first ballot of votes has been cast," he said. "A supermajority of 69 votes is required for passage. We have ... let me see here ... eighty-seven *Aye* votes, two *Nay* votes, and two counted as *Present*. The Proclamation of Secession is hereby adopted," he said, with a mixture of emotions – both elated and somber. He was excited for what the passage of the document meant for the people of Wyoming. He was equally concerned about the consequences.

The group roared its approval. Hats flew into the air, and delegates congratulated one another for the historic vote.

"Yes, we have approval of the proclamation," said Sumner again. "Of course, this resolution is supposed to be approved by the U.S. Congress under the U.S. Constitution. However, since there is no U.S. Constitution, and we do not recognize the USSA Constitution that this state never ratified, we hereby proclaim independence from that state – the United Socialist States of America. The independent Republic of Wyoming shall be duly formed as a sovereign nation and will seek a seat at the World Council, separate from that of the USSA.

"We have drafted a constitution for the new republic, which will be read at the next meeting and debated. After ratification by a majority of the districts, we will move to create our own currency, the Buffalo Dollar; provide for our own defense by turning the State Guard into our own sovereign military; provide for domestic tranquility by using existing state laws as the basis for those of the republic; provide for justice, using our the existing civil and criminal court systems; protect life, liberty and property, as originally promulgated by the U.S. Constitution using local and state police; and provide for the general welfare, in the more limited sense as originally intended by the Founding Fathers–that is, those few, basic and necessary things the U.S. government was supposed to provide, but failed to do so.

Sumner stood smiling before the group and held up his hand. "I am proud of all of you for voting your conscience. You have made history tonight. Now, let us pray ...

"May God, the Almighty, guide us as we plot a new course for the people of the Republic of Wyoming, and may He protect us and our families as we begin this journey. We are sure to face seemingly- insurmountable obstacles and the possibility of retaliation from our enemies, both from within and without. But give us the strength to resist violence, if possible, and to endure. If confrontation is required, let us stand on the side of righteousness to defend the freedoms we hold dear and that have been the core of our principles for generations. Amen."

******

327

CH 47 Black Tea and Brandy

Minister Griffin carried out his part of the bargain, asking that the black tea served at the state dinner for the Uzbekistani president, Tahir Safaev, be served extra-strong. He had told the White House staff that the president liked his tea strong, and that had been good enough for them.

The night was a lavish event, as white tie dinners usually were. President Safaev did not wear tails, but then neither did Fourier, who preferred a winged-collar, white-tie combination with vest instead. The president's wife, Zilola, wore an emerald-green, long-sleeve, lace evening gown with a high-neck collar. All looked elegant as they walked down the grand staircase of the White House to the entrance hall where *Hail to the Chief* was played, along with the anthems of the two countries: the *Star Spangled Banner* and the *O'zbekiston Respublikasining Davlat Madhiyasi*. The tradition of *Hail to the Chief* played by the Marine Corp band had been replaced with a small, chamber orchestra from the nearby Kennedy Center for the Performing Arts, as Fourier had felt the military band was too threatening.

After the receiving line and speeches by each of the heads of state, the dinner began. Decorated with large porcelain vases covered by Asian and Middle-Eastern mosaics and filled with a dazzling array of colorful flowers, the tables were opulently set with rich Baccarat crystal glasses, fine Wedgewood china, layers of silverware that banded each dish, fine French white linens with intricate lace patterns, and candles – thousands of white and gold candles that gave the State Dining Room the feeling of a White House set in the 1800s.

Presenting only a five-course meal, the calligraphic menu was beautifully presented, resting on top of gold charger plates that were set for each guest. The procession of foods began with raw, Blue Point oysters with Mignonette sauce – not ethnic, but a favorite of President Safaev's -- a doughy chuchvara as an appetizer, followed by shurpa or fatty mutton soup with vegetables and other ingredients. The main dish was that of the traditional palov, but with lamb, carrots and onions. Desert was an assortment of dried fruits and nuts. It was all to be choreographed like a hit Broadway show, and although there were a few guffaws here and there, no one noticed, especially not the First Citizen.

Safaev sat to the right of Fourier, and with their translators they spent the evening chatting about how remarkable America had become now that Fourier was at the helm. Fourier enjoyed having guests who were sycophantic to his accomplishments and his persona. He was bigger than life, and he always wanted to make sure everyone around him knew it.

Griffin sat with his wife at a table farther away from the main grouping. He was placed with other, lesser dignitaries of Uzbekistan. In the eyes of most, he was merely a placeholder, someone whom the new constitution specified as a secondary alternative should something unfortunate happen to the First Citizen. However, nothing was certain anymore, especially after the unilateral dismantling of the founding principles of the nation. No matter what the constitution then-in-place stated, there were no longer any absolutes when it came to succession of power. Off-handedly, Fourier had twice suggested that his successor should be his wife, Patricia. It was an odd thing to say. For if there were anyone more feared than Fourier himself, it was Patricia. Accused of being behind some of his more heinous acts, she had the face of an angel, but the heart of a monster. Yet, there were two angels at Fourier's table that night – the other was Ratner. She had managed to weasel a chair at the head table, while Griffin had been stuck farther away from power. When not occupied by trite conversation with Safaev's wife, Patricia chatted with Ratner. It wasn't much more meaningful, but Patricia needed to put on the show of being a gracious hostess.

After the first two courses, the waiters, dressed in black tuxes and starched shirts, came from the kitchen carrying pots of the black tea in their white-gloved hands. Griffin watched as they poured from the exquisite, eighteenth-century porcelain pots, careful not to spill any of the hot, black liquid. Those from the Uzbek contingency quickly took their cups and sipped, but Fourier seemed to ignore his, preferring instead to keep drinking his red Bordeaux.

Minutes passed, and Fourier, deep in conversation with his guest, continued to disregard his other libation. *What if he doesn't drink it?* Griffin thought, beginning to panic. *I don't have a plan B.* Griffin saw the opportunity fading and glanced over at Ratner, hoping she was watching and looking for some sign that she *did* have a backup plan. He found that he wasn't alone in his concern; she too was fastidiously watching Fourier's every move while Patricia conversed with Safaev's wife. Griffin sent a digital message to Ratner's wristcom, a small-screen PCD worn around the wrist.

What's the plan? It read.

Ratner was cool to the touch, perhaps even ice-cold. Little bothered her. She merely glanced at the message and resumed her watch, ignoring any reply. Still, the tea was getting cold, and it was becoming less and less likely that Fourier would take it. Griffin decided he had to do something before the chance slipped away for good.

Griffin wiped his chin with his napkin and then placed it on the table in front of him. He took a deep breath and grasped the tiny earlobe handle on the teacup, pushing his chair back to stand up. But from across the room, there was a loud noise, as plates from a serving tray crashed to the floor. It was right next to Ratner's chair, and she jumped up, brushing off her gown. Griffin hadn't seen anything spill on her, but her act was convincing.

"I am so sorry," said one of the attendants, face reddened as he awkwardly tried to clean up the mess around the table.

"That's quite alright," said Ratner with all eyes turned toward her and the calamity. "These things happen. But I will need a fresh napkin and someone will have to replace my chair, I'm afraid. I'm sure the stain will come out of the upholstery."

Ratner looked around, acting sheepishly as if the event had spontaneously occurred. Then, she picked up her tea cup and said, "Well, as there's nothing more I can do until my new chair arrives, I ask the First Citizen if it is acceptable that I propose a toast from my Ministry of Unity to our guests and their great nation of Uzbekistan?" She waited for some subtle response from Fourier, hoping her ploy would work.

Fourier smiled disingenuously, shook his head and said, "I appreciate your offer, minister Ratner. However, I do not feel it is appropriate at this time."

It was the only time Griffin had actually seen angst on Ratner's face. It was as if she had, indeed, played her last card and believed she'd lost.

But Fourier then stood up and raising his wine glass said, "Minister Ratner was about to make a grand point, but I believe it is something that should be said by the head of state. My dear guests …" Fourier said. However, he stopped, realizing that everyone else had tea cups in their hands. Following Ratner's lead, he put down his wine glass, replacing it with his own teacup. Lifting it in the air, he continued. "On behalf of my First Lady, our Ministry of Unity and all Americans, we are resolute in our friendship and ties with our brethren in Uzbekistan. You see, we believe there is a kindred spirit that unites all of mankind. We are but drops of water in a greater ocean. Individually, we have no weight and no force. Together, we are mighty. Little else on Earth wields the power of the oceans, and countries big and small have an effect on what happens here. For example, all nations have witnessed the effects of global climate change on everything around us. We are only as strong as the weakest among us in preventing these changes. Our Ministry of Unity is designated to unite the people of America – of this great United Socialist State, and my Administration is succeeding. In the same way, we hope to be unified with the people of your great country, President Safaev. Let both of our countries enjoy lasting friendship and years of prosperity."

Fourier spent the next five minutes talking about himself and how his policies had been good for America, especially the Uzbekies who lived in the country. Citing made-up statistics, clichés and old campaign slogans, he painted a glorious picture of a place that only existed in his mind. But when he had finished, Fourier put the teacup to his lips and took a sip. Surprisingly, he did not put it down, but rather drank the rest, having apparently liked the taste after all.

Things settled down once again, and the evening went on smoothly for the next hour while the guests ate, drank and acted like they were enjoying the company of others, whether they were or not. Griffin began to relax and had a few more drinks to relax his mind, now that the stressful part of the night was over. Lubricated and speaking freely, he chatted with several other members of the Cabinet and the Uzbeki delegation, laughing on command and looking serious when the moment required it.

As the intermezzo sorbet was distributed to help guests cleanse their palettes after the previous course, the Chief Usher made an announcement. "The First Citizen has asked that I inform you of an addition to the night's menu. As we on the White House staff have labored to prepare the exquisite dishes that you have enjoyed from the nation of Uzbekistan, the First Citizen felt that the White House should offer a signature dish from America. We hope you enjoy it."

The waiters brought out dried fruit and nuts on large, silver trays intended mainly for those from Uzbekistan. However, there were other attendants, intermingled, who carried smaller trays – these held pies, glorified with a fizzling, sparkler-lit candle.

"What are they serving?" asked Griffin, apprehensively, after pulling over one of the waiters.

"Oh, it's the apple pie. The First Citizen hasn't done this for a while, but given the remoteness of Uzbekistan from the rest of the world, he thought President Safaev would enjoy it," said the tall, young man carrying one of the attention-grabbing trays.

Apple pie? thought Griffin, beginning to feel his stomach tie-up in knots. A cold sweat came over him, as if he had come down with a severe case of food poisoning, and once again, panic set-in. *Sh*t!* he muttered to himself. *What the hell do we do now?* His hand shook as he reached for his scotch and downed the entire glass. He summoned a waiter to ask for another. *Everyone will be dead shortly after midnight,* he thought. *We will have killed everyone!*

Breaking protocol, he got up from his table and walked over to the head table where Ratner was still sitting. She shook her head as he approached and quickly sent him an electronic message that stopped him in his tracks.

It read: **Stop! Don't come over here or you'll lead both of us to the gallows. I'll meet you as we both return from the restrooms. Do not come near my table!**

Griffin walked past the minister toward the men's restroom, while Ratner got up just after he had vanished from the room. A few minutes later, Griffin came out and began checking the messages on his PCD, as Ratner exited from the women's facilities.

As calmly as he could, he whispered, "What the hell do we do now?" He continued looking at his phone.

"There isn't anything we can do. It is what it is. People are already eating the apple pie. I guess we will just have to chalk it up to food poisoning. It looks like, in the end, we will still be in charge ... it's just that we may have started a war with Uzbekistan in the process," said Ratner.

"But you and I won't be dead. Won't that look suspicious?"

"Just take some of the apple pie. We'll have to take a small bite of it – enough to get sick, but not to kill us," she answered, looking at him, unflinching.

"How much is that? I don't know how much that would be?" Griffin said anxiously. There was sweat beading on his forehead, and he took his handkerchief to wipe his brow. "If I take too much, it will kill me too!"

"Calm down, Bailey. You must get yourself under control. If we just take a little bit – less than a spoonful, we should be fine."

"A spoonful?"

"Yeah, just take a little less than a spoonful! Now we have to get back in there before it anyone notices we're out here talking," she added, before walking away.

Griffin went back to his seat and fixated on the narrow wedge of apple pie that sat on a white desert plate in front of him. *Now I know what Socrates must have felt before he killed himself*, he thought. He watched circumspectly as Ratner took her fork and broke off a piece of the pie before poking it with the tines. Without hesitating she popped it into her mouth and swallowed, never once glancing over at him. He did likewise, making sure his piece was small. He figured he could fake more of an illness if the portion he ate wasn't enough to do the job. He wouldn't be able to "unfake" anything if he erred the other way -- by taking too much. His first reaction was to pick up his teacup to wash it down, but thought better of that. Instead, he chose is the scotch and finished off another glass.

Meanwhile, they had forgotten about Fourier, who was still monopolizing President Safaev's time, chatting away about himself and his philosophies. *Had Fourier eaten any of the pie?* Griffin asked himself. *Surely he had, as he had been the one who'd requested it be served*. But the minister wasn't sure, and he couldn't get up again to check. All he could do was watch until the plates were cleared and see if he could spot anything left on the plate.

Only twenty minutes later did the waiters clear the tables of the deserts, but it was too far away for Griffin to tell whether Fourier had taken any of the apple pie, or Patricia, his wife, for that matter. Ratner had been closer, but he saw that she wasn't paying that much attention to the First Citizen or Patricia as they had desert.

At the end of the dinner, the Chief Usher again appeared and announced that the entertainment of the evening was going to be held in the East Room. "The very famous singer and song writer Adam Bristol will be providing the concert for all in attendance this evening," he said. "If you would kindly make your way to the East Room, Mr. Bristol will begin his performance shortly."

Everyone rose from the tables and began moving toward the large, elegant East Room with its magnificent crystal chandeliers, gold brocade draperies, ornate colonial moldings, and portable, wooden stage hauled in from a local warehouse for use in such occasions. Griffin only hoped that the festivities would conclude well before the four-hour, post-desert, death-watch period. Guests keeling over and dying on the floor of the White House would be hard, even for this Administration, to spin to their favor. But to Griffin's relief, the singing was brief, as Bristol had an early engagement the next morning and had to catch his private jet out of town. However, uncharacteristically, Fourier invited Griffin and Ratner to his private dining room for a late-night cocktail, telling them that he was still too wound-up from the evening to go to bed.

But it wasn't just the three of them. Patricia; Trevor Allen, the Chief of Staff; and minister Welbourne were also asked to join him. They all sat down upstairs in the residence quarters on the third floor and took their final drinks from the attendant who had come up to see if they needed anything else for the evening.

"No, I think that will be all, Simmons," said Fourier. With collars unbuttoned and ties undone, the men helped themselves to the humidor and lit up Cubans, blowing smoke out into the sacred space around them.

"Things went quite well tonight," said Fourier. "I'll be honest, I wasn't sure what to expect from a bunch of sheep herders." His remarks were biting and harsh. It was obvious the First Citizen had taken a few too many to drink, and his guard was down. Everyone laughed at the joke, including Ratner.

"I actually thought the dishes were very good," said Patricia. "Not that I'm going to add mutton to the list of regular White House dishes any time soon." That too brought a chortle or two.

333

Fourier fingered his Calvados brandy snifter, twirling the golden-brown liquid around the sides like a pro. He took a sip now and again and then kept the bottom of the glass warm with the palm of his hand. "So, Angel, what do you think of the latest proposal from the self-proclaimed Russian Czar … sorry … I guess he goes by the title General Secretary now, doesn't he?" asked Fourier.

Ratner held her small glass of Sambuca and took a sip before answering. "If I may speak openly, First Citizen."

"Of course," he answered, putting his feet up on the low table he sometimes used to separate the two sofas that straddled the new First Citizen seal woven into the carpeting.

"I think it's important that we be liked in the world," she answered. "For too many years, I believe we've been the neighborhood bully. It's time we mend fences and make things right with others. Once we've repaired our image, we'll be able to work closer with all of these governments. At this point, decades of pushing our own values down their throats has only alienated them. If we can show them they can trust us, we will be fine. They'll admire us!"

"Yes, quite right," said Fourier, nodding his approval. "I'll be proposing that we give the Russians more aid and that old NATO antiballistic missile systems still in place in the Northern Islamic Republic be removed. We must show a good faith effort to appease them. We must prove we mean them no ill will."

"Quite right, First Citizen," said Griffin. "Russia has been attacked from all sides throughout its history. If we just stand down, I think they'll come our way."

"The total, unilateral elimination of all of our nuclear warheads must be part of this," said Fourier. "If Russia knows we are serious about removing all nuclear bombs from the face of the earth, they will follow our lead. It just takes someone to start the process. That's what leadership is about," said Fourier, taking along drag on his cigar.

One of the White House attendants came up the stairs bearing a tray. "It's time for your midnight treat," said Patricia with a smile. "Every night, Jack takes his brandy and a chocolate sweet. We both know that it isn't good for us, but you have to live a little too. Please, everyone, help yourselves. I made sure there was extra for everyone tonight."

The silver tray was presented as the waiter bent slightly at the waist to show them his temptations. There was an assortment of chocolate-drizzled cookies, candies, and even chocolate-covered strawberries.

"The strawberries are how I make sure I get my fruit for the day," said Fourier, picking up two and placing them on the desert dish provided.

The others went for the array of cookies and candies that beckoned their sinfulness. Griffin was also a notable chocoholic, as was Patricia. Ratner, on the other hand, waved off the temptation. "I'm just too full from dinner," she said, preferring to nurse her drink instead.

Already two in the morning, Griffin worried when the effects of the lethal concoctions of the evening would kick in, but no one seemed affected. He looked at the clock and apologized. "I'm sorry, but it's late, and I have an early morning meeting. You'll excuse me then?"

"Ah, you're just a *wus*," Fourier said but then chuckled. "But, you know what? I think I'm about shot for today too." Then he quickly added, "No! I didn't mean that kind of *shot* – no need for the Secret Service," he said laughing. They all chuckled too, but it was a sign the party was ending.

The party broke up as Griffin and Ratner left at the same time, sharing a limo ride home. Griffin suggested that they find a hotel, but Ratner told him she didn't think that was such a good idea, given what was expected in the morning.

"What do you think will happen?" Griffin asked her.

"I don't know," she answered as they pulled up to her Georgetown townhouse. "It's all up in the air now, with that apple pie thing. I assume there will be mass hysteria in the morning. If the Uzbeki delegation is dead, there will be hell to pay for us. But what's worse is if we lose all of our ministers. The economy will take a hit, no doubt, and foreign governments will have to be reassured right away that the USSA is still in control of its government. But then again, you will be in charge; won't you?" she said, grinning at him. "You're going to have to call the shots as soon as this stuff breaks in the morning. Will you be ready?"

Griffin sat in the limo, half-drunk and half-stunned by the realization that he might suddenly be thrust into the number one spot within a few hours. He was unprepared. He was scared.

"We will need a joint statement from the White House and your ministry," said Ratner, coaching him through things. "You and I will both speak, and I will formally turn over the power and authority to run the government over to you, since there won't be anyone else to do that. I've already prepared the my remarks. All I have to do is read it to the media. Then, you'll need to calm the nation and tell them you will maintain the path Fourier has put us on. People have to be reassured and calmed."

"Call me if you hear anything, Okay?" Griffin asked, rolling up his window and watching as Ratner turned and walked confidently toward her townhouse.

"Sure," said Ratner, not intending Griffin to hear her.

Griffin rolled up the window. He felt queasy and light headed. The burdens of the Oval Office were immense, suffocating. They were already affecting him, and he had yet to assume command. He hoped the sickness would pass quickly, not only from what he'd eaten that night but from what he was afraid he'd face in the morning.

*****

CH 48 The Republic of Wyoming

After the secession proclamation, the delegates who had made history at the rail station stayed in town to debate the final details of the new constitution prior to its ratification. Drafts had been circulating for weeks prior to the secession vote, but there were still many points to which they had yet to agree.

But there were other unknowns potentially of even more consequence. The biggest was what Washington would do knowing Wyoming had seceded. How would the Administration react? Would they use military force? If so, how strong, when and where? Many at the convention had worried about retaliation. Sumner too was fearful of the coming days and weeks. The split-away state was now at its most vulnerable. Between its secession and its reconstitution, Wyoming stood naked before its former federal master.

News of the secession proclamation hit SI-net websites within hours of its signing. All of the conservative blogs picked it up and even some moderate ones. Shock spread throughout the country as the impossible had happened. The fact that it had come to a point when a state would *actually* secede from the country was unfathomable. Not since South Carolina in 1860 had it occurred, and the pain and suffering that had followed that event had long been chiseled in prose, verse, lyrics, and lamentations.

"So, what do you think they will do?" Shea asked Sumner, just prior to their constitutional meeting. It was an unusually warm, sunny morning in April, only a day after the proclamation signing, and Shea had found Sumner already battling others over the next course of action.

Sumner put down his cup of black joe and grimaced. "It's odd – really odd. I just thought there would be an immediate reaction, other than the lambasting and jaw-flapping that's going on in Washington. Sure, Congress and Fourier are livid over what we've done and have been railing on us all day, but that's been about it. They're about taking some action against us, but I don't see any coordinated effort. Right now, there's a lot of confusion in their ranks."

"Are you going to follow the plan everyone agreed to before the convention?" Shea asked.

"That's just the thing," said Sumner, "I've got delegates who are backing away from us now. They're frightened and don't want to poke the monster anymore than they have to. I think they have buyer's remorse, but they shouldn't. What we did, we had to do. It was right for us – right for Wyoming."

"But we had a fully outlined plan of what we were going to do after we passed that secession paper? We have to stay the course. We have to do what we said

337

we would do," said Shea. "Sumner, you have to get out in front of this thing before it gets out in front of you."

Sumner breathed a heavy sigh. "I know you're right. It's one thing to plan it and to believe what you're doing is the right thing. It's another thing when you're there and have to do it." He leaned-in toward her and said, "Hundreds of thousands of lives are at stake based on how we go forward with this. Isn't it natural to want to be careful with those decisions?"

"Yeah, but when you're the leader, you have to be decisive. Once you make reasonable efforts to hear all the arguments and they're freely debated, then someone must be make a decision and implement it," said Shea. "More lives will be at risk if you don't!"

"Where did that come from? Sun Tzu?" asked Sumner, referring to the ancient Chinese war strategist.

Shea laughed. "Yes, it came from Sun Tzu Shea," she answered, winking at him.

"Very funny," retorted Sumner.

"But it's true. We decided on the plan. Has anything happened that would force us to rethink it?"

"No."

"Then, what's the problem? You haven't been reluctant to move forward before?"

Sumner poured a little more milk in his coffee and stirred it with a spoon. "Is it really that easy?" he asked. He took a long slurp and let out another sigh. "I was in business for years. I was in Congress for more years. Then, I started GOFLA and organized this group here in Wyoming, my home state, to secede from the Union. None of those things endangered anybody's life. No one was going to die if I made the wrong decision. Now, it's different."

Shea understood what he was saying. She put her hand on his. "Listen, JC. How many books on the Revolutionary and Civil wars, the Spanish American War, World War I and II, the Korean and Vietnam conflicts and the Middle East wars have you read?"

"More than I can remember," said Sumner.

"And in all of them, did the generals face decisions that they knew would end in soldiers dying?"

"Of course, that's what happens in war. People Die."

"But leaders lead. Those generals had to make impossible decisions. They had to decide who lived and who died – all for the greater good. Isn't that right?" Shea pressed him.

"Yes."

"And isn't there a greater good here?"

"Of course. And I get your point. It's true that we have to fight, but do people here really have to die?" Sumner asked. "If we do it right, no one will have to die."

"But we can't go into this thinking that, can we? Don't we have to realize that we've made our pact, and that pact is one of sacrifice – including our very lives. Maria has already sacrificed hers, and you know deep down others will too. This will not be a bloodless action. You and I both know that."

Sumner nodded. "You're right. Of course, you're right. And, the only thing I can do is make decisions that minimize those."

"Right, just as all of those generals did in those wars. They didn't want to sacrifice any more men than they had to. But they knew that those who were sacrificed were necessary so that fewer would die later. Again, it's all for the greater good."

"I appreciate your words, Shea. I've taken them in. It's time now that we get to our meeting." Sumner stood, put down his coffee and began to leave. He wasn't used to someone talking to him in that way. Then, he abruptly turned and smiled. "If I'm the major general, then you must be my second-in-command, but my first and only *aid-de-camp*," he said. "Thanks."

"Then, let's do it," said Shea. Then, she smiled back. "Let's get this party started!"

***

As demanded at the secession convention, ratification of the constitution required the approval of fifty-six delegates, in essence, the state senate representatives and some house representatives from each of the thirty senate and sixty house districts. They met at the governor's mansion at the insistence of the state's former governor, Nellie Taylor, who retired after the state's powers were eroded under the new USSA Constitution 2.0.

The first order of business was the actual signing of the Proclamation of Secession that had been passed the prior week. One by one, the delegates picked up a symbolic quill pen and signed the symbolic parchment; they also signed the real, electronic version. After each signature, the convention recorder, sprinkled sand across the page as they had done almost three centuries earlier in Philadelphia. Once the requisite signatures were obtained, Sumner held up the parchment.

"I wish to proclaim that we have formally declared our independence as a sovereign state, free from the shackles of the United Socialist States of America. And, as the Republic of Wyoming ....

"We the People of the sovereign state of Wyoming, hereby declare our independence from the tyranny of that which has come to be known as the United Socialist States of America. As a result of the oppressive taxation, malfeasance of trust, corruption of power, illegal confiscation of property, unjust imprisonment of the citizenry, misuse of the public treasury, delegitimizing of elections, and stripping of every moral and legal freedom held dear to the denizens of that once great land, the United States of America, we cannot accept – and shall no longer tolerate – the abuse of power by those officials of government ...

"... Therefore, this new nation-state, the Republic of Wyoming, is duly consecrated in the spirit of that which came before us and was born on September 17, 1787, with the adoption of the original United States Constitution, to become the United States of America, a once-great country that has ceased to exist. However, it is those founding principles upon which we will build a new society, established for the preservation of God-given freedoms which no man may take for granted. We, as people of Wyoming, are willing to stand up for those freedoms for which so many Americans have died during the course of nearly three centuries. We owe them our eternal gratitude for giving us this second chance at life without oppression and repression. We may only pray to the Almighty that we make good this time on those elusive dreams held by our forefathers. We will use all of our faculties, resources, and opportunities to ensure freedom for the people of Wyoming. We stand resolute and united in this cause ..."

It was a solemn moment. No one clapped or cheered. The group was strangely silent. Everyone there knew what they had done and what it meant. The fear they would no longer be safe seemed raised another octave. Might they no longer feel secure with their families or find comfort and sanctuary within their own homes? They had become enemies of the other state, the USSA, and it would remain a large shadow that would loom overhead every day like Damocles' sword.

After signing the proclamation, the delegates voted Sumner as president of the Constitutional Convention and Shea as its vice-president and secretary. With the help of others, Sumner had worked diligently on the new constitution based on the original one of 1789. There had been many iterations and many disagreements. Progress had been made. But more was needed.

The real debate focused on the revisions some wanted to make to the original U.S. Constitution. However, to avoid the mistakes of the past, many changes felt necessary and other provisions added. The group proposed several ideas for the convention delegates to consider:

First, a balanced budget, without debt, unless three-fifths of the districts voted for emergency spending that exceeded budgetary requirements. Then, budget deficits could not exceed five percent of the overall budget, with cumulative debt never to exceed ten percent of the republic's annual output of products and services.

Second, term limits for all politicians, varying by position. Compensation for positions would be set to four times the poverty level, providing comfort but not allowing politicians to vote pay increases unless the country as a whole was doing well.

Third, Supreme Court decisions could be overturned by a three-fifths vote of the legislature or two-thirds of the district governments.

Fourth, equal rights bestowed on all, regardless of race, ethnicity, gender, age, or any other category previously viewed as discriminatory. None had priority over any other. And all such groups forever would give up any claims of restitution for past governmental indiscretions.

Fifth, a fourth division of government would be established, independent of the others. The Bureau of Statistics & Metrics would have no governing authority, but would be responsible for providing unbiased and accurate statistics and informational data on the economy and operations of all branches of government. Its chairman would be nominated by the House and approved by the Senate. The chairman would hold the position only for seven years, unless impeached by the legislature and found guilty of prejudicial bias or some high crime by the Supreme Court.

Sixth, terms of the president and legislature would be changed. The president would be limited to one, eight-year term; the House members to three four-year terms; and the Senate to two six-year terms.

Seventh, a line-item presidential veto would be instituted.

Eighth, there was no provision for a vice-president. Instead, the post of Secretary of State would be chosen as the first replacement for the president should he or she become incapacitated or die in office. Thereafter, it would be the House Speaker, the Senate Majority Leader (not the Senate Pro Tempore), and then the remaining Secretaries of Departments in order as set by the constitution.

Ninth, the process of impeachment was changed to include judicial, as well as legislative action to remove a president for 'high-crimes' against the nation, omitting reference to 'misdemeanors.' Although the legislative process from the original U.S. Constitution was kept, a provision was offered to permit two-thirds of the local governments (districts) to bring legal action against the president in the Supreme Court to request removal.

Tenth, the president could be subject to a 'confidence' vote by both houses every two years at the time of a national election; however, the requirements proposed were stiff – more than 60 percent of the House and 66 percent of the Senate were required to oust a sitting president.

The constitution was going to be limiting just like the first one. But just as the first one, it would be broad enough to offer flexibility for future decades and, hopefully, centuries to come. It permitted only a few specific actions by the republican government, ensuring that no despotic tyrant could assume control and derail what was intended to be a government of the people. All other functions were left to the local governments.

Still, there were other matters that the delegates argued heatedly over. They included:

One -- Taxation only to provide for the basic essentials of the new republic, namely, its defense, coinage of money, and the limited operation of government functions. User fees and other revenue generating methods would provide for other activities used by constituents.

Two -- The formation of republic-level government departments to require the vote of two-thirds of the districts within the new republic.

Three -- Catastrophic health care would be provided or supplemented where the inability to pay was proved. This would include pre-existing conditions.

Four -- Unions were permitted only if approved by a majority of workers at a workplace and could be later revoked by the same majority. Silent balloting was permitted. Unionization of public safety, education or government positions was prohibited.

Five -- Education was mandated through high school, but the curricula was left to the districts. Students were permitted to apply to any school they chose using a voucher system, and underperforming schools were allowed to fail and close. No teacher unions were permitted.

Six -- Class-action lawsuits would be prohibited unless they met extraordinarily high thresholds, and losing plaintiffs in civil litigation were subject to paying all legal fees – curtailing contingency cases that were 'no lose' propositions for the plaintiffs. Limits to appeals would also be instituted for criminal cases so such appeals would not span years or even decades.

Seven – Citizenship would not be granted automatically for children born in the country to non-citizen parents. No longer would anchor babies be permitted.

By the end of the three-day event, much had been accomplished; yet, much was left to be done. Many details and *"wordsmithery"* were still needed and many more hours of debate required. However, the basic framework had been established.

But even as the new constitution was being hammered into form, other constructs demanded immediate attention. One was an opposition party. The events at the former Cheyenne state house had shocked even the most hard-core Leftists. Worried about what their Leftist party had helped create, they tacitly supported the actions of the new Freedom Party or abstained. However, they insisted on setting up their own new party, which they called the Eagle Party. This acted as a necessary counterweight to the views of the Freedom Party, keeping everyone in check.

A second exigency was to refashion the former state's government into a national, sovereign one. Although not the highest physical priority, the rebuilding of the seat of government was a critical, psychological one. The republic needed a symbol of its new-found authority and independence. Therefore, the Sumner ordered the rebuilding of the statehouse in Cheyenne, near the site of the catastrophic explosion months earlier. In addition, state agencies were being reorganized around a federal model, eliminating duplication and waste and bidding out many functions to private businesses. Contracts were written with performance clauses mandating that vendors meet certain objectives and within pre-approved costs. Overruns would be absorbed by the vendor if there were no changes in the project's or program's scope. No business could have connections to anyone in government, and each agreement was to be reviewed annually by the Bureau of Statistics & Metrics, the BSM, based on the results of the services rendered. If a private business failed in its performance, it could not re-bid any government contract for five years.

Reorganized agencies were given annual goals of performance based on their mission statements in serving the public. The president, with the concurrence of the chairman of the BSM, set forth service and resource utilization goals to be achieved by each. Monies were limited, and agencies were measured on the effectiveness of how they used resources they were given. If certain objectives were not met, the BSM could force the president to replace the head of the agency. No government pensions were allowed; instead, retirement accounts were funded by tax-free contributions made by the workers themselves. The BSM also conducted surveys of private industry to set pay levels for all government positions – thus maintaining parity and competitiveness between private and public sector jobs.

In the end, the Constitution of the Republic of Wyoming incorporated many of these changes into a framework already built from the original U.S. Constitution. The founders of the new republic believed it was an improvement over the original – changes needed after nearly 270 years. But they were also realistic, understanding that nothing was perfect. Changes to it would be pushed to the people rather than being entrusted to the central government branches as it had been in the original constitution. Although the original permitted a state convention, it was arduous. The Wyoming Constitution would permit changes only by legislative convention or by a national referendum, both of which mandated at least 60 percent approval to pass.

Change was inevitable, but those working to construct the constitution for the Republic of Wyoming hoped this one would be the last one ever needed.

***

Finally, the new constitution was completed, approved and ratified. It was a momentous day as the delegates watched Sumner unroll the momentous document from a scroll. The same quill pens used to sign the Secession Proclamation were used to ink the Constitution of the Republic of Wyoming.

Shea stood beside a simple, Amish-style oak table and handed a feathered pen to each delegate. It was old fashioned, but everyone had wanted it done that way. All fifty-six of the delegates found a place on the last page to sign, just as the same number had on the original.

Sumner waited for the last delegate to finish her strokes on the paper and then stepped forward, taking the quill and leaning over to brandish his *JC Sumner* into the place marked President of the Constitutional Convention toward the top. He then turned and handed his pen to the woman beside him. Just below Sumner's signature, Shea more carefully let her name flow across the page, authenticating it as Secretary of the Constitutional Convention.

Sumner held up the scroll. It was nightfall, and a spring breeze was blowing through the windows behind him accompanied by the chirping of crickets. "I always wondered what was going through Benjamin Franklin's mind at age of eighty-one when he signed the U.S. Constitution. Tears ran down Franklin's cheeks as he, with some assistance, placed his name on that cherished document. He had seen much during his lifetime, and he had worried that day might never happen. Whether his tears were of joy or of trepidation for what lay ahead for the newly coined United States of America is uncertain. But, what he was thankful for was that he was able to see the birth of a nation. Tears are not running down my cheeks, but I too have a mixture of emotions right now," said Sumner. "This is our baby," he added, gently shaking the paper in his hands. "It is up to us to guide it, nurture it, care for it, and help it mature into the type of nation we truly want it and intent it to be."

"Countrymen!" Sumner then shouted. "God bless you all, and God bless the Republic of Wyoming!"

This time there were cheers and whoops of jubilation and excitement over what they had accomplished. Shea had ordered cases of champagne be put on ice, and when the ink had dried, they began opening the bottles and celebrating their success.

***

There was one more day added to the docket to review the plan going forward. Sumner took Shea's advice and presented the plan as a *fait accompli* rather than re-open it to discussion. Under the plan, the delegates were to become the members of the lower and upper houses of the Republic's legislature forming the House and Senate, respectively. Elections for their positions would be held within six months. Likewise, the position of president would be voted on by the people of Wyoming, in a general election to be held concurrent with other federal and local offices. The delegates overwhelmingly elected Sumner as the interim-president. He was the obvious choice, and no one offered a serious consideration of a challenge. The post of interim secretary of state went to Lawrence Ingram due to his extensive work at the United Nations and as ambassador to what used to be called England. Sumner pushed and got his nominee for interim attorney general – that was Shea. Other key positions were also selected, including those of the Supreme Court, which held only five seats, instead of nine.

It was a new day; a new time. And although the calendar showed the same year – 2049, April had ushered in a different era from that which had staggered in on New Year's Day. One with endless possibilities and dangers.

As interim president, Sumner's first order of business was to communicate to the surrounding states that the Republic of Wyoming wished to co-exist peacefully with its neighbors and that there would be no significant change to those relationships. Even so, Sumner called-up the republic's army – the former state's National Guard – and put them on standby, just in case Washington ordered troops from one of its nearby bases to crush Wyoming's defection. Sumner was concerned with how the other states would react to the secession. To be vigilant, he sent aerial drones to patrol the borders with Nebraska, Colorado, Idaho, Montana, South Dakota and Utah.

But within days of the Constitutional Convention, all but Colorado had signed armistice agreements with Wyoming, vowing non-aggression. In fact, many within those states began forming their own groups, petitioning to join the Wyoming republic.

Only Colorado was openly hostile to the new nation, immediately moving the state's National Guard to its northern border with Wyoming and asking Washington for more troops. But the rift was more complicated than that. Old schisms between people in the big cities and those in the rural countryside had often created friction and factionalism. There were some northern counties in Colorado, such as Weld County, that were sympathetic to Wyoming's cause and were actively seeking to join them. Several other counties near Nebraska also asked to be annexed into the republic. Cheyenne struggled with all of the requests while, at the same time, trying to create its own sovereign government. For the time being, all it could do was to take the proposals "under review" and consider them for provisional statehood, but that would be well after the Wyoming general elections, set within the following six months.

South Dakota and Idaho were the first to ask unofficially for statehood within the new Republic, followed by Nebraska and North Dakota. Once they were given "provisional" status, those states moved quickly to hold secession conventions of their own. The outlying counties of Colorado were also given provisional status and would be admitted as the state of North Colorado.

It had taken less than thirty days and already the new republic was growing. From the sole state of Wyoming, it would soon become a nation of five states when they came on board. Sumner had also learned directly from the former governors of other states, that there would be twelve more petitions to join the Republic within the next few fortnights.

"It's overwhelming," said Sumner, looking at the list of petitions stacking up on his computer. "I just never thought it would spread so quickly. I thought we would have to go it alone for a while – you know, as others watched and waited to see how Fourier would react. Instead, because of the silence, the other states are seeing that it can be done. One can secede and succeed at the same time."

"But don't you think it is odd that there's been very little reaction out of Washington? It's as if they don't care," said Shea, sitting with the interim-president for their daily meeting.

"Maybe they believe we will just implode on our own, collapsing from our inability to get world credit or raise an army or … well, something. I don't know what to make of it either, but it makes me nervous."

"Do we have any information on what's going on from DC?" asked Sumner.

"No. It seems many are puzzled by the inaction coming from the White House. They haven't seen Fourier in weeks. In fact, they haven't seen much of anyone. Apparently, Fourier's been ill, but his spokesperson says its nothing serious – that he should be back at things soon. However, if he's been sick for weeks, it would seem a bit more concerning. But then again, maybe that's the ruse they're using to plan something big against us. What do you think?"

"I don't know what to think either, but we need to plan for the worst. When do you meet with Josh Templeton to go over your defensive plans?"

"Right after our meeting. Would you like to sit in on my meeting with the Secretary of Defense?"

"Absolutely. I hope you don't mind?"

"I think it will be good to get your perspective. Sure. The more the merrier."

Templeton arrived on time and came in with his joint chief's head, General Artemis Ward. Both were intense, career men who had dedicated their lives to the military. Templeton had served in the near-Armageddon war in the Middle East back in the 20's and had continued to rise up through the ranks to full colonel before getting booted out of the armed services for his political views by Fourier. He had gotten into politics and hadn't looked back.

Ward was tough as nails. Often compared to George Patten, except without the "social niceties," he was one with whom few wanted to tangle. Yet, he knew his position, and his years in the military had taught him to respect authority. Templeton was his boss, as was Sumner. But Ward truly had respect for both of them, so he was happy to be on a team in which he believed with all his heart and soul.

"So General, what do you think of the current inaction from Washington? What do you make of it?" asked Sumner, looking up from the computer screen that hovered in front of his eyes. He was sitting at his desk and reviewing the latest report filed by his defense secretary.

"Mr. President," said Ward, "I'm not sure what to make of it. But I think it's a political, not military strategy. All I can tell you is what we're doing to increase our defenses and early-warning systems to prepare us for an attack."

Ward spent the next thirty minutes covering the overall approach he was using to defend Wyoming. But in the end, his words were not encouraging.

"But, Mr. President, I must tell you that if the USSA wants to invade and crush us, they can. We do not have the resources or technology to fight them. Their military power, while nowhere near where it was at the turn of the century, is still formidable against a single state. The best we can hope for is they have figured that an invasion will result in thousands of dead which won't look good politically for them. Since they see everything through a political lens, that's what I'm banking on."

"I see," said Sumner. He thought for a moment and then added, "But you said that we don't have the technology to fight them. Is that right?"

"Yes, sir."

Sumner turned to Shea and smiled. "I think I know how we can beat them if they decide to take back Wyoming."

***

Several weeks passed, yet there was still no sign that tanks were being readied by Washington to lead an assault on the new republic. *Could it be that instead of an Abraham Lincoln in the White House, they had a Franklin Pierce or a James Buchanan at 1600 Pennsylvania Avenue?* thought Sumner, referring to the ineptness of the two presidents who preceded the most famous, the sixteenth. But there were things going on within the halls of power in Washington that few knew, especially not J.C. Sumner. Timing was everything, and the new republic had hit the "crease" at the right place and time. Things did not seem right in the White House, but no one knew exactly why. The attention of the Congress, the Cabinet, and others in D.C. was focused on Wyoming, but that wasn't true with the White House. The Administration was nowhere to be seen or heard. Supposedly, they were attending to Fourier's illness. But as the emperor lay stricken, the rebellion continued to spread and spread rapidly.

No one knew the answers. But, all they could do was prepare for the worst and pray for the best.

*****

CH 49 Lasting Hangover

It was Saturday morning, and things were different. Ratner's chauffeur, Winston, was not waiting for her outside her townhouse as he normally would. Typically, he would arrive at seven o'clock and stay, biding his time patiently until eight when she would stumble out of the brownstone and find her seat inside the SUV for her ride into work. But oddly, the night before, he had been told that he wouldn't be needed until later in the morning. "I'll be sleeping in tomorrow," Ratner had said that night as she wobbled toward her home. "You can come at, well let's say eleven. How does that sound?"

However, Ratner's PCD sounded at seven that morning. It was a call from the White House.

"Minister Ratner, this is Minister Chin. We need you to come to the White House at once. A car will be there to pick you up in ten minutes." Chin was the Minister of Domestic Policing, or what was the FBI.

Ratner was prepared for the call, but she had imbibed in a bit too much drink the night before, and she was paying for it now. She took a deep breath and made sure she sounded appropriately alarmed. "Can you tell me what this is about?"

"No ma'am. You have to come to the White House. Again, a car will be waiting outside."

Ratner dressed and as she descended the narrow, walnut stair case of her house to the main floor, there was a knock on the door. Grabbing her things, she closed the door behind her, making sure the surveillance cameras and detection systems were all activated. Things would not be the same when she returned.

***

Inside the limo was Chin and two assistants. Each had tablets and other *com* devices to be able to brief Ratner on the status of the fluid situation. As soon as she was inside, she turned to Chin and asked, "What's going on? Why am I so urgently needed at the White House?"

"First Citizen Fourier is dead," said Chin, calmly from behind the safe walls of his dark sunglasses. "So, is the First Lady. We haven't been able to determine the cause of death, but apparently, they relate to the state dinner that occurred last night – the one you attended."

At first, she wondered if she were being taken in for questioning. But those fears subsided, when Minister Chin added, "We must find out what you know about last night's dinner. You will be questioned as soon as we get to the mansion."

"Was it food poisoning then?" she asked, assuming this would be the most obvious cause.

"We don't know," said Chin.

"What about the others? Were there others affected by the dinner? Was anyone from the Uzbeki delegation affected?" she asked, sounding concerned.

"Not that we can tell. We contacted everyone from the dinner last night. There were only a few casualties."

"Who?" she asked, most interested in the answer to that question. She trembled with nervous energy and excitement to hear the news. She had expected Fourier and Patricia to be dead — that was what had been planned. It was the others she was less certain about.

"The First Citizen and First Lady; the Chief of Staff, Trevor Allen, Dutch Welbourne, and Bailey Griffin, the Tax Minister. All were found dead in their living quarters this morning. Apparently, all died from eating something the night before. A very bad case of food poisoning we think, but of course there will be an investigation."

"Oh, god, how tragic!" said Ratner, shaking. "This is just awful! And I assume that I'll have to take the oath of office right away in order to prevent a vacancy of the office, I would understand that."

"That will be discussed at the White House, minister," said Chin.

"But how, under such circumstances can I be asked to do that? I guess I'll just have to go ahead with it, until we figure out the long-term course of action here," she said, bringing up her best acting voice.

"Quite right," said Chin. "It is very tragic. It's a good thing the new constitution has you as the next in line. It makes the transition easier, as you are aware of what is going on in the First Citizen's office already."

"Yes. Yes, I do," she answered. Ratner turned her head and stared out the blackened windows as she passed the common people walking aimlessly in the street, without a purpose and without a leader. She smiled. *It is mine, now,* she mused. *All mine. How stupid people were and how naïve about the thirst and drive for power. Thank God for such people,* she thought, *and thank God for chocoholics.*

#####

About the Author

The author has written numerous novels, many of which are trilogies or multi-volume sets, and span several different types of book genre from fantasies and murder mysteries to horror stories and allegories. He has been cited for his creativity and fresh approach in each of the book categories for which he has written. This is the only novel series Gregory Phillips has penned using that *nom de plume*. Each genre is inked using a unique pseudonym most fitting to that style writing.

Phillips lives with his family in the Chicago area.

Go to www.blueMpublishing for more works by this and other authors.

THE NEXT BOOK

ATLAS in ASCENDANCE - America at War - Book III

Volume III, *Atlas in Ascendance*, brings this story to its fiery conclusion. The Republic of Wyoming must face the full wrath of the USSA. Conflict is inevitable as the breakaway state seeks to establish itself peacefully, while its former owner will not allow it to go away quietly. Angel Ratner unleashes even tighter rule over the country while Sumner takes over as president of the new and growing nation. Shea struggles to adapt to her new role within the government and is shaken by revelations about Patrick, her former husband.

*****

Blue M Publishing

FIND US at: www.blueMpublishing.com

www.ingramcontent.com/pod-product-compliance
Lightning Source LLC
Chambersburg PA
CBHW070307280626
47159CB00017B/347